Hazardous Pay, Shirt Talk and Twenty-Four Other Stories

Hazardous Pay, Shirt Talk and Twenty-Four Other Stories

By

Ivan Prashker

ARPress
ILLUMINATING IDEAS
EMPOWERING VOICES

ARPress
45 Dan Road Suite 5
Canton MA 02021
Hotline: 1(888) 821-0229
Fax: 1(508) 545-7580

Ordering Information:
Quantity sales.Special discounts are available on quantity purchases by corporations, associations, and others.For details, contact the publisher at the address above.

Printed in the United States of America.

ISBN-13:   Paperback   979-8-89389-101-0
              eBook   979-8-89389-100-3

Library of Congress Control Number: 2024905221

Many of the stories in this book, slightly revised, have appeared in the following publications: *Adelina, Bellevue Literary Review, Gallery, Harper's Magazine, Ladies' Home Journal, McCall's, Midstream, Playboy, Redbook Magazine, Rooster, The Best American Short Stories, and War, Literature & the Arts.*

For Crede, Jack, Mark, Michael, and Chaitanya, and in Memory of Alan Einhorn Barrie and Mario Puzo

Contents

I. Childhood

The Doll

～⚞～

"I'll be home about eleven," Harry Rosen said, kissing his daughters goodnight. "If you want anything, Mrs. Larson will be in the living room." Mrs. Larson had been their housekeeper for almost a year. "Sweet dreams."

Sandra was ten, Arlene three years younger. They shared a bedroom in a large, high-ceilinged seventh-floor apartment in the Nineties overlooking Central Park. Arlene soon fell asleep next to her Raggedy Anne Doll, Lenesa. Sandra tried to find her favorite, most comfortable spot in bed, although she knew she couldn't possibly fall asleep until her father returned.

Her mother had died two years ago and her three-year-old brother had died the following year of polio. Because all her classmates' mothers and brothers were still living and her father always seemed to be saying *kaddish,* Sandra knew she was different.

She was smart, a reserved girl, usually the smartest or next smartest in her class. Her brown hair was bobbed and she had her father's pale blue eyes. Arlene, on the other hand, had her mother's rosy cheeks as well as her mother's bubbly, expansive personality.

Their father was going to the opera that night. A wealthy hat manufacturer, Harry could afford the best of seats, and Sandra wondered if he was going to take his girlfriend Carol. He'd been seeing Carol for three months, although she hadn't been around the last couple of weeks. Maybe they'd be getting together again tonight.

Both Sandra and Arlene liked Carol, who also wore her hair bobbed and giggled a lot. Anyway, Sandra hoped the opera, with or without Carol, would cheer up her preoccupied father.

Sitting in a green velvet chair near the front door, Sandra used to wait for him when he returned from work on weekday nights. Arlene would be in their bedroom playing with Lenesa, Mrs. Larson in the kitchen keeping their supper warm and listening to the radio.

Neither of the girls liked Mrs. Larson, who was weepy and manipulative. A Norwegian in her sixties, she'd been married to a sailor who'd died at sea.

From the beginning, Mrs. Larson tried to get Sandra to tattle on Arlene and vice versa, prompting Sandra to warn her younger sister, "Don't be fooled by her tears, Arlene. We have to stick together, or she'll make us hate each other."

"I could never hate you, Sandra, I love you," Arlene had affirmed, throwing her arms around Sandra's neck. Since their mother died, they'd become especially close.

Suddenly Arlene moaned in her sleep, and Sandra found herself wondering if her sister would still resemble their mother years from now. It was something to hang on to, like a tree in a flood, or even a favorite book.

That night, Sandra heard the front door open. She could have sworn her father was talking to a woman whose voice she didn't recognize. It wasn't Mrs. Larson, who croaked like a frog, nor was it Carol, who talked with a squeak. This woman had a rich, deep voice, a resonant voice, and Sandra wondered if her father had returned with one of the opera singers.

She went over to Arlene's bed and woke her. "Daddy just came home. Let's run inside and kiss him hello." Knowing a strange woman was with him, Sandra was far too shy to do it alone.

And without either of them putting on their slippers, the girls raced into the living room. Sandra flung herself into her father's startled arms. So did Arlene.

He'd been standing opposite their dark gray couch, talking to a strange woman who was sitting and drinking ginger ale. The woman had raven hair and brown eyes shiny as agates. Sandra's spine tingled; she knew the stranger was beautiful.

Suddenly the woman looked shocked, as though Harry had forgotten to mention that he was the father of two young daughters.

Kissing the girls clumsily, Harry seemed terribly distracted. Then he remembered to introduce them. "This is Sandra, my oldest, and Arlene, who's seven. Girls, I'd like you to meet a friend, Rachel Kluger. My daughters," said Harry, rubbing his small hands nervously.

Blinking as if she had something caught in one eye, Rachel stood up and said hello in a slightly strained voice.

"Girls, it's late," Harry finally had the sense to declare, and he accompanied them back to their bedroom.

"Did you like her?" Sandra whispered after Harry had wished them sweet dreams again, closing their door.

"I think I like Carol better," Arlene said judiciously. "Is this one Daddy's new girlfriend?"

"I don't know," answered Sandra.

"Can Daddy have more than one girlfriend?" Arlene asked, yawning.

"Sure," declared Sandra, although she really wasn't that sure.

In a few minutes, she heard Arlene falling back asleep. Sandra kept listening to Rachel leave, but it was very late now, and she felt herself growing drowsy.

Next morning, no one, including her father, mentioned last night's visitor. While Arlene seemed to forget Rachel entirely, Sandra, who couldn't stop thinking about her, was deeply relieved Rachel didn't show up the following week or months.

Neither, for that matter, did Carol or any other woman.

***

A year passed. It was the first Sunday in June, a beautiful, warm spring morning, and Harry had taken his daughters rowing in Central Park. He was a short man, a Sabbath observer, with thick, curly hair, who wore a red tie and a diamond stickpin just below his tie knot. He'd been particularly cheerful the last few weeks, Sandra noted, was even whistling when they returned from Central Park.

"I want you girls to look especially nice this afternoon, because I'm bringing over some friends to have tea and cookies with us," Harry said.

That probably explained Mrs. Larson's taking yesterday off rather than today, and now she made sure Sandra and Arlene put on their best dresses. Sandra asked if Mrs. Larson knew who her father's guests were.

"Girls, no disrespect, but your papa's a very secretive man. I was going to ask you the same question."

Waiting for him to return with his mysterious guests, Sandra sat in her favorite green velvet chair and kept glancing at her Mickey Mouse watch.

A few minutes after three, the door opened and Harry walked in. Accompanying him was Rachel and an older woman the girls had never met before.

Harry reintroduced Rachel and introduced the older woman as Rachel's mother, Mrs. Kluger, whom he kept calling "Fanny." She was in her fifties, shorter than Rachel, Sandra observed, but possessed eyes as dark and shiny as her daughter's.

"Can I sit with you on the couch?" Arlene asked Fanny, who had the kind of enveloping smile all grandchildren adore.

"I wish you would," said Fanny, smoothing her gray hair which she wore in a bun. The mother of six, she was far more comfortable around small children than Rachel, who was her oldest daughter and worked as a model in the fur district.

While Harry went to get the tea and cookies, Rachel said awkwardly, "Sandra, your father told us you were going to camp soon. What's the name of the camp?"

"Walden." Sandra had recently learned that one-word answers often satisfied adults whom you didn't really know.

"I was a sparrow last year, this year I'm going to be a robin," Arlene informed everyone cheerfully.

For their guests' sake, Sandra felt obliged to explain that the camp was divided into age groups, sparrows being the youngest. She herself was going to be a finch this year.

A minute later, Harry came into the living room, carrying a sterling silver tray with cups of tea and cookies molded in the shape of hearts. The tray had an embossed "R" with curlicues, and Harry was smiling. Sandra couldn't remember the last time she'd seen him so happy.

Tea consumed a pleasant half hour, after which, Harry, proud of his panoramic view, casually offered to show his guests the rest of the apartment.

Seen from the seventh floor, Central Park was a sprawling mint-green oasis, dwarfed by the brick and stone of surrounding high-risers. Glancing out the window, Harry's guests could see an oblong-shaped playground directly below them, dotted with swings, seesaws, and a sandbox.

The master bedroom was huge and also overlooked the park. The room Sandra and Arlene shared was considerably smaller. Mrs. Larson slept in the third bedroom, which used to be Sandra's brother's. There were three bathrooms, plus a dining room and a large kitchen with a bay window. The walls were all painted white. For some reason Rachel seemed to take special interest in the furniture.

"It's a lovely apartment, Harry," Fanny said after they'd completed their tour. "I can see why you like it so much."

"What do you think, Rachel?" Harry asked.

"The view's wonderful, the apartment's spacious. And three bedrooms—pretty spectacular."

Throughout their hour-long visit, Sandra remained uncomfortable because of the way both women conversed with her father. They seemed to know him very well, which made her sense something familiar was happening that she couldn't put a name to. She'd had that same feeling when her mother and brother had entered the hospital. Then, too, she was unable to measure each event, gauge its proper weight or accurately position it within the circumference of her experience.

***

Yet nothing out of the ordinary occurred during the next few weeks. And then, before Sandra realized it, her father was taking her and Arlene down to Penn Station the last Sunday in June. Walden's excited campers were leaving for Pittsfield that morning, their trunks and duffel bags having been shipped the beginning of the month. The train ride would last four hours.

More than a hundred nervous and happy girls gathered under Walden's green and white banner hung in a designated area along the balcony overlooking the terminal's Grand

Concourse. The harried camp director, who had a clipboard framing a typewritten bunk list, was distributing name tags.

"You're going to have a wonderful summer," Harry told his daughters, kissing them goodbye. "And the apartment is going to be freshly painted and have new furniture when you return."

Hearing their father's surprising news, Arlene clapped with delight while Sandra, who'd learned to be fearful of change, turned her head in dismay.

Their train left a little after ten. Sandra could tell when they reached Connecticut because of the preponderance of Connecticut license plates an hour later. Because her head had been pressed against the train window practically since they'd started, no one noticed tears streaking her face.

The camp was kosher, two miles from the center of town, and bordered a lake. Six girls and a counselor were assigned to each bunk, which was painted white and had green shutters. The tennis courts were near the mess hall, about ten minutes from the main campus, which was down a hill lined with blue spruce trees.

A week after the girls had settled in camp, they received two picture postcards with striking shots of Niagara Falls on the back. Harry had written an identical message to each of his daughters: "Got married, on honeymoon, hope you're enjoying camp. Love, Daddy."

Arlene was convinced that Harry had married Rachel's mother, but Sandra insisted, "No, no, Daddy married Rachel. Her mother was too old for him."

It was strange that he hadn't written exactly whom he married, hadn't mentioned his new wife by name. Stranger still, Sandra thought, that he hadn't told them he was planning to get married before they'd left for camp.

"Do you think Rachel has any children, and will they come to live with us?" Arlene asked.

Sandra didn't think so, although there was no way of telling from Pittsfield.

"I guess that means Mommy's never coming back," Arlene said.

Sandra blinked twice. "But she's dead, Arlene."

"I know, I know. But I kept thinking that as long as Daddy didn't marry again, there was always a chance it might not be true."

The following week, the camp director called Sandra into her office and asked if something had recently happened to disturb Arlene.

"What do you mean?" asked Sandra, who'd grown increasingly suspicious of adults, all adults.

"Arlene's been getting into fights and arguments with her bunkmates and her counselor. Yet last year, when she was younger, I don't recall her doing that even once. Nor did she at the beginning of this summer. So, Sandra, do you know if anything recently happened to upset her?"

It was probably the cards postmarked Niagara Falls, but Sandra was hardly prepared to discuss her father's remarriage with someone as remote to her as the camp director, and she said no, she had no idea, none at all.

That night, however, Sandra had second thoughts, then debated for days whether to tell the truth, or as much of the truth as she thought she knew. She was torn, because while she felt badly for Arlene, the possibility of having to confide in a strange adult petrified her.

Then, almost magically, her father came to the rescue. Or at least it felt that way the afternoon he called, telling Sandra, "You and Arlene will be coming home from camp early this year, after the first week of August rather than at the end of the month with everyone else. The reason is, I've bought you both a lot of new presents, fixed over the apartment, and want you to have time to see and enjoy all our new things before school starts. It'll be a new beginning for all of us, Sandra, a fresh start." He didn't mention his remarriage.

"Oh, Daddy, I love you so much!" Sandra burst out, relieved she didn't have to tell the camp director about Rachel.

When he picked them up at Penn Station the beginning of August, Sandra had never seen her father looking better. He was sunburned and smiling. "You won't believe how nice our apartment is, how many changes we made while you were away."

Their building was twenty years old. The first two of its floors consisted of gray stone, the rest was of white brick. It had a stately inner courtyard, with two shiny globes of frosted glass that illuminated the swinging double door at night.

Rachel, who'd been waiting anxiously, greeted each of the girls politely, saying, "I know we're going to become good friends."

Sandra didn't recognize the apartment. Two splendid Oriental carpets decorated with birds and cages covered the living room floor that used to be bare. The room itself was painted a bottle green. Gone was the large brass lamp near the living room window. Gone were the brown drapes. Gone were the framed pictures of her mother and brother. And where was Mrs. Larson? Gone, too, it seemed. Her former bedroom was painted the same bottle green of the living room and had been converted into a kind of study, with a victrola, stacks of opera records, and leather-bound books lining the walls. Disoriented, Sandra and Arlene stared at each other.

"Would you like some milk and cookies?" Rachel asked them.

But the girls felt too unhinged to be particularly hungry.

Saying he had to call his stockbroker, Harry disappeared into the master bedroom. But even before that, he'd stayed in the background and seemed to want to remain there.

"We'll do things together during the next few weeks before school starts," Rachel said. "Go to museums and concerts, the Central Park Zoo. We'll go shopping and buy you lots of pretty dresses," and it sounded to Sandra as if Rachel thought they hadn't bought any new dresses since their mother died. "We'll get to know each other during the next month and have fun, too," Rachel promised. "I'm looking forward to it."

"Is it okay if we go to our bedroom?" asked Sandra, anxious to see what changes had been made there as well.

"Sure, you don't have to ask, it's your room." Rachel smiled, and Sandra thought her face appeared even more beautiful now than it was that unforgettable night more than a year ago.

In the girls' room, painted a dusky rose, Sandra saw rectangular boxes of Chinese Checkers, a Monopoly game, lots of new books and crayons, also a small container of paints and an easel. There was a pink dollhouse in the corner, and large new dolls sat atop each bed.

Arlene's was a fairy godmother. She had blonde hair, blue eyes that closed, and her face was hand-painted. The doll wore a cylindrical hat that came to a point and a long blue dress that skimmed her shiny black shoes.

Sandra's doll had a silver bracelet with the name "Juliet" scrawled across its length. Her hair was brown and so were her eyes. Her dress was a satiny gold.

As for the girls' old dolls, games, and books, it was as if they'd never existed. Gone! They were all gone!

Arlene couldn't believe it, and when she tried to find her favorite, Lenesa, but finally realized that doll had been thrown away with everything else, she whispered in despair, "But I love Lenesa, I love Lenesa!" Arlene's lower lip trembled, and the pain inside her heart seemed to clench and churn at the same time.

Sandra might have tried calming Arlene if her treasured copy of *Little Women* hadn't also been discarded.

Arlene bit her lower lip to keep from crying. "How could Rachel throw Lenesa away?" she asked, bewildered. "Lenesa didn't belong to her. I'll never forget this, never forgive Rachel! *How could she do it?*"

And without waiting for an answer, Arlene raced into the kitchen. Returning, she closed their bedroom door and threw herself upon her new doll, stabbing it repeatedly with a bread knife until she pierced where she thought its heart might be. She was only eight, but the accumulated rage she'd felt at having lost not only Lenesa but her mother and brother seemed to have fused in an unusually frightful way.

Watching her, Sandra stood mesmerized, too shocked to interfere.

When, at last, Arlene's fury finally spent itself, she said regretfully, "Oh, Sandra, I shouldn't have done that. Daddy's going to be so angry at me now. What am I going to do?"

Trying not to panic, Sandra said, "We've got to find a shopping bag and take the doll away before Daddy and Rachel can see it."

Getting a large paper bag from the kitchen proved no problem. Choosing the opportune moment to slip out of the apartment was another matter. They left while Rachel was using the bathroom and their father was still talking to his stockbroker. Sandra quickly said that she and Arlene wanted to take a walk, reacquaint themselves with the neighborhood and would soon return. Harry blew them a kiss and waved goodbye.

To ensure the doll wouldn't be found near their apartment, they walked all the way to Eighty-sixth Street, crossed into Central Park, and tossed the bag into a chain-link trash basket opposite the Reservoir.

Before returning, Sandra said they'd have to tell their father and Rachel that they'd gone to the park to play with Arlene's new doll, but a mean old drunk stole it from them and ran away. "If you still feel like crying, Arlene, that's the time to do it," added Sandra shrewdly.

Arlene nodded, before throwing her arms around her sister's neck. "Oh, Sandra, I don't want to go home," she said.

"Me, either," Sandra confessed. "But we have to."

Unfortunately, that was exactly what Arlene didn't want to hear, and pushing Sandra away, she cried out, "I want my mother!"

A number of people turned around, and one sympathetic woman even came over and asked if anything was the matter.

"Poor thing," Sandra said, trying to sound more grownup than she felt. "Her mother died three years ago, but she still can't accept that means it's forever..."

***

Of course, all that happened seventy-odd years ago, a lifetime really, before parents became more sophisticated, before they knew and understood children better. Or at least that's what I tell myself each time I reflect about the summer my mother and father married and my sisters' hearts continued to break. They're both grandmothers now, by the way, and I usually see them every Passover at Sandra's. It's there Arlene, still bubbly and expansive, invariably confides, "I was glad when you were born, Eric, glad Daddy had another son." We're sitting side-by-side, around a large festive table, and there are twelve, maybe fifteen others in the room. But when Arlene starts telling me what my father was like before I was born and he kept trying to put their lives back together, it seems as though it's just the two of us.

"Ma, don't do it!" I always want to shout when my sister gets to the part where Rachel throws Lenesa away. "They'll hold it against you forever! For Christ's sake, don't!"

"Forgive me, Eric," Arlene whispers, sensing my anxiety and reaching for her wine glass. "But it's as if it all happened only yesterday."

Peter

Peter Ritter, a chunky, bright, nine-year-old boy who lived near East End Avenue in New York City, was jumpy all that day in school. His mother had been killed in an auto crash ten months before, and because the next day would have been her birthday, he couldn't seem to get her out of his head. What a relief for him at three o'clock when, along with the other nine-year-olds, he charged out of the building into the freedom and autumn sunshine of the street.

His books bouncing in one hand against his thigh, Peter ran all the way home. He caught his breath in the lobby downstairs. As soon as he got into the apartment, he made for the kitchen. There he found Marjorie, the housekeeper, sitting at the table, studying the day's racing form. She was a tall, skinny woman in her late forties; his father had hired her a month after his mother's death.

When he came into the room, Marjorie tossed her racing form against the sugar bowl and gave him a mighty grin. Peter smelled whisky on her breath.

"Learn anything interesting today, Pistol Pete?" she asked.

Then she stood up and got a container of milk out of the refrigerator and filled a glass for him. She had a habit of asking a question and then turning her back on him. Peter, a serious boy, believed that only people's faces deserved answers; backs didn't qualify. Anyway, he'd been so tied up in knots all day in school that it was impossible for him to have learned anything, let alone anything interesting.

He thanked her for the milk and walked out of the kitchen. Marjorie watched him heading toward his bedroom and felt like giving him a smack where it would do the most good. The nerve of the squirt, not responding when she spoke to him! "Spoiled rotten by his father," she said to herself.

Peter closed his bedroom door behind him and put the glass of milk on his desk. Then he opened the closet and took out his camp duffel bag. Reaching to the bottom of it, he touched the gold-framed photograph of his mother and yanked the picture out past bundles of camp clothing.

A month after her death, Peter's father had packed away all the photographs of his wife. He'd put newspaper around the frames to protect the glass, then piled them one on top of another in an old suitcase. Before closing the suitcase, though, he went to the liquor cabinet and poured himself a stiff shot. And that was when Peter made his move. He grabbed one of the pictures, and while his father's back was still turned, retreated with his treasure into his bedroom; there he hid the photograph in his duffel bag. When he came out of the bedroom some minutes later he saw his father snap the suitcase shut, but because a single picture of his mother now rested in the bottom of his duffel bag, it wasn't so bad watching his father carry the suitcase down to the storage room in the basement of the building.

Peter looked at his mother's picture and traced with one finger her long, black hair, which almost reached her shoulders. He drank the glass of milk Marjorie had given him and stared and smiled at his mother. She was wearing a white blouse open at the throat, with a necklace of pearls and matching earrings. She had a full, dark, beautiful face, and though Peter couldn't see it, people said he resembled her.

Suddenly he heard the phone ring, and like an alarmed thief he ran to the closet and thrust the picture back into its hiding place. He didn't close the closet door a moment too soon, for Marjorie entered his bedroom without knocking just as Peter skipped to the window overlooking the East River, on the other side of his room.

"Your father's on the telephone," Marjorie said. "He wants to parley with Your Majesty."

"Thanks, Marjorie," he said, and walked with as much sang-froid as he could muster into the kitchen. He was sure she hadn't spotted him fooling with the duffel bag. He had no doubt that had she seen him near the closet, she'd have become suspicious, investigated and reported her findings to his father. In fact, he suspected her of telling tales about most of the things he did.

In the kitchen Peter reached for the phone. "Hello, kid," Marty Ritter said. Ritter worked for a large advertising firm and busied himself making piles of money. "Listen, Peter," his father said now, "I called to tell you not to wait for dinner with me tonight because I've got to stay in the office and work late. I'll probably be home after you've gone to sleep, but I'll see you tomorrow morning before you go to school. If I'm not up, wake me right before you leave like a good kid. Okay?"

"I wish you'd come home and eat supper with me tonight, Daddy," Peter said. "Tomorrow's Mama's birthday."

"I know what tomorrow is, Peter," his father said tensely. "But I've got to work late. I have to get this job done tonight or we won't be eating dessert next month."

"I don't want to eat by myself tonight, Daddy."

"Then break bread with Marjorie!" his father snapped. "Listen, kid, I can't help it. I'll make it up to you this weekend. We'll do whatever you say. Go to a ballgame, a movie—both of them, if you want—whatever you say. Try to understand," he pleaded. "I couldn't take it, being in the apartment tonight."

"Why?" Peter asked.

"We'll talk about it some other time. 'By, kid," his father said, hanging up.

After a while Peter put the receiver back on the hook. Marjorie was watching.

"My father has to work late tonight and won't be home for dinner."

"Your father works too hard," Marjorie said. "You don't appreciate what he does for you."

Peter winced. "I'm going down for a walk, Marjorie. I'll be back soon."

"Just don't be late for dinner," she called after him.

When Peter emerged from the apartment building, one hand was clutching the change in his pocket. He knew from the feel of the coins that he had enough money to make the telephone call. He passed a group of boys playing punchball in the street. One of the boys called to him. Peter waved but kept walking. Soon he came to a candy store. Inside, he saw that all three telephone booths were empty.

He was planning to call his aunt Phyllis, his mother's twin sister, who lived in Queens with her husband and three children. He'd called her five times before. Five other times he'd heard her say hello, after which he hung up. He called because he enjoyed hearing her voice; it reminded him of his mother's.

Being her twin, Phyllis naturally looked a lot like her late sister, and Peter often wished he could see his aunt. But whenever he suggested that they invite her over to the apartment, his father turned the idea down cold. And whenever his aunt invited them for dinner or to spend the day, his father said, "You go, kid. I'll give you money to buy them a house gift and to take a cab both ways." But Peter was a timid boy, and though he wanted to see his aunt very badly, he couldn't get up the nerve to make the trip alone.

Reaching for his change now, Peter chose the middle telephone booth. He tried to make himself comfortable, but his throat remained stubbornly dry. His hands shook as he held the phone, deposited the coins and dialed the Queens number he'd committed to memory months ago. Then he took a deep breath.

The phone rang twice before his aunt answered it. She said hello and Peter sighed.

Then his aunt was saying, "Look, this is the fifth or sixth time you've called, whoever you are, and I'm getting tired of it. You're the same one who's called before—don't deny it. What are you trying to do, frighten me?"

This was the first time she'd become angry when he called. Peter didn't know what to do. He wished he could say something to explain, but it was as if his jaws were bound together.

"I'll tell you what I think," his aunt was shouting. "I think you're a rotten burglar, and you keep calling to see if I'm home. Well, burglar, as soon as I hang up on you, I'm dialing the police. And if you ever bother me again, they'll trace the call and grab you!"

The anger in her voice sent a shiver racing down Peter's spine. Before his aunt could break the connection, he hung up. Then bolted from the telephone booth. He had the presence of mind not to run once he hit the street, for he didn't want to draw attention to himself. But he couldn't help hurrying from the candy store to his building.

Without bothering to say hello to Marjorie, who was sitting at the kitchen table, marking her racing form, he went directly to his bedroom and shut the door. His heart was pounding violently, and he tried to calm himself by lying on his bed.

The walls of his room were decorated with colored photographs of major-league baseball players: Willie Mays spearing a line drive over his shoulder, Mantle belting a homer at Yankee Stadium, Sandy Koufax following through after blazing a fast ball past a late swinging hitter. Peter looked Koufax in the eye. "I didn't mean to do anything bad, Sandy," he said.

He wished he had the courage to call his aunt and explain why he'd dialed her number six times but never said a word to her. He wished he had the courage, but he knew he didn't. After a while he rolled over on his stomach. Then he got the idea of writing his aunt a letter. It would certainly be easier explaining himself in a letter than having to say the words over the telephone. When he'd gone to camp this past summer he'd written several letters to his father, so he knew how to write one—where to put the date, what to say in the beginning and how to sign off.

Feeling a sense of relief, he hopped off the bed and got some lined, loose-leaf paper out of his notebook and a ball-point pen from his desk. Then he sat down and began to think about what he'd write. He had a lot of things to say, and he wanted to organize them in his head first.

He'd tell her how much he enjoyed hearing her say hello, that it meant a lot to him because she sounded so much like his mother. He'd explain that this was why he'd called her six times. He'd tell her that he wished he had a chance to see her and hoped she'd understand that he just hadn't got around to it yet. He wouldn't be disloyal to his father and write the truth.

Then he would ask how his uncle and cousins were. He'd describe how school was going for him. He'd write something like, "I used to have trouble with penmanship, but that's improved a lot. My last report card I got a good mark in penmanship. I passed all my subjects. It used to bother me that I was the shortest boy in the class last year. They line you up by size all the time, so you can never forget you're the shortest. But this term I grew faster than the two other boys, and now I'm the third shortest, and that makes me feel much better about everything. Maybe next year these two other boys will outgrow someone else. As long as it's not me, I hope so. I figure I've had my turn being shortest."

Peter sat back against his chair, satisfied with how the letter was taking shape in his head. It all sounded pretty good, he thought. He knew that once his aunt received the letter, she'd tell the police to forget about listening to her incoming calls.

Pen in hand, he began to write. "Dear Mama," he scrawled. "I'm fine. How are you? I'm the one who's called you six times…"

An hour later Marjorie barged into his room and announced that supper was ready.

"What are we eating?" Peter asked.

"Lamb chops and French fries," she said. "Does that satisfy Your Majesty?"

Leading the way to the kitchen, Peter was smiling. Marjorie thought that her last crack had somehow given him pleasure. But Peter was happy for another reason. His letter, safely hidden next to his mother's photograph in the duffel bag, was signed, sealed and ready to be mailed. And nothing, no one, could stop him from sending it to his aunt tomorrow.

The *Minyan*

Monday after school, Richie and I went to smoke a couple of cigarettes in Riverside Park, where neither our mothers nor any pain-in-the-ass neighbors were likely to spot us.

It was mid-October, a week after the Yankees had beaten my beloved Bums in five. We had started smoking that September, shortly after coming home from camp. I don't know why, but we both liked Lucky Strike, maybe because of the catchy name.

Both Richie and I had plenty of homework, so neither of us was anticipating playing stickball that afternoon. Just time for a relaxing smoke down the park before hitting the books back home. I had a report due the following morning on Thomas Paine. The prospect of a math test tomorrow was driving Richie crazy, so he had a lot of crap to memorize that night.

"I figure Palladino for five-seven, one-forty," Richie said. Lester Palladino was his math teacher. It was funny about Richie's being able to look at someone and accurately guess the guy's height and weight—funny, because he was having such a terrible time in math.

And talking about height—we'd stood exactly the same that June. But by September I'd shot up three inches, Richie only an inch. And that was also driving him so crazy he'd begun drinking tiger's milk, having read somewhere that it helped you grow faster than cow's milk.

"Hey, just study tonight instead of watching television, and you'll pass Palladino's crummy little test," I said, cupping my hand and lighting up. The first inhalation was still kind of harsh.

"Who's worried?" said Richie, blowing a smoke ring like a pro.

Inhaling, I let the smoke curl from my nose. Across the Hudson, I could see the unlit SPRY sign. It wasn't dark yet.

"That Rita Glasser," Richie was saying, attempting a second smoke ring. "Boy, she's got a nice body, sexy as hell." Rita was a girl in Richie's class whom he'd liked for years. She'd also grown a couple of inches this summer which, I suspected, was the real reason he was consuming a quart of tiger's milk each day.

"We ought to go on a double date one of these days," Richie suggested. "Me and Rita, you and Joanne Stemmer."

I liked Joanne a lot, but because I was painfully shy, I shrugged, flipping my half-smoked cigarette away. "I really don't like Joanne that much. Nothing sexy about her at all," I said.

"Ah, Eric, she'll develop, she'll mature. Give her another year." And not wanting to embarrass me, Richie changed the subject, saying, "Hey, there's supposed to be a good action movie at the Symphony this week—*Gunga Din.*" He stamped out his cigarette. "Let's go Saturday."

"Sure," I said, grateful he'd stopped mentioning Joanne. We crossed the Drive, heading up the hilly street before West End Avenue.

"Say, what's the name of that movie again?" I asked before we parted in front of my building. Richie lived a block away, on 105th.

Upstairs, my grandfather was drinking tea with my mother. He often stopped for tea before going on to pray in *shul.* He was in his early eighties, a tall, slender man who didn't have a beard but didn't shave either. I used to love rubbing my face against his chin, feeling the bristles.

Grandpa wasn't wearing a hat but his *yarmulke*. He had wispy hair, a large, thick nose, and cheated at casino because he couldn't stand for a kid to beat him.

"How you feeling, Grandpa?" I asked.

He nodded, smiling, and I could see his gums. For as long as I could remember he'd been toothless.

"So, how was school?" he asked in Yiddish, rubbing his teary eyes.

"Yeah, okay," I shrugged. When I'd broken my leg nine years ago, it was my grandfather who'd carried me to the orthopedist. He may have had no teeth, but he was a strong old guy.

"Eric, before you start your homework, I want you to go to Daitch," my mother said, handing me a five-dollar bill. We needed milk, farmer cheese, and a rye bread. The crust there was terrifically crunchy, and I always ate both ends of the sliced loaf on my way home.

"Maybe I'll leave with Eric now," my grandfather said, finishing his tea and putting a fedora on over his *yarmulke*.

Daitch was at Broadway and 106th, my grandfather's *shul* on 108th between Broadway and Amsterdam. We walked side-by-side. Looking over at him, I was reminded of an old Indian chieftain—ageless, endearing, and homely. Although he was my mother's father, because he spoke singsong Yiddish and was always unshaven, he seemed like someone from another world and I loved him for his strangeness.

"See you tomorrow, Grandpa," I said in front of Daitch, kissing him and feeling the familiar stubble near his chin.

The book report on Thomas Paine proved harder to write than I'd anticipated, and I didn't finish until after ten. I handed it in Tuesday morning soon after my social studies class began. Mrs. Rabinovitch, the teacher, was pretty, but I didn't like her because when you weren't around she'd criticize you to your classmates.

Social studies preceded my lunch period, and I was always hungry when I got to the cafeteria. My mother had packed a couple of peanut butter and jelly sandwiches and an apple.

Richie and I didn't share the same homeroom, but we used to meet for lunch and I was sitting with him, finishing my second sandwich, when a messenger came over and said I was to accompany him back to the principal's office. "Jesus, what did I do wrong?" I wondered.

"I told you not to make fun of Rabinovitch, that one of her pets would squeal on you," Richie needled, as I gathered my books, then tossed him my apple.

"Make believe it's Rita Glasser," I told Richie. "That's the closest you're going to get to her."

***

Meanwhile, my father was waiting for me outside the principal's office. "Daddy?" I said with a smile, astonished to see him.

"Grandpa had an accident and he's in the hospital," my father announced. That's when I realized my dad was pale, minus his usual ruddy color. "I want you to come home with me," he said.

"Sure," I agreed, starting to feel nervous, and we immediately left school. Rather than walk five blocks, we surprisingly caught a cab.

"Grandpa going to be okay?" I asked in the taxi. "What happened?"

My father said that he fell in *shul* early that morning and must have hit his head. When two other old men entered the synagogue, they'd found him unconscious near the ark. One of them called for an ambulance. Grandpa, my father said, was still unconscious.

But arriving home, I immediately spotted a sheet covering the hall mirror, knew that meant Grandpa was dead, and hurried into my parents' bedroom. My mother was crying.

"I told Eric that your father fell, hit his head in *shul.*" Something about the abrupt way my father said it made me stare at him.

My mother stood up and put her arms around me. "Grandpa didn't fall," she began to explain. "Somebody killed him with a lead pipe in *shul.* It's in the afternoon papers, and we didn't want you possibly seeing the headlines on the way home."

Killed? Murdered? But he was an old man, over eighty, it made no sense. "Who'd want to kill Grandpa?" I asked, starting to cry. "Why?"

That's when the phone rang and my father went inside to answer it. When he came back, he said it was the police. They wanted a family member to go down to the morgue to make an official identification. Because my uncle Danny wasn't in New York yet and my father was the only male member of the family around, he told the cop he'd be right down.

But my father was a diabetic, who took insulin and had lapsed into shock twice last year; and remembering that, I dried my eyes, saying, "I'll go with you, Daddy."

My mother shook her head, but my father said, "Rachel, I really don't want to go down there alone."

Two detectives from the 24th Precinct were waiting for us at the medical examiner's office. One of the cops looked at me, then whispered something to my father. Frowning, my father told me to remain in the anteroom. "I appreciate your coming with me, Eric but I want to do this myself." Then the shorter cop led him into a second room.

When my father returned a few minutes later, he looked even paler than before. "Let's get the hell out of here," he said.

Outside, because my father seemed distracted, I hailed the cab.

"I couldn't identify Grandpa's face," my father told me in a hollow voice. "The guy beat him so badly, he was unrecognizable. I had to identify him from his clothes, his high-button shoes."

"Daddy," I said reaching for my father's hand as the cab cut through Central Park. "Please don't go into shock again, okay?"

Grandpa was to be buried next day, Wednesday. A couple of hours before the funeral, one of the detectives who'd met us at the medical examiner's office called, saying he and his partner wanted to come over, and they showed up at our apartment fifteen minutes later.

The taller detective's name was Hillard. He had a wart near his nose. The shorter one's name was O'Brien, and he spoke with the same thick Irish brogue as Mike Quill, the labor leader who was always threatening to strike the subways on New Year's Day.

O'Brien asked if we knew my grandfather's friend, Myer Zeigler. Of course we knew him. Old man Zeigler lived directly across the street from us, in Two-Forty-Five. He was rich, owned a button factory, and attended the same *shul* as my grandfather. He was also Richie's grandfather, on Richie's mother's side.

Hillard said they'd learned from an informant that Mr. Zeigler's son, David, Richie's uncle, was a compulsive gambler who'd run up a large debt that the old man had refused to pay. Was it possible the killer had confused Zeigler with my grandfather?

"They don't look anywhere near alike," I said. Richie's grandfather had a white mustache and, unlike my grandfather, always dressed well, favoring bowties. I couldn't remember or imagine my grandfather ever wearing a bowtie, let alone dressing well.

O'Brien said, "We're thinking it's also possible that the murder was a warning to Mr. Zeigler—that he better pay his son's debt or he's next. Anyway, if information about Mr. Zeigler or his son comes your way, be sure to let us know without letting them know. It could be important."

Later, I noticed both detectives at the funeral. Also, four of my closest friends, sitting together at the rear of the chapel. They were all wearing their *bar mitzvah* suits, white shirts, and ties. An old, bearded rabbi spoke in Yiddish for almost an hour. But he spoke as if he had marbles in his mouth, and I don't think I understood ten words.

Because I'd had a bad dream and couldn't eat, my mother let me stay home from school the following day. She, her sister, and brother were sitting *shiva* over at my grandfather's. They wore slippers and sat on wooden boxes. Relatives and neighbors came and went, bringing baskets of fruit and boxes of candy. Same thing next day.

***

Late that afternoon, the men got together to conduct a service but found they were one short of a *minyan*, the quorum of ten adult males required so that my uncle could say *kaddish*. Having turned thirteen, I was considered an adult and therefore made the ninth. "I'll go downstairs and find one of my friends," I said. "He'll be our tenth."

The guys were on 106th, in the middle of a stickball game, five to a side. Home and second base were a couple of sewers. First and third were in chalk, so was the inning-by-inning score, sketched out in the gutter near home plate. We were mostly the same age, so any number of my friends could have returned with me. When I walked over to Richie, explaining the situation, he said, "Sure, I'll be your number ten, let's go."

But between the time I'd left and returned with Richie, three old men from my grandfather's *shul* had arrived, so there were more than enough now for a *minyan* without us. Among the three was Richie's grandfather, who was wearing a polka-dot bowtie.

As soon as he saw his grandson, old man Zeigler said to him in a voice brimming with anger, "What are you doing here?"

Flustered, Richie explained that I'd gone down to get a tenth because there'd been only nine for a *minyan.*

"So that makes it okay to come here wearing old, shabby clothes?" Zeigler's voice coiled with sarcasm. "This is a house of mourning. Grandson, what do you use for brains?"

"But, Mr. Zeigler, Richie was in the middle of a stickball game," I said. "He did me a favor leaving the game to come up here. Why are you talking this way to him?"

The old man, however, gave me a dirty look, as if I wasn't much better, and who was I to question his authority anyway.

"You're a disgrace to me, a disgrace!" Ziegler hissed, and suddenly he lashed out, slapping Richie, just like that, for no good reason. Richie turned a nail-polish red.

I spun around, but none of the others, including my parents, interceded. I couldn't believe it. They all sort of looked away, down at the floor or at each other, as if politeness required their making believe they weren't present. Even my mother, my cherished mother.

"Why do you keep standing there like the dummy you are?" old man Zeigler taunted Richie. "Go! Leave this apartment! Disappear! Vanish! Evaporate! Out of my sight!"

Each command was like another slap, another stinging blow to Richie's face, and it suddenly occurred to me maybe that was what the old man had wanted to do to his son, the gambler, that smacking Richie was a kind of consolation prize he couldn't pass up.

When Richie finally turned, leaving the apartment, I trailed after him.

There were more than ten men now, a *minyan;* they no longer needed me. Besides, after what had just happened, who wanted to stick around?

"Gee whiz, Richie," I said when we got downstairs, "you okay?"

Richie's face had turned from bright red back to normal, yet when he looked over at me it was as if I'd just done something terrible—set him up or let him down, maybe both. "Why didn't you at least tell me my grandfather was up there?" he asked angrily, as we headed in the direction of Broadway. "You're supposed to be one of my best friends. We're supposed to stick up for each other, supposed to be able to trust each other."

"But your grandfather wasn't there when I left," I tried to explain, "and I don't think the way you're dressed is so terrible."

Suddenly Richie grabbed my shirt and started shaking me. "I was your guest, in your grandfather's apartment. Why didn't you stop him? I feel so embarrassed."

"Listen," I said after Richie finally let go of my shirt. "The cops think your grandfather was the guy the murderer was after because he refused to pay your uncle's gambling debts.

They said not to tell you, Richie, but it's your grandfather who may have caused everything, everything!"

As soon as I said it, I knew it was wrong, not because the cops didn't want Richie to know but because it wasn't fair. Not to old man Zeigler, who didn't kill anybody or run up any gambling debts, nor to Richie, because he was already feeling rotten and telling him about his grandfather, springing it on him like that, was the equivalent of piling on.

Richie looked like he wanted to die. "You're just saying lousy things about my family because you didn't really help me. I thought you were different, Eric, but you're just like all the other jerks taller than me. You take advantage, and how am I supposed to trust you anymore?" Then he began walking down Broadway. He had a funny walk, like a rooster, a bantam rooster. "Go to hell!" he shouted over his shoulder.

Meanwhile, it was growing dark and people were spilling out of the nearby subway kiosk, on their way home from work. I kept standing on the corner, hoping Richie would circle back. But nothing doing. My circumscribed world of family and friends was fragmenting as never before, and how was I going to put the remaining pieces together again when, because of gaps beyond my ability to bridge, the rest no longer seemed to fit?

Realizing my mother would start worrying about me, I decided to return to my grandfather's and began walking up the block. Suddenly a howling wind shot off the nearby river into my face, hurtling between apartment buildings and the confining tunnel of a one-way side street. The buildings seemed to sway, to rock and shake, as if they were all going to tumble down on me, and I ran, making an anxious right at West End Avenue. There, the wind no longer howling, I tried to stop feeling panicky, tried to catch my breath. I blinked once, twice, even said a belated prayer, the *Shema*, only that didn't seem to help much either.

And still feeling agitated, I crossed West End. It was then I saw in the dim glare of an orange moon a profile of my grandfather's large nose and sunken mouth, his homely, ageless face. He was wearing a *yarmulke*.

"Old chief!" I exclaimed, astonished to see him. "Revered and honored elder!" His profile was slightly hazy, but it was definitely my grandfather, couldn't have been anyone else. Not with that bulbous nose.

Turning, he looked at me, his face slowly coming in focus, and I could clearly make out two rheumy eyes, stubble shading his chin, his pink, toothless gums.

"Old chief, old chief," I said, lifting my arms to embrace him. "I never thought I'd see you again."

Room 503

The dream was always the same: in the dim glare of an orange moon, I could see the profile of my grandfather's large, bulbous nose and sunken mouth, the bristles on his chin, his homely, ageless face. He was wearing a *yarmulke*. Turning, he faced me. He was smiling. I saw his toothless gums and remembered how he'd dunk his toast into his tea; he couldn't eat it otherwise. But when he gestured that he wanted to embrace me, I ran away as fast as my pumping legs allowed, through confining one-way side streets, across brightly lit Broadway, dodging buses and horn-blaring yellow cabs, until I reached Riverside Park, then down the stairs and on to the park's lower level, only stopping when I approached the river and could see the friendly, blinking lights of Jersey on the other side of the calm black water. Quickly I began shedding my clothes, before swimming to the opposite shore.

But that's when I'd wake, and it was always with a pounding headache. The headache would last hours, sometimes a day, leaving me tense, nervous, and high-strung.

It was 1949. I was fourteen. My grandfather had been murdered, beaten beyond recognition early one October morning in a small Orthodox *shul* on the Upper West Side, and I couldn't seem to come to terms with his awful death.

At first, I didn't mention the dream or headache to anyone, but when it got so bad that I couldn't go to school, I had to tell my mother. She was upset but not surprised. Since my grandfather's death, she was afraid to go outside once it got dark. Of course, she'd hoped her fear would abate and my headaches disappear, but when the dream and pain persisted over a course of weeks, she insisted I see the doctor. I didn't want to and kept putting her off. But six months after my grandfather's death, I had the worst headache of all—it felt as though my skull was being squeezed inside a vise. Next morning I found myself in Dr. Felder's familiar office.

Sophie Felder had been my pediatrician since I was born. Her husband, Morton Gerrin, had been my mother's obstetrician, and husband and wife shared a Park Avenue office in the mid-Seventies. Their waiting room was filled with adolescents, young children, squealing infants, and pregnant women. Miss Reedy, their receptionist, was a fanatical Dodger fan who had red hair and freckles.

Sophie Felder, no baseball fan but an opera buff, was a wonderful woman and a terrific doctor. Doctors still made house calls then, and though you might be running a high fever and feel miserable when she arrived, you absolutely knew you were going to feel better soon, because Dr. Felder was in your bedroom, incapable of disappointing you.

She was on the heavy side, medium height, and not particularly good-looking. Had wide brown eyes, a nice mouth, and a soothing, lovely voice, deeper than most women's. She always ran behind schedule, both in her office and when she made house calls, because she never rushed a patient or an anxious parent. On her way out, Dr. Felder would ask to use your phone, so she could apologize to her next patient's mother for the delay. I'm sure I wasn't the only one of her young charges who loved and admired her extravagantly.

My mother, I knew, didn't feel the same about Dr. Felder's husband. She thought that tall, good-looking Morton Gerrin practiced medicine—unlike his wife—for the money and prestige of being a doctor, and she never went back to him after I was born. She said that while he was a good doctor, he wasn't her kind of doctor. It was only later that I understood what she meant.

During my appointment, my mother told Dr. Felder that I'd been having bad dreams and headaches since my grandfather died.

After examining me, Dr. Felder said she thought I was okay and the headaches would go away. But just to be on the safe side, she was going to take blood and send me for X-rays. "Eric, don't be nervous about these tests," she said. "I'm almost certain they're going to show nothing. I just want to be completely sure."

***

In between the time I had the blood test and went for the X-rays, a story mentioning Dr. Felder appeared in the *News*. She'd been driving near a construction site one afternoon, just after a hard hat had been pinned under a collapsed steel beam in an underground shaft. Waiting for an ambulance that seemed to take forever, one of the other construction workers stopped Dr. Felder's Buick because of her MD license plate. She pulled over and was rushed down the narrow shaft. The hard hat was conscious but in shock and pain. According to the *News*, Dr. Felder gave him a shot to deaden the pain, then insisted on remaining with him, at considerable risk to her own safety—the weakened shaft could have collapsed on both of them. Mayor O'Dwyer called her "a hero."

When she phoned a few days later, never mentioning the *News* but saying that my blood test and X-rays revealed nothing wrong, my mother thanked her. Dr. Felder added that if my headaches persisted, she wanted me to come to her office again.

The following week, I had the dream and a headache. Then the same thing again the week after that. And for the first time since I'd been going to her, I was afraid Dr. Felder didn't know how to help me.

"Eric, why do you think you keep having the same dream?" she asked. I was her last office patient that afternoon. It was almost 1:30. We weren't in one of the examining rooms but sitting opposite each other in her wood-paneled office.

"I don't know why the same dream keeps coming back," I said.

She asked if I liked my grandfather.

"I loved my grandfather. He lived a block away, and I saw him the afternoon before he died." Then I told her how, when I was five and had broken my leg, he carried me to the orthopedist. Yet, playing casino with me after, he still used to cheat because he hated losing to a kid.

Dr. Felder smiled. Smiling, she looked prettier than she really was. "Are you afraid that what happened to your grandfather might happen to you?" she asked.

"No, not really. Although my father did tell me never to forget that Jews not only got murdered in Europe but in America, too."

That was when Miss Reedy reminded Dr. Felder, "You're running late for lunch and your first house call is scheduled for three."

But Dr. Felder waved her away, saying to me, "Eric, I remember that your grandmother died years ago. Did you have bad dreams then, too?"

I shook my head. "No, but this is different, Dr. Felder. My grandfather's face was beaten so badly my father had to identify him by his clothes. Besides, they still haven't found the guy who did it."

Before Dr. Felder could respond, her husband looked in on us. "Sophie," he said with obvious exasperation, "if you can't make lunch in five minutes, I'm going to have to leave without you."

She apologized with a smile, but said, "Perhaps you ought to do that, Morton."

"Oh, for Christ's sake!'" he snapped, walking away. I had the feeling that, although he delivered babies, he didn't particularly like children.

I started to get up. "Maybe I ought to leave now."

"No, Eric, I want you to stay," Dr. Felder insisted, gesturing for me to sit down again. Then she said, as though she were thinking out loud, "I could always send you to a psychiatrist. But I don't think you really need one, and I believe you'd gain a lot from this experience by working it out for yourself." This reminded me of the time, three years ago, when she told my mother after I'd gotten into a fight and my chin was lacerated, "Stitches aren't the worst thing in the world, Mrs. Rosen. They'll remind Eric that not only can life be violent, but that he can survive its violence."

Now she leaned back in her chair, and rubbed her wedding ring with her right thumb. I wondered if she was thinking of her husband. But then she said, "I see so many terrible things at the hospital each day, Eric, and I know that when your grandfather was murdered you experienced something terrible, too, the first really awful event in your life, and the first is especially upsetting, painful to absorb. But I also think you'll find a way soon, and it would be useful for you to know you can deal with something like this on your own."

I loved it that she was sympathetic but didn't pamper me, nor had she encouraged my mother to be overly protective. Also, she never used words I didn't understand or reasoning I couldn't follow. She spoke as if we were equals. I knew we weren't, but it was as an equal that I had the presumption to ask, "Were you frightened when you stayed with the construction worker down that shaft?"

Although she appeared surprised by the question, she said, "I certainly was frightened. But I've learned that as long as being afraid doesn't prevent me from functioning, it's not so terrible."

Pressing her, I asked how she was able to remain down the shaft despite her fear.

She gave herself a minute to reflect, then said, "Before the ambulance arrived, the man held my hand and we kept talking. This seemed to give him comfort. After that, it wouldn't have occurred to me to leave him in the shaft, even with someone else."

I nodded. "Maybe something will happen to me soon that will also be stronger than the dream about my grandfather."

***

That was early May. I wish I could report that a transforming event quickly took place to make the headaches go away or lessen. But nothing happened, and I began to think that Dr. Felder should have sent me to a psychiatrist after all, that I couldn't handle this on my own.

Then, one Saturday later that month, I was hanging around the basketball courts on Riverside Park and 110th, when some older guys I knew asked if I wanted a game. It was half-court, three on a side. They needed a sixth.

I was okay in basketball, but nothing special. I didn't have a particularly accurate outside shot and could only drive going to my left. But I held my own that afternoon, scoring the first and last baskets, plus one in between. My team won, eleven-nine. After the game, one of the guys on the team, Jimmy Kindler, happened to say if he didn't go to a hooker every other week, he got terrible headaches, too.

Jimmy was sixteen. I was still fourteen and hadn't come close to getting laid. But I thought that if this worked for Jimmy, it might also work for me, even if this wasn't the kind of remedy Dr. Felder might have prescribed.

As someone who wanted to believe he could tell right from wrong, I preferred making my own mistakes. On the other hand, I lacked even the initial, fumbling experiences when it came to sex. But the way Jimmy talked, going to a hooker seemed the equivalent of taking a kind of super-aspirin, which sounded like the sort of thing someone shy like me would be able to manage.

That explains why, when we began walking home, I mentioned my headaches to Jimmy, then asked if he really knew a hooker and how much she'd charge.

Jimmy was tall and thin, had a beaky nose and wavy hair that resembled Brillo. He stared at me as if he thought I was kidding. "How old are you, Eric?" he said with a sarcastic grin.

I looked younger than I was, but told him, "Almost sixteen, why?"

"You're full of shit!" he said.

"Look, I didn't ask your permission to get laid, just where to go. You sounded like you might know. You want to act snotty, fuck you, too!" And I started walking away.

"Hey, don't get so touchy. I was only teasing."

Maybe he remembered that I'd scored those three baskets, the last of which, a curling lay-up after going baseline, won the goddamn game. We were walking along Broadway, approaching pocket-size Straus Park. I slowed down, letting Jimmy catch up.

"There are a couple of hookers at the Marseilles Hotel, twins—Marie and Colette," he finally said. "They call themselves, 'The Fabulous Jolly Sisters.'" Jimmy laughed, as if he'd just told a joke, a joke I didn't understand.

"Actually, they're kind of famous, known all over the city," he threw in, as if he decided he'd gone too far, even if I hadn't appreciated his humor. "You have to make an appointment, call the hotel, Room 503. They charge twenty dollars."

The Marseilles was on the corner of Broadway and 103rd. A lot of Europeans had lived there since the end of the war. "They refugees?" I asked.

"Hungarians from Paris. The only thing is, you can't say I'm the one who recommended them," Jimmy insisted, clearly afraid I might make a fool of myself and embarrass him by association. "If they ask, just say you overheard some guy talking in Stanley's about how great they are." Stanley's was a cafeteria on the other side of Broadway. "Room 503, okay?"

"Sure," I said, wondering where in God's name I'd get hold of twenty dollars. It seemed like a fortune to me.

***

I gave it a lot of thought that night, and decided the following day to cash in one of the $18.75 U.S. Savings Bonds I'd received when I was *bar mitzvahed.* I had ten of them in a safety deposit box at our bank, and I had one of the keys, in case of an emergency.

Trust me when I say I was prepared to cash in the rest, one at a time, if going to a hooker every other week meant getting rid of my headaches. Of course, if my mother ever learned about it, she'd have had a heart attack. Nor had I figured out what to do after the last bond was gone. But that was at least five months away, and I was confident something else would occur to me by then.

After cashing in the first, I called the Marseilles, asking for Room 503. Sure enough, a woman with a French accent answered. But then, I'm ashamed to admit, I lost my nerve and hung up. That was the moment when I realized this was not going to be as easy as taking a super-aspirin.

Next morning, I decided to sneak up to the fifth floor of the Marseilles. I knew that once I saw someone close to my age entering 503, I'd tell myself, "Hey, if he can, why can't you?"

I'd been to the Marseilles before. An automatic soda machine stood near the newsstand opposite the reception desk. My friends and I occasionally went for a Coke there following a day of stickball.

It was early Saturday afternoon when I entered the hotel lobby and got myself a soda. Then I looked for the nearest flight of stairs. Using the stairs would be easier than taking one of the elevators; I wouldn't have to nervously tell the operator the floor I wanted.

There were a couple of stairways in the hotel, and I spotted one to the right of the reception desk. Sipping a Coke, I casually headed there. It couldn't have been easier, and I was practically patting myself on the back when I reached the fifth floor.

Room 503 was the second door from the end, down a long, dimly lit hallway. Luckily, it was also near a second stairway. If I stood in the stairwell, in the shadows, I could see those entering and leaving without the other person being aware of me.

Within five minutes of positioning myself, I spotted State Senator Leonard Tamken knocking on the door. He was a short, fat guy with a red face, a flashy dresser, who wore a white carnation in his lapel and lived in the neighborhood. I had once seen him in his apartment: his younger son, Steve, was my age and had hung around with me and my friends a couple of years ago.

Senator Tamken going to one of the hookers I'm hoping to see, I thought, Jesus Christ!

This was a revelation. I'd been under the impression hookers were meant for older bachelors and younger guys before they married. No one ever told me differently. Yet Senator Tamken had a wife, was in his fifties, and the father of two.

Tamken remained inside for almost an hour. I couldn't imagine what was taking him so long, and I began to wonder if maybe he'd died in there. But when he came out of the room, he was smiling ear-to-ear, looking anything but dead.

Barely five minutes later, surprise number two materialized in the person of a New York Football Giant, only I'm not going to mention his name.

During the football season, the team lived three blocks away, at the Whitehall Hotel. You'd see the players on their way to breakfast Sundays before they headed out to the Polo Grounds for an NFL game that afternoon. You couldn't possibly mistake them for anyone else. They had immense shoulders and walked in groups of three or four, which only seemed to highlight their unusual bulk. And now, my God, there was one of them, not twenty feet away, his neck thick as a fire hydrant. Curiously, he stayed less than a half hour and looked disappointed when he left.

The third guy, who appeared within ten minutes, was one of the barbers from the shop around the corner on Broadway where I'd gone for a haircut the week before. An older man than the first two, he was close to seventy, with a mustache and snow-white hair. Because of his age, call him surprise number three. He wore a red tie and blue suit, as if he was going to a party, and kept smoothing his mustache before he finally cleared his throat and knocked on the door.

I didn't recognize the fourth man, which was a relief, because I was beginning to worry that my father or uncle might be next, and I probably would have burst into tears then.

Not wishing to dwell on the possible appearance of a family member, I distracted myself by wondering if the Jolly Sisters ever took customers simultaneously, the way the barbers around the corner did. So far, they hadn't, nor had I caught a glimpse of either sister. Were they pretty? What did they wear? And what did they say when you walked in? Although I realized I hadn't a clue, and my confidence had been hemorrhaging since I'd first recognized Senator Tamken, I still hoped I'd find the nerve to see this damn thing through, because the dream was no fun and the headaches worse.

Fortunately, it was Saturday, and I had all afternoon to work this out. Yet how could I possibly have foreseen that the fifth man would not only make time irrelevant but prove the biggest surprise of all? On the other hand, maybe I shouldn't have been stunned after having seen Senator Tamken. But observing Morton Gerrin, Dr. Felder's husband, knocking on 503 literally took my breath away.

I knew that he lived close by, in the Nineties near Central Park, and I guess—as Jimmy said—the Fabulous Jolly Sister had a citywide reputation. As for Dr. Gerrin, how could he have anticipated that one of his wife's pediatric patients would be lurking in the shadows, commanding a perfect view of those entering the inner sanctum?

Of course, seeing Dr. Felder's husband immediately made me think of her, and I found myself quickly retreating down the stairs, as if not only Gerrin was betraying his wife but I was somehow on the verge of betraying her, too.

***

That afternoon, walking alone in Riverside Park, I understood that no matter how many headaches I'd have, I wasn't ready to step into Room 503. To actually involve myself with the same hookers used by those considerably older guys would have been silly really, like trying on a pair of shoes four sizes too large.

I suppose it's ironic how things eventually turned out. Because after that unforgettable Saturday, each time I thought about my grandfather, I also thought about 503. And while the two became inextricably joined, Room 503 ended up far more compelling. Instead of continuing to dream about my grandfather, I began to dream of entering 503, where I got to know Colette and Marie. And when I'd wake, it wasn't with a headache but with the stickiness of an orgasm and a smile as wide as Senator Tamken's.

While my sense of relief was enormous, I couldn't forget about Dr. Felder. The urge to help or comfort her wouldn't go away. I seriously considered writing an anonymous letter, mentioning Gerrin and the Hotel Marseilles. But how do you disclose to someone you admire that her husband is an intimate of the Fabulous Jolly Sisters? In the end, I found that ratting even on a jerk like Gerrin was just too sneaky. Maybe when I was eighteen, I would find an excuse to tell him that if he ever two-timed Dr. Felder again, I'd knock him on his ass. But that was four years away and didn't help Dr. Felder now.

What I decided was to write another kind of letter, still anonymous, because she might otherwise wonder why I wrote it, and under the pressure of her questions I might have told her everything.

Dear Dr. Felder, I printed, because I was afraid she would recognize my scrawly handwriting. *Who I am is unimportant, because I'm sure most of your patients feel about you as I do. If you're ever in a tight spot, count on me. But what I really want you to know is that even if I'm unaware you're in trouble, or you're unaware you're in trouble, I'm still with you.* That's what I wrote, short and convoluted, my heart plastered all over it.

Next time I saw Dr. Felder was in September, just before school started. Thank God I didn't spot Gerrin in the office they shared. I might have lost it then, even if I did feel a lot older since all this began. You never know.

Examining me, Dr. Felder asked about my headaches. I told her they were gone. She smiled and nodded, touching my shoulder as though she was proud of me. But shortly before I left, she looked into my eyes in a strange, probing way, a way I'd never seen her look at me before.

At first, I couldn't figure out why. Then it occurred to me that she must have drawn a list of the ten most likely patients who might have written that besotted, unsigned letter. I imagined that my name was posted there, fifth or sixth, somewhere in the middle.

What can I tell you? What can I say? Making that list, her hand brushing my shoulder—both, both meant the world to me.

The Doubleheader

Not too long ago, I received a condolence card. It was a strange experience because no one I knew had recently died. The background is pale blue and on the front is a vase with two darker blue irises.

"May love bring you comfort and time bring you peace," were the words printed inside the card. It was signed, "Rose."

As soon as I saw Rose's signature, I burst out laughing. Rose is the ninety-something mother of a good friend I made about thirty years ago. She lives down in Florida. A diehard Red Sox fan, Rose was commiserating with me, if that's the right word, less than a week after the Marlins knocked off the heavily favored Yankees in that year's Series. Savoring the card, I'm reminded of what the formidable Leo Durocher once said of the even more formidable Jackie Robinson: "You want a guy to come to play. But this guy just didn't come to play. He came to stuff the goddamn bat up your ass!"

Anticipating how much it's going to amuse me each time I see it, I placed Rose's condolence card on my dresser. "Good Lord," I think, "ninety-two, ninety-three? What was she like twenty years ago?"

Next to the card happens to be a more-than-sixty-year-old photograph of five boyhood friends. I know exactly when this picture was taken—September 6, 1948. I know, because I took the picture minutes before we'd jumped into a cab on our way to Yankee Stadium for a Labor Day doubleheader against the Philadelphia Athletics. It was in the midst of a torrid pennant race, the Yanks that morning a half game behind Rose's beloved Red Sox, Cleveland trailing New York by three or four games.

As you've probably gathered, baseball's meant a lot to me over the years, another reason I find Rose's card so rich and September 6, 1948 a day I'll never forget. But first I think I ought to tell you about the five boys in the picture.

The photo was taken in front of an apartment building on the southeast corner of 103rd and West End Avenue. My friends are smiling and form an inverted T, three of them squatting, one, leaning over, his hands on his knees, the last sitting on a stone ledge outside a dentist's ground-floor office window.

This last is Harry Kotlowitz. Wearing a white tee shirt, he's tall and wiry, although Harry's long legs are hidden behind the boy whose hands are braced on his knees. Kotlowitz bat and threw left-handed, was probably our best hitter and had a good arm, his only weakness being lack of foot speed. He also played the piano beautifully, had a couple of warhorses, and I must have heard *The Hungarian Rhapsody* a hundred thousand times.

Hunched over in front of Harry, hands on his knees, is Richie Graf, our prime organizer, concerned about time, place, who'd be coming to the game, who wouldn't. On the short side, Graf did stretching exercises in the futile hope they'd help him grow. He also used to chew soda rather than simply swallow it. At the time, Richie and I were tight, and when he was a captain and chose sides, he'd say to the other captain, "Give me Eric, you can have the next two."

Squatting below Graf is Alex Novokov. Alex lived on 109th and was the only non-Jew among my close friends. Stronger and wilder than the rest of us, he often seemed tense, wound up, maybe because he was our outsider. His father came from Armenia, and Alex had high cheekbones and narrow eyes. I'd call him "Novocaine" sometimes, just to get a rise out of him.

To Alex's right is Gerard Schumann, whom we all called "Gee." He had the sweetest of temperaments, was genuinely endearing, thin, pale, and presented a shambling walk. Which probably explains why his favorite Yankees were bruisers like Charlie Keller and Cliff Mapes. Gee had a sly sense of humor, loved to kid around and laugh a lot, although I never heard Gee, unlike the rest of us, say a mean word about anyone.

On the other side of Alex is Ira Zeller. In the winter, Ira's mother would smother him in a blizzard of mufflers, warm hats, sweaters, and woolen gloves. Ira was skinny, fidgety, and spoke with machine-gun rapidity. He was particularly close to Gee and Alex; they were in the same class in junior high. It was Ira, Gee, and Alex who came up to my apartment the night before my *bar mitzvah* that June, giving me a Louisville Slugger, an American League baseball, and a copy of Joe DiMaggio's *Lucky to be a Yankee.*

I had four or five other good friends, about ten in all, but those in the picture constituted the core group, certainly the group that attended that memorable doubleheader.

***

The day before, Sunday, we had arranged to meet on the corner of 103rd and West End at ten-thirty. The Stadium would be mobbed, they were expecting more than 70,000, and we wanted to arrive at least before twelve to get decent general admission seats which cost $1.25 in those days.

As I said, the pennant race that September was sizzling along, and the three contending teams—New York, Boston, and Cleveland—were setting attendance records. The players had caught pennant fever, too, with DiMaggio about to knock in more than 150 runs, Boston's Ted Williams hitting something like .370, and Cleveland's playing manager, Lou Boudreau, batting over .350.

Next morning, five of us showed up by ten-thirty. The only one who didn't was Harry Kotlowitz.

Harry was born in Antwerp, but his family had fled Hitler, arriving in New York during the spring of 1941. His father was a diamond merchant, short, bald, and stocky, his mother was tall, pretty, and read movie magazines. Because she served Harry steak and French fries just about every other day, I used to think, "What a lucky stiff Kotlowitz is." He had an older sister, Monique, and a brother, Avrom, eleven years younger.

That August, Kotlowitz's parents and two-year-old brother had gone back to Belgium to visit relatives who'd survived the war. Avrom had been named after an uncle who hadn't. Harry, on the other hand, had been placed under the thumb of his sister, with whom he didn't always get along, and we should have guessed Monique was probably causing the hangup.

"Goddamn, it's getting late," Richie Graf says, glancing at his watch. Richie, whose precision and punctuality could be irritating, hated having to wait for anyone.

"Maybe Harry's not feeling well," Ira says sympathetically. Sympathetically, because Ira used to get lots of colds, which is why his folks bundled him up so often.

"No, Harry would have called if he was sick," says Gee, the voice of benevolent reason.

"So, let's go up and get him," I suggest.

"That prick makes us late, I'm going to be really pissed off," says Alex.

"Hey, we're not going to be late, we're still early," Gee calms Alex down. He often did.

"Eric's right, let's go get him," Graf urges.

So, we pile into one of the building's two elevators and ride up to the tenth floor. With five of us jostling, horsing around, the elevator seems terribly confining.

Kotlowitz answers the door, a look of exasperation and embarrassment straining his face, as the five of us surge into his apartment.

"Ah, Harry's wonderful group of friends," his sister Monique greets us sarcastically. She's a good-looking girl, with honey-brown eyes and a round face, big chest and narrow hips.

"Hey, Harry, what's the holdup?" Graf asks impatiently, ignoring Monique. "We're going to be late we don't leave soon."

"The holdup is, Harry's not going if I'm not going, because I'm not giving him the money to go," Monique says, hands on her hips.

Did I mention she's two years older and, naturally, considers Harry's boisterous friends hopelessly childish.

"You want to go with us? What do you know about baseball?" Ira asks in his typical rat-a-tat way. Of course the implication is that she'll be a drag, cramp our style, ask stupid, nonsensical questions especially when the ball's in play and the crowd's going crazy. Monigue actually tagging along? A girl? A freaking girl?

We look at Kotlowitz for direction—it's his sister, after all—but Harry seems in a quandry, doesn't appear to have a clue. "Goddamn it, Monique, give me the lousy money," he finally says. "You're making me feel like a jerk in front of my friends,"

"Because you don't want me to go with you, you *are* a jerk," she replies, "And I'm not giving you the money. If I can't go, you can't go."

Gee tries to reason with her, saying, "This isn't the usual kind of game, Monique, but a Labor Day doubleheader, and the Yanks are only a half game out of first, so the pennant might very well be decided today. If it was the beginning of the season, or the Yanks weren't so close to first, then maybe you could come and everyone would feel relaxed about it. But today..."

It's obvious Monique hasn't the faintest idea what Gee is talking about, and even if she did, it would hardly convince her.

"Why don't you just take the money from her?" Alex suggests.

"You mean I should hit her and take the money, overpower her?" Kotlowitz responds angrily. He and Alex rarely see eye-to-eye.

"Yeah," says Alex, shrugging. "That's what I'd do if she was my sister."

"Well, Harry's got to do something, it's getting goddamn late," Graf insists, checking his watch again.

Monique is watching us, scanning the room. She seems to be enjoying our communal perplexity.

Gee says, "Maybe if we all chip in, we'll have enough to buy a ticket for Harry."

"Good idea," I second the motion and start taking out the few bills in my pocket.

"No, I got a better idea!" Kotlowitz says, racing off toward his bedroom.

Meanwhile, we're still standing in the hall, and I glance to the left, in the direction of the living room. It's the one room in the apartment we're prohibited from entering; Gee has christened it "The Forbidden Room." It houses a wooden cabinet with a glass front. Inside the cabinet and scattered throughout the room are glass figurines that Kotlowitz's father fears that we, in our boyish, roughouse manner, might accidentally break. Hence, his edict, strictly enforced, that Harry's friends are never, ever to enter the living room.

Kotlowitz finally rejoins us in the hall, waving his piggy bank high above his head. We hear the jangling coins. "I got at least five hundred pennies in there. Let's get the hell out of here!" he says, a look of vast relief burnishing his previously saturnine face.

"Hey, sweetheart!" Graf shouts, giving Monique the finger.

I pat Kotlowitz on the back, proud he's able to cope, and we race out of the apartment, laughing and hollering.

Downstairs, I say, "I want to take a picture."

"But we're late," Graf argues.

"I don't care, I want to take a picture so we can remember today. It's a historic occasion. Kotlowitz outflanked his older, pain-in-the-ass sister, and we were there to see it."

So, the guys quickly form an inverted T, Kotlowitz sitting up on the ledge, and I snap the picture, the picture I still have on my dresser next to Rose's perversely amusing condolence card.

After the picture, we decide it'll save time to take a cab rather than head for the subway. If we split the fare six ways, it can't be that much. Besides, we're all feeling pretty good in the wake of Kotlowitz's triumph, why not splurge, live a little...

A roomy Checker cab stops, but when the driver sees there are six of us, he says, "I can only take five, it's against the law to take six." He's a fat guy in his forties, has a mustache and a big scar on his forehead where, I think like a wise guy, his brains must have fallen out.

Gee says, "One of us will sit on the floor, no one will see, plus we'll give you an extra large tip."

"Come on, mister, we're New Yorkers, we know how to deal with this," Kotlowitz adds. Hearing him, I'm happy to realize that Harry's morale's been restored.

The driver ponders the possibilities, like he's deciding the world's fate.

"Okay, okay, get in," he says with a deeply pained expression, as if he's still got a wisdom tooth that hurts or suffers from chronic hemorrhoids.

Of course, no one sat on the floor. That was just something to say. If the guy wants an extra large tip, it's understood he's got to be a good sport, act like a gentleman.

***

We swing across town, through Central Park, over to the East Side, making good time. But traffic slows to a crawl as we cross the Harlem River and enter the Bronx. When we arrive at the Stadium, it's a veritable mob scene, long lines of thousands of happy fans waiting to buy tickets. Kotlowitz's broken his piggy bank by now, and he must have something like a hundred pennies in each of his four pockets. It's almost funny. You can hear them rumbling around each time he takes a step.

We stand together at the rear of what we conclude is the shortest line. All around us guys are discussing the pennant race. To our dismay, we learn that the schedule after today favors Cleveland. Eighteen of their remaining twenty-three games will be against the league's four least talented teams while the Yanks still have to face Ted Williams and company eight more times.

But our spirits soon lift when someone else says Vic Raschi's pitching the opener today, Eddie Lopat's going in the nightcap. Along with the Chief, Allie Reynolds, they're the Yanks' three best pitchers, so we're in for what figures to be a terrific afternoon, and we decide to just take this old pennant race one day at a time.

Although the lines are huge, they're moving along at a nice steady clip. A few mornings from now we'll all be back in school, so this day might just be our last really satisfying one before the long winter break at Christmas. By now, Kotlowitz's imbroglio with his bossy sister is an amusing footnote.

Our line continues to move along briskly, and soon we're actually standing in front of the ticket seller's kiosk, handing over our money and buying our tickets. That is, we're all buying tickets except for Kotlowitz, because the jerk selling them refuses to accept, let alone count, the more than hundred pennies Harry frantically keeps trying to shove across to him.

Kotlowitz is astonished! So are the rest of us. After all that struggle and anguish, is he really to be denied entry just feet from the pearly gate?

Mister, Kotlowitz implores, please, my sister wouldn't give me the money. I had to break open my piggy bank. You've already sold my friends their tickets. You can't do this to me. It's not fair.

The ticket seller can't believe Kotlowitz. The lines are immense, and this crazy kid actually wants him to count pennies? Angrily, he tells Harry to get off his goddamn line, or he's going to call a cop. A cop, you stupid kid!

We stand to the side, enveloping Kotlowitz protectively. He's our buddy, we're not going inside without him. Not yet anyway.

There's a desperate look in Kotlowitz's eye. It's the same look he had back in his apartment when Monique stamped her foot and said, "If I'm not going..."

Suddenly Kotlowitz's eyes light up as he sees a ring of concession stands across the street where you can buy ice cream, hot dogs, peanuts, soda, jockstraps, whatever. Kotlowitz starts counting his pennies, giving each of us thirty, forty of them. "Go to three or four of those concessions," he says excitedly, "and give them eleven pennies for a dime; maybe one'll even take twenty-seven for a quarter. We'll meet back here in no later than ten minutes."

Why it didn't occur to one of us to give Harry a dollar bill just then, I can't explain. Go figure. Maybe because he was more fun doing it the hard way.

Anyway, we race across the street, under the El, dodging beeping cars, each of us hitting a different concession stand, where we do Kotlowitz's inspired bidding. And less than ten minutes later, we regroup, handing Kotlowitz the dimes and quarters that will, pray God, earn him the general admission ticket we've already purchased.

Kotlowitz wisely chooses a line other than the one where his hundred-plus pennies had been so brutally rejected. No point in tempting fate by confronting that lump of inhumanity a second time. We hold our collective breath as Kotlowitz finally hands over his change minus that one crummy bill which would have saved us all so much grief. But, hey, no problem! Kotlowitz is issued his general admission ticket as if he were General Eisenhower in mufti. We hurry together into the Stadium, into the House that Ruth Built, racing up the gangway leading to what we hope will be terrific seats in the upper right field grandstand.

***

It was always such a thrill, that first sight inside the big ballpark, the sheer immensity of it. Those days, home plate to the bleachers was almost five hundred feet. It was a triple-tiered arena shaped like a horseshoe, the upper deck trimmed with a sixteen-foot copper frieze that gave the place an unusually distinctive look, like an amphitheater maybe out of King Arthur.

We grandly decide that the morning's been an adventure as we settle into our narrow, wooden-slatted seats, each of us buying a scorecard at the first opportunity. We're knowledgeable fans, know how to keep score, and plan to mark our cards just like the older guys sitting near us, who are already lighting up smelly cigars and drinking from large paper cups of foamy beer.

The visiting lowly A's, wearing their gray traveling uniforms, are taking batting practice, and you can clearly hear the sweet crack of the bat as the hitter inside the cage connects with one meatball after another.

Hungry, we take out sandwiches we've brought along. As always, my cherished mother stuck in a raw carrot. "Ma," I used to think, "if carrots are so great for your eyesight, how come I'm the only kid on the block who ever brings one?"

All around us the Stadium's filling up. Next day, I learn I was one of 72,859; it was the Yanks' largest turnout of 1948, and, as an added bonus, we witnessed Hank Bauer's first major league game.

Bauer was a six-foot outfielder who went about a hundred ninety, an ex-Marine. He had a large nose, a square, almost Slavic-looking face, and the rugged features of a boxer. The opener that Labor Day was not only his first game, but he was batting third, in the heart of the lineup, between Old Reliable, Tommy Henrich, and the one and only Joe D.—pretty fancy company bracketing your major league debut.

Nor could he have begun much better, because in the first inning, after Stirnweiss doubles and Henrich makes out, Bauer singles in the first run, then steals second, scoring the Yanks second run when Johnny Lindell also singles to left.

"Hey, Bauer looks almost as good as Stirnweiss," I kid Kotlowitz, who's sitting to my left. This calls for an explanation.

Growing up, Kotlowitz had three heroes—Yankee second baseman George Stirnweiss, whom he mistakenly thought was Jewish, Knick guard Max Zaslofsky, whom he correctly thought was Jewish, and conductor Arturo Toscanini, whose religion for some reason didn't seem to matter.

It was Ira Zeller who'd read in the *News* last month that Stirnweiss was a devout Catholic who attended daily mass, and Ira, catching my drift, asks disingenuously, "Hey, Harry, Stirnweiss still your favorite Yankee?"

Poor Kotlowitz, I forgot to mention, is sitting sandwiched between us.

"Screw off, Ira!" he says.

"How come you like Toscanini, he's not Jewish," I say.

Shaking his head, Kotlowitz decides not to respond this time. It's two against one, he realizes, and he's caught in the shitty middle.

"I wonder what your sister's doing back home," Richie Graf belatedly jumps in. Richie is sitting on the aisle, his favorite seat. He's always been such a finicky guy.

"I still would have taken the money from her," says Alex, from the other end of the row.

"Ah, words of wisdom from Novocaine," I grin. "Then she tells her father when the old man gets back from Europe, and where does that leave Harry?"

"Up the creek," says Gee, sitting to my right.

God knows, no great colloquies there, but I never felt so at ease, so comfortable with another group the rest of my life, and I was sure we'd all be friends forever.

Meanwhile, the A's tie the game in the top of the third, but the Yanks regain the lead with two runs in the bottom of the inning. Vic Raschi keeps getting in trouble, but he proves especially tough with runners on base.

Raschi, for those who never saw him pitch, was a big righthander who threw a hard, heavy fast ball and was ace of the staff that year. Before warming up, he used to sit alone, psyching himself by growing angrier and angrier at the other team.

In case you're interested in the final score, Tommy Henrich hits a homer in the eighth, icing the game, 6-4, and Raschi goes the distance, notching his eighteenth win of the season.

"Attababy, Vic," we congratulate each other after the last out, slapping hands down the line.

"Just imagine if Bauer turns out as good as DiMaggio," says Richie, as we all stand, stretching our legs. Bauer has gotten two other hits, made a strong throw from right, and not only stole a base but appeared capable of covering a lot of ground.

"Hey, that was one game, probably beginner's luck," says Kotlowitz, who considers himself an astute observer of the national pastime. "Pitchers get to know him a little better, see what his weaknesses are, he'll have to adjust, and not every player can do that."

Up on the huge scoreboard, beyond the bleachers and above the Ballantine Beer & Ale sign, we note with disappointment that the hated Red Sox have also won their opener, beating the not-so hot Senators. So that means the Yanks are still a half game out of first.

"Think Bauer's happy back in the old clubhouse?" Gee asks. "Three hits his first game, big crowd, Labor Day doubleheader. What would you guys give to be in Bauer's shoes?"

For a second, everyone smiles, even Alex. Bauer is probably twenty-five, twenty-six. If he doesn't feel like a million bucks just now, his career as a Yankee ballooning in his imagination, he's probably missing a marble or two.

"Me, I'd still rather be Joe DiMaggio," Kotlowitz pronounces, "even if he is nearing the end of his career."

"You're Joe DiMaggio," I say, imitating Jimmy Cannon, the famous sports columnist of the *Post*. "You're the greatest player I ever saw and the loneliest man on the face of the earth. You hit in fifty-six straight games, and you have the ulcers to prove it was no walk in the park. You're an aristocrat in temperament, yet you've given this scuffling but endlessly fascinating city an aspect of class it would otherwise not have. You're Jolting Joe DiMaggio, best I ever saw, and I keep waiting for another like you to gladden my lonely afternoons."

"Hey, I like it," says Richie Graf, applauding.

"Not bad, Eric," Ira nods, judiciously, "except for maybe 'gladden.'"

"Watch your ass, Cannon," Gee grins. "Our buddy Rosen is coming up fast on the inside."

Out in the Yankee bullpen, we see Steady Eddie Lopat warming up for the second game. We all buy ice cream. Then Alex tries to get one of the vendors to sell him a beer, but the guy tells him to come back in five years.

"Don't you want to see my draft card?" Alex kids him.

"What for—the Boy Scouts?" the vendor shouts over his shoulder.

Lopat, a lefty, is a junk-ball pitcher, terrific contrast to Raschi. He has a great slow curve and has learned to vary speeds but maintain the same motion. He was, we're given to understand, a thinking man's pitcher, who outsmarts the opposing team's hitters.

The only trouble is, the A's don't bother thinking much in the nightcap, scoring four runs in the first, and the Yanks are never in the game, By the fifth inning, the score is 6-2 and percentages tell you the home team, who's won nine straight, is not going to win this one. The only good news is that Bauer finally gets another hit, so that makes four for the day, and by then fanny fatigue has set in with a vengeance. We're all ready to go home. Too bad the Yanks aren't going to capture the second game. But it's been a great afternoon, a lot of fun —Kotlowitz's pennies frosting on the cake—only let's take off before trying to board the next Manhattan-bound train becomes a nightmare. Forget about getting a cab.

***

Back at West End and 103rd, Harry says to me, "Hey, Rosen, I want to lend you a great record I received last week." Kotlowitz has belonged to a record club for years, and I'm just starting to collect them. "It's Schubert's *Trout*, played by the Budapest String Quartet. Just tremendous. Come on up with me now, and you can keep it for a week. You're going to love it, Eric."

It's late, after six, and my parents are probably waiting for me to eat dinner, but Harry sounds so full of enthusiasm it's hard to say no. If I was eighteen, it might have occurred to me he wanted someone with him, didn't want to have to face his wildly unpredictable sister alone, at least initially. But I'm not old enough to figure that out. Besides, getting the record isn't going to take that long, and I live only a block away.

But when we get upstairs, we're surprised to hear frantic whispering coming from Kotlowitz's parents' bedroom, then some scrambling sounds, prompting Harry to look nervously at me.

"Monique, you in there?" he calls out.

Within seconds, this guy with big shoulders walks out of the bedroom, hitching up his pants and adjusting his belt. He's an older kid from the neighborhood, Elliot Horowitz, a classmate of Monique's, and he has a big smirk on his dark face. Behind his back, we used to call him "Elliot the Ape."

Harry, who never liked him, says, "What the hell you doing up here, Elliot? What the hell you doing in my parents' bedroom?"

But Elliot doesn't answer, he just keeps walking, opening the front door, and leaves the apartment.

"Monique?" Harry calls out again, marching forward anxiously. I trail close behind him.

His sister is sitting on the near corner of her parents' double bed. She's dressed, smoothing her skirt.

"I told him to leave an hour ago," she says, "that you were on your way home from the ballgame. But he wouldn't go."

Kotlowitz keeps blinking, wondering what I'm wondering. "Jesus," he says, "Elliot's one of the guys in your class you can't stand. Why would you even think about making out with that stiff?"

Monique shakes her head. Then she sobs once or twice, brushing away her tears with an abrupt, angry gesture. She's like an actress, sad one moment, furious the next.

"You don't understand, Harry," she eventually says. Then she points to her parents' bed. "They're having a good time in Antwerp. You were with your friends at the ballgame. It's lousy when it's a holiday and you're left alone, So I thought, 'The hell with everybody.' Only you've got to promise not to tell Daddy. He'll kill me if he ever finds out."

"Yeah, sure, I promise," Kotlowitz says. They're both frightened of their father, who has a bad temper.

Suddenly Monique, her eyes growing larger as she focuses on me, jumps up and hurries over to where I'm standing, back near the door. Yet she appears neither angry nor surprised to realize I'm there, saying in a merely practical way, "You've got to promise, too, Ira. You can't tell anybody about this, okay? Nobody. Not your other friends, not my parents, not your parents. This has got to be our secret—yours, mine, and Harry's,"

"His name is Eric, not Ira," Harry corrects her with a frown.

"I mean Eric," she says.

"Sure, I promise," I agree, wondering about Elliot the Ape. Has he promised, too?

For a minute, Monique seems to study me, as if she isn't sure I'm trustworthy. She keeps staring and staring, and the intensity of her look begins to frighten me. Then she says, "Wait here a second," and she hurries out of the room.

I look over at Kotlowitz, but he appears slightly dazed. No doubt he expected some typical rebellious Monique stunt, but this as yet unfulfilled one obviously throws him.

When she comes back, she's holding one of the figurines her father was so afraid me or my friends would break if we were allowed to socialize in "The Forbidden Room."

"Here's a present," says Monique, handing me the figurine.

It's a beautifully shaped piece of glass of a man on a rearing horse. The man holds a lance in his free hand, a kind of medieval helmet slung low over his eyes. "I'm giving you this present," Monique is saying, "and in return you really have to swear never to tell anyone."

"I swear, I already swore," I answer. "But I don't want your present. Your father'll probably miss it." The truth is, I hate the idea she thinks she has to bribe me. Kotlowitz is my buddy and she's his sister. That's enough.

But Monique insists. "You have to take it, you can't say no." Her hands on her hips, I'm reminded how she looked when she refused to give Harry the money for the ballgame. "Damn it, don't make me angry," she says. "I do crazy things when I get angry."

"No kidding," I think, looking over at Kotlowitz again.

"Take it," he urges, not wishing to tempt Monique into performing a second desperate act. "There are so many figurines inside, my father's not going to miss one. And if he does, too bad!"

So, swallowing my pride, I accept the figurine and start to leave.

Surprisingly, Monique walks me to the door, kissing me abruptly before I leave. First time any girl ever put her tongue in my mouth, "You're a nice kid, Ira," she says. "And I'm not going to forget you're doing me this favor."

She can't remember my name, but she's going to remember me doing her this favor? Not exactly the perfect end to what had been a swell day, and it disturbs me for a long time; I mean, especially Monique's kissing me that way. And I dream about her for months, have wild sexual fantasies about which I never tell anyone because, damn it, she's Harry's sister...

***

Hard to believe all this occurred a million years ago.

Incidentally, for those fans who weren't around then, Cleveland won the American League and World Series that memorable year. But the Yanks won the next five Series, then again in '56 and 1958.

And if memory serves right, our man Bauer got ten hits in '58, including five homers, leading the Bombers to a thrilling, come-from-behind triumph.

I should probably leave this besotted reminiscence at that. But remembering Rose's condolence card, I can't resist; I go over to my dresser, pick up the card, and kiss it, saying, "That's seven Series in ten years, which ain't chopped liver, Rosie, not too shabby." And smiling like an idiot, I can't help thinking, "That last crack to ninety-plus Rose—some nice Jewish boy I've turned out to be, huh?"

II. The Holocaust

R&R
The Uninvited Guest
Gieseking
Gloves

R&R

⤜❧⤐

The Bauman sisters, Eva and Angela, were the first of twelve women who entered the bus. They sat by themselves on the long, wooden-slatted bench in the back. There they'd be able to talk in relative privacy. Eva was twenty-three, Angela twenty-one. Angela was pretty, Eva the smarter, more worldly one.

Eva had received a letter from their mother, Trudy, that morning, asking that she look out for her younger, more impressionable sister. The world being in such a mess, Trudy wrote, Angela could easily find herself in trouble.

Two days ago, Angela had received a similar, cautionary letter from their stepfather, Walter, whom both sisters detested. Walter had even more crudely referred to the perils facing Angela, begging her for her mother's sake to always think first of the family's good name.

"Imagine that jerk writing me such a patronizing letter," Angela told Eva. The principal reason Angela left home last month was that she could no longer bear to continue living under the same roof as ham-fisted Walter. It was the same reason that had driven Eva away two years before, even if there was a war going on.

Walter had married their widowed mother a decade ago, or a couple of years after their cherished father, Albert, a schoolteacher, had died of a heart attack at the age of forty. Walter was a policeman, a big, red-faced, hefty fellow who loved beer, potatoes, and sausages in that order. He was the complete opposite of their refined, wisp-thin father, whose great passion was listening to music composed by Mozart. The contrast between the two was so striking, it often bewildered the sisters, until Eva deduced at a blossoming fifteen that it was precisely the contrast that explained their mother's decision to marry Walter. Widowed early once was enough: Trudy didn't think a robust fellow like Walter would also die an unanticipated death.

Almost immediately upon entering the bus, the Baumans could hear the other women beginning to gossip, talk shop. They were all in their twenties, typists and stenographers, on their way to a nearby Alpine lodge.

It was a Saturday morning, spring, and the women were being treated to a day in the country where they'd be entertained, encouraged to relax, fed a light lunch and dinner.

"It's called R&R, rest and recreation," explained Eva with a sisterly smile. Eva had attended two of these pleasant interludes before; but this was going to be a first for Angela, who asked what the last time was like.

"Really a lot of fun," Eva answered. "The lodge is near a river, it's pretty there, and you can go for a nice walk. Inside are a couple of pingpong tables and a billiard room. We sat out on the deck, I remember, enjoyed the sun and ate blueberries. There was even a guy with an accordion, who not only sang but got everyone else to join him in sing-alongs. Food was good, too."

"Good morning, ladies!" their driver suddenly called out, inquiring if everyone was comfortable. It was the first of three buses, actually. The other two were filling up with men, who were also being taken for R&R that day. The men were older, mostly in their thirties and forties.

Their bus started down a hill, and relaxing, Angela asked, "What do you hear from Felix?"

Felix was Walter's son from his first marriage. Sadly, Felix's mother had died giving birth to him. He was a year younger than Angela, with whom he'd competed for Trudy's attention when they were kids, which probably explained why they'd never hit it off and didn't keep in touch.

Eva, who didn't have that problem, said Felix wrote that he loved Paris and was going to hate having to leave it. He'd sent each of them, as well as Trudy, a bottle of French perfume for Christmas. Inducted into the Army last year, Felix hoped to make the military a career.

"Angela, by the way, never tell Felix how much we both dislike Walter," her older sister suddenly counseled.

"But, Eva, Felix can't stand him either."

"I know," Eva acknowledged. "Still, Walter's his flesh and blood, and it would upset Felix to hear how much we detest his father. And not only upset him, but he'd come to resent us for it."

"Oh, let's not mention Walter anymore," said Angela, wrinkling her pretty nose. "I want to enjoy today." She'd been living and working alongside Eva for less than a month, so their being together still retained the fresh appeal of something new, an appeal she didn't wish tarnished on this bright, sunny morning.

They passed a farm, saw a couple of cows munching grass and a beautiful white horse walking toward a barn that had a red roof. Hardly any surprise, for the soil here was known to be rich and abundant, good farm country.

A woman sitting three rows ahead of them opened a window just then. At the same time, two others sitting up front began singing "My Funny Valentine." They were joined by a third woman with a much deeper voice, who sat on the other side of the bus. A strawberry blonde with dazzling blue eyes, she turned around and waved her arm, encouraging everyone else to participate in the singing.

Angela responded by immediately humming along. She'd always had a number of friends and being accepted as one of twelve now held great allure. On the other hand, Eva merely smiled, not only because she couldn't carry a tune but she had a less accommodating personality, was often secretive and moody.

It was the song that prompted Angela to ask, "You and Max still thinking of getting married?"

Max had been Eva's boyfriend since high school. The problem was his parents didn't like Eva, especially Max's possessive mother, who thought her darling boy could do a lot better. Like Felix, Max was in the Army, only currently stationed in Milan.

"I wrote Max a week ago and told him it was time to make up his mind—yes or no," Eva reported. "But who knows with Max? He wants to marry me but is still afraid of offending 'mother dear.'"

"Well, Martin's a little like that, too," Angela said, nodding sympathetically. Martin was one of two boyfriends Angela was presently interested in. His father owned a chemical factory, where Martin was employed as an engineer. Her other boyfriend, Alfred, aspired to be an actor. Angela's good looks meant she'd always attract men. Her problem was she never could decide who among them she liked best.

The women up front began singing another song. It was "Tea for Two," and this time almost everyone seemed to join in from the beginning, as if the group was tuning up for the sing-alongs most of them still remembered fondly.

"What did they serve last time?" Angela asked after the singing died down. "Eva, you remember?"

"Let me think." Frowning, Eva resembled their late father. The last year of his life, when the politics back home had turned increasingly violent, he'd frowned a lot. Suddenly Eva smiled. *"Sauerbraten* with dumplings,*"* she said.

Angela knew why Eva smiled. *Sauerbraten* was one of Eva's favorites.

"As good as *mutti's?"* Angela asked.

"Are you kidding? Come on," said Eva, shaking her head. "No, not close." Their mother was a terrific cook. It was one of the reasons Walter had married her. A burly fellow like him loved food, not liked but loved it.

"Time before that they served *Weiner schnitzel* with red cabbage," Eva remembered.

Angela began licking her lips. "Oh, boy," she said. *"Weiner schnitzel."*

"We'll probably wind up with something like *weisswurst* and potato salad this time," Eva said teasingly, and the sisters laughed together. Unlike Walter, neither of them liked *weisswurst.*

Still, both were happy to be on the same bus, sitting side-by-side. They'd always been close as sisters, especially close after their father had died and heavy-handed Walter had entered their lives. They'd learned that it was important to stick together then because their mother often sided with her second husband when he'd object to something one or both sisters did at home.

"God knows, I don't miss Walter, but I do miss *mutti* and her cooking," Eva said, looking out the window as they drove past a second farm that had another barn with a red roof.

"Do you miss home?" Angela asked softly.

Home was Murnau, a small town in the Bavarian Alps near Munich.

"Once in a while," Eva acknowledged. "So I try not to think of Murnau or about *mutti* too much."

The bus slowed down, stopping opposite a Catholic church where a funeral had just taken place. A group of men in dark jackets, supervised by a priest wearing his surplice, were placing a coffin in a horse-driven wagon. The bus waited for the wagon and emerging mourners to depart before continuing. In the distance, Eva could see the Sola River, which meant the lodge was close by, and she remembered the letter from home she'd received that morning.

"Angela dear, there are going to be more than a hundred guys at the lodge, ten men to every woman," Eva said. "I guarantee at least five of them will offer to take you to Cracow next weekend, show you a great time. Most of them haven't seen their wives for months, which means they're horny as hell. So, a word to the wise, Angela—don't let *any* of them hit on you."

Angela looked at her older sister and tried to smile. But like most pretty young women everywhere, she didn't enjoy being told what to do. Yet if she couldn't trust Eva, who could she trust?

"All the big shots will be there," Eva said, and knowing her sister, Eva decided to throw in a few names, in the vague hope that would further impress Angela, convince her to act more intelligently than was occasionally her wont.

"Baer, the commandant, and his adjutant, Hocker, will certainly show up," Eva intoned. "Knittel, in charge of political education, Harjenstein, who commands the garrison. Also the doctors—Kremer, Breitweiser, Clauberg."

The funeral cortege began to move, turning in a direction away from the river, and soon their bus started up again.

"My big sister, my big sister," Angela said, patting Eva's hand reassuringly.

"*Mutti* would never forgive me if you got pregnant here," Eva confessed.

Their bus swung off the main road and approached a gravel path that led directly to the lodge. Trees lined either side of the path. They could hear pine cones crunching and gravel spinning as the bus began climbing up a slight hill.

"One of the doctors is really cute," said Angela, who couldn't resist playing the mischievous princess. She'd noticed the fellow a week ago when he'd smiled at her. "Really good-looking."

"Who do you mean?" Eva asked sharply.

"I'm not sure of his name, but it begins with an M— Mendel, Mengel, something like that. Long eyelashes, beautiful eyes."

The bus came to a stop in front of the lodge, its door scraping open with a hiss. Angela could see folding chairs with striped canvas seating lined up neatly on the beckoning rustic deck.

The women up front began filing out. They were greeted by the same accordion-toting officer as last time, who welcomed them now with the always popular "Beer Barrel Polka." He had a cheerful, rosy face and was smiling broadly, his peaked cap worn rakishly aslant, over his right ear. But the SS insignia on his black collar was perfectly straight, militarily correct. So were his highly polished jackboots.

As the sisters walked to the front of the bus, Eva belatedly said the doctor's name was Mengele and for Angela to strictly keep hands-off because someone else was sleeping with him.

"Who's that?" Angela had stopped walking.

So did Eva, who stared at her. "You can't ask me that, Angela."

Momentarily confused, Angela remarked that the smell coming from the camp that morning had been unusually pungent.

Eva shrugged. "Oh, another month," she said, "you'll hardly be aware of it."

"Is that what happened to you?" asked Angela, relieved they were no longer discussing Mendel, Mengel, Mengele, whatever his stupid name was.

"That's what happened to me," Eva affirmed. "I don't think about it, don't talk about it. I've put it out of my mind."

Nodding, Angela resumed walking down the aisle. As she stepped out of the bus, an SS photographer asked her to smile. The adjutant, Hocker, had told him to click away, that it would be good for morale, and the shutter-happy guy must have taken a hundred, two hundred pictures that day. Maybe more.

The Uninvited Guest

In 1947, I was twelve years old and a confirmed thief. My parents had fled Kolo, a two-bit Polish town on the Poznan road to Warsaw, just before Hitler began unleashing his hordes. But our journey to the States was a tortuous one, and we did not reach New York until the summer of 1941, almost three years after we'd started.

No doubt this nerve-racking odyssey contributed to the seemingly endless number of illnesses that plagued the youth of my younger brother Stefan—asthma, rheumatic fever, shingles, a stomach constantly offended by the mildest of baby foods. Stefan, born in 1938, was three years my junior, the second and last child of my parents, Josef and Wanda Fershon. I, Miriam, was the fourth member of our often discordant quartet.

Just getting us safely to the States seemed to have consumed most of my father's resiliency. He spoke little English, which complicated his ability to hold, let alone get, a decent job. In Poland, he'd been a high school teacher, but the best he could manage that first year in New York was one ill-paying janitor's position after another—jobs he invariably lost when his incredulous bosses discovered that the most menial of blue-collar tasks proved beyond his scholar's blundering fingers.

What saved us, in the sense that my family was finally assured of bread and a roof over our heads, was my parents getting to know the Pollocks, an elderly couple who owned a candy store on the Upper West Side not too far from pocket-size Straus Park. The store was becoming too much for them, and they suggested my parents take it over on a trial basis, with the idea of eventually buying the Pollocks out.

Now the prospect of running a store that sold penny candy and comic books to unruly pups, as well as newspapers and Cokes to their rich, stuck-up parents, pleased neither my mother nor my father, who considered themselves above providing such mundane services. But what with my brother's growing medical bills—bills my fiercely proud father insisted on paying promptly and to the last penny—they really had little choice, and soon the three of us were taking turns behind the soda fountain, my mother and me wearing flowered aprons reaching below our knees, my father insisting on a beige-colored jacket above his starched white shirt and tie.

It was an old-fashioned candy store, the kind you don't find too many of in New York these days. It had a long marble counter, with metal-rimmed seats small boys loved to set spinning. The counter was lined with open boxes of cookies and candies, and two tall plastic cylinders of pretzels. The favorite drink of the day was the celebrated egg cream, which consisted of no eggs but a little milk, a lot of chocolate syrup, and seltzer, plain but invigorating.

Lining the back wall, opposite the counter, were the magazine racks filled with comic books, *The Saturday Evening Post, Life, Look, Collier's, and Time.* This was before the advent of television, and weekly magazines were very popular then. Like everyone else, I particularly remember and was struck by the *Post's* covers painted by Norman Rockwell. Depicted was an America of infinite goodness and generosity, an America of simple but enduring values, an America I hadn't discovered yet but believed was out there—beyond the steel canyons of the city, beyond the majestic river separating New York from New Jersey, beyond even the Appalachian and Blue Ridge Mountains—the golden America of small towns, the hinterlands, the country's unmistakable heart lacking which, I thought, the great republic would have been only another Babylon. That was partly why I'd become a thief—

I'd wanted to flee the grinding candy store, my awkward parents and sickly brother, crossing the Hudson and climbing over the mountains, until I found that quaint hamlet where people were as kind and generous as those seducing Norman Rockwell's benevolent imagination.

My thievery consisted of taking money from the candy store till. I started with pennies and nickels, working myself up to dimes and quarters. I never had the nerve to touch a dollar bill, although when my nickels and quarters added up to dollars, I certainly took the coins to a bank, exchanging them for paper money, which I then secreted in an obscure pocket of a tweed jacket hung in the closet of the bedroom I shared with my brother.

Of course, one of the reasons I stole was that I resented Stefan terribly. That sickly kid dominated my parents' attention as much as the candy store, and between the two I became quite lost in the shuffle. I also stole because I was ashamed that my parents spoke a fractured English and the best my stumbling father could do was run a candy store, while the fathers of my classmates were smooth-talking doctors, lawyers, and big shot black market operators.

Invariably, I sought an imaginary hole behind the counter when any of my classmates entered the candy store. The boys would often show up just as it was getting dark, too dark to continue playing stickball or touch football in the street. Sweaty and excited from that day's strenuous games, they'd munch pretzels and steal candy, drinking one soda after another, utterly ruining their appetites for dinner.

The girls in my class were more conceited than the boys, and when they sat at the counter, decorously sipping their Cokes and Pepsis, they almost always gave that pitying, condescending look I learned to despise. I would force myself to stare them down, my eyes filled with unremitting hostility. I hated servicing them, and if either of my parents was around when they came in, I made a point of having my mother or father do their bidding.

They lived, my classmates, in fat brick buildings on West End Avenue. The rooms had high ceilings and some breathtaking views of the sun-speckled hills on the Jersey shore. The buildings were patrolled by doormen dressed in peaked caps and black uniforms padded with silver epaulets. Occasionally, I was invited by a preening classmate up to her apartment. But, unwilling to return the invitation by extending the slightest hospitality in our own cramped, third-floor walk-up, I only went once, never twice.

My mother, who sensed better than my father, how ashamed I was of our miserable circumstances, once said to me, "We almost died in Europe. You don't know how lucky you were to get out in time. Instead of feeling angry and humiliated, you should be grateful!"

But I heard, not her words, only her thick accent, and in my mind's eye I saw the depressing candy store, and it seemed to me a prison. Then I looked about me in our apartment which never reflected a single ray of cheerful sunlight, and I thought, "You be grateful, Mama—be grateful for both of us! I've better things to do." Naturally, I made a point that day of taking double the amount of change I usually filched from the till.

I developed a technique of keeping the money while I was in the process of making change for a customer. Say a father of one of my classmates had just bought a *Times*, which cost three cents those days, and had given me a quarter. I'd dutifully put the quarter in the till, returning him the proper change, and quickly slipped the two other pennies into my apron pocket before turning to face either my parents or the next customer, my huge eyes batting innocently.

I was a pretty girl, as pretty as any of the Judys, Carols, and Arlenes in my class. I had almost jet black hair and matching dark eyes. A man I went with years later told me I had the kind of velvety eyes that intrigue and excite a man—whatever that means. On second thought, a lovely come-on line, whether he meant it or not.

Though I was thin and somewhat of a problem eater, when the boys in my class teased or pushed me, I invariably pushed back, flashing my incisors. The boys were taller and stronger, but I was afraid of none of them, and when they hit me with snowballs, unlike the other girls who cowered or tried to flee, I would run directly at them, knocking over the weakest and pushing his startled face into the biting snow. The others would have to drag me off before I'd let go. What a strange creature I must have seemed to Jerry and David, to Sandy and Richard.

On the other hand, I wasn't the first refugee they'd ever encountered. Many such lived in the commodious Hotel Marseilles, which stood on the corner of Broadway and 103rd Street. You knew they were refugees from their long coats and tight, double-breasted suits. They also seemed smaller than Americans, and many of them displayed a tiny gold mine in their mouths when they spoke or smiled.

They'd stand in fraternal circles, either on the corner of Broadway or in front of the hotel entrance, discussing the latest tragedy gripping Europe's charnel house. How most of them lived and who supported them were questions I didn't consider those days. But then, these refugees were a particularly resourceful lot anyway, and surviving in New York must have been small potatoes to people who'd out-foxed and outrun gimlet-eyed hunters wearing jackboots and SS brassards. In that sense, of course, my parents were also survivors. But, believe me, that earned them not a single Purple Heart from yours truly.

***

We were not religious people but would go through the motions during the Jewish holidays to please my mother, whose bearded father had been a Chasidic master. Naturally, my mother insisted on having a Seder during Passover.

Donning his hardly worn *yarmulke*, my father read from the prayer book, answering the Four Questions recited to him by my brother. Stefan, resembling his old man, had watery blue eyes and wheat-colored hair.

My father had closed the candy store late that afternoon, pasting a sign in the window saying the store wouldn't be open during the next two days. My mother had insisted. Each of them claimed many lost relatives, and during the Seder, my mother would sob, her shoulders trembling, then race into the bathroom. We would hear her trying to smother the sounds of her weeping by turning on the shower. Stefan and I shrugged at each other. People we once knew, yet barely remembered, had died during the war. But, pray, what had they to do with us, citizens of the New World, daily imbibers of homogenized milk, no less?

My father's clenched fists turned white each time my mother rushed from the table, but he managed to keep reciting from the prayer book, and I remember thinking, "Thank God he hasn't stopped," because I was starving, and you had to read through a good portion of the service before it was permissible to begin serving the meal.

I wore a pink blouse with frilly sleeves. Stefan had on a blue shirt stiff as cardboard. It was April, and those were the first new clothes we'd gotten since September, when school began. Blouses didn't mean much to me those years, but I didn't have to be a clotheshorse to be aware how much better dressed were my classmates. Another cause for envy, no doubt, though I'd have been the last to admit it.

When my mother came out of the bathroom, my father said, "Wanda, Wanda, your repeated weeping will frighten the children." He said it quickly in Polish, perhaps hoping that neither Stefan nor I would understand him.

My mother nodded, glancing at me, then took Stefan's hand and began stroking it. She was always reaching out to her precious, but Stefan's customary response was a bug-eyed look on his pinched blue face. Still, my mother did not let go of his hand even as we sipped the wine that tasted sweeter than grape juice, then chewed the matzos and bitter herbs. Two candles flickered from the center of the table.

When it was time for my mother to serve the meal proper, my father said, "Miriam, help your mother in the kitchen."

I left the table with my patented long-suffering sigh. In the kitchen, while my mother was dishing out overcooked carrots and peas and cutting up the chicken, she asked me, "Do you remember your grandmother and grandfather?"

I had last seen my mother's parents when I was three. How could she possibly expect me to remember them? But I said, "A little bit, Mama," hoping that answer would satisfy the tearful woman.

When she didn't respond, I looked up at her. She'd closed her eyes and was rocking back and forth. Her lips were moving; probably she was praying. Of course, my mother's elderly parents, incapable of physical labor and living within a stone's throw of Treblinka, must have been among the first to inhale the gas.

Meanwhile, the roasted chicken smelled unbearably delicious, and I wished my mother would hurry her prayers because in another minute I'd begin eating in the kitchen, before the others had been served. Opening her eyes, my mother must have seen the famished, selfish expression on my face, because she nodded curtly.

"This plate is for your father," she said. It held the biggest piece of chicken. "That is for Stefan." It held the next biggest. Naturally.

***

There is a point in the Passover service, after the meal has been served and the third cup of wine emptied when, not only is the fourth cup filled but a goblet as well, the goblet then placed in the middle of the table as one of the younger celebrants goes to the front door, opening it for Elijah the Prophet. Stefan was nodding half-asleep, which explains why I was chosen for the dubious honor of greeting our invisible sage. My stomach full and whistling to myself with great good humor, I skipped down our gloomy hall, narrow as those threading a railroad flat.

Imagine, if you possibly can, my surprise, my astonishment, my stunned disbelief, when I saw standing outside our door the first truly beautiful woman I'd ever encountered. "Elijah the Prophet?" flashed crazily through my mind.

She had blonde hair reaching her shoulders and violet eyes, and she was wearing a trench coat. Realizing that prophets don't wear trench coats, I came to my senses. The woman began breathing heavily, as if she were out of breath and had just reached our third-floor walk-up. But even then I'd realized she must have been standing outside our apartment for a long time.

"Ah, you must be Miriam," she said, in as accented an English as my parents', and I understood that she was, like them, a refugee.

"Papa, Papa!" I called out, grasping that I was at a certain disadvantage.

Hearing the urgency in my voice, my father hurried to the door. "Josef, it's Eva, Eva Baorske," the woman announced herself.

"Eva! Eva!" he whispered, lifting both hands to his gaping mouth. Then he called out, "Wanda, Wanda!" and we could hear my mother rushing to join us.

"Eva! Eva!" my mother exclaimed, immediately recognizing and embracing the woman. Eva reached down, stroking my dark hair.

"We'd heard you'd survived the camps and had come to America, but no one knew where you had settled," my mother told Eva quickly.

My father took Eva's trench coat and handbag, and we all ushered her into the dining room. One of the candles was still burning. Stefan had fallen asleep at the table, his head resting in the cradle formed by his gaunt arm. Of course, my parents woke him so that Eva might greet our little prince.

Though our small dining room table was already crowded with four, my mother placed another setting for Eva, next to mine, and began plying her with food. They spoke, my parents and Eva, mostly in Polish. Eva, I learned, also came from Kolo, living on the same street as my parents, and had been great friends with them before the war. She'd miraculously survived three years in one of the most gruesome of the concentration camps. God only knows how. Probably her stunning good looks helped. She certainly had a Slavic beauty's face, framed with high cheekbones.

Eating the chicken and carrots, she told my parents that she'd arrived in New York a year ago, settling in a small apartment in the Bronx. She worked as a receptionist for a young dentist, in an office near Yankee Stadium.

"But why didn't you get in touch with us before now?" my father inquired.

"I did not wish for you to see me as I looked then," she said. "I was a real mess, skin and bones. I must have put back thirty pounds since then," she added with a proud smile. Her teeth were the whitest I'd ever seen, almost pearly. I didn't realize they must have been false teeth—no real choppers could have looked so perfectly white. Probably her dentist-employer had made them for Eva.

"Your mother and father, your sisters, Eva, did any of them survive?" my mother asked tensely.

"I'm the only one," Eva answered without histrionics.

She had eaten quickly, as if she'd been afraid the food would be snatched from her plate after a certain time had elapsed. My mother asked if she wanted any more chicken, but Eva held up her hand, saying, "Enough, Wanda, more than enough. I often eat too much, and become ill." Eva cleared her throat. "Besides, there is a reason for my coming tonight."

My parents stiffened where they sat.

"The money," my mother barely whispered.

"I know things can't be easy for you in this strange country, especially with two growing children, but I need the money for an operation," Eva said.

"Operation?" Josef groaned. Looking at her, it must have occurred to him that she seemed in splendid health compared to his anemic Stefan.

"What's the matter with you?" Wanda asked boldly.

Eva lifted the sleeve of her dress, carefully displaying the ugly row of numbers tattooed along the inside of her right arm. I couldn't take my eyes from them. Against the timid background of pale living flesh, the numbers struck me as wormy—a kind of colony of maggots.

"A doctor, a plastic surgeon, says he will remove them for five hundred dollars," Eva said. "Perhaps when these numbers will no longer be on my arm, I will know a moment's ease. If I don't soon, I'm afraid I'll go quite crazy."

When my parents were in the process of fleeing Europe, it seems they were short of funds, and Eva, alone of their friends, had given them the equivalent of four hundred dollars. "You'll repay me when all this nasty business about Jews will have passed into the dustbin," she'd told Wanda and Josef confidentially.

My mother glanced down at her thick hands. "Eva," she said, "our Stefan has been chronically ill since we left Poland, and the meager amounts we've been able to save go toward paying his doctors. We might have to send him to live in Arizona next year, the best climate in this country for asthmatics. Believe me, Eva darling, if we had the money we would give it to you in a second. How could we not? You are our friend, and we owe you our lives."

The despair that raced across Eva's beautiful face was striking, but just as powerful was the shame flooding my father's eyes. And unable that Passover night to honor a debt to an old friend who'd suffered unspeakable humiliations, my proud father bowed his head.

"Now that we know you are in New York, of course we will start saving to repay you," my mother told Eva. "Perhaps it will take us a year. And perhaps our Stefan will not have to go live in Arizona, then sooner. Oh, Eva, surely we will have the money for you by next Passover."

Although my father lifted his head, he couldn't look Eva in the eye. "Would your doctor perhaps perform the operation if we signed some sort of promissory note?" he asked.

Eva shrugged. Knowing she wouldn't be getting the money tonight nor in the near future, she seemed to have lost interest. "Unfortunately, nothing is accomplished in America without proper funds. Have you not found that so, Josef?" Eva might have been discussing the price of bread.

I could tell that my parents wished she would leave, and the guest herself seemed awfully uncomfortable. It was painful watching the three of them sitting there, trying to converse politely, and slipping away from the table I went into my room. Stefan was in bed, crying out in his sleep. Were the demons in his dreams the same one-eyed monsters who, dominating my nightmares, threw me into the roaring oven? How strange, but to this day I've never asked my brother.

I thought of my parents' fractured English and our dreary apartment, of my patronizing classmates and the candy store, I thought of my parents doting on sickly Stefan and having little time, let alone love, left for me. But even at twelve, I suppose, I was a sentimental fool, because I got the crumpled bills I'd been saving to run away, money it had taken me years to save, or since we'd been operating the candy store. I had between thirty and forty bucks—a fortune to a twelve-year-old—and my hands were shaking as I hurried into the hall, found Eva's handbag, and quickly stuffed the bills between her lipstick and powder box. "Papa," I thought, "surely even you can lift your proud head a little higher now."

When she left our apartment later that night, Eva promised to keep in touch, as did my parents, but so far as I know they never saw each other again. What happened to Eva? Did she have her operation? Is such an operation possible? Was she ever able to blot the concentration camp from her memory? When my parents tried finding her to repay their debt, as I'm sure they must have, what did they learn of Eva's fate?

I'd give a lot to know the answers to those questions, but whenever I posed them, my parents quickly changed the subject. Which leads me to fear that something terrible probably happened to Eva, although I'd like to believe she also crossed the river and climbed the mountains, finding ease and comfort in that never-never-land of a Norman Rockwell village that had so captured my fancy during our first years in America.

Is there anything I've forgotten to mention? Nothing I can think of offhand, except perhaps to say that after Passover, I never did dip my hand into the till again.

Gieseking

Tall and spare, Irving Goff had a small head and a bobbing Adam's apple. He favored bowties, wore rimless glasses, and looked like a middle-aged whiz kid. In Goff's junior high English class, you read and compared sonnets written by Milton and Shakespeare. Mr. Goff would give you a quote, for example, "If winter comes, can spring be far behind," and ask you to write an essay analyzing the line. He not only taught on a college level, but turned out to be more stimulating than most college professors Michael later had.

Yet one particular morning, he happened to say in passing that President Franklin Roosevelt was probably the greatest president in American history. That was when Leon Kleiner, who had a photographic memory and a high I.Q., blurted out that Franklin Roosevelt was a moral failure.

Leon had entered Public School 165 that September, after having been expelled from two of New York's finest private schools.

"We raise hands and get recognized before speaking out in this classroom, Leon, remember?" Mr. Goff reprimanded him.

Undeterred, Leon jumped to his feet. Born in France of Austrian parents, he'd come to New York in 1941 and spoke English now with only the slightest of French accents. But to his classmates, he'd remained an unreconstructed newcomer, the classic outsider, a bit of an oddball.

"It is incumbent on me to inform you, Mr. Goff, that by mid-1944 both Churchill and Roosevelt knew about the concentration camps," Leon said rather formally. "At the time, roughly nine thousand Jews were being exterminated each day. Yet not once did the R. A. F. or the U.S. Air Force bomb either the ovens burning the bodies or the rail lines leading to the camps. Not once, Mr. Goff. And they knew, they knew," Leon declared, his voice acquiring an authority unusual for a boy of thirteen.

"How can you be so sure what Churchill and Roosevelt knew in 1944?" Mr. Goff asked, more like a prosecutor than a teacher.

But refusing to back down, Leon answered, "The Polish underground, my dear Mr. Goff, had issued desperate pleas to bomb the rail lines. Word had reached London and Washington. It's been amply documented."

"Okay, let's say for the sake of argument Churchill and Roosevelt knew," Mr. Goff answered in the reasonable voice of a man now willing to consider all possibilities. "I served in the Army, Leon, don't believe you did. Has it occurred to your purely civilian cast of mind that the Allies could not send planes because it was technically impossible as a military operation?"

"Mr. Goff, Mr. Goff," said Leon in an equally reasonable voice. "Low flying R.A.F. planes blew open the doors of a prison in France, rescuing important officers of the French Resistance. It wasn't done vis-a-vis the concentration camps because neither leader who could have done something about it gave a damn. Roosevelt, this country's greatest president? Perhaps if two and two equal five..."

***

Because it was the only time Michael Steinmetz remembered Mr. Goff losing an argument, he made a point of walking home with Leon that afternoon. Leon lived on 107th, Micheal 105th, so heading away from school together seemed perfectly natural.

Yet no one had acted even remotely friendly toward Leon before that day. The reasons being, not only did Leon seem to prefer keeping his distance, but he was perpetually moody, hated punchball, and knew all the answers.

"Hey, Leon, how come you're so knowledgeable about Roosevelt and the concentration camps?" Michael asked when they reached the corner of Broadway. A curious, occasionally thoughtful boy, Michael had a higher than average I. Q. but was no genius.

"Maybe because I make it my business to know about things like that," Leon answered, surprised that unprepossessing Michael, of all people, had taken enough interest not only to walk home with him but pose the question.

"Yeah, but why do you make it your business?" Michael's parents had wept the day Roosevelt died. Was there really something evil or sinister about him they did not know?

Rather than answer directly, Leon said, "Where's your father from and when did he arrive in this country?"

Michael's blue eyes blinked with unaccustomed suspicion. Yet he quickly answered that his father was born in Poland, arriving here in 1900. "But what's that got to do with it?"

Leon offered a smug smile, another reason the other boys avoided him. As for the girls, they weren't interested in Leon because he wasn't particularly good-looking nor came close to what they considered cute.

"If your father hadn't come here in 1900," said Leon, gesturing with a pointy finger, "if you were born in Poland and had remained there, you'd have been among the first to go up in smoke." Leon had stopped walking, practically spitting the words out. Then he added, almost as an afterthought, "You and I, Steinmetz, aren't so different, after all."

Michael didn't know whether to take it as a compliment or an insult. "What's that supposed to mean?" he asked.

"It means we're both damn fortunate to be alive!" And baring his teeth, Leon added, "Of the nineteen Jewish boys in my class in France, seventeen died at Dachau. That's seventeen, my friend, one, seven! Each time I think about them it makes me sick. A couple of those boys were first cousins."

"Maybe instead of feeling sick, you ought to feel grateful that you're still living," said Michael, trying to offer helpful advice like his mother. And maybe, Michael thought but did not add, that would also make you come off a lot less smug.

But Leon could only shake his head in disgust as they stood under the marquee in front of the Olympia Theater. "Listen, while I always had more than enough to eat, while I slept warm and safe on 107th, seventeen boys I knew were murdered. Why was I and one other kid spared, while those seventeen died? What makes me so damn special? Most of them were nicer than me, one was even smarter. And by the way, how come you're living and Jewish boys from your father's hometown are dead? What's so terrific about you?" Leon paused, catching his breath before grabbing Michael's sleeve. "Tell me, Steinmetz, have you ever considered any of this one crummy day of your sheltered life? No! Hell, no! I should be grateful, I should be grateful!" Leon pronounced scornfully, imitating Michael's high-pitched voice. "You sound like a rich, dopey American, without a sense of either history or tragedy. Save your silly advice for those jerks with whom you play that stupid punchball, okay? Okay?"

And talking about punchball, the school yard with the squared-off punchball box faced 109th. When a game was in progress, Leon preferred standing in a corner by himself, kicking a volleyball against the wall as if it was a soccer ball, or dribbling the ball in place, alternating his feet.

One morning, a boy from another class named Tommy Phelan tried to take the volleyball away from Leon. Michael happened to be standing nearby, waiting to get into the next punchball game, when he heard Phelan tell Leon to give him the lousy volleyball or he'd smash Leon's big Jewish nose. What happened next astonished Michael. Leon docilely handed over the ball. Only when Phelan reached for it, Leon hit him in the face, bloodying the kid's mouth.

Michael had never seen a Jewish boy hit first. Jewish boys Michael knew, himself included, always tried to talk their way out of having to fight, or simply fled if they could. But Leon Kleiner, not a particularly athletic sort, not only threw the first punch but kept hitting a stunned Tommy Phelan, actually chasing him out of the schoolyard. Michael stood there, mouth agape: throwing that first punch was even more impressive than taking on Mr. Goff.

Unfortunately, envy mingled with admiration when Michael approached Leon a minute later, saying, "That kid you just beat up has an older brother who goes to Ascension." Ascension was the parochial school across from 165, over on 108th. "The older brother's going to be mad as hell, a Jewish kid hitting Tommy first, and come looking for you."

Leon smirked. "Yeah, so what's he going to do, kill me? Everybody dies." It sounded like a line he'd once heard in a movie.

"But aren't you scared?" Michael said. He was a boy who could be maddeningly curious, ask literal-minded questions at exactly the wrong moment.

"Probably I'll be scared when I see him," Leon confessed. "But so what?"

"Yeah, but what are you going to do when he comes after you?" Michael persisted. Leon was his size, after all, and Michael knew what he'd do in Leon's shoes—run! Run as fast as his pumping legs could propel him. "They're bigger, stronger, and always more of them," Michael added spitefully.

Leon held out his hand. "You don't see it shaking, do you?"

Despite this bitter exchange, Michael again found himself walking beside Leon after three o'clock, scared out of his pants but hopelessly intrigued. Leon was probably a little crazy, but there was something irresistible about him, that is, if you were thirteen and valued brains and courage above all other combinations.

Call it luck, bad or good, depending on your point of view, but who does Michael see approaching them on 108th that very afternoon, but four Irish kids, including the slightly battered Tommy Phelan, who was pointing Leon out to his older brother, Jackie.

Knowing what was about to happen, Michael, despite being intrigued, began backing off. At the same time, he heard Leon hissing under his breath, "Steinmetz, damn it, don't run away! Whatever else you do, don't be a Jew who runs!"

And instead of waiting for the Irish kids to advance upon him unchallenged, Leon walked directly toward Jackie Phelan, who looked a lot like his brother. Same red face, same lantern jaw, only he was an inch taller than Tommy and maybe ten pounds heavier.

Heading straight for Jackie Phelan, Leon dropped his books. Then he began fumbling in his pocket. Still, he kept advancing. Jackie Phelan seemed surprised, both that Leon had dropped his books and that he'd kept coming. Then Phelan also dropped his books as the other Irish boys peeled away, giving Jackie plenty of fighting room. But striking boldly, Leon got in the first punch again. Only this time, my God, he was wearing a pair of brass knuckles! Michael saw the snappy gleam the knuckles made when Leon threw that surprising right lead. Jackie Phelan, his nose gushing blood the color of a fire engine, staggered back.

"You sneaky little Christ killer!" he shouted, blood streaking his starched blue shirt and navy tie.

But Leon didn't stop; got close enough to use those brass knuckles again, this time drawing blood from Jackie's mouth.

Stunned by Leon's aggressiveness, Jackie seemed disoriented. So did the other Irish boys. A Jewish kid not only hitting first but using brass knuckles? Impossible! Out of the question! Maybe this guy wasn't Jewish, after all. Maybe he only sort of looked it. Maybe he was really Italian.

Recovering from shock, Phelan's friends insisted that a bewildered Jackie nurse his wounds and fight another day. It was awful watching him bleeding from both his mouth and nose. And protectively ushering Jackie away, one of them uttered over his shoulder, "Watch yourself, Jewboy, you won't always land that lucky first punch."

As for Leon, he waited calmly, rubbing the brass knuckles against his thigh as the Phelan entourage retreated toward Amsterdam Avenue. Then he went back and picked up his books.

"Well, I'll give you this much," he finally addressed Michael. "At least you didn't run away."

Rooted there, Michael, couldn't help wondering why Leon had courage while he lacked it. Who doesn't want to be brave? They were the same size, damn it! So then what explained this essential difference between them? Probing for an answer, Michael asked, "Leon, you ever been beaten up?"

"It's *because* I've been beaten up that when I know I'm in for a fight I want to throw the first punch," Leon replied with the authority of Mr. Goff discussing a Shakespeare sonnet. "And if the other guy's bigger, then I want to hit him with something besides my fist. Makes a lot of sense, don't you think? Perfectly logical if you're someone as unathletic as me. You got to learn from history, Steinmetz, your own as well as the world's, right? Right?"

*　*　*

It was after Leon had routed the Phelan brothers, neither of whom, incidentally, sought a rematch, that Michael began spending a lot of time with Leon. Boys of thirteen, boys in their young teens before they start thinking of girls, have this passion for friendship. You can hear it in the pleasure of their laughter when they're together; and you can see it when they're walking down the street, their arms linked about each other's shoulder. So it soon was with Michael and Leon.

In spending a lot of time with Leon, Michael often found himself up in Leon's apartment. which had a great view of the Hudson River and Riverside Park. There he heard both Leon and his parents begin a sentence in English, continue it in French, and conclude it in German. They performed like a trio—a trio of linguistic musicians.

Leon's father, Michael soon learned, was, in fact, a real musician, a cellist with the New York Philharmonic. Before that he'd played with the Paris Opera and the Vienna Philharmonic. He was bald and had a walrus mustache, the lobe of his left ear missing, sliced away by a shell fragment he'd attracted fighting in the trenches for the Austrian Army during World War I.

Leon's mother was a blonde who had a round face and loved New York's bustling Upper West Side with its countless movie theaters and myriad candy stores. America's limitless choices were wonderful, she often said, so was the quality of food here. As if to prove her point, the woman made terrific brisket; and happy that Leon had finally secured a school friend, his first in New York, she was constantly urging Michael to remain for lunch or dinner.

Given his father's past, it should come as no surprise that it was Leon who introduced Michael to classical music. They would sprawl on the floor in Leon's bedroom, listening to Schubert's *Trout* and Beethoven's *Pastoral*, as Leon would explain what made each piece so thrillingly compelling. Michael learned a lot those afternoons from Leon about music. Leon, it seemed to Michael, was a born teacher, as good as Mr. Goff.

One day, word reached New York that the pro-Nazi pianist, Walter Gieseking, was planning to make an American tour in early 1949, his first in ten years. During the war, Gieseking had given innumerable concerts under Nazi auspices, coedited a Nazi music magazine, and had concluded his correspondence signing off, "Heil Hitler!" But scheduled to perform before a sold-out audience at Carnegie Hall, Gieseking now claimed, prior to the commencement of his American tour, that he was only a German artist above the seamy game of international politics.

Yet Michael clearly remembered hearing Leon's father say the afternoon before the pianist's New York concert, "What kills me about Gieseking, what upsets me more than anything else is learning that he played Debussy in Munich while everyone in the auditorium heard the screams of Jews crying out for water in sealed railroad cars. The cars were off on a siding, waiting to proceed to nearby Dachau, and that night Gieseking, by all accounts, played movingly, the audience calling for encores. Why do I find I cannot reconcile myself to those accounts? Why do I find I cannot make sense of them?—carloads pleading, howling for water, and Gieseking, a very great artist, hearing those cries but continuing to play beautifully. How is that possible? How could he have continued playing?"

Suddenly, Leon's father shook his massive head, raising both hands above his shoulders before slamming them against his thighs. "Beautifully!" he uttered again, only this time the word seemed to inflame, like salt in a wound. Seeing a grown man looking so pained, as well as so perplexed, was awful, and no one knew quite what to say, how to comfort him. Not his loving wife, not his precocious son, certainly not Leon's young friend, Michael.

***

Next morning, Monday, Leon was morose in school, taciturn and apathetic. Michael tried to engage him several times, especially between classes. But Leon kept shrugging him off, gave monosyllabic answers, and seemed to retreat into a shell. It was only after school, at three o'clock, that he rejoined the land of the living by suggesting they go down to Carnegie Hall. "Maybe we'll spot Gieseking," he said. "I know what he looks like from old pictures. Besides, it ought to be interesting. Veteran groups will be picketing."

They dropped off their schoolbooks at Michael's apartment, before taking the subway to Columbus Circle. From there they walked over to Fifty-seventh and Seventh. Pickets were already marching outside the hall, behind wooden barricades. Many wore their World War II overseas caps. They chanted, "Adolf and Walter, joined at the altar!" One carried a sign that read, "Gieseking will play a funeral dirge for six million Jews tonight!" Another held a second sign that read, "Ilse Koch plays next Saturday!" Uniformed cops were everywhere.

"Who's Ilse Koch?" Michael asked.

Leon seemed surprised by the question but answered patiently, "A Nazi guard at one of the camps, who made lampshades from the skin of dead Jews."

A notice posted outside Carnegie announced that the hall was a democratic institution, and since the U.S. government had allowed Gieseking to enter the county, management saw no reason to bar him from playing.

"Come on," Leon urged Michael, "let's go around to the backstage entrance." He knew exactly where to go because he'd once accompanied his father when Mr. Kleiner appeared at Carnegie with the rest of the Philharmonic. "Maybe we can sneak in," Leon said. Last week, they'd sneaked into the old, rundown Thalia on Ninety-fifth off Broadway, catching a French film showing a woman completely nude.

But two burly cops stood at Carnegie's backstage entrance, blocking off the swinging door.

Without preamble, a small group of men emerged from behind the door. They were all wearing hats and bulky winter coats. Two leading the procession had gold badges pinned to their lapels. Following them was a man with a briefcase, wearing a homburg. Next to him walked a tall, husky fellow with a dimple in his chin and bright blue eyes. Bringing up the rear was a third official also displaying a gold badge.

"The guy with the dimple in his chin," Leon hissed, "that's Gieseking."

To Michael he looked more like a fullback than a pianist—big shoulders, thick neck, meaty face.

"Hey, Gieseking!" Leon called out in German. "You heard my cousins pleading for water that night you played Debussy in Munich! They were on their way to Dachau, and you heard them, you lousy swine!"

Gieseking paused, staring at Leon before smiling.

"What are you laughing about?" Leon continued in German. "Think it's funny?"

But Gieseking smiled again, silently mouthing the words, "Heil Hitler!"

Leon turned to Michael, muttering in barely suppressed fury, "Did you see what that worm just said? Did you see?" And leaving his feet, he flung himself at the passing Gieseking as if he was shot from a cannon.

It was the Phelan brothers reprised and happened so quickly, neither the two cops nor the men wearing gold shields were able to prevent Leon not only from knocking Gieseking down but grabbing him around the throat.

Shouting, they began trying to pull him off the pianist, who was flopping on the ground like an expiring fish. But they couldn't seem to get Leon to release his grip. Then one of the cops began swinging his club, hitting Leon near his eye and causing an immediate gush of blood. Still, Leon wouldn't let go, and the cop raised his club to hit Leon a second time.

But blindsiding the cop, Michael knocked the club from his hand. It was sheer instinct: Leon was his friend, and Michael didn't have time to become frightened.

Almost immediately, Michael felt someone flinging him aside. Sprawled on the ground, he saw three men finally pry Leon off Gieseking, who kept reaching frantically for his throat. Then one of the men wearing a gold badge yelled to the cops to bring Leon and Michael inside, and Michael felt slightly dazed as the shorter cop yanked him to his feet.

The fellow carrying the briefcase turned out to be Gieseking's American lawyer, and once everyone managed to get beyond the backstage entrance, he immediately announced that his client, wanting no further publicity, would forgo pressing any charges. Gieseking, massaging his throat, began arguing violently. But his lawyer shouted back that if he ever wanted to play in the U.S. again, he better forget about what just happened. Pressing charges against two children would absolutely turn all Americans against him.

"Rotten little scum, you're right," Gieseking grudgingly agreed.

At the same time the taller cop conveyed Leon to the nearest city hospital, Michael was shoved into a windowless room that had a large 1949 calendar and a gray desk with a red telephone. Ten minutes later, one of the men wearing a gold badge entered the room, identifying himself as an agent of the Immigration Service. "You're free to go," he announced, after taking Michael's name and address. "Only don't ever let me catch you jumping a cop again, or I'll toss your skinny Jew ass in jail and throw away the key. You hear me loud and clear, kid?"

***

That night, although he felt scared and a little numb, Michael did not tell his parents what happened because he was afraid his mother would cry. He called Leon's apartment after dinner, but the phone just rang forever. Getting any homework done now was out of the question, and he hid Leon's schoolbooks under his baseball glove and a pair of blue Keds in the back of his closet.

The following morning, on his way to school Michael was startled to see a headline in Tuesday's *Times* that read, "Gieseking Agrees To Quit U.S. Without Giving Concert Here."

It seems that although Gieseking had been granted a visa by the State Department, the Immigration Service was now prepared to determine whether he was an "undesirable alien." Their investigation would take perhaps a month, during which time Gieseking would be quarantined at Ellis Island. Rather than agree to remain there, the *Times* reported, Gieseking had decided to return to Europe. No mention was made of the thirteen-year-old who'd assaulted him.

Yet Leon did not attend school that day, nor did anyone answer the phone when Michael later called that afternoon nor answered the door when he went to their apartment either. It was as if the family had disappeared, evaporated, which left Michael confused. No charges had been filed, this was America, not Hitler's Germany. Where were the Kleiners?

Meanwhile, Wednesday's *Times* showed a picture of Gieseking boarding a flight back to Paris. The pianist said, "I've been treated too roughly here," a quote which made Michael laugh. "Everywhere in Europe they ask for concerts, and I give them," Gieseking continued. "This is the first time in my life I have not been treated as an artist should be treated." More important to Michael, he still hadn't learned anything about Leon's whereabouts.

In the end, it took until Thursday morning before Leon, wearing a large bandage over his left eye, intercepted Michael as he walked through Straus Park on his way to school.

"Leon, where've you been?" Michael asked him excitedly. "Gee, I'm so glad to see you. I tried calling."

"We need to talk, I've been waiting for you," Leon said in an unusually subdued voice. "You'll probably be late for school this morning, okay?"

"Sure, sure." Michael was so happy to see him, to know that Leon was alive and reasonably okay, that being late for school mattered little next to his relief and pleasure in seeing Leon again. In the three, four months they'd been hanging around together, he'd come to love the guy. Not only was Leon smart as hell and courageous, but he'd treated Michael as a true friend, a perfect equal.

"Let's sit down here," Leon said, pointing to an empty bench in the park, as people kept hurrying past on their way to the 103th Street subway kiosk.

"Your eye okay?" Michael asked, staring at the bandage.

"They told me at the hospital that if the cop hit me there a second time, he would have blinded me. So thanks for jumping him."

Michael shrugged. "You were bleeding; I just didn't want him to hit you again."

"Well, it took a lot of guts." Then Leon smiled, patting Michael on the back, and it was one of the great moments of Michael's young life.

"The second thing I have to tell you is goodbye," said Leon, and had he slipped on his brass knuckles and struck Michael's nose the effect could not have been more devastating.

"Goodbye? Goodbye? But why?" Michael asked, stunned. "Why?"

Leon sighed. "This may be a little hard to understand," he said, and he looked thoughtful but uncertain, as if he didn't quite grasp it himself. "Do you know what the German word *Judenrein* means?"

When Michael shook his head, Leon explained that Hitler wanted to make Europe *Judenrein*, free of all Jews, even if that meant killing them.

"I still don't understand," said Michael, impatiently.

"I know this will sound odd," Leon said hesitantly. "But, you see, it's been bothering my father since the end of the war that we're still living here, because to him that means Hitler won. Then Monday, after Gieseking, my father said, 'In America they protest, but in Europe they let him play. I can no longer forsake Europe, leaving it to the Giesekings of the world.' What can I tell you?" Leon said. "That's my father, my noble father. Neither me nor my mother want to go back. To my surprise, I've come to love New York, even quaint 165, come to love that we've become close friends."

Feeling awful, Michael looked away, down at the ground. Didn't Leon realize that close friends are rare, and losing one is lousy?

"Listen," said Leon, gripping Michael's hand. "You were with me when I jumped Gieseking. And you weren't only with me, but you saved me from losing an eye. Don't you understand? That means we're always going to be friends. Always."

Unfortunately, what Michael understood was that Leon's imminent departure was incredibly painful to accept. Besides, what was the point of remaining friends if you couldn't continue spending time together?

Yet Michael could see Leon anxiously waiting for some sign of concurrence, or the merest hint of comprehension, and wishing to please him, Michael finally nodded, though he found the words impossible to say.

"Okay," Leon responded, believing that Michael had gone as far as he could. "Okay." Then he stood up, so did Michael, and they shook hands in the formal way of schoolboys trying to act like grownups.

"I've got to get back to my apartment," Leon said. "A car's picking us up and we're flying to Paris at one. But I simply had to see you first, couldn't leave without saying goodbye, had to thank you for saving my eye."

Realizing this was it and not wishing to part on what he took to be a fraudulent note, Michael confessed, "Knocking that club out of the cop's hand, I acted braver than I am. I just didn't have time to be afraid."

"Same thing happened to me when I jumped Gieseking," said Leon, the last thing Michael remembered Leon saying to him.

It was, thought Michael, the kind of response only the most generous of friends would think to offer and Michael never forgot it.

Later, he recalled standing there and taking a deep breath, not only watching Leon leave the park but staring after Leon for a long time before it belatedly occurred to him that if he didn't get started soon he was going to miss Mr. Goff's ten o'clock English class.

Gloves

The Bear Stearns stockbroker Jay Weiss had cut the article out of the *Times* last winter, stuck it in the blue "Miscellaneous" folder he kept in his rolltop desk, and promptly forgot about it. The article was about a man named Michael Gorzki, who lived on the Upper West Side, did odd jobs, and was a neighborhood character. Gorzki wore a red beret and was often found presiding in the luncheonette at Broadway and 114th. There, known as "The Professor," he argued with Columbia University students, urging them to overthrow a social system that encouraged greed and selfishness. Then for a month each fall Gorzki disappeared, traveling down to the Bowery where you'd find him offering warm gloves to homeless alcoholics soon to face another of New York's bitter winters. According to the *Times*, Gorzki had been doing it from Thanksgiving to Christmas, and for years men along the Bowery referred to him as "Gloves."

He was a tall, powerfully built man, although the picture in the *Times* showed a gentle-looking Gorzki wearing his beret and thick glasses. When Jay knew him forty-five years ago, Gorzki wore neither. But it was, Jay felt certain, the same Michael Gorzki: the name was too unusual, the resemblance too striking for him not to be.

One reason Jay had remembered Gorzki so well was not only had they attended the same boys' camp in 1950, but they were the identical age, celebrating the same birthday, July 22nd. Jay remembered, because it was the custom at the camp for others to sing "Happy Birthday," presenting him with a birthday cake, which he and Gorzki had had to share that year.

Another reason Jay remembered was that they were probably the two most unhappy boys at Camp Cherokee. Jay did not know the reason for Gorzki's unhappiness that summer, but what explained his own was that his parents had gotten a divorce that spring.

Cherokee was one of those rich Jewish boys' camps located in the hilly Berkshires, where the food was delicious and the grounds stunningly beautiful. Mountains bracketed a pebbly lake, silver birch trees reflected in the water's glassy surface. The facilities included a chlorinated swimming pool, a baseball diamond that had a sloping left field, and three red-clay tennis courts. The counselors, college students, had muscular calves and could smack a waist-high softball a country mile. Caressingly warm during the day, the nighttime sky brimmed with chilled stars that seemed so close you could practically pluck one to save for good luck.

Presiding over this memorably Edenic estate was its owner, Larry Gottchalk. Although Larry was an assistant principal in the Bronx during the school year, it was Cherokee's cachet and well-being that elicited his deepest feelings. You often saw him driving a black Cadillac, giving prospective parents his fabled "Million Dollar Tour."

Or he could be observed prowling the campgrounds, picking up a delinquent candy wrapper here, a discarded letter from home there. And, oh, God help the boy who thoughtlessly violated camp property.

That July, Michael Gorzki was one such, caught by the nature counselor in the act of breaking two branches off a Colorado blue spruce tree near the peeling shower house. That night, Larry made a terrible example of him.

Gorzki, who'd come over from Europe a few years after the end of World War II, was fifteen then and still spoke English with a heavy Polish accent. Yet he was forced to stand on a chair and admit guilt in his stammering English before the rest of the camp after dinner. Then he was told that the next time anything remotely similar happened, a really awful punishment would follow, possibly expulsion. Finally, Larry announced that Gorzki's father, a prominent doctor, would immediately be billed for damage to the tree. "We do not abuse camp property at Cherokee," Larry proclaimed, "we cherish it."

Unfortunately, the following week the arts-and-crafts counselor discovered yet another tree that had two branches freshly torn from its trunk. Only this time no one had spotted the miscreant, and in his fury and frustration Larry Gottchalk decided it had to be Gorzki again.

That night, the boy was forced to stand near the head counselor's table while the rest of the camp dined on rare roast beef and French fries. Then he was ordered by Larry to confess his guilt. When Gorzki insisted it wasn't him this time, Larry answered that Camp Cherokee was prepared to remain in the mess hall until hell froze over, or Michael Gorzki found the courage to tell the truth and take his punishment like a man.

A half hour came and went, but rather than confess Gorzki remained standing, the expression on his face a muddy compound of sullenness, bewilderment, and unrepentance.

"Well, fellows, what's it to be?" Larry addressed the restless boys, almost two hundred strong. "Does Michael Gorzki have your permission to keep us in this mess hall just because he's a sneaky coward and no one saw him break the branches off a tree we all love?"

"No, no, no!" the boys began to shout in unison. Having had to sit quietly for the last half hour, they were bored silly and it was a huge relief just to make some noise. Besides, the activity scheduled for the evening was a Hopalong Cassidy movie—a cowboy film they'd be prevented from seeing if Gorzki stubbornly maintained his innocence.

"Come on, Gorzki!" the most popular of the seniors called out. "We all know you did it!"

"Confess, confess!" shouted one junior after another.

God knows the reason, but Gorzki seemed to nod then. And catching him nod, Larry Gottchalk beamed, pulling out the chair of shame for Gorzki to mount so that all could not only hear but also see him as he publicly proclaimed his guilt.

Gorzki stood on the chair, quite alone. Yet he seemed to take in every face before he spoke, his stony eyes panning each table like an unblinking camera. And it was only then that he shouted in his faulty English, "I do not break branches this time! I do not break them!"

Surprised and outraged, Larry Gottchalk began shaking his chair and shouting back, "You lying, miserable refugee!"

That's when Gorzki leaped, knocking Larry to the ground. Then, before anyone could intercede, he began choking the camp owner.

***

Pandemonium broke out. Boys stood up and cheered. For whom? For what? Did they really know? Did they really care? Counselors from the nearest tables rushed over, coming to the aid of the startled camp owner, who was gasping for breath and beginning to turn dangerously blue.

It seemed to take forever, but they were finally able to pry Gorzki away before he strangled Larry. As four struggling counselors dragged a thrashing Gorzki out of the mess hall, the wimpy camp doctor hurried to Larry's side. So did Larry's howling wife, who'd been summoned from the nearby camp office.

Of course, Gorzki disappeared from Cherokee that evening. Larry Gottchalk survived his assault but had to be taken to Pittsfield General Hospital, where he remained overnight for observation. As far as Jay Weiss ever learned, no charges were filed against Gorzki, and for years no one seemed to know what happened to him. It was as if he'd disappeared off the face of the earth. That is, until Jay had read the article in the *Times* last winter. Then, six months later, Jay happened to spot the clip again a couple of days before his sixtieth birthday, and reading the article a second time, it occurred to him it might be amusing and distracting to see Gorzki after such a long interval.

Anyway, feeling particularly frisky the following morning, Jay found himself obtaining Gorzki's number from 411. "I probably shouldn't be doing this," he told himself prankishly, as he dialed Gorzki's apartment.

The man on the other end answered after the first ring. "Yes?" he said in a nasal voice that sounded more New York than European.

Introducing himself, Jay confided that if he wasn't mistaken, they'd been bunkmates at Camp Cherokee in 1950.

"Jay Weiss? Jay Weiss?" Gorzki said in a suspicious voice after a minute. "Oh, yes, I remember you."

Recalling that they had the same birthday, tomorrow, Jay said it might be fun if they got together then for lunch.

"Short guy and your parents had just gotten divorced," recalled Gorzki, a man accustomed to rummaging in his past.

"Hey, that's some memory," Jay said with a laugh meant to flatter.

They talked for a few minutes, Jay again suggesting that lunch might be special on their joint birthday after not having seen each other for almost fifty years.

At first, Gorzki seemed reluctant, but Jay was a salesman, a good one, and the more he kept talking, the more he sensed Gorzki becoming increasingly curious. Finally, Jay heard Gorzki saying, "Well, okay, Weiss. If you really want to get together tomorrow..."

Jay said he worked for Bear Stearns, and they were located at 245 Park. Gorzki was to go to the lobby, where he'd be given an elevator pass. He was then to go to the seventh floor, the executive dining room. The receptionist there would summon Jay, whose office was on a higher floor.

"You'll need to wear a jacket and tie," Jay instructed. "I hope it's okay if I call you Michael. Please call me Jay. Twelve-thirty tomorrow convenient for you?"

***

When the receptionist sitting outside the executive dining room phoned the following afternoon saying that a Michael Gorzki was waiting for him, Jay grinned as if he were patting himself on the back. Then he straightened his paisley tie and slipped into a gray pinstriped jacket.

In the reception area on the seventh floor, Jay saw a tall man with a pepper-and-salt beard. Gorzki, who'd posed beardless in the *Times* photograph, was wearing an old tweed jacket, thin yellow tie, and chino pants. He looked barely respectable, or just about what Jay had expected.

"Michael?" he said, extending his hand confidently. "Jay Weiss, nice seeing you again after all these years."

Gorzki was four, five inches taller than Jay. He had dark, almost black eyes, and seeing him again, Jay recalled that as a kid Gorzki had a habit of staring at people until they turned away.

"Happy Birthday," Jay told him with a dazzling smile.

"You, too," Gorzki replied with a lopsided grin. Two of his front teeth were still crooked.

Jay guided his guest toward the dining room, where they were met by a slim blonde with terrific legs, who led them to a table near a window. "This okay, Mr. Weiss?" she asked, but Jay didn't even bother answering her. Manners were not exactly his strong suit.

Their table was covered by a white damask tablecloth and had a pink carnation in a thin transparent vase. The waiter, a Pakistani, wore a tuxedo and asked in a high voice starched with an English accent, "What can I get you gentlemen to drink?"

"Name your poison, Michael," Jay encouraged him.

After his guest ordered a glass of red wine, Jay said alcohol made him dizzy in the afternoon. Besides, he had two important calls to make to Kuwait at three. "Club soda for me," he told the waiter abruptly.

A number of nearby tables were occupied. Most of the men, like Jay, wore conservative ties and business suits. Other than the leggy blonde, no woman graced the clubby, rectangular dining room.

Jay said that he'd read about Gorzki in the *Times* last winter and had considered calling him then, but decided to wait until it was almost July 22nd. "Thought you'd probably be more receptive to coming down here on your birthday." Then he asked if Gorzki was married and what he'd been doing since they last saw each other. Jay, who'd been selling securities since 1960, had developed a silky manner of speaking that made him sound casual yet polished.

On the other hand, Gorzki, smiling self-consciously, said sociability was not his forte and he'd always lived alone. As for how he supported himself, the *Times* article was perfectly accurate—he was a kind of neighborhood handyman.

Reunions have their inevitable moments of awkwardness, and one unmistakably occurred when Gorzki stiffly asked Jay about himself. While the question sounded a lot flatter and more wooden than it needed to, Jay was only too happy to respond that he had been at Bear Stearns since 1972, lived in the leafy suburb of Manhasset with his wife Marcy, and had two sons. One had just started working for Proctor and Gamble in Cincinnati; the other was attending the Wharton School of Business. "Just your typical American success story," said Jay, half-kiddingly.

When the waiter gave them menus a minute later, Jay explained that because the aforementioned sons were taking him to dinner that night, he'd only be eating a tuna salad now. But he suggested that Gorzki order the lamb chops; they were thick and delicious.

"You know, when I read that article about you, it naturally brought back memories of Camp Cherokee and 1950," Jay resumed after they ordered. "I've never forgotten that encounter you had with Larry Gottchalk."

Although Jay had hoped that naming Gottchalk might somehow strike sparks, he found himself disappointed because his guest merely shrugged, saying, "Lucky for him and me the others quickly interceded. Another ten seconds, and I'd have choked that sadistic fool to death."

It was immediately after the waiter brought their food that Jay told his guest, "I've a confession to make—it was me who damaged that second blue spruce tree for which you were blamed. Because my parents had just gotten divorced, I was angry, confused, destructive."

But leaning forward, Gorzki's only reaction was to begin eating. "You're right," he told Jay, pointing enthusiastically to the lamb chops with his fork. "They are delicious."

At first, Jay wondered if his guest had actually heard him. Then, annoyed because he realized he'd been quite unable to provoke Gorzki, Jay decided to add, "I was afraid back in 1950 to admit I did it; afraid that that clown Gottchalk would humiliate me rather than you."

Yet Gorzki continued eating as if his sole concern was that someone might come along and prematurely snatch away his plate.

And it was only after he'd polished off the tiny boiled potatoes, Julienne carrots, and last bite of pink meat that he looked up at Jay, saying inquisitively, "Weiss, really, why did you call me down here? Surely not to tell me you're sorry after forty-five years?"

Jay had eaten only half his tuna salad. He'd found it increasingly irritating that an accomplished salesman like himself had so far failed to engage, let alone manipulate such an obviously unworldly man as Michael Gorzki.

"I'll tell you why I got you down here," Jay said, making it sound as though the moment of truth had arrived at last, although, if truth really be told, it was simply the first thing Jay could think of to say. "Bear Stearns owns this building, and I know the guy who hires the maintenance people. They offer a terrific health plan, and I could put in a good word for you, Michael. It would be a way of making up to you for what happened at camp. Of course, you'd have to shave your beard. They have a dress code—no beards, no hair below the neck, no men's earrings."

Gorzki's reaction can only be described with the greatest charity as a barely patient smile. "Listen, my friend," he eventually said. "I'm not interested in your wonderful health plan. Besides, whatever happened at Cherokee, you don't owe me a thing."

"Well, I guess that means I'm just going to have to feel guilty each time I think about you now." It was the kind of response Jay's wife often used when she attempted to emotionally blackmail him.

"Oh, Weiss, Weiss," Gorzki said, and for the first time that afternoon he actually seemed to come alive. "You really mustn't talk to me about guilt. A self-satisfied fellow like yourself hasn't the faintest idea what certified guilt's actually like. I, on the other hand, am an expert in that wretched department." And he laughed an utterly bitter laugh, harsh and uncompromising.

"Pardon me for breathing," Jay said angrily. "Pardon me for daring to presume in the presence of a national authority. Self-proclaimed, that is."

"But why feel so offended just now?" Gorzki asked with an exaggerated shrug. "I'm not offended you have a wife, two sons, lots of money—all of which I don't have. Why should you be insulted that I suffer from real guilt and you plainly do not."

"You know what I think?" Jay said, sorry he'd ever seen the article about Gorzki, let alone asked the guy to lunch. "I think inviting you here was a huge mistake."

"Oh, it was, it was," Gorzki acknowledged, nodding. "But I haven't eaten such delicious lamb chops in ten years, so I don't consider it a total waste. At the same time, it really bothers me that you've reached age sixty with not a single line indenting your smooth face." And at that moment, Jay reminded him of those unseasoned college students up a Columbia he enjoyed debating.

"Tell me," Gorzki continued, after taking a breath and smiling, "would you consent to hear how a terrible action early in life can dominate one's existence, not be a mere footnote, the way I'm a 1950 footnote to the glorious saga of Jay Weiss, successful American stockbroker?"

Unnerved, Jay muttered, "What I think is I ought to say good riddance to you right here, right now."

"No, what you ought to do is sit back and listen," Gorzki told him. "Maybe you'll learn something. By the way, do they serve brandy here? I'll need a strong drink or two to loosen my tongue."

Jay debated for almost a minute whether to toss Gorzki out or take his advice. Finally, he called their waiter over,saying his guest wanted a brandy, and could he have a glass of water with a lemon wedge. Something unpleasant, probably the fishy, half-eaten tuna salad, was making his mouth taste awful.

**

"Nice brandy, " Gorzki acknowledged with a smile after taking a sip.

"You were going to straighten me out," Jay said challengingly. "You were going to educate me, remember?"

"That's not so easy," Gorzki confessed, taking another sip. "Not nearly as easy as talking about dear old Camp Cherokee."

"This better be good," Jay threatened, "or I'm going to laugh in your face the way you laughed in mine."

"You're not going to laugh in my face," Gorzki promised, finishing off the brandy with a flourish before signaling the waiter for a refill.

After the waiter brought a second brandy, Gorzki took a sip and gave a reassuring stroke to his neatly trimmed beard.

"I come from a town outside of Warsaw," he began with a sigh. "My father, as you might or might not recall, was a doctor. When the Nazis occupied our town, he was ordered to care for the German commandant and his family. The Nazis choose wisely, because my father was a very good doctor. They could have selected others who weren't Jewish, but they chose my father.

"One morning, my father learned that all the Jewish children were going to be swept up in a Nazi raid and shipped off to one of the concentration camps. How he learned about it I don't know to this day. Maybe the commandant hinted what was going to happen; maybe my father was in the right place at the right time.

"I was eight then, my younger brother Arthur, seven. My father hid us in an attic on a deserted farm he owned just outside of town. He told us not to leave the attic under any circumstances. The Nazis would make their sweep, ship out those they caught, and my father would then make arrangements for me and my brother to live with a Catholic family in another part of the country. He said we would have to care for ourselves until it was safe for him to come for us.

"It was January, bitter cold. We had been provided with bread, water, two large pails to use when we needed to relieve ourselves. My father had tried to think of everything. But after he left us, my brother realized he'd forgotten to wear his gloves.

"As I say, it was bitterly cold, and my brother's hands were freezing. He asked me to sneak back to our house and find his gloves. I refused, reminding him our father said we must not leave our hiding place. My brother asked if I would share my gloves with him. Again, I refused. I had remembered to bring my gloves; he was at fault in forgetting his. Arthur was often careless about such matters, and this would be a good lesson for him, I thought, one he would not soon forget.

"You can probably guess the rest," Gorzki said, looking up at Jay, and his dark eyes never seemed as black. "Arthur sneaked back to our house while I was sleeping, before the Nazis had completed their sweep. Seeing him, an antisemite alerted the Germans, who made my brother lead them to me. Thrown together with the others in the school auditorium, we were all scheduled to leave for the concentration camp that night.

"When my father found out, he rushed over to the commandant's office, pleading for our lives. The commandant thought a moment, debating what to do, finally telling my father, 'I will give you the older one back. You're a clever man,' he said. 'See to it he's not found again. I will not save him a second time.'"

Gorzki leaned back in his chair, reached for the brandy, and took a long swallow.

Then he closed his eyes, breathing deeply. When he opened them, he said, "Now that's the real thing, Weiss, a prelude to lifelong guilt, not that watery Cherokee romance you were telling me about a little while ago."

Because it was impossible to disagree, Jay not only found himself hating Gorzki but also wishing the guy would instantly disappear, evaporate, vanish.

"I can see from your face that you absolutely no longer wish me to remain here," noted Gorzki, almost kindly now. "I recognize the expression, because all my life I seem to be someone who makes others uncomfortable."

Then he finished the second brandy, nodded, and repeated that the lamb chops were delicious, a real treat.

Jay watched him leave without accompanying Gorzki to the elevator. "I was looking for a little diversion on my birthday, something different, out of the ordinary," he thought. "But I got more than I bargained for." And shaking his head,

Jay swore he'd never do that again, telling himself to forget that Camp Cherokee's Michael Gorzki ever turned up.

***

Yet for the next several months, and to his considerable surprise, Jay found himself increasingly troubled. Because he had a limited imagination, he couldn't trace Arthur Gorzki's tragic route on that frigid day Arthur had sneaked away from his father's farm. Instead, Jay dreamt repeatedly of his own son when the youngest was seven. He saw the boy without gloves, crying from the cold as he walked through downtown Manhasset, and in the dream, Jay clearly saw himself also walking past his weeping child.

Each time he had the dream, Jay woke, cursing the day he'd ever thought of getting in touch with Gorzki, and to calm his nerves, he often took a large drink of Scotch.

"What does this lousy dream mean, and why do I keep having it?" Jay wondered, shaking his head. "It's a stupid dream, makes no sense, because I'd never walk past my own shivering seven-year-old son. Maybe, to be perfectly honest, I'd walk past some other shivering kid, but never my own. Not in a million years!"

Unfortunately, it never occurred to Jay that because he'd still walk past someone else's shivering child, even after having heard Gorzki's terrible confession, the dream stubbornly refused to go away. It kept recurring two, three times a week. Oddly, it was the first recurrent dream Jay had experienced in years that had nothing to do with the fluctuating stock market. Naturally he told no one about it, not even his wife, nor did he consult a shrink. Jay wasn't the consulting kind.

He was a stockbroker, a practical, can-do guy, a businessman. Surely, Jay reasoned, there was something he could think of—a device, a process, a self-help manual—to stop the dream from returning. But when he tried to come up with a solution, something specific, his mind seemed to freeze and he drew a blank.

"Gorzki, Gorzki, damn you!" he'd moan irrationally. "You got me into this mess, you're going to get me out of it!"

***

Even so, it took until the end of October before Jay finally began shopping various men's stores, where he bought enormous quantities of gloves. The gloves didn't have to look great or be expensive, but they did have to be warm and they had to come in all sizes. Jay stocked the gloves in his garage. When Marcy inquired about them, because he doubted she'd understand, he told her that one of the big shots at Bear Stearns had asked him to contribute an item of clothing to the poor that Christmas. He chose gloves, and it was only after he'd spent the suggested, obligatory sum of ten thousand dollars that he stopped piling up the boxes.

The following week, he contacted a messenger service and asked that they send their most responsible employee. The man would need a car or truck, Jay said. The responsible employee showed up at Jay's home on a Saturday morning in December. Snow covered the ground. Jay helped load the man's truck, which was a small U-Haul. Then he gave him of copy of Gorzki's picture and jotted down Gorzki's address.

"I want you to be there before seven tomorrow morning," Jay said. "Then I want you to wait for Mr. Gorzki to come out of his building. Gorzki's probably got a beard now and he'll be wearing a red beret. Just to be sure it's him, though, ask his name. Say you read about the gloves in the *Times* and want to contribute some."

"Wouldn't it be easier if I called and told him I'll be bringing the gloves over?" the messenger suggested. He was in his fifties, a somewhat fussy man who had a thin, ginger-colored mustache and wore a navy watch cap.

"No," Jay answered, "because I want everything to suit Mr. Gorzki's convenience, not yours or mine."

"Well, if you don't want me to call, what about I ring his apartment when I arrive there?" The attractive part of being a messenger was that it kept him on the go, and he was someone who hated sitting around, hated being inactive.

But Jay said, "Mr. Gorzki might be sleeping, and because I don't think he's someone who sleeps well, I don't want him even possibly disturbed."

Somehow Jay had sensed it was as important to be considerate of Gorzki as it was to buy the gloves, and for a minute, perhaps more, he stared thoughtfully at the snow covering his front lawn. It had fallen during the night, eight, nine inches, and it was still beautiful, white and fluffy, even magical. But the temperature was beginning to drop. Single digits were predicted, and soon the snow would turn into glassy sheets of treacherous ice.

Jay thought about Gorzki's brother, and he wondered if it was as cold on the day Arthur had slipped away from the farm as it promised to be tomorrow. Then he thought about the men on the Bowery who called Gorzki "Gloves." The two were inextricably linked in his mind, as no doubt they were in Gorzki's, and now Jay added to them his bad dream. It occurred less than three times a week but still appeared often enough to prove unsettling.

If Gorzki needed to give gloves to alcoholics for a month each year to get through the rest of his life, maybe if Jay more modestly supplied some of those gloves this year, the bad dream would eventually go away.

Of course, that was the general idea, or as far as Jay could take the dream. On the other hand, looking up at the messenger, he did say, "The only thing you can't tell Gorzki is that the gloves come from me. You can't mention my name," and he found himself smiling. He was smiling because a part of him just then wanted the gloves to strike Gorzki as a kind of miracle—one box after another, hundreds of them, a veritable blizzard of gloves, all sizes, all colors, warm gloves, one pair to a customer. "Just step right up, take a look, try them, keep them, wear them! Oh, please, for God's sweet sake, give me the supreme pleasure of seeing you wear them." And if their donor remained unknown, Jay wanted to believe, if he remained a mystery, the blizzard of gloves had a good chance of intriguing Gorzki, of maybe even making his tortured memory a little less painful. "What the hell, why not, why not?" Jay muttered, and letting himself get carried away, he reached out, slapping the messenger's truck twice for good luck.

"Okay, okay," he finally told the guy. "You're on your way." It had, thought Jay, who wasn't a particularly religious man, the terse, metrical appeal of a streetside blessing, an abbreviated benediction.

III. US51426447

Fortunes of War
Hazardous Pay
P.O.W.
The Lawyer
Van
Garrison Revisited

Fortunes of War

❧

General Mark Clark and his staff entered Rome from the south, in a ragged convoy of jeeps, passing through the Porta Maggiore. They were heading for the *municipio* on Capitolone Hill, the historic seat of Roman power, where the Italian resistance leaders would officially turn over the city to the Allied Armies. It was a sunny June morning, and the Eternal City had just been torn from the grasp of the hated *Tedeschi,* which was how most Romans referred to the German troops.

But the convoy soon became lost in St. Peter's Square, and many of the streets were blocked off by flag-waving men and rapturous-looking women. So it took the general somewhat longer than he would have liked before he found his way. Three stars glinted off his soft cap, which he wore tilted to the right. He was a lanky man, with a long face and dark eyes, and there was a kerchief under the open collar of his shirt.

Reaching his destination, Clark climbed to the top of the stairs, where he took out a map and began issuing instructions to his corps commanders, Truscott, Keyes and the French general, Juin. "It's a great day for the Fifth Army," he announced for the benefit of the grinding newsreel cameras. His personal photographer jumped around him, clicking his camera with the rapidity of a machine gun.

Standing near the ancient balustrade, within hearing distance of Clark, Captain Gene Colucci, a recently appointed legal officer attached to the general's staff couldn't help smiling ambivalently. He had no love for Clark, whom he considered a publicity hound and something of a fraud; at the same time, he admired the general's crude determination. Clark had wanted his Fifth Army to go down in history as liberators, and through luck, persistence and possibly disingenuousness, he'd beaten the straining British Eighth Army to the gates of the city that had witnessed the crowning of Charlemagne as well as the martyrdom of the early Christians. "Hell," Colucci thought, "even a son of a bitch of a general is entitled to his moment in the sun."

He pushed his way back down the stairs through the crowd and found his jeep. It seemed a good time to drive through Rome, and Colucci, who'd been born there twenty-eight years before but left for America when he was three, wondered if he'd remember any of the landmarks. Fat chance.

He'd written his mother a couple of months ago back in New York, asking if there was anyone she wished him to look up in her hometown. He'd only been half-serious, but she'd responded gravely, "Do not frivolously open wounds it has taken me twenty-odd years to close through enormous will and effort."

She'd fled from Italy, with only the clothes on her back and her three-year-old son, leaving behind her brutal womanizer of a husband, and their two-year-old daughter. "I would have died if I'd remained with your father," she once told her son. "As for the little girl, God have mercy on me, but she was simply an innocent, a victim. I could not wait, and I had passage money for only one of you, and no woman in her right mind parts with her male offspring, the pride of her life and motherhood." Still, not once during the last twenty-five years, had she tried to find out what fate had befallen those she'd abandoned. And without even divorcing her first husband, she married the barber, Salvatore Colucci, and both she and Gene adopted his name.

Colucci started the jeep. He knew that most of the officers on Clark's staff were planning on staying in the fancy hotels on the Via Veneto for the next few days and he thought the intelligent thing might be for him to make a beeline for the

Excelsior. Last week he'd heard a correspondent say that before the war it was the best hotel in town.

The streets were still thronged with shouting people and confetti rained down from the buildings. Partisans wearing red, white, and green brassards and carrying rifles, roamed the city on the lookout for fascists and fifth columnists. Gene had never seen so many priests before, they seemed to have fallen from the trees. Buxom women in tight skirts jumped into jeeps and straddled tank turrets, kissing GI's while growing visibly excited by the purring beneath them of U.S. government vehicles.

The contrast between the exuberance in the streets and the suave, slightly superior clerks in the Excelsior couldn't have been more startling. Just that morning German officers had hastily checked out—their names and rank were on the same page in the register Gene signed—yet the hotel clerks acted as if today was like any other suggesting they were either great snobs or consummate actors. Gene, given his scant familiarity with them, couldn't decide which.

After getting his gear squared away in his room, Gene treated himself to a bath in the biggest tub he'd ever seen. Three men his size could have shared it in comfort. He hadn't realized he'd been quite so dirty, but soon it was as if someone had squirted a jar of ink into the water.

Gene had dark eyes, black hair, and a swarthy complexion—a true son of Roma—and looking at himself in the bathroom mirror, he said, "Hometown boy makes good!"

He'd never had much trouble getting his way with girls back in the States, and he was looking forward now to trying his luck in the city of his birth. Besides, Roman women were said to be bold and knowledgeable in bed, and Gene, who hadn't slept with a soul since he'd been in a North African bordello six months ago, was one terribly horny fellow.

First, though, he checked the phone book in his room. His father's name was Paolo Barbetta. His sister's, Mirella, but neither was listed in the directory, and Gene felt more relieved than anything else. He knew he wouldn't have been able to resist looking them up, despite what his mother had written.

GI's were roaming the streets, cut off from their officers, and enjoying the heady confusion liberators have always experienced. Old men grabbed Gene's hands and kissed them, old women burst into grateful tears at the very sight of him. Young girls thrust bouquets of violets into his masculine hands. He offered thanks in such fluent Italian that their eyebrows arched with surprise and pleasure. A murmurous sound seemed to impregnate the streets, and the closer he walked toward the center of the city, the louder the noise became, swelling into an exultant and sustained roar.

It seemed to Gene that he'd become an expert on sounds this last year. Take the S mines he heard when he landed in Sicily. Those babies issued a pop noise when you stepped on them, shooting a container five feet into the air, where they exploded, scattering hundreds of deadly steel balls. Altogether different from the whine of a Kraut 88, which grew into a sudden rush of air, finally sounding as if God, kicked in the belly, was desperately sucking in to catch his faltering breath.

Gazing about him, Gene couldn't help wondering how many of Rome's multitudes had ever heard those sounds. What did Mussolini urge Italians before the war—live like lions? They sure didn't look very lion-like to Gene today. But then, he didn't know of the Roman waiters, who brought German officers the worst dishes on their menus, claiming they didn't understand pidgin Italian. Nor did Gene know of the torture chamber in the jail on the Via Tasso, where the sixty-five-year-old leader of one of the partisan groups had wads of cotton stuffed into his ears and set on fire because he refused to tell the fascists where to find his comrades. Nor did Gene know of the nuns who'd hid many of Rome's frightened Jews, keeping them from being shipped to the crematoriums belching their endless plumes of flesh-smelling smoke. Gene was a decent enough fellow, but he couldn't help feeling slightly superior to the forebears he'd just helped liberate.

***

The whores, when Gene saw them, were standing near the Piazza Venezia. There were three of them. Each wore a tight skirt, a blouse with padded shoulders, and wedge-heel shoes. It seemed to be their uniform. The one who caught his eye must have been twenty-five and vaguely reminded him—dare he admit it?—of his mother. She had her high cheekbones and chestnut-colored hair. Her name, she said, was Maria.

"I have a room at the Excelsior," Gene told her.

"Ah, the Excelsior," she said, impressed, and gestured grandly to her two friends. They seemed sad-faced and more reserved, smiling timidly at Gene. *"Ciao,"* Maria waved goodbye, and took Gene's hand, thrusting her bosom forward. Perhaps he was her first American. Perhaps she'd been uncertain how a GI would act. But her confident walk seemed to suggest that an American who spoke impeccable Italian couldn't be all bad, despite what the sneering Germans might have been telling the girls the last several months.

When they got to the Excelsior, the lobby was crowded with officers of the Fifth Army, most of whom were drinking to their victory over both the Nazis and the British Eighth Army. Bold *contessas,* as well as the high-priced call girls, made the rounds, but Gene didn't see a woman prettier than the one holding his arm, and he did not stop to talk to any of his comrades. He wouldn't mind perhaps drinking, even dancing later, but now he had one matter on his mind, and the girl could tell how excited he was by the way he kept nervously licking his mouth.

Nevertheless, she first insisted on washing herself, then him. "So that neither of us will get the sickness." Her ministrations seemed knowing, and he wondered not if but with how many Germans she'd slept. Not that he blamed her; one had to survive. Perhaps she'd even slept with some of the Kraut officers whose names he'd seen scrawled in the hotel register that morning.

Maria had beautifully proportioned breasts and eyes shaped like almonds. As he almost knew he would, he came only a minute after entering her. He waited without embarrassment to get his second wind before mounting her again. This time he was in control and, shutting his eyes, pumped away contentedly.

"Mother of God." she whispered in his ear. "You're like a bull."

It sounded like a line she offered every stiff she'd ever slept with and, without breaking stride, he couldn't help smiling.

She raked his back and made spurious love sounds, yet her hips maintained the steady grind of a professional, and he fitted inside her like a hand wearing a perfectly matched glove. Her neck smelled of fresh bread, and this homey scent charmed him.

Still, when he finally let himself go, he seemed to explode, and the authenticity of his passion became contagious, for without any tricky stage gestures, she urged in her naturally dark contralto's voice for him to please, please don't stop.

Later, she told him that her own passion hadn't been this aroused in more than a year, or just before the Nazis had taken over Rome.

"I could sleep with them, but I never could quite let myself go, not like just now." She went into the bathroom for some water.

Outside, there suddenly sounded a cacophony of bells. It occurred to Gene he was hearing the booming *ding-dong* made by the great chimes of St. Peter, although he wondered if even the clamorous sounds from Vatican City, located on the other side of the Tiber, carried so far.

Gazing with pleasure at the woman as she emerged from the john, Gene decided to call room service and order a simple meal. He did not wish to take her downstairs now and share her even with his comrades' eyes.

"The water supply must be very low, for the faucets stopped working as I finished washing." Maria told him.

He shrugged. After living in the Italian hills for weeks, a faucet that stopped running was but a minor inconvenience. "I'd like you to stay the night," he told her.

Considering his request a just tribute to her skills and looks, she nodded, and they quickly settled upon a decent price.

***

That night, Gene slept like a baby. His dreams were rich and sweet. He dreamt of his mother's pasta smothered in tomato sauce, capers, and glistening black olives. He imagined Brooklyn girls, who wanted him to believe they were virgins but whose panties flew from their powdered thighs at his slightest touch. He dreamt of his corpulent, kindly stepfather, taking his ease in front of his barber shop in Little Italy, the sun slanting through the buildings and anointing him with bars of beneficent light.

In the best of all possible worlds such dreams unreel endlessly, but toward morning Gene and the woman were rudely awakened by sounds of water and heaving pipes.

"What the hell is that?" he said, sitting up.

"Ah, mother of God!" Maria shouted, jumping out of bed and racing into the bathroom.

When she returned, she had a sheepish look. "A thousand pardons, captain. I forgot to turn off the faucet yesterday, and the water supply must be normal again." There was only a slight stream leading from the bathroom to the bedroom, and Maria, down on her haunches, did the best she could wiping it away.

"Don't worry about it," Gene said, urging her back to bed. Hell, the Excelsior was hardly in a position to sue him.

Marie dried her feet before slipping between the crisp sheets. She was no longer sleepy. "Tell me." she said, "I was too shy to ask yesterday, but where did you learn to speak Italian so well, in school?"

"School? No," he laughed. Then he said he was born in Rome but left for America as a little boy with his mother. And reaching for his pants, he took out his wallet and showed her a picture of his mother taken when he was home during his first furlough.

Looking at the picture, Maria frowned with concentration. She got out her own wallet, showing Gene a much older photo of a woman she said was her mother.

Though it was the picture of a considerably younger woman, the resemblance was striking, and slowly sitting up in bed, Gene gazed at the prostitute with a slightly stunned expression. "What did you say your name was?" he asked, his voice unnaturally tense.

Looking at the two photos again, the woman confessed, "Maria's not actually my name. It's Mirella. Mirella Barbetta. Why do you ask?"

Gene paled, his eyes rolled around a couple of times, and he thought he was going to pass out.

"Are you ill?" the woman asked. She touched his hand. "What's the matter?"

Amazed she hadn't made the connection yet, he said in a hushed voice, "My adopted name is Gene Colucci, but I was born Gino, Gino Barbetta."

She slapped her mouth with one hand. "Gino? Gino?" she whispered. She placed her hands over her trembling breasts. "Gino, my brother from America?"

When he nodded, trying to smile, she burst into tears, throwing herself upon him.

"Mirella, Mirella," he said, stroking her lovely hair. "My little sister, Mirella," Then, looking about him and realizing they were stark naked in bed together, he leaped from beneath the covers, grabbed his clothes and ran into the bathroom.

Trying to get over his initial shock, he tossed cold water into his face. His first calm thought was, "Christ, what a great piece of ass, and I'll never get to bang her again!" But immediately realizing how unworthy that reaction was, he cursed himself, saying, "You piece of shit! Shame on you, shame on you!" Then he reached for his clothes.

When he returned to the bedroom fully dressed, Mirella was in her skirt and high heels and just buttoning her blouse. "Gino! Gino!" she said again, throwing open her arms and embracing him.

"You know," he told her, "before I went downstairs yesterday and met you, one of the first things I did in the hotel room here was look up you and our father in the phone book. But there was no listing.'"

Mirella's passionate face darkened. She bit her lips, then cleared her voice. "Our father was a fascist, a fascist who betrayed Jews, Gino. The partisans killed him six months ago. I was not sorry. Had you known him, you wouldn't been either."

Reaching for his sister's hand, he changed the subject, telling her about their mother and stepfather.

"We'll arrange to have you flown to the States, Mirella. That won't be possible right away, but this lousy war can't last forever, maybe another year. But I'll write our mother today and tell her I've found you. I won't tell her how we met, but I'll certainly say you're alive and, well, a beautiful woman." He began laughing, and his sister gave him a playful tap on the chin.

"I still can't believe this is happening, Gino," she said, "although I've often dreamed of seeing you and my mother. I don't believe in God, but this must be His doing."

After breakfast, Gene asked her to remain in the room, saying he'd be back in an hour. He wanted to buy some gifts and knew the city's most elegant shopping street, the Via Condotti, was within walking distance. During the Germans' last days in Rome, the shop windows stood self-consciously bare, but the day the Allies entered, fine leathers, wools and lingerie magically appeared.

Gene bought his sister a brown leather handbag, some lingerie and a sweater, and opening her presents, she was like a small child at Christmas. Her eyes danced and her hands fumbled. "Ah. Gino, Gino, you have a wide heart! I knew my brother would!"

Mirella put on the stockings and transferred her money and cosmetics into her new bag, looking admiringly at herself in the mirror as she gaily swung the bag from side to side. Pleased with her gifts, she kissed her brother on the mouth.

"I'll be able to give you some money, but until we're able to get you flown to the States, how will you support yourself?" he asked.

She looked at him suspiciously. "I've always gotten along, Gino."

He felt an awkwardness. "I mean do you think you'll be able to get a job, a regular job? Can you type? What is it you like to do?"

"Do? Do?" She lifted her head proudly. She was glad to have found her brother but that hardly meant she either wanted or needed his questions or advice.

He hoped she understood his meaning but suspected otherwise. And the thought of his fellow Fifth Army officers sleeping with Mirella, whether they knew Gene was her brother or not, filled him with revulsion. "Look," he said, "I'll send you all the money I can each month but wish you'd no longer earn money as you do now." He'd tried to phrase it as delicately as possible but suspected he'd sounded maladroit. "You're my sister, I have protective feelings toward you."

But studying him, one hand on her chin, she took a step backward. "You arrive one day, tell me you're my brother and tell me how I should live, what I should and shouldn't do?"

He could see her getting angry—his mother also got red when she became angry. "Look, I've been with these soldiers in the hotel now for years. I know them well. A lot of them are real bastards. and it would pain me knowing you're sleeping with such slobs."

Mirella shook her head from side to side. "Gino, Gino. You and our mother leave me with a brute of a father for twenty-five years, and your first day back you write me a book of rules?" She waved a finger at him. "It's not alone because you're my brother and a naive American, no. You're also a conqueror and that's what conquerors immediately do, make rules for others."

He held up both hands, denying her charge. "You're making me sound like a bad guy. Mirella, when I only want what's best for you."

"Oh, foolish boy, all tyrants talk that way!" she exclaimed. "Besides, who knows how long today's liberators will be in a generous frame of mind? What you wish is particularly stupid now, because I might be able to make as much money today and tomorrow as it would take me a month to earn otherwise. A month!"

He reached into his pocket and thrust a fistful of bills upon her. Then he also insisted she accept a carton of Lucky Strike Cigarettes. "Only please, please don't sleep with any of those men. Tonight, we'll have dinner here and talk again. We'll have had time to think of what's happened, how we found each other and what kind of good consequences can flow from our having met."

He sounded more like a lawyer than a brother, and she was noncommittal about how she'd spend the rest of the day, though she promised to meet him for dinner that night at nine. At the door, he gave her a brotherly kiss.

But alone now, he anxiously wondered how things would work out and how his mother would take the news. He decided to hold off writing her until he first had dinner with Mirella and they came to a definite understanding. Then he realized he had not asked for her address before she left. Suppose they missed connections tonight? How would he find her again if she didn't return to the hotel? "Idiot!" he said, pounding his head with both hands. He knew that, given their miraculous meeting, he should have been feeling exultant, marveling how fate, luck, whatever, had brought them together; but his thoughts that morning were troubled. Maybe his mother, who never wished to explore the past, had been right all along for reasons that defied pure logic but abounded with common sense.

**

It was later that morning, that a colonel ran through the Excelsior lobby, shouting, "It's official! Eisenhower just announced the invasion of France!"

The lobby became very still, and Gene instantly realized that news of the Italian campaign would now vanish from the world's front pages. One of the purposes guiding the armies driving up the Italian peninsula had been to draw as many German troops as possible away from the defense of northern Europe, against which the Allies main thrust had always been projected. And now, remembering how rough the landing at Anzio had been, Gene said a silent prayer for the poor bastards struggling to gain a toehold on the treacherous French littoral. A lot of good men were going to die today, had already died, and though the invasion news excited him, it also stirred his deepest fraternal feelings.

But less than an hour after hearing about the Normandy landings, Gene saw a barrel-chested major whom he despised picking Mirella up outside the Hassler Hotel, and suddenly the invasion in France became no longer a reality but only a distant abstraction. Probably Mirella didn't think Gene would be there to see her going about business. More likely, she didn't care, because when she happened to notice him watching her negotiating with the officer, she brushed him off with a wave of dismissal, then took the major by the arm and led him into the Hassler.

This particular major was one of those martinets armies through the centuries seemed to be cursed with, a man who constantly bullied those below him in rank but couldn't be mere obsequious when it came to anyone from light colonel on.

Gene had to lock both hands around his belt to prevent himself from racing after Mirella and beating her black-and-blue. Had his mother been in his place, he was sure that's what she'd have done. As for his brutal father, who knows the violent course of action that Roman lion would have chosen?

In any case, Gene wasn't a man used to be being taken lightly by women. And now, walking back to the Excelsior, he kept seeing Mirella waving to him disdainfully, and he worked himself into an absolute fury, cursing the day his mother told him he once had a sister with eyes shaped like almonds.

And still furious, Gene determined to stand Mirella up that night. He knew that if she came to his room at nine o'clock, he was quite capable of striking her, even of throwing her across his bed, and God knows what would have happened next. As for how things turned out tomorrow, at that moment he couldn't have cared less.

He left his room an hour before Mirella was due to show up, driving past the Pantheon to the Via Vittorio Emmanuele, where the Grand Hotel was located. Gene had little appetite for food that night, but he sat in the bar and sipped an endless number of brandies. It was there he overheard two correspondents discussing the Ardeatine Caves Massacre.

Earlier that year, during the last week of March, it seemed 32 German troops, marching to their posts, had been ambushed by Roman partisans. Lusting for vengeance, the

Germans decided to execute ten Italians for every German killed. Death lists were hastily drawn up that night, and innocent suspects languishing in their jail cells were roused. The condemned were then taken in a convoy of trucks to the Ardeatine Caves on the outskirts of the city. SS officers chose individual victims, forcing them to kneel in the cave before dispatching them with a bullet in the neck. After the bodies began stacking up, the newest victims were made to kneel atop those already shot. The grisly work consumed hours. Then the entrance to the cave was dynamited, sealed up. Priests were said to have heard faint cries from the dying hours later.

Though he was quite drunk, the story had a sobering effect on Gene, and he decided to hurry back to the Excelsior. Perhaps Mirella was still waiting for him.

But it was shortly after midnight when he arrived, and there was no sign of her, neither in the lobby nor upstairs near his room. He fell on his bed, telling himself he needed a few minutes to rest before returning to the street, perhaps Mirella was hanging around on the Via Nazionale, where he'd picked her up, or perhaps she was streetwalking near the Hassler. But a few minutes stretched into hours, and he slept the night through in his uniform.

***

He woke in the morning with a rotten headache, and his mouth felt fuzzy. Remembering Mirella, he jumped to his feet. He could have sworn someone was cracking open his skull as he inched his way toward the bathroom, where he shed his clothes and took a cold shower. It helped a little. He dressed quickly in a fresh uniform. Perhaps Mirella had left him a message between now and the last time he had checked.

His heart raced with excitement when the snotty clerk handed him an envelope upon which was scrawled a handwriting he didn't recognize but guessed was his sister's. The envelope felt heavy. Tearing it open, a cross and chain fell out. *My dear Gino,* Mirella wrote. *I give you this cross as a memento of our meeting. God keep you safe until this horrible war is over and you return to our mother. I feel one day we shall meet again somewhere. Your sister, Mirella.*

The cross was made of some kind of metal, and though Gene considered himself an unbeliever, he unhesitatingly swung it around his neck and under his shirt.

On the Via Nazionale, Gene thought he recognized one of the timid, doleful prostitutes who'd been with Mirella the day he'd picked her up. "Excuse me," he said, approaching the woman. "But you're a friend of Maria's, and it's important I see her. Do you know where she is?" He handed the prostitute a pack of cigarettes.

The smokes cheered the woman up instantly "Oh, Maria's left for Naples this morning," she said with a smile.

He asked if there was any forwarding address. The prostitute told him she knew of none, but was sure to see Maria when her friend returned to Rome. Getting out pen and paper, Gene scrawled his APO number, then his mother's address. He took out all the money he'd brought with him and placed both the money and the addresses in an envelope which he scaled. He told the prostitute that if Mirella received the envelope intact, he'd reward her handsomely.

The prostitute smiled reassuringly and thanked him again for the cigarettes. But as soon as Gene turned the corner, she tore open the envelope and withdrew the money, tossing the address into the confetti-strewn gutter.

Though Gene tried for years to find Maria, he never saw her again, nor did he ever mention having met her to his mother. She, in her bitter wisdom, would have told him, "You wanted to meet her and so were punished by the fates for raking up the past. Foolish boy masquerading as a soldier, didn't your mother warn you?"

Hazardous Pay

Wanting to beat the rush, the general exodus, they left the Plaza Monumental Bullring before the last fight, heading over to the whorehouses on Carr Porvenir. There were three of them, draftees from New York, and each would be completing his military obligation at Fort Bliss, leaving the Army before the end of the year.

Bliss was less than ten miles from El Paso, and El Paso was a short walk over the Santa Fe Bridge to Juarez. Juarez was Mexico—all bars, brothels, and the bullring. Maybe things are different now, but that's the way it was in the spring of 1954, less than a year after the cease-fire had been signed, ending, in effect, the Korean War,

The oldest by a few months was Rollie Sanger, the company clerk. He was prematurely bald, heavyset, and his father, a teenager during world War I, owned a string of drycleaning stores back in Queens.

Sanger's closest Army buddy was Gerard Lohmann, whom his friends called Gerry. Lohmann, the mail room orderly, was born in Berlin, migrated with his family in the late Thirties, and wound up living near the George Washington Bridge. His father had fought in the German Army and was badly wounded at Verdun in 1917.

The youngest, Hal Weiler, was the tallest of the three. He'd been a copyboy at the *Mirror,* which was why his company commander, Captain Roosma, had made him an assistant editor of the *Fort Bliss News.* Weiler's father, a Brooklyn-born dentist who treated indigents for nothing, had also fought in World War I. "You need at least two friends in the Army," he'd advised his son the night before Hal was inducted down at Whitehall Street, "One Jew to cover your ass, the other to cover your ass in case the first guy forgets."

At the whorehouse, his friends let Lohmann pick first. The girls, teenagers and women in their twenties, were seated on two couches against a stucco wall.

Lohmann, short and horny, liked women taller than himself. "It's like riding a horse then," he'd say with a toothy grin, although Weiler seriously doubted that Gerry ever rode a horse in his twenty-three years. Not surprisingly, Lohmann chose a skinny girl with exceptionally long legs. She looked all of fifteen, but when she stood up, towering over him, Lohmann leered in anticipation.

On the other hand, Sanger liked them solid. "What's your name, honey?" he stopped in front of a wide-hipped girl who looked about twenty. She had big brown eyes and a slash of purple lipstick. Evidently, she didn't understand English, and the girl next to her muttered in her ear. Smiling, the anointed one announced, "Maria, Maria."

Extending his hand and misnaming her, Sanger said, "Hey, Marie, we're going to have a ball. You treat old Rollie right, and he's going to treat you better than any other guy you've ever been with. And that's a promise from a guy who doesn't make many."

Weiler watched them walking hand-in-hand down the hall. Then he gazed at the women still sitting on the two couches. There must have been six or seven of them, A few he'd remembered from the last time. Others, like the two his friends had chosen, were new. Weiler never picked any of the younger-looking ones; didn't want to feel he was taking advantage of a kid.

The last woman seated on the second couch seemed older, in her late twenties, had black hair, and wore a loose green dress with yellow polka dots. Weiler, who hadn't chosen her last time, remembered that she'd vaguely reminded him of his conceited cousin Rose, who lived near Coney Island and had recently married a pulmonologist.

He gestured politely, as if to say, Okay this time if you come with me? Nodding, she stood up, walked over to him, and boldly took his hand, leading him to one of the empty rooms in the back.

The rooms all had crosses on the wall over the bed. The crosses always gave Weiler a creepy feeling, as if God was watching him. Saying her name was Fermina, the woman held out her hand, and Weiler gave her the required five bucks.

Fermina was all business. She got out a large enamel pan, filled it with soap and water, and told Weiler to get undressed. Her English was better than Weiler would have guessed, and only after she carefully inspected and washed him thoroughly, she takes off her dress, slip, and lies down.

Entering her, Weiler tried to think of something totally asexual, like his favorite team. He alternately pictured Robinson stealing home and the prince of Flatbush swinging from the heels. That was Duke Snider. But, as always, Weiler came in less than a minute.

"Jesus Christ," he thought, "I'm hopeless."

Embarrassed, Weiler waited outside the building for the others, smoking and muttering to himself.

Sanger emerged next, all smiles, his bald head crowned with a halo of sweat. A few minutes later, their buddy Lohmann joined them. "Oh, God, she was terrific," Gerry kept saying. "I love it when their long legs wrap themselves around you. How was yours, Rollie?"

Sanger made a fist, kissed it, and jerked it away.

Heading for the Santa Fe Bridge, they stopped for a beer. Naturally that was Sanger's idea, and he chugalugged two, "Which one did you fuck, Hal?" he asked Weiler politely.

"The one in the green dress seated at the end of the second couch. Great lay, hell of a woman," Weiler enthused, wondering if they were all full of shit or was it just him?

***

Next morning, Monday, Weiler was told to report to the company commander. Harry Roosma was in charge of Post I & E, Information and Education, It was a headquarters company, a service unit, and Roosma was a high school history teacher from Rhode Island, a member of the Army Reserves, who'd fought in World War II and been recalled within months after the Korean War began.

"Sit down, corporal," he said, after Weiler saluted. Roosma had a tapering, bony face, pale blue eyes, and wore rimless glasses. Weiler hadn't the faintest idea why he'd been summoned. He 'd done nothing wrong that he remembered, nor was he aware anyone was sick back home. Yet company commanders weren't in the habit of calling in corporals to chat about the weather.

"One of our cooks, PFC by the name of Otis Trueblood, new man, has been AWOL the last couple of weeks, and battalion recently had local authorities arrest him in his hometown. I've been ordered to assign someone to bring him back to Bliss, and you've been elected."

"Me?" Weiler tried to remember if he knew Trueblood, or recall what the new man looked like. But the cooks kept to themselves and lived in a different barracks, "Why me, sir?" Weiler heard himself asking. "I've never done anything like that before, bring back an AWOL."

"I know, Weiler, I know," Roosma said, frowning. It was the first time Roosma ever had to retrieve an AWOL, too. "But I have to send someone. I don't want to send a private, and, frankly, the sergeants would be pissed if I assigned one of them. So it came down to the corporals, Weiler, and you're the tallest. Anyway, I trust you more than I trust the others."

Weiler almost laughed. The captain barely knew he existed.

Roosma directed Weiler's attention to a map of Texas spread across his desk, First he pointed to El Paso, which was in the western corner of the state. Then he pointed to a small, circled town, which was southwest of Dallas, between Dallas and Houston, not too far from the Louisiana border, "Sorry to have to tell you, corporal, but that's more than six hundred miles from here. Big goddamn state, Texas." The town's name, incidentally, was Palestine.

Weiler was directed to catch an early morning Greyhound tomorrow to Dallas, where he'd transfer to a Trailway that would take him the rest of the way. The trip, including the layover, would consume between twelve and fourteen hours, "Take something to read," Roosma advised. Weiler was to check in with the local sheriff the following morning, and make arrangements to return with Trueblood on Thursday.

Sergeant Harmeling, the supply sergeant, was now going to drive Weiler over to the post stockade, where he'd pick up a weapon, shackles, and be given a list of instructions by a Captain Stargel, the stockade exec. Assuming all went smoothly, Weiler was to return to the company orderly room that morning. Harmeling would wait for him. "Any questions?" Roosma asked.

***

Harmeling, a redhead with a long nose and freckles, had two years to go before retirement, and, like a lot of chronic complainers took unusual pleasure in other people's dismay.

"You sure don't seem a happy soldier, Weiler," he observed with a smile on their way to the stockade, "But look at it this way, corporal: There are three things you don't want in this man's Army—gonorrhea, diarrhea, and Korea, and escorting an AWOL ain't one of those."

"Hey, that's pretty funny, sarge, comforting, too," Weiler said. Only he wasn't laughing nor was he terribly comforted.

At the gate outside the stockade, they were stopped by a couple of MP's. Harmeling said they were told to pick up a weapon and shackles, Captain Stargel was expecting them. One of the MP's phoned inside and got an okay to let them proceed.

Captain Stargel was built like a Dallas linebacker, with wide shoulders and a barely discernible neck, "You ever fire a .45, corporal?" he asked Weiler with a mountainy twang.

"No, I haven't, captain."

"Well, we're going to take you back to our little firing range and get you qualified, trooper."

The .45 scared the hell out of Weiler and felt a lot heavier than it looked. Stargel showed him where the safety was and told him how to load. Then Weiler fired off six rounds, using both hands.

Although he never came close to hitting the target, the captain said, "AWOL's are harmless, soldier, you'll do," putting a check next to a box on a list he held in front of him. Then Stargel read from an index card he withdrew from his wallet.

"I'm giving you a list of how to proceed once you take charge of the prisoner. It behooves you to study this list before you reach your destination. If the need arises, I order you to use your weapon. In addition, I order you to keep your prisoner shackled from the time you take possession of him until you deliver said prisoner back here to Bliss. Now you need to sign on the bottom line for the weapon, ammo, and shackles, Weiler. Your company commander will give you food and travel vouchers and Fourth Army orders authorizing you to take charge of the AWOL. Have a pleasant trip, corporal."

That night, his friends, Sanger and Lohmann, tried to cheer Weiler up, saying it would be an adventure, a break from the Bliss routine, something to tell his grandchildren.

"Hey, if it sounds so terrific, what about one of you guys volunteering to change places with me?"

Sanger laughed, his belly bouncing, "In your dreams," he said, "your dry ones."

"Listen, Hal, we'll celebrate when you get back, all get laid Saturday," Lohmann announced. "My treat." A talented cartoonist, he'd sold his second to the *Saturday Evening Post* a few days before.

While his friends took off for a movie that night, Weiler went to sleep early. Sergeant Harmeling had been assigned to drive him into El Paso before five-thirty next morning.

***

The Greyhound left for Dallas a little after six. Weiler had brought along a fried egg sandwich and a container of coffee, the egg tasting of lard. The bus was almost empty when it started but gradually began filling up as it seemed to make about a million stops. The towns had strange names— Fabens, Sierra Blanca, Toyah, Pecos, Odessa. "My God, what's a Russian seaport doing in the middle of Texas?" Weiler wondered.

Taking Roosma's advice, he'd packed a big fat novel to help kill time. It was Saul Bellow's *The Adventures of Augie March,* which had come out the previous fall. Weiler had loved the first three hundred and fifty pages. They took place in and around Chicago and were filled with rich, larger-than-life but believable characters. Then Bellew has his protagonist take off on a half-cocked, farfetched trip to Mexico with a girl Augie barely knows, the girl wanting to tame an eagle. And picaresque hero notwithstanding, the book starts sounding literary, symbolic, and begins to sputter and sag. In Weiler's humble opinion, anyway.

When the bus reached the town of Big Spring, which was about halfway to Dallas, people used the bathroom and bought sandwiches for lunch. But Weiler decided to skip lunch, the egg sandwich for breakfast having given him heartburn. At least, he thought it was the egg sandwich.

Back on the bus, Weiler told himself that in six months he'd be out of the Army. He wanted to be a journalist, a reporter, and was fortunate to have written a number of stories for the *Fort Bliss News.* It was an eight-page weekly, had a staff of six, and he'd learned a lot—how to crop pictures, design layouts, how to write a lead and make captions fit. Now if he could just bring Trueblood back to Bliss without a hitch, he'd be able to return to the newspaper, complete his Army tour, and revert to civilian life with a number of articles to show when he went looking for a job.

Picking up Bellow's novel again, Weiler soon learned that Augie's new girlfriend had enjoyed getting away with him down to Mexico, but when the eagle refused to be tamed and Augie proposed marriage, she rejected Augie out of hand. Weiler guessed that meant an imminent return to Chicago, and he wondered how the resilient, restless Augie would have comported himself escorting a prisoner from one end of Texas to the other.

A kind of interesting, maybe even amusing, supposition, Weiler reflected. Yet not a minute later, John Wayne replaced Augie as a measure of comparison. It happened this way. Weiler had been looking out the window and the passing countryside—flat, brown, and seemingly endless—suddenly reminded him of a hundred sprawling Westerns, from one of which emerged, with that characteristic rolling strut, big John himself, sitting next to Weiler now and patting his own .45 as if it were an old friend. "The first time Trueblood gives you any lip, belt him on the side of the head with your gun. Problem solved," big John winked.

Well, that's the way Weiler's imagination often operated, books and movies popping up, mixing and melding with real life.

"The only trouble is," Weiler pinched himself after a while, "I'm not Augie March, let alone John Wayne, just a New York guy out of my element, seriously miscast, wrong goddamn corporal for this stupid escort role." In fact, if he wasn't wearing his fatigues and Army boots, Weiler would have felt genuinely petrified. Funny that wearing the uniform helped keep him relatively calm. And funny, too, that his final destination was to a whistle-stop called Palestine. Although, as he got closer to it, the countryside did gradually turn from uneventful brown to biblical green, and the air became far less dry, even downright humid. Yet something, he decided, other than heartburn kept bothering him, and it wasn't the weather, but he couldn't give it a name.

Then, late that afternoon, Weiler remembered that his father treated indigents for nothing, and he told himself that if Trueblood tried to escape, forget about Augie March or John Wayne, forget about Captain Stargel, he'd fire the .45, but only into the air, only into the goddamn air.

Of course the last hour was the worst, seemed longest, took forever.

***

"Palestine!" Weiler muttered, taking a quick look after getting off the second bus as the sun was starting to descend. "Some promised land!"

There was a tiny railroad station with a checkered Purina sign, a barber shop, the jail, which was a red-brick building with bars over its windows, a grocery store, Rosebud's Good Eats Cafe, a clothing store, and the Pioneer Station Hotel. Talk about proverbial one-street towns. "Get me out of here!" Weiler thought.

But the Army in its wisdom had booked a room for him, and fly paper hung from its ceiling. The bed was a narrow, metal-framed affair, covered by a torn blue spread. There was a Bible on the side table, along with a lamp that had a crooked orange shade. Hanging from a nail near the table was a single worn towel that had a green stripe, on which was printed, "Property of the Pioneer Station Hotel." As if anyone with half a mind would choose to walk off with it.

Weiler made sure to put the .45 under the bed, so that he couldn't possibly shoot himself by mistake in the dark. Then he lay on the bed, without getting into it. Fearing bedbugs and devoutly wishing he was elsewhere, he doubted if he slept three solid hours.

***

"Hey, corporal, got your nigger for you!" the sheriff declared early next morning when Weiler entered his jail.

"I beg your pardon," Weiler said, a confused look flooding his hazel-colored eyes.

"Your nigger. Say, you're the corporal come to take Trueblood back to Bliss, right? Your nigger."

"You got to be kidding!" Weiler thought. He hadn't remembered nor had anyone thought to tell him that Trueblood was colored, a black man. Not that, coming from New York, he had anything against black guys. But why hadn't anyone told him? Texas was segregated, and it was sure to complicate the return trip to El Paso. "Goddamn Army," Weiler thought, "get your head out of your ass..."

The sheriff, whose name was Billy Joe Gibson, was tall and thin, looked a little like Randolph Scott who'd starred in a lot of Grade-B cowboy movies Weiler had been fond of as a kid. Gibson wore khakis, a silver star near his heart, and a pearl-handled gun in a tan holster. He was grinning now, a mean little grin. "You didn't know Trueblood was a nigger? They didn't tell you?" Then he started laughing, as if it was the biggest joke in the whole wide world. Not ha, ha, ha, but hee, hee, hee.

Weiler nervously cleared his throat.

"You got a copy of your orders, corporal?" Gibson finally asked when he stopped laughing and pinched his nose to keep from having to blow it. "Some authorization to take this boy off my hands?"

Weiler unbuttoned his fatigue pocket, reached into it, and handed over a single sheet of paper. He had three copies left.

"Harold Weiler," the sheriff read, glancing at the orders. Gibson had a lined, leathery face, and Weiler's name seemed to intrigue him. "Where you from, corporal?"

"New York, New York City," Weiler said.

"Oh, hell," the sheriff said, grinning again. "Nigger like Trueblood ain't going to be no problem for a smart New York fellow like you. No disrespect intended, but you wouldn't be a member of the Jewish church, would you?"

Weiler nodded guardedly.

"I ask, because I always wondered what the words 'High Holydays' meant. Read that once, and always wondered?"

Weiler sighed. "It's just a couple of religious holidays, like Christmas and Easter."

Because he'd expected a far more exotic explanation, Gibson frowned, then asked abruptly, "When you planning to take this nigger back with you, corporal?"

"Early tomorrow morning. Want to catch the seven o'clock bus to Dallas."

Gibson nodded, putting the copy of Weiler's orders on his desk. "Want to see your boy, take a look at him?" It hadn't occurred to Weiler to ask but seemed, now that Gibson mentioned it, a good idea.

They walked to one of the cells in the back. It was separated from the other cells behind a kind of steel partition.

"On your feet, nigger!" Gibson said to Trueblood when they entered his cell, "This corporal from New York is taking you back to Bliss tomorrow, and he wanted to see the whites of your eyes."

But it was Trueblood's smell, not his looks, that immediately seized Weiler's attention. The smell was overwhelming and seemed to come in waves, or each time Weiler took a breath, and at first, he thought he was going to puke. It was obvious that Trueblood hadn't taken a shower for days, maybe a week. Curiously, the smell didn't seem to bother the sheriff at all.

Trueblood was wearing his uniform, his Class A's, but the uniform was filthy, full of stains, He wasn't as tall as Weiler, but much wider. Not so much fat as wide, He had a pug nose, big lips, and his skin seemed to be blue-black, resembling an eggplant.

"We're leaving early tomorrow morning, Trueblood, going back to Bliss," Weiler finally said, trying not to inhale too deeply.

"Yes, sir," answered Trueblood.

"I'm not a 'sir,'" Weiler responded, "My father's a 'sir' and Captain Roosma's a 'sir.' But I'm an enlisted man, same as you, only a corporal, okay? So don't call me 'sir.'"

"What I call you?" Trueblood asked suspiciously.

"'Corporal's okay, My name's Harold Weiler, Either one of those is okay, too." The smell started to get to him again, and Weiler wanted out of there in the worst way. "I'll see you tomorrow, Trueblood. We're making the seven o'clock bus to Dallas."

Then he walked back with Gibson to the sheriff's office. "Sheriff," Weiler said, "Trueblood needs to take a shower before he leaves here tomorrow."

For the first time since they met, the sheriff's thin lips began to look like a pair of knives. "What shower? What are you talking about, corporal?"

"He stinks to high heaven, hasn't taken a shower in days. I've got to sit next to him for twelve hours tomorrow, sheriff, maybe more, and my nose won't make it back to Bliss he doesn't leave here cleaned up."

But Gibson insisted, "Hey, corporal, that's the way niggers smell. Ain't you ever been around them in New York? Or maybe they smell different up there? Besides, even if he took a shower, he'd still be wearing those shitty clothes, and what do you think they smell like? Your girlfriend's perfume?"

Weiler thought a minute. Then he pointed to the phone on Gibson's desk, "I need to call my captain collect, sheriff, okay?"

Still angry, as if he'd been tacitly accused of being incompetent, the sheriff nodded grudgingly. "You do that little thing."

Explaining the situation to Captain Roosma, Weiler proposed buying Trueblood a set of underwear, jeans, a tee shirt, and a pair of socks. If that was okay, could he also dispose of Trueblood's uniform? And if that was also okay, would the captain authorize that Trueblood first take a shower so that the trip back to Bliss would be as problem-free as possible?

Roosma was no genius but he was no idiot either. "Save the receipts and let me speak to the sheriff," he said.

That morning, Weiler picked out a pair of jeans, size 42, socks, a pair of shorts, and a tee shirt in the clothing store a half block from the jail.

"You the soldier taking the nigger back to Bliss?" the cashier asked when he paid for the clothes. She was a pretty girl, about twenty, with long, curly black hair and violet eyes that reminded Weiler of Elizabeth Taylor's. Wincing inside, Weiler hated hearing the word "nigger" coming from a woman that young and pretty. Yet he nodded now, accepting the change. But when her hand accidentally brushed against his, he found himself wanting to smack and fuck her at the same time. "It's because I'm anxious, nervous, don't want to goddamn be here," he thought.

***

Next morning, Weiler was wearing the .45 in an Army holster strapped around his waist. It rested on his hip and felt heavy, uncomfortable. Unlike the sheriff, he wasn't used to it and wished he could have taken Trueblood back without having to wear it. But his printed instructions could not have been more explicit.

"I got your boy smelling like a rose, a goddamn rose," the sheriff said with a grin when Weiler came to pick up the prisoner, and they went together to get Trueblood from his cell.

Trueblood was wearing the jeans and tee shirt Weiler had purchased for him yesterday, and although he hardly smelled like a rose, Weiler could take a breath near him now without gagging.

"I'm sorry, Trueblood, but we both have to wear this," Weiler said, getting out the shackles, Not wanting to do it awkwardly or fumble them in front of Gibson, Weiler had practiced in his hotel room last night, applying and withdrawing them repeatedly, the shackles making a metallic, clicking sound.

Looking from one to the other, the sheriff couldn't stop smiling. "Now, nigger," he said, addressing Trueblood, "the corporal there is wearing a gun. And he's wearing that gun because if you try anything foolish he's going to fill you full of holes. And you know what's going to happen he fills you with holes? All your nigger blood is going to run out and you're going to turn into a white man. A white man! Hee, hee, hee," he laughed his loony-sounding laugh.

Then, still enjoying his little joke, he slowly turned to Weiler. "Corporal," he said, "I need you to sign some release papers," and the three of them proceeded to walk out of the cell, Gibson leading the way. They stopped opposite the sheriff's desk. There was a picture of Gibson's wife in a red frame with gilt trimming near his calendar. She was wearing a cowboy hat, twirled a gun, and looked about as friendly as a snake.

Weiler quickly read the papers and signed them. He probably didn't read them carefully enough, but he wanted to be sure to catch that Dallas bus.

The sheriff accompanied them to the bus stop. A couple about to enter the cafe across the street stopped to watch.

When the bus arrived a few minutes later, the sheriff spoke to the driver, explaining that Weiler was taking a nigger soldier back to Bliss. Shackled together, they'd have to sit next to each other. Fortunately, it was early and the bus would not be crowded.

"Now what the hell am I supposed to do, Billy Joe?" the driver complained. "Put them in the nigger section or the white?" He was a short, fat man with an enormous gut. Must have weighed an easy two-fifty. "I ain't no Solomon, sheriff. You tell me where to put those boys."

The sheriff, having anticipated the question, handed him a roll of string, "You put them in the back of the white section, Frankie, and you rope off the area with this string. Nobody can sit in the seats directly in front of them and nobody can sit in the seats behind them. Then you give the corporal the string so he can give it to the El Paso driver. Okay, *amigo?*"

And winking, he turned to Weiler. Staring at him, Weiler found himself staring back. The sheriff was one of those guys who liked to stare but didn't like others responding in kind. "I just did you a big favor, corporal. Saved you a lot of hassle. Surprised, huh?" he said, tauntingly. "Ain't you going to thank me?"

Sensing trouble, Weiler cautiously said, "Sure." But, no pushover, that's all he said, and the brevity of his response seemed to piss the sheriff off even more.

"Don't you want to know why I did you that favor?" Gibson snarled.

Realizing that the sheriff was determined to make a scene, Weiler, refusing to panic, smiled. "Sure," he said again, trying to sound more confident this time.

"Because," Gibson declared, "*I-hate-niggers!* But I don't want a smart Jew corporal from New York thinking we're all dumb animals down here. Now, your nigger took his fucking shower an hour ago. But he stink yesterday and he's going to stink again soon, because that's the way they smell. That stink of theirs is natural with them, Right, nigger? *Right?*"

But before Trueblood could answer, Weiler, who hated being bullied, or seeing anyone else being bullied, jerked Trueblood away, saying, "He's my prisoner now, sheriff, I just signed for him, and we're out of here," and they started to board the bus.

The sheriff, unaccustomed to asking a black man a question that remained unanswered, made an angry move for his gun, thought better of it, and yanked his hand aside.

In the bus, Weiler waited for the driver to show them where to sit. But the driver had turned a milky white, because for a second, he thought the sheriff was going to blow both soldiers away.

Now, exhaling, the driver moved down the length of the bus, stopping about three-quarters of the way back. Then he pointed. But Weiler said, "No, the other side. He's got to sit near the window, because I need to be on the aisle." The driver frowned but didn't argue. A white couple who'd been sitting toward the rear of the white section moved to seats up front.

When the bus finally started a couple of minutes later, both Weiler and Trueblood felt relieved. "Some fucking town, huh, corporal?" Trueblood whispered.

The bus drove for more than an hour, slowly taking on more passengers. Both blacks and whites stared at Weiler and his prisoner. They pointed, whispered, and kept staring. Weiler felt increasingly uncomfortable; God knows what was going through Trueblood's mind.

A little old lady with white sneakers and white hair got on the bus in a town called Terrell; she looked about eighty and wore a blue dress with small red flowers and matching red buttons. When she tried to sit in the seat directly in front of Weiler and his prisoner, she came in contact with the string and started blinking. Sensing her confusion, the driver hurried back, explaining why she couldn't sit there. But the old lady couldn't seem to understand what he was saying, and she took a few steps back, staring first at Weiler, then at Trueblood. Never in her long life had she seen a black man sitting next to a white in a bus before, and the sight amazed her, her blue eyes, one of which seemed clouded with a cataract, growing larger and larger.

The driver whispered in her ear again, placing his hand on one of her elbows and tried to ease her away. But she shrugged him off, as if the sight of Weiler and his prisoner was one so unique, so fascinating that she needed to absorb it a while longer.

Finally, the old lady decided to speak. "Is he dangerous?" she asked Weiler quietly.

Weiler shook his head, "No, ma'am. He's not dangerous."

She pointed to the shackles, "Why's he shackled to you then?" she asked, as if it wasn't very kind of Weiler trying to deceive a woman of her advanced years.

Weiler shrugged. "It's just a precaution, ma'am. Nothing to worry about."

For a minute, she grew thoughtful. Then she smiled, patting Weiler on the shoulder, "I'm proud of you, soldier," she said. "He looks very dangerous, like a gorilla, and I'm sure you're just being modest. Your mama must be proud of you, too."

At that moment, Trueblood turned, looking out the window. He didn't want the others to see his face, because the inside of his head felt as though it was ricocheting like a pinball. "You may have lived a long life," he wanted to tell the old lady. "But you one big fool, cause I'm no damn gorilla..."

***

The Dallas terminal was crowded with a noisy Boy Scout troop about to board a bus bound for New Orleans. They kept pointing and grinning at the escort and prisoner who had a half hour wait for the next Greyhound to El Paso. The only really good thing about the layover was soon after they got off the Trailway, Trueblood, needing to use the john, announced, "Sir, I got to pee."

Turning to him, Weiler said curtly, "I told you yesterday, I'm not a 'sir.' I'm a corporal, or Hal, or Weiler, Anything but a 'sir.' I can't stand those guys." Of course the real problem was there was a bathroom for colored and one for whites, and which could a shackled Trueblood use now without getting them both lynched?

Spotting a local cop, Weiler walked over to him, Trueblood in his wake, "Officer, I'm taking this prisoner back to Fort Bliss," Weiler said. "But he needs to use the bathroom and I'm under orders to keep him shackled, me beside him. Which bathroom can he use?"

The officer had a face as red and round as a tomato and wore a peaked cap low over his forehead. "I'd say you had a decided problem, soldier. That is, your prisoner sure does. Don't you, boy?" he giggled, staring at Trueblood. "Got to take a wicked one, and nowhere to take it. Now ain't that something—"

"No offense, officer," Weiler interrupted him, "But we need to catch the next bus to El Paso, and my prisoner has this urgent need. So if you'd be kind enough to tell me what to do, I'd be grateful."

Because the officer didn't appreciate being prodded, he asked, squinting, "Where you from, corporal?"

"Omaha, Nebraska," Weiler lied. He'd learned from Gibson, anywhere but New York.

"You sure don't sound like a guy from Nebraska," the officer said, squinting again. Then, because he had a short attention span, he seemed to lose interest, "Okay, you wait here, I'll get us a nigger deputy. Then you unshackle your boy. We know how to handle this sort of thing in Dallas."

Soon the deputy showed up. He looked a lean fifty with a grey mustache, was wearing jeans and a star, and toted a shotgun.

"Jesus Christ," Weiler muttered, staring at the shotgun.

They walked over to the men's room for colored only, where Weiler removed the shackles.

"It's all right, bro," the black deputy told Trueblood. "You pee to your heart's content. Just don't try running away, or I'll blow your nigger head off. We straight?"

"Yeah, we straight," Trueblood muttered, opening the door.

Weiler quickly used the other men's room, and ten minutes later the three of them came together again.

"He took a nice big dump, too," the black deputy reported, grinning, "and washed his hands like his mama taught him."

Weiler put the shackles back on.

"What this black brother do?" the deputy asked. "He kill somebody?"

"No, nothing like that," Weiler said. "Just went AWOL."

"And they sent you all the way from El Paso to bring him back for that? My, my, Uncle Sam sure a mean old uncle. Well, brother, you take care now and behave yourself. Nice meeting you, corporal."

"Yeah, same here," Weiler said, rolling his eyes and deciding in the short time they had left to buy sandwiches and a few candy bars. Who knew when they'd stop and have another chance to get some food.

He bought four ham and cheese sandwiches. It was all they had ready that early. "What kind of candy bar you like?" he asked Trueblood.

"Milky Way," said his prisoner, only the way he said it sounded like one word.

"How many do you want?"

"How many you get me?" Trueblood was smiling. It was evidently his idea of a joke, "Ten," Trueblood said, far more relaxed now than he was back in Palestine. "I want ten."

Weiler shook his head, grinning, as if he'd just gotten the joke, "I'll get us five." He didn't want Trueblood becoming sick in the bus. "Three for you, two for me."

"More for me than for you?" Trueblood said, "You sure a strange white man."

"What the hell," Weiler said. "It's your lucky day."

***

Boarding the El Paso bus, Weiler recalled the ball of string the Trailway driver had remembered to give him when they'd reached Dallas; and as clearly and quickly as he could, Weiler not only told the new driver what the problem was, but, handing over the string, described its solution.

"I was in the Army myself, understand orders," said the guy from Greyhound. "But sure would hate the duty you have now." He walked with a pronounced limp, and leading them back into the bus, showed them where to sit, roping off the immediate area around them. "Got shot up at Bastogne, that's why I limp," he told Weiler, one soldier to another, "Earned me a Bronze Star and Purple Heart there."

The bus was about half filled when it left Dallas, and by this time Weiler was used to people pointing at him and Trueblood, as well as the whispering and the stares. He didn't like any of it any better now, but it was no longer a novel occurrence, and he was able to ignore most of it more easily.

"Tell me when you start getting hungry," he said to Trueblood.

"What they going to do to me back at Bliss?" Trueblood asked.

"Nothing," Weiler said. Then he reconsidered, saying, "You're a PFC, so they'll probably take away your stripe, and for every day you went AWOL you'll have to spend two in the stockade. At least that's what I think."

"That's something, not nothing," Trueblood said. "Fucking Army. You like the Army, corporal?"

The morning ritual in Weiler's barracks was, reveille sounded and each soldier called out the number of days he had left to serve. It was like a bouncing ball, cynically traveling from bed to bed. "No, I don't like the Army," Weiler said.

Trueblood grinned. "Maybe we ain't so different, corporal."

Weiler certainly didn't agree with that, but there was no point in debating the issue. And certainly not now. The bus, after all, was headed for El Paso, unlike Palestine, the real promised land as far as Weiler was concerned; and once in El Paso and back to Bliss, he'd hand Trueblood over to the MP's, and that'd be all she wrote. *Finito,* done, mission accomplished.

"Why'd you go AWOL, Trueblood?" Weiler wasn't particularly curious, but maybe it would help pass the time.

"My papa a son of a bitch," Trueblood answered, "always beating on me and my mama. Meaner even than Sheriff Gibson. I hate my papa, hate him more than I hate the Army. Had to get away from him." But a friend, it turned out, had called Trueblood and told him that his father was going to kill his mother if Trueblood didn't return from Bliss and get his mother away from the old man, too.

But when Trueblood came to the rescue, his mother refused to leave. She seemed resigned to being beaten or worse. Trueblood swore he'd kill his father if anything happened to his mother, but his father laughed in his face. "He still young man, forty. Still kick my ass. My mama only thirty-six. Had me when she was sixteen," Trueblood said. "Life suck. Sometime, wish I was dead."

Sighing, Weiler decided he'd heard enough and got out Bellow's *Augie March.* It was more than six hundred pages, and Weiler had about a hundred-fifty to go. Augie was back in Chicago, the girlfriend in Mexico, remember, having given him the old heave-ho; and for a while the book, instead of jerking around, began to pick up real steam again. That wasn't, by the way, the opinion of most critics who'd loved every word. But Weiler was in the habit of making up his own mind.

"That the Bible?" Trueblood asked.

Frowning, Weiler put the book down. He'd want to read now, not talk.

"Book look as big as Bible."

"No, it's not the Bible. It's a novel, a story, came out a year ago."

"You read all that book?" Trueblood inquired. He wasn't making fun, it just seemed to him hard to believe that someone could or wanted to read a book that big.

"Yeah, I like reading novels, stories."

"Say, corporal, you come visit me in the stockade, okay?"

The request came out of left field, and Weiler grinned.

"Sure," he said, shrugging.

But his body language was all wrong, and Trueblood insisted, "No, I mean it, mean it. You not only tell Gibson, 'Fuck off,' but you first white guy treat me square in a long time."

"Okay," Weiler agreed, "I'll come visit you." It wasn't the flattery, it was that he wanted no trouble on the bus.

"You promise? You gotta promise. Then I count on you. I gotta count on you, count on fucking someone."

It was, Weiler thought, almost like talking to a child, a kid, an adolescent. "Yeah, I promise," he shrugged.

***

The remainder of the trip was long but uneventful, and they arrived back in El Paso shortly before nine. Sergeant Harmeling was there when they got off the bus.

"Usually," he complained, "the prisoner is brought back to the orderly room, so the CO can see for himself, the MP's from the stockade come get him. But Captain Roosma's a reservist who doesn't know his dick from his elbow, and I was detailed to pick you up at the bus station and bring you both directly to the stockade. Beginning to feel as though I was a taxi driver rather than an SFC with two years to go before making twenty."

"Oh, give me a fucking break," thought a tired Weiler.

At the stockade, two MP's quickly took charge of Trueblood and led him away. They both looked big and mean. Captain Stargel, the same who'd qualified Weiler on the pistol range, now signed for the .45 and the shackles. Come to think of it, he looked pretty mean, too.

"How was your trip, corporal?" he asked pleasantly.

"It was fine, sir, no problem," Weiler answered, because why bother? Why say the sheriff was a little nuts and Texas wasn't much better? What was to be gained? Besides, yawning, he badly wanted to hit the old sack.

Stargel smiled. "You're entitled to twelve hours' hazardous pay, and don't drink it all at once, hear?"

Weiler stifled another yawn. "Loud and clear, sir."

On the drive back to the company area, Harmeling said, "Boy, that Trueblood looked like he was going to faint when those monster MP's took over, By the way, Captain Roosma said to tell you to report to him first thing tomorrow after breakfast."

***

A couple of Army manuals resided in their forest-green covers in a small bookcase behind Roosma, while a framed picture of President Eisenhower hovered on the wall above him. Eisenhower was sitting at his desk in the Oval Office. It was almost ten years to the day that, as Supreme Commander, he'd led the Allied Armies on to the heavily fortified beaches of Normandy.

"Sit down, Weiler." Captain Roosma said next morning, after returning Weiler's salute, The map of Texas was still on his desk, folded in half this time. "Everything go okay yesterday?" he asked,

Weiler nodded. "Trueblood's in the stockade, sir, and I returned the .45 and shackles to Captain Roosma." Still half-asleep, he had named the wrong officer.

"You mean Captain Stargel," Roosma corrected him, and Roosma sort of twisted from side to side in his swivel chair. There was a pained expression on his face. "Listen, Weiler, I hated having to send you to bring Trueblood back. I'm sorry, you didn't deserve it."

Weiler didn't know how to respond. Captains rarely apologize to corporals about an assignment they're compelled to make. Besides, *who* deserved it and what exactly had they not deserved?

"I wasn't sure if you remembered that Trueblood was a negro, and I probably should have told you. But if you hadn't remembered and I told you, I figured it would only add to your worries before you left."

Weiler still didn't know what to say. It might have helped had he known that Roosma's superiors judged that Roosma was right only half the time, yet as a reservist and commanding officer of a service unit he couldn't do too much harm when he was wrong.

"Sheriff Gibson called yesterday afternoon," the captain finally got around to saying. "He told me never to send you back there again. Not that I would. Said to tell you that if he ever laid eyes on you again, in uniform or out, he'd blow your head off. I take it there was a serious confrontation."

So that explained the apology. "It was about my calling you and wanting Trueblood to take a shower, sir," Weiler reported. "The sheriff wasn't too crazy about the idea; claimed that all negroes naturally smell. Another dumb prick abusing his authority. So, what else is new, sir?"

Roosma wasn't sure he liked the implications of what he'd just heard or Weiler's informal frankness. Well, it never paid being too nice to an enlisted man, even if you might have taken advantage of him, and now Roosma stood up. The interview was over. Or not quite.

"I passed on the warning about never returning to Trueblood's hometown, corporal," and the captain made it sound like a formal announcement. "Not that I think you would. But I passed it on. So my conscience is clear. Now why don't you take the rest of the day off, Weiler, tomorrow morning as well." They worked Saturdays until twelve at Bliss. "I'll call your sergeant at the newspaper and tell him to expect you reporting back to duty Monday morning."

It was when Weiler left the orderly room that he began to feel queasy. The whole experience, going and coming, had been nerve-racking as well as depressing, and the sheriff's vicious threat just seemed to cap it all in a particularly miserable way. "Boy what a screwed-up country," Weiler thought.

He decided to spend the rest of the day in the post library. Weiler took out a number of books and flipped through the pages, until he found an odd paragraph that struck his fancy. But he couldn't really seem to focus, nor did he bother going to lunch. He didn't want to see anyone, didn't want to have to salute, or say a word to a soul. Besides, it was awfully hot outside. Bliss always seemed to be hot, hot and dry. Only in the mornings, before the sun came up, was there ever a decent, occasional breeze. But the air-conditioned library was just what the doctor ordered now, cool and quiet, and, most important, Weiler felt safe there.

***

Gerry Lohmann hadn't forgotten his promise to treat his buddies to a Saturday roll in the hay. And, Lord knows, had he forgotten, Rollie Sanger would have reminded him. You told Sanger it was your treat, no way he'd let you off the hook.

Both Sanger and Lohmann had tried getting Weiler to talk about Trueblood, but Weiler refused, turned them down cold, telling them, "I don't want to talk about him. I want to forget about the whole lousy deal." That was a lot to forget, including being scared to death Gibson might just be wacky and hateful enough to come looking for him.

"What the hell, you did your duty," Sanger acknowledged generously. "Brought the *shwartze* back and deposited him in the stockade."

"Hey, do me a favor, Rollie, don't call him a *shwartze*, okay?" *Shwartze* was a Yiddish word for someone of color.

"Jesus, Hal, come on," Sanger threw up his pudgy arms. "My father employs a lot of them in our drycleaning stores. In fact, my father thinks the heat from the pressing machines doesn't bother them in the summer like it does whites, which is why we hire so many of them."

"Rollie," Weiler began to say. "Oh, forget it, just forget it." Sanger was hopeless, and his father didn't sound much better.

A block from the whorehouse, Lohmann started rubbing his hands in anticipation. Weiler couldn't help staring at him. Lohmann saw him staring, grinned, but kept rubbing his hands.

"What can I tell you, Hal?" he said. "The anticipation just excites the hell out of me, and who cares what Rollie calls your boy?"

***

It was a Monday night, a couple of weeks later. Lohmann had gone home on a week's leave, and Sanger and Weiler were on their way to a movie, Movies were cheap on post, cost a quarter, and better them than getting drunk or avoiding a fight in an El Paso bar with yet another G.I. who thought he packed a right like Marciano.

"I'm not supposed to tell you, Hal, but your *shwartze* hung himself in the stockade," Sanger said. "One of the captains there called Roosma this afternoon. I eavesdropped, heard the whole conversation."

Weiler stopped walking. "What'd you just say?"

"Trueblood, the *shwartze* you brought back a couple of weeks ago."

Weiler couldn't believe it, yet instinctively started walking away from the movie theater as groups of soldiers wearing civvies kept surging toward him. They seemed innumerable, a blur, indistinct.

"Where you going?" asked Sanger anxiously, trailing after him.

But it felt as if something heavy just hit Weiler on the backswing, smashing into his shoulder, and his head began to spin from the aftershock. Afraid to stop, he kept walking, stumbling forward.

Soon a guy with a bristling crewcut told him to watch who the hell he was cutting off, and only then did Weiler come to an abrupt standstill.

"Hal, for crying out loud, you're going to get yourself in a jam," Sanger warned him.

Weiler said he couldn't help himself, that he felt sick, nauseous.

"But he was a black guy you barely knew," Sanger pointed out.

Sighing, Weiler tried to make sense of what had happened, or at least understand why it was bothering him so much. But it didn't take a genius or too long to figure that one out. Of course, he knew why.

"I did something, Rollie, said something I shouldn't have," he told Sanger.

"What are you talking about?"

Just as Weiler knew that two plus two equal four, he knew that it was a mistake to tell Sanger, but who else could he confide in, and soon he heard himself saying, "Trueblood asked me to visit him in the stockade, Rollie, and I told him I would. But it was one of those half-assed promises that I kept putting off because I'd didn't really want to, because I'd hoped to forget about him, forget about everything that happened those two days. There's a screwball sheriff out there who told Roosma he'd kill me if he saw me again, and mostly I want to forget about him. I just want to go back to writing for the *Fort Bliss News*, just want to complete my lousy two years and get out, free and clear. But how the hell am I going to do that now, Rollie? How am I going to be able to forget about any of this terrible crap?"

Sanger made a face as though it was he, not Weiler, who'd just swallowed something irremediably bitter. "Man, that's crazy," he said, "I remember Trueblood. He was dumb, dumb as hell. They don't come any fucking dumber. He wouldn't have remembered you, Hal, let alone your so-called promise. Besides, who takes promises like that seriously? Come on, let's go to the movie, you'll feel better after. I'm one of your two friends here at Bliss. I wouldn't kid you."

But Weiler said that he'd sat next to the guy for more than twelve hours less than a month ago, they'd been shackled together. "And now, the guy's dead, was only nineteen or twenty, maybe I *could* have helped him but didn't, and now

I feel lousy. What's so crazy about that? What's so wrong about that?"

"You don't understand, Hal, you can't feel lousy because you got to forget about him," Sanger insisted, "They want to keep it quiet, they don't want anyone to know. Roosma had to be informed; but enough people know, there might be a stink, an investigation. So it's practically an order that everyone forget about it."

Weiler stared at him. "If no one else is supposed to know, why'd you just tell me?" he asked.

Sanger took a step back, and for a minute he seemed confused, didn't know how to respond. Then he grinned, saying, "Oh, come on, Hal, you know me. I had to tell someone, and Lohmann wasn't around, so you were it. Besides, you seemed to have sort of liked the *shwartze,* felt protective toward him. So I figured you'd want to know, and what are buddies for? But listen, us Jews got to stick together. So if Roosma ever brings the subject up, we *never* talked about it, Hal, *never* discussed it. Never, Never! Okay? Understand?"

***

The picture was a contemporary Western starring Spencer Tracy, *Bad Day at Black Rock.* Sanger loved it, and to please him Weiler said the movie was okay. After all, they were buddies, right? But it didn't make Weiler feel the slightest bit better after, and the rest of week was just as bad—he still felt lousy. Same thing that weekend. Something indigestible seemed stuck inside his chest, like that fried egg sandwich the morning after he'd boarded the Greyhound to Dallas. And Monday night, he even dreamed about Trueblood, who kept bleating like a disappointed kid, "But you promised, you promised..."

"Go to hell!" Weiler muttered, turning over. "Get away from me! You're fucking poison, Otis!"

Funny, strange he said that. Or maybe not so funny, not so strange. People are such a bundle of contradiction. How else explain that four days later, Friday, a small item appeared on the back page of the *Fort Bliss News*, announcing the death of Otis Trueblood, 4025 Service Unit, Post I & E, and, oh, Jesus, the shit that hit the fan that charged Friday morning.

P.O.W.

~⊰≋⊱~

When the first American P.O.W.'s leaving Hanoi were shown on television recently, Edith Arkin, a sixty-five-year-old widow, sat glued to her TV set. Her son, Jack, had been reported "missing in action" five years ago, and since then she'd prayed every day for his safe return. And now, watching those liberated P.O.W.'s, she'd have given anything to see her son walking among them.

Earlier that week she'd bought a new dress, new shoes, a new bag, everything matching. She'd wanted to look her best when she greeted her son on his safe return, for she knew in her heart he'd be among those eventually coming home. She'd tried to remember the type of clothing he admired and which pieces of jewelry he'd complimented her on wearing. Not that she was rich or owned much jewelry. But she'd always tried to look her best, and prided herself on aging gracefully. As her best friend once put it, "Edith is what's known as a fine woman, and she looks it."

She had large brown eyes and a shapely mouth. Her nose was slightly on the flat side, and the cast of her face was round and full. Her hair was almost totally white. Edith never was much of a reader. For entertainment and to keep up with what was happening in the world, she watched a lot of television. But that week, when the papers were filled with news about the first batch of repatriated soldiers, she made it a point to buy all the available papers, and avidly read each news item about the P.O.W.'s. That, plus watching as many film clips taken in Hanoi as possible, was almost a full-time job.

One afternoon, while Edith was listening to a special CBS report about the physical condition of the first group of returning P.O.W.'s, her phone rang. "Hello, Edith, it's me,

Annie," said her ex-daughter-in-law. "I was thinking of you today and wanted to say hello." Annie had divorced Jack three years after he'd been shot down in Vietnam and had remarried last year.

"It's nice of you to call, Annie," Edith said suspiciously. She'd tried to sympathize with Annie in the years since her divorce. But blood is thicker than water, and in the long run she couldn't help feeling that Annie had let her son down.

"I'd like to come over and see you tonight, Edith," Annie said. They hadn't seen each other in almost two years.

"I've been tired this last week, Annie. I'd really prefer being alone tonight." The truth is, she couldn't forgive Annie for remarrying.

"I'd just stay a few minutes, Edith. We've always liked each other and been friends. Please, for old time's sake."

"Some other time, Annie," Edith said, without meaning it.

Annie sighed, disappointed because, as she'd said, she'd always like Edith.

"I'm sorry, Annie, but I can't help myself. Or maybe I don't wanna help myself, okay?"

"Sure, okay," said Annie. And, getting the unmistakable message, she hung up, tears clouding her eyes.

***

You probably don't remember now, but before the second batch of American P.O.W.'s were released, there was a delay, and for a few uncertain days relatives of the P.O.W.'s still held by the North Vietnamese feared the worst. Then the Secretary of State, in Paris at the time, was given new and firm assurances by the other side that the second contingent of American P.O.W's would be repatriated just a few days beyond the original release date.

Edith suffered terribly during that uncertain time. It was as if God was teasing her, along with the other mothers and wives, and she was powerless to do anything about it. But she told herself, "If you keep wanting something badly enough, it *will* really happen. It's the people who give up, who can't stand long and painful disappointments, who lose out in the end."

Edith lived in a four-room apartment in Kew Gardens. Her best friend, Rose, also a widow, lived on the same floor. "Keep your chin up," Rose kept telling her, especially this last month.

Edith and Rose used to sit, weather permitting, on benches in a park two blocks from their apartment building. Four or five of the other women from the building used to sit with them. Edith thought she was lucky to have such good friends. She had missed sitting with them these last weeks, because, though the weather was mild for this time of year, she had avoided the park. She had neither the time nor the patience for it.

It seemed that all her attention was focused on the faces of the second group of P.O.W.'s as they disembarked from the planes that had flown them from Hanoi to Clark Air Force Base in the Philippines. They all appeared so happy to be free and to be among friends, Edith wished she could reach out and touch them; touching them, she could almost believe she was touching her son. According to the arrangements worked out with their captors, the P.O.W.'s were to be released about once every two weeks, in batches of four. So, although Jack wasn't among the servicemen in the first two contingents, Edith still believed she'd see her son's smiling face in one of the two groups yet to be released.

Some newspapers were beginning to carry stories that certain of the returning P.O.W.'s had been more cooperative with the enemy than was prescribed in the military code. And there were those in the Pentagon who wanted such personnel court-martialed. Word had even leaked out that some of the repatriated servicemen themselves were bitter toward comrades who'd voluntarily signed anti-American statements.

Edith tried to guess who among those already freed looked even remotely like a traitor. And she wondered if Jack's life had been made more miserable because of such treachery. If there was a traitor among the men who'd returned, Edith, from the bottom of her heart, wished him no good.

To distract herself, Edith went to her closet and looked at her new dress and shoes. She wanted so much to look her best when she greeted her son. Would he choose to stay with her when he was well enough to leave the military hospital where he'd be stationed? She hoped so, and, to avoid being caught unprepared, she'd made the spare bedroom cheerful by buying a bright new bedspread; also a new AM/FM radio and a lamp with a brass base,

Edith made a point of keeping the door to the bedroom closed whenever any of her friends or neighbors visited the apartment. Last week, for instance, after she'd returned from buying the radio and lamp, Rose rang her bell. Edith checked the door to the spare bedroom before letting even her closest friend into the apartment.

Rose said she hadn't seen Edith all day. "Where've you been?"

"Shopping," Edith said, without mentioning the radio or the lamp.

Rose was glad that Edith had gotten out of the house and only sorry that her friend hadn't asked Rose to accompany her downtown. "Did you buy anything?" Rose asked.

"No, just looked around," Edith said. "It was nice to get out of the house for a while."

An hour later, feeling ashamed, it occurred to Edith that that was the first time she had lied to Rose since they became friends, and, hating herself she dearly wished she hadn't felt compelled to lie.

***

When the third batch of American P.O.W's were released in the middle of the month, Edith read the papers avidly and watched her TV screen with frightening absorption. Now, if her doorbell or phone rang while she was in the midst of catching a P.O.W. report on the news, the door and phone went unanswered.

One night, Edith's brother, Al, called her five or six times, but no one picked up the phone. Soon after the ten o'clock news was over, Rose rang Edith's doorbell. She told Edith that her brother had been trying to reach her most of the evening, and because he'd gotten no answer he'd called Rose and asked her to make sure Edith was all right.

"He must have been dialing the wrong number," Edith shrugged. "I've been here all evening."

Rose wanted to say, "But he had the operator call you the last two times." However, she thought better of it.

"Thanks for coming in," Edith said. "I guess I better call Al now, or he'll be worried."

The following day, Rose called Edith's brother herself. "I'm concerned about Edith," Rose said. "She's been under a terrific strain since the P.O.W.'s have been in the news so prominently, and no one seems able to reach her. It's as if she's living in her own private world."

Al said he'd noticed the strain in Edith's voice the last few weeks, too. "I was going to visit her last week, but business has been so hectic. I'll make a point of catching her as soon as possible."

In between the time Rose called Al and Al arranged to visit his sister in her apartment, Edith read a story in the paper which told how torture broke down the will of many of the P.O.W.'s. One navy pilot was forced to sit on a stool for three straight weeks. And whenever he tried to sleep, a guard woke him by hitting him under the nose. Other P.O.W.'s were forced to kneel on concrete floors for days, their knees swelling like inflated balloons.

Edith knew her son to be forceful and independent. Even as a boy, Jack could be stubborn, and if a test of wills was involved, he hated to lose. Now, Edith tried not to imagine the tortures he underwent, and she wondered if breaking a man would leave his mental abilities confused for all time. She thought she could bear Jack's losing an arm or a leg, but it frightened her to consider his coming home mentally unbalanced.

Each morning, before attending to any of her other chores, Edith would dust and sweep the spare bedroom. On the dresser was a piece of cardboard. WELCOME HOME JACK had been printed on the cardboard with a red crayon, "Just let him come home safely," she told herself, "and I'm quite sure that everything else will work out."

When her brother called during the last week in March and said he wanted to drop by that night, Edith tried to talk him out of it. He'd come alone, he said, she wasn't to go to any trouble. "I haven't seen you for a while and would just like to say hello in the flesh," Al said.

Al was three years younger than Edith, and had been in the Army during World War II. Before enlisting, he'd had an ulcer, and a doctor cousin had told him the ulcer could give him a medical deferment. But Al said, "No thanks. There are too many slackers ducking the Army as it is."

"But you have a legitimate excuse," the doctor said.

"Well, then maybe my going evens it up a little for one of those jerks who can go but is weaseling out."

"You're a stubborn fool," the doctor said kindly.

"It must run in my family," Al said. "My sister's the same way."

And, wouldn't you know it, Al kept remembering how painfully stubborn Edith could be while driving over to her apartment from work that night. But when he got there, first thing he said was, "Please excuse me for not coming over sooner." He looked at Edith, trying to detect signs of a nervous breakdown, whatever they might be. Then he glanced around his sister's apartment; the place appeared neat and clean, Edith seemed to be functioning okay.

Meanwhile, Edith put on the kettle for some tea and took out half a cheesecake from the refrigerator. In the kitchen, Al spotted a pile of newspapers. While she poured tea for them both, he casually flipped through the top paper, a month old. All the news items relating to the returning P.O.W.'s had been circled in red. Putting the paper down, Al suddenly felt flushed and decided to wash his face.

He went out into the hall. He hadn't been in Edith's apartment for more than six months, and instead of going to the bathroom, by mistake he opened the door to the spare bedroom. Flipping on the light, he realized he'd made an error, and was about to turn it off when he noticed the Welcome Home Jack sign on the dresser. He must have stared at the sign for a minute before putting out the light and closing the door. Then he saw Edith, watching him from the kitchen.

"Edith, Edith, you mustn't do this to yourself," he couldn't help saying.

"You've no right to spy on me, Al," she said angrily.

"Edith, why do you torture yourself like this?" Al said. "Jack's dead. He's not coming back. His plane was shot down five years ago, and if he was captured or is alive, you'd have had word by now." Al went over and took his sister's hand. "You'll wind up in a mental hospital if you don't accept your son's death."

Edith pushed her brother away from her. "Al, did I ask you to come over? Do I bother you? Do I complain? Do I make a nuisance of myself? Please, drink your tea and you're welcome to some cheesecake, then go home to your wife. You're a hard worker, Al, you probably had a rough day at the store, go home and rest, Al." She walked back into the kitchen and sat down at the kitchen table. Al trailed after her.

"Edith, Jack's dead," Al said again, considering his alternatives. He could tell his sister to see a psychiatrist. He could try to get her admitted to a hospital tonight. He could really keep in touch with her, maybe visit her again this weekend, or generally play things by ear. Besides, didn't he have his own troubles?

"You've done your duty; you're a good brother," Edith said, reading his mind. "Go home, Al. No one can help me, just my son, he's the only one."

***

The last batch of returning American P.O.W.'s from the New York area was scheduled to arrive at McGuire Air Force Base shortly before six on a Sunday evening. Relatives of the P.O.W.'s crowded behind restraining ropes. They were standing about fifty yards from the approximate point at which the hospital plane would come to a halt. They'd been instructed by the military public relation officers that each P.O.W. would have his name announced, after which he'd emerge from the plane and salute the welcoming military brass. Then, when all the P.O.W.'s had left the plane, they'd be taken to waiting rooms at the air base, where their relatives might see them in comparative privacy. To prevent confusion, to keep things organized, the relatives were asked to please cooperate.

Among the relatives were young wives wearing corsages, tiny children, and elderly parents. Edith stood toward the rear of the crowd. She wore her new dress and new shoes, and she carried her matching bag. Her brother stood next to her, pawing at the ground nervously with one shoe. Al had visited Edith earlier that afternoon, and she'd told him she planned to go out to the air base. Did he want to go along for the ride?

More worried than ever about her, Al found he couldn't say no, and he'd held her hand during the two-hour drive from Kew Gardens. And he was still holding her hand when they heard a couple of M.P.'s saying to each other that among this returning batch of P.O.W's were two reputed traitors, enlisted men who'd been shunned by the others since the group had left Hanoi last week.

Presently, the plane landed and maneuvered itself near the crowd of watchful relatives. A band struck up "The Star-Spangled Banner." The first P.O.W.'s name was announced: he was a colonel, and he came striding out of the plane dressed in a new uniform, combat ribbons festooning one side of his chest. He saluted the three officers standing at the foot of the plane. Then, before anyone could stop her, the colonel's wife broke past two M.P.'s and flew into her husband's arms. Her impact knocked the colonel's hat from his head. One of the generals nearby bent down, picked up the hat, and held it patiently for the colonel. The colonel's wife seemed to set the tone for the other wives. Each of them embraced her husband almost as soon as the man stepped out and away from the plane.

The last repatriated soldier to emerge was a P.F.C. He was no more than twenty-two, and he was very thin. After he saluted the welcoming officers, he did not look up expectantly, like the others, to see if any kin was there to meet him.

"That's it," Al said softly. "He's the last one."

Edith let go of her brother's hand. Then, without a word, she started threading her way toward the front of the crowd.

Al tried to keep up with his sister, but a solid wall of people got between them. "Edith, where you going?" he called out.

But Edith didn't even bother answering him. She made her way purposefully past the M.P.'s and officers, and walked over to the young soldier, who stood quite alone now.

Looking at Edith suspiciously, he said with a soft southern drawl, "I think you've mistaken me for someone else, ma'am."

She kissed him on the cheek. "It's no mistake," she said, and tried to smile.

But it was, the soldier thought, the saddest smile he'd ever seen. And, momentarily forgetting his own troubles, he reached for her hand and held it as if Edith was a close relative—an aunt, his favorite cousin, a sister, even somehow his mother who died giving birth to him.

The Lawyer

"At least kiss your father goodbye this time," Dave Koussevitsky heard his ex-wife say quietly to their daughter, Diane. "He's been good to us."

"Funny, I heard you tell one of your friends just the opposite last week," Diane snapped. She was fourteen, an age when all adults seem violently hypocritical. "You're so crazy about him, why don't *you* kiss him goodbye?"

"You're still his daughter, I'm his *ex*-wife," Julia said, barely able to control her anger. They were talking in the kitchen. Dave had gone to the bathroom, and they hadn't heard him approaching the kitchen again. But he'd heard them, every word.

Now, as always when something happened that might have upset him, Dave told himself, "It's crazy to expect more from life than life can reasonably offer." And he decided it was a propitious time to check his answering service. He went into Julia's bedroom, where he picked up the phone.

It was a Saturday afternoon, and a congressman he was defending in federal court next week was in the process of deciding whether he wanted to cop a plea. It was Dave's experience that more than a few nervous clients needed a lawyer's reassurance particularly over the weekend before their trials were scheduled to begin. But the only message Dave's answering service forwarded was from a Mrs. Laura Bassini, who'd left her number and asked Dave to call back. The name, though, rang absolutely no bell, and though he jotted down the lady's number, he was in no rush to return the call. Not Dave, who avoided surprises like the plague. Strangers who sought him out were third-degreed by his secretary first.

Alerting Julia and his daughter by clearing his throat, Dave made his way back into the kitchen. A year or two shy of forty, he was no more than five pounds heavier now than when he'd graduated from law school. Which figured, because he believed in keeping in good shape and played tennis once a week all year round. His daughter he visited once a month, and always in her mother's apartment.

In the kitchen, he saw Julia urging Diane with her eyes to kiss him. Diane resembled her mother. The same oval-shaped face, blond hair, and long, shapely legs. Dave wondered with amusement, not if she'd broken any hearts yet, but just how many. He decided to get her off the hook with her mother, saying, "Diane, if you want to go to ballet next week and have any trouble getting tickets, call my secretary. One of the choreographers at Lincoln Center is a client and owes me a favor." And before she could thank him, or tell him to go to hell, or whatever, he kissed her. Proud of his tactfulness, he turned to Julia with a smile and said, "Take care of yourself, ex-. I'll be in touch."

"You take care of yourself, Dave," Julia said. She was looking better now than she had during any other time since their divorce, and Dave had to assume that her love life was on the upswing. Knowing Julia, he hoped the guy was serious, for the guy's sake.

***

Outside, Dave hopped a cab that took him over to the East Side and a little farther uptown. He had an apartment overlooking the river. He liked to think that it was tastefully furnished. He had an original Degas and Pissarro in his living room, on either side of a china closet filled with sterling silver embossed with the letter K—stuff he'd inherited from his parents, both of whom had died during the past five years. The only picture in his bedroom was a large photograph of his mother. Every once in a while, he found himself stroking the glass covering her face.

Dave didn't have many friends, but he felt close to two men, one of whom he'd grown up with, and he was seeing a lot of a woman whose name was Sybil Lavin. She was 31, had a wicked pair of hips and was an associate producer of a CBS television program he couldn't stand. Sybil had been married to a surgeon who'd thrown her over for his nurse.

Dave had handled her late father's estate. He liked Sybil in a casual way, and they enjoyed seeing each other. But Dave believed that anything permanent between them was out of the question, if only because he was compulsively neat and Sybil, though meticulous about her appearance and clothes, was a slob around the house. More important, Dave wasn't really prepared to struggle through the strain of living with another person. Why should he? Professionally, personally, he was doing okay.

After visiting his ex-wife and daughter, Dave always made a point of spending the night with Sybil, and they had a date tonight. So he wasn't too surprised soon after he returned to his apartment when the phone rang, and he heard Sybil say on the other end, "Hello, Counselor."

"Sybil, we're still on for tonight, no?" he asked nervously. Last month, after he'd seen his ex-wife and daughter, Sybil had broken a date with him at the last minute, and getting through that night alone had been sheer murder.

Instead of his taking her to dinner, Sybil wondered if it was okay if she came over to his place early, where she'd cook them dinner. There was a Pakistani recipe she'd clipped from the *Times* this week she'd like to try.

He thought about the mess she'd make in his kitchen, but remembering how miserable he felt sleeping alone last month after visiting his daughter, he said, "Sure, sure. Come on over and cook to your heart's content."

The food seemed fine when they ate it, but during the early hours of Sunday morning, they both felt violently sick and kept rushing each other out of the bathroom. Neither of them fell back asleep until it was almost seven, Which was why, when Dave's phone rang a little before ten, they both groaned in disgust simultaneously.

"Doesn't whoever's calling know it's Sunday?" Sybil moaned.

Dave's eyes felt bleary, the taste in his mouth terrible and his gut still tender. "Yeah? Yeah?" he said, picking up the phone. It was Mrs. Corry, his secretary, who'd been called by his answering service. A Mrs. Laura Bassini had called and said it was important to get in touch with Mr. Koussevitsky.

"Listen, I've never heard of this Mrs. Bassini, whoever she is," Dave said. "Mrs. Corry, you call her, and don't fill me in on the gory details unless it's an absolute emergency. And as I'm still recovering from an almost fatal attack of food poisoning, it'll have to wait till tomorrow even if it is an emergency." And he put down the receiver without waiting for Mrs. Corry's no-nonsense reply.

"What was that all about?" Sybil wanted to know.

"I don't know and I don't want to know," Dave said. "How do you feel?"

"Don't ask," she said. "Let's go back to sleep. Maybe when we wake up it'll only seem like a bad dream."

He patted her dark hair twice and smiled sympathetically. But closing his eyes, he swore that he'd never let Sybil cook him another meal, no matter how lonely he felt.

***

Dave arrived at his law office before nine Monday morning. He still felt weak on his feet. He was scheduled for a 9:30 appointment with the congressman he was defending in federal court that week. But now Mrs. Corry reminded him about the woman who'd been trying to get in touch with him over the weekend. "She sounded like an Italian who's visiting the States, a tourist," Mrs. Corry said. "Just don't be too surprised if she shows up this morning; she sounded determined."

"But did you find out what she wants?" he asked impatiently.

"The woman wouldn't tell me," Mrs. Corry said, frowning. Mrs. Corry had white hair, which she wore in a bun. Although her hairstyle made her look old and timid, she was a spunky woman, and it was obvious from her expression now that she thought Dave had had an affair with Mrs. Bassini during one of his trips to Europe. Didn't he remember?

Dave looked at the woman's name scrawled across the top of Mrs. Corry's legal pad. No, he was sure he'd never heard of Laura Bassini. "Look, I've a busy day ahead of me and I'm still not feeling so great, so if and when this sixty-four-dollar mystery does come to the office, be a sport, Mrs. Corry, and try to find out what it's about."

Mrs. Corry filled her cheeks with air. Then, expelling the air, she made a puff sound. She'd worked for Dave for five years and felt she could take certain liberties with him. This despite the fact that he didn't look well this morning and she was always acutely aware of how desperately he avoided surprises; she'd never known a man who so badly needed to be in control of himself and of what was happening around him. She'd worked for other lawyers, and knew them for a cautious breed, but none of the others matched Dave when it came to sheer wariness. "I'll do the best I can," Mrs. Corry said, shrugging.

"That's the old fighting spirit," Dave said, shaking a limp fist.

The congressman arrived more than a half hour late. Dave just loved waiting for clients. A tall man in his fifties, the congressman wore a tailored suit and carried a Gucci attaché case. While he might have passed for a prince of men the evidence presented to the grand jury, which had indicted him, indicated that he was a greedy and petty man who'd accepted bribes from construction companies for years. Last Friday Dave had advised his client to cop a plea. The congressman, turning pale, said he'd think about it over the weekend. His trial was scheduled to commence Thursday, which meant that time was growing short, especially if the congressman decided to let Dave try to negotiate for a light sentence in return for a guilty plea.

Settling himself in the leather chair facing Dave's desk, the congressman smiled. His teeth were capped, he had wavy, carefully combed hair and the smell of his aftershave lotion clung to the air. "I've given a lot of thought to your advice, Counselor," the congressman said in his booming baritone. "The only trouble with my copping a plea is that I'm an innocent man."

Dave said with calculated cruelty, "No, Congressman, you're not innocent. You're guilty as hell. And they've got the goods on you, got them cold."

The congressman wasn't used to people talking to him this way, and his jaw trembled imperceptibly. "You don't like me very much, do you, Counselor?"

Permitting himself to smile, Dave said with a kinder tone than he'd intended, "You make nine-thirty appointments and waltz in here after ten. No, I don't like you very much, Congressman."

"How do I know you're not selling me down the river, then?" the congressman said angrily.

"Let's get something straight," Dave said evenly. "I'm giving you my best advice and judgment, not because I like or don't like you, and not because I believe or don't believe you, but because one of the few things I take seriously in life is my job. And your case happens to be one, among others, that furnishes me with the occasion to do my stuff, exercise my best judgment. Do we understand each other, Congressman?"

But the congressman remained silent. His nostrils flared, and it was obvious he'd have given a lot to have been able to smash Dave in the face.

"I've asked you a question, Congressman, and I want an answer," Dave said coldly.

The congressman nodded.

"I still don't hear you."

"We understand each other," the congressman muttered.

"Fine, swell," Dave said. "Now, as I hinted to you for two weeks and finally told you last Friday, I've weighed all the factors in your case carefully, and in my judgment the very best thing you can do is authorize me to bargain for a light sentence in return for a guilty plea."

The congressman fell back against his chair. Though all the fight seemed to go out of him, he still didn't give Dave the go-ahead.

"I need another day to think—"

"No," Dave interrupted him. "Your way or my way, and that's all I want to hear from you now."

"Okay, okay, your way," the congressman sighed.

"Congratulations, Congressman," Dave said affably, extending his hand. "You just made a very wise decision."

And ten minutes after his client left, Dave put in a call to the assistant U.S. attorney in charge of the congressman's case. "Rudy, make my client an offer I can't refuse," he said.

"Hungry for a powwow?" Rudy said.

"Not me, Rudy, it's the congressman," Dave said. "Seems the man's a great believer in touching all the available bases."

"Sure, Counselor, sure," Rudy said—like Dave, jockeying for position even before their get-together. Then they sparred for another two minutes, before agreeing to meet the following morning in the U.S. attorneys' offices.

Putting down the phone, Dave asked Mrs. Corry for a cup of tea.

"Tea?" she said, making a face. "But you're a confirmed coffee man."

"My stomach still feels as if it was run over by a Mack truck. Which reminds me," he said, picking up the phone and calling a nearby florist. He ordered a dozen roses, telling the florist the card should read, "It's roses, Sybil, on the assumption you're still in the land of the living. Lilies only if and when I hear otherwise."

***

Dave drank tea only when he didn't feel well. That, hot cereal and soup. The few times he drank tea he invariably thought of how his grandfather used to drink it—in a glass, with the spoon in the glass and a cube of sugar clenched between his toothless gums.

He was just finishing his own tea—drunk from a cup, milk, no sugar, thanks—when the mysterious Laura Bassini showed up at his office and insisted on speaking to him face-to-face.

Mrs. Corry seemed puzzled. "She still won't tell me why she wants to see you, and though she's not pushy she won't take no for an answer, either."

"What's she like?" Dave asked suspiciously.

"I'd say between fifty-five and sixty. An Italian woman visiting the States, like I thought."

The name still meant less than nothing, and his secretary's thumbnail sketch wasn't the least bit helpful.

"Well, it doesn't sound like she's going to whip out a gun and shoot me," Dave said. "Okay, Mrs. Corry, show her in but hang around near the door."

Laura Bassini wore a wedding ring. That was the first thing Dave looked for and saw. Her hair was dark. She was dressed well, but not showily. She wore a cameo pin on the jacket of her suit that reminded Dave of one his mother used to wear. He had a good memory for faces and had seen a younger version of Laura Bassini's somewhere but couldn't place it yet. "My name is David Koussevitsky," he said, asking the woman to sit down.

But she remained standing. She looked at him without responding, then slowly looked around his office. Presently her eyes became very still. She was staring at the photograph of Dave's dead uncle Morris, which was hung next to his diploma. Morris had died of cancer in 1947, He'd contracted the illness in the Army during the early months of 1945, in Italy.

"Italy," Dave muttered, and suddenly remembered that Morris had had an affair with a woman named Laura in Italy during the war. And when Morris had returned to the States, though he was incurably ill, the woman had wanted to come with him. They'd corresponded during the next year and a half, and after Morris had died Dave's father, Morris' brother, had written to Laura, informing her of Morris' death.

"I was going to ask if you were related to Morris Koussevitsky," the woman said with a smile. "But I see Morris' portrait on your wall and I need not ask."

"Please sit down," Dave said, catching his breath. Before closing his inner office door, he winked at Mrs. Corry, letting her know that everything was under control.

"I knew Morris in Italy," the woman said. She watched Dave carefully, trying to gauge the effect her words were having. "He mentioned your name in one of his last letters, and the Italian consulate was kind enough to trace you for me." She spoke English quite well. "I've been trying to get in touch with you since Saturday."

"I've been out of town and quite busy," Dave said smoothly. "But you've found me, and I'm very glad to meet you."

She asked him to call her Laura.

He felt like a bastard but couldn't help wondering if the woman was working up her nerve to put the bite on him.

When she inquired about his parents, he told her that they were dead and that he was Morris' closest surviving relative. He felt the woman looking even more intently at his face now, trying to discover, he supposed, his slightest resemblance to Morris.

"Do you know about me?" Laura asked shyly.

Nodding, he said, "I have the letter you wrote my father after learning of Morris' death." He didn't mention the two love letters Laura had written Morris in 1946, which were also in his possession. How long was it since Morris had died? Twenty-six, twenty-seven years ago? That long?

Laura told him she'd come to New York with her husband ten days ago. It was their first visit to the States and, likely, would be their last; they were not rich people. They were flying back to Italy tomorrow evening. She'd wanted to find Dave, she said, or any other of Morris' close relatives, but had been timid at first. Then, when she'd shed her timidity, she had had some difficulty in making contact with him.

To make up for not having responded to her phone calls, Dave asked if he could take Laura and her husband to dinner that evening.

But she said with a smile, "My husband would not understand."

Dave knew that Italian men had a reputation for jealousy and possessiveness, but Laura had known his uncle more than twenty-five years ago. Then Dave wondered if she'd meant that her husband, seeing Dave, would think that he was Laura's recently acquired New York lover.

"I have a favor to ask," Laura said.

Dave pressed his back comfortably against his chair. Wasn't a favor what he'd anticipated? Yet he decided he liked the woman and knew he'd give her money. The only question was, how much.

"I would like you to take me to the cemetery where Morris is buried."

Her request surprised Dave, and at the same time he realized he shouldn't have been surprised. Then he thought, "Perhaps she'll ask me for money *after* paying her respects to Morris."

"I know that you are a busy man," Laura said. "But I would consider it a great kindness for you to take me to Morris' grave."

Dave knew there was no way he could manage it by tomorrow evening, but he consulted his calendar just to make sure. He had to be in court that afternoon, and the following morning he was set to see the U.S. attorneys about the congressman's case.

Looking up, he told Laura that, unfortunately, his schedule was very tight for the next two days. "I'd like to take you to Morris' grave, and I think I'd be able to manage it Wednesday or Friday," he said. "Could you possibly leave for home later in the week? You and your husband could remain at the hotel as my guests."

"No, I am sorry, that is quite impossible," Laura said, shaking her head.

Thinking fast, Dave decided he'd have Mrs. Corry hire a chauffeured limousine, and she would ride out in his place to the cemetery with Laura tomorrow morning. When he explained what he planned to do, he sensed Laura's disappointment, though she was too much the lady to accept his offer other than graciously. He wanted to apologize for not being able to accompany her himself, but he hated apologies, both giving and receiving them. Instead, he called Mrs. Corry into his office and told her to order the limousine. He suggested that Mrs. Corry and the chauffeur call for Laura at her hotel early the following morning. But Laura said she preferred to have the car meet her in front of Dave's office building.

"Fine, okay," Dave agreed, wondering if she was ashamed of the hotel where she was staying. Then he said he would, if it was possible for him and convenient for Laura, try to speak to her tomorrow afternoon; or, if she preferred, he would try to see her again sometime tomorrow before she left for Italy. He was trying to let her know that if, indeed, money was in the back of her mind, he was prepared to give her whatever she asked for.

"Rather than you call me, I would prefer calling you," she said.

After all the arrangements were made, he walked her to the elevator outside his office. And just before the elevator stopped for her, he found himself kissing her cheek.

She touched his face. "You have Morris' eyes," she said.

He wanted to apologize to her again, but not trusting himself he hurried back inside his office. There, he said to Morris' picture, "I'm boxed in by a tight schedule. For crying out loud, you were a lawyer—if you don't understand, who would?"

***

That night, after eating a light supper—his stomach still felt queasy—Dave went over all his papers relating to the congressman's case. He wanted to be on top of the material and so use his knowledge to the congressman's best advantage. But his usual powers of concentration failed him, and every so often he found himself thinking about Laura. Once he thought about calling Sybil, to find out how she was feeling. But if she wasn't feeling well, she had to know he wasn't in such great shape either. Why hadn't she called him? Hadn't he sent her flowers and shown his concern?

He went to bed shortly before one but found he couldn't sleep. Thoughts of his parents, his daughter, Morris, his failed marriage, his childhood—everything seemed to crowd in on him. He got up and went to the hall closet he used for storing old papers and legal briefs. There he found a torn manila envelope with the notation in red grease pencil: MORRIS' LETTERS.

They were letters written mostly to Dave's parents during World War II. How proud Dave had been that Morris was a soldier, he remembered, especially after his father had been rejected by the Army.

Dave's father had saved many of his brother's V-Mail letters, and Dave had kept them after his parents died. He found the one he was particularly looking for, written to Dave's father soon after the death of Dave's grandmother. It was dated February 17, 1945, Somewhere in Italy, and read:

"... Don't sorrow at the fact that I was not there to do her honor. I've never been far from her and all of you in my thoughts since I've been here. Please don't grieve too much. Never feel that we have lost our blessed mother. You can't lose something that is part of you..."

A shorter note on the second page was addressed to Dave. Morris wrote:

"Don't cry that Grandma has gone away. She will always be with you in her love for you. Treasure and love your mother, for she is more like Grandma than anyone else I know."

There was a time some years ago when many people Dave knew complained of their families. Dave figured they were exaggerating; also it seemed fashionable to knock one's kin. But even if only a part of what they said was true, Dave knew he'd been born lucky: Morris was a terrific man, and he'd been Dave's uncle, almost a surrogate father; as for Dave's mother, two days before she died he'd told her in the hospital, "When I was a kid, the other boys envied me because you were my mother. Have I ever told you, Ma, how much I've always been proud you're my mother?"

Dave wondered why the people closest to him now didn't engender the same feelings he once had. Had he changed so radically? Or was love perhaps easy for a child but infinitely more difficult for an adult, because life grinds down people's ability to feel? But Dave was now the same age as Morris when Morris had known Laura and when he'd written those letters after learning of his mother's death.

"What's the matter with me?" Dave said. "What's been happening to me over the years?" He lit a cigarette and poured himself a drink. He stared at the young blade in the Degas painting in his living room. "You ever feel this way, you son of a bitch?" he said. After a while, he realized that if he was to function even marginally tomorrow, he'd have to get some sleep. But it took him three stiff shots before he calmed down enough to lie down again, let alone fall asleep.

Nevertheless, there was a bounce to his step when he went to his office early the next morning. He was prepared to look over his mail, then meet with the U.S. attorneys an hour later in their offices. But when he saw his secretary waiting in the limousine for Laura, he couldn't bear the idea of Laura's driving out to Morris' grave accompanied only by a stranger,

He walked over to the car and told Mrs. Corry he'd changed his mind: He'd accompany Laura to the cemetery. Would she call the U.S. attorneys and tell them a personal emergency had arisen and he'd be in touch with them in the afternoon? And if the good congressman called, he was also to be told of a personal problem.

Mrs. Corry looked at her boss as if she didn't recognize him. "You don't usually flip-flop like this," she said.

Shrugging, Dave said, "This is special, I guess."

When Laura showed up, she too was surprised to see him.

"I was able to clear up this morning's appointments last night," Dave said. "So I'm going to be able to ride out to the cemetery with you, after all."

"I'm more than glad," Laura said, smiling. "Your coming with me makes me happy."

Dave helped her in the car. It was an air-conditioned Cadillac. The chauffeur asked if he could take off his hat before he started driving. "Sure," Dave said, who hated hats himself.

On the way to the cemetery, Laura asked Dave about his life. He told her he had a daughter but was divorced. She told him she had one child, a son, whom she'd named after Morris.

Dave confided, "You know, one of the main reasons I'm a lawyer is that Morris was one. And one of the main reasons I served in the Army when I could have ducked the draft is that Morris had been in the Army."

Laura smiled. "I think that means we both were able to value all the good qualities of Morris' character."

"This will probably sound a little sententious, but I'm sorry about how things worked out for you and Morris."

Laura wasn't exactly sure what the fancy word meant, but still, she said, "What can you do against the fates?" she asked.

It was, Dave thought, the kind of question an American somehow wouldn't have posed.

"Nothing!" Laura said, answering her own question. "Nothing!"

Dave wondered what Laura's husband was like. Did he resemble Morris? Did he know about Morris? Was Laura happily married? Dave had to assume that her life would have turned out differently had Morris been well after the war and married her. And Dave's life—would it, too, have taken a decidedly different turn if Morris was still living?

Presently the Cadillac crossed a small, shaky-looking bridge and rolled past the spiked gates of the cemetery. The chauffeur put his hat back on before jumping outside the car to open the door for Dave.

Dave helped Laura out of the ear. He noticed for the first time the single, long-stemmed rose she held. "It's this way," he said, and they started walking in the direction of the cemetery office.

From the parking lot past the cemetery office to the family plot was a ten-minute walk. And soon they saw, near a curve where two roads joined, a monument with the name KOUSSEVITSKY carved into the stone. Morris' grave was the one next to Dave's grandmother's. Dave put his hand under Laura's elbow and guided her closer to Morris' footstone. They could see clearly now Morris' name in English and Hebrew, and the dates of his birth and death. The grave itself was covered with a thick bed of dark-green ivy.

"Morris," Dave heard Laura say softly. She reached down and brushed away a clump of dirt staining a corner of the footstone. "Oh, my poor Morrie," she said, falling to her knees. She dropped her bag and the rose beside her, and began caressing the footstone as if it were a man's head, his face. Then she rolled off her knees, resting her weight on one thigh, and, leaning over, she kissed the footstone.

Dave had never seen anyone mourn so passionately, and he took an involuntary step backward. He thought of asking Laura if she wanted to be left alone but found himself too curious to leave her. Then he watched incredulously as she rested her check against the footstone and extended her body parallel to the length of Morris' grave. He couldn't take his eyes away from her.

After a while, Laura sat up and turned to him. "Surely Morris is in a high sphere, and from there he may look down on earth and protect us," she said. She wasn't in the least self-conscious, her voice steady, and she wasn't crying either.

"Let me help you," he said, offering her his hand.

She took his hand and got to her feet.

He picked up her bag and the rose and handed them to her. She placed the rose next to Morris' name on the footstone. Then she closed her eyes. She had very long eyelashes. What was she thinking? What was she remembering? What wasn't she thinking?

And standing next to her, Dave couldn't help wondering if anyone, twenty-five years after his death, would visit his grave and mourn him with even a quarter of Laura's feeling. Would Sybil? She hadn't even called to thank him for the flowers, let alone to find out how he was feeling. Would his ex-wife? But that wasn't even a serious question. His daughter? No way. Would anyone?

He took Laura's hand again and held it tightly as they walked back to the parking lot. They did not say anything to each other. The chauffeur saluted them before opening the door.

On the way back to the city, Dave asked Laura if there was anything he could do for her, He meant giving her money, but he didn't say the word.

"But you have taken me to Morris' grave," she said, implying that that was quite enough.

"I mean besides that," he insisted.

"But that is all I have wanted since I have been in New York."

Then he asked if he might have her address in Italy. He occasionally went to Europe, he told her, and the next time he was in Italy perhaps he could see her. She gave him one of her husband's cards, but he could tell she wasn't counting on seeing him again.

Putting the card in his inner jacket pocket, Dave told himself he must try to be a better man—at the very least, a more attentive father. And if he couldn't make it with Sybil, really make it, he must soon begin looking for someone else.

When they got back to the city, Laura asked to be let out on Park Avenue and 57th Street. Dave helped her from the car.

She took his hand. "Remember me from time to time as I will remember you and poor Morris," she said.

He kissed her again. "I'll remember you," he promised. "How could I not?"

***

That afternoon, Dave met with the assistant U.S. attorneys handling the congressman's case. Dave was up against three of them, and they took turns trying to wear him down. The assistant U.S. attorney who most wanted the congressman to serve a lengthy prison term had once cheated on an exam and had been suspended from law school. Dave brought up the law school incident Tuesday afternoon. It was a rough ploy, but it got Dave most of what he wanted for the congressman, and the deal was consummated Wednesday night.

A reporter who'd been tipped off about the plea-bargaining session cornered Dave outside the U.S. attorneys' offices. "You look beat, Counselor. Think you got your client a good deal?"

Dave felt exhausted, but he considered the reporter's question for almost a minute before answering. Then he said very deliberately, "I think I got my client a sweetheart of a deal."

Thursday's afternoon paper carried the story, with Dave's quote punctuating the key paragraph.

Professionally speaking, Dave was pleased with the deal he'd gotten the congressman. But reading Thursday's paper a second time Friday morning he experienced a sudden letdown. Guys who make sweetheart deals for crooks aren't the ones remembered twenty-five years after they're dead and gone, he told himself, nor do women like Laura caress their footstones as if it was the man's hair, his head, or his cherished face.

"Right, Laura?" Dave said. "Right, goddamn it? Right?"

Van

I served in the Army from 1958 through 1960—two years that, like a lucky pair of dice, fell between the Korean and Vietnam wars. Fate, history, whatever had conspired so that between the time I was drafted and the time I was discharged, America remained at peace. Although, just as I was concluding basic training at Fort Dix, some trouble did occur in Lebanon, and a rumor circulated that if President Eisenhower decided to send troops there, we'd be among the first to go. But the crisis passed, and I was assigned, instead, to Headquarters Company, 1st Radio, Broadcasting, and Leaflet Battalion, Fort Bragg, North Carolina. It was a soft, psywar unit, though our barracks were situated next to Special Forces', which even then was considered among the Army's elite fighting contingents.

I put my time in the military, coping with its pervasive boredom and chickenshit rules. Weekends, when I had enough money, I'd rent a hotel room Saturday afternoon in Fayetteville, the town about fifteen miles from Bragg, and spent most of the Saturday and Sunday there. Trying to unwind, I'd listen to the New York Philharmonic for two hours and fall asleep reading a book. I had my own john. Blessed privacy made Saturday and Sunday in Fayetteville the high spot of the week.

The town had recently built a new library of terra–cotta bricks and long, sun-splashed windows. There was a nearby copse of trees and a small stream. The side street where the library was located struck me as a kind of oasis among the neighboring bars, pizza joints, and movie houses strung like glaring light bulbs along the town's main drag.

It was in the library one Saturday afternoon during the spring of 1959 that I first noticed Van. He was a Vietnamese officer. Those years, a number of foreign officers were being sent to the Special Warfare Center School at Bragg. Among other things, they were taught the latest in counterinsurgency and the finer points of survival training.

Van was twenty-five then, a couple of years older than me, a slender man, about five-five. He was fascinated by our Civil War and read Bruce Catton, Douglas Southall Freeman, and just about anyone else who wrote about Jackson, Lee, Stuart, and Longstreet. The subject of good and honorable men fighting for a less than good and honorable cause obsessed him.

Waiting for the elevator to my hotel room later that afternoon, I saw Van coming out of the hotel's coffee shop. He was carrying a couple of library books. So was I. He nodded to me, and I nodded back. He'd probably noticed me in the library. Neither of us was wearing a uniform, and I didn't really know then if he was stationed at Bragg, whether he was an officer, or what country he came from. We were simply two guys in a dinky Army town who'd sought out Fayetteville's library and only decent hotel, the Prince Charles.

I ran into Van the following Monday, on my way down to the personnel section where I worked as a clerk. He was in uniform this time, a captain, and heading over to a nearby Special Warfare classroom. Recognizing me, he not only returned my salute but again offered that friendly nod we'd shared in the hotel lobby two days before.

The following Saturday, we got to talking. I was in the Fayetteville library, browsing near the shelves where they kept their most recent acquisitions when Van came over, said hello, and asked if I'd like to have a drink or some coffee with him. He spoke English surprisingly well.

Officers, foreign or otherwise, weren't in the habit of befriending lowly PFCs those days. "You're the first guy I've noticed from Bragg who not only likes to read but enjoys the privacy of a hotel room weekends," he explained. "I'm the same."

A kindred soul in the middle of nowhere? Maybe, and because I had another year to go at Bragg, I said, "I duck the bars in town because there are always fights. But coffee sounds fine."

He extended his hand. "Duong Van Thi, only call me 'Van,' it'll simplify things."

"Goren," I said, "Michael Goren," and we shook hands.

We went to the coffee shop in the Prince Charles. No one wore uniforms there, nor were any drunks from the 82nd Airborne looking to prove they were the toughest cowboys this side of the Iron Curtain.

Van said he'd attended and graduated from The Citadel, a military school down in South Carolina, which explained why he spoke English so well. His father was a general back in Saigon.

I asked if he missed being away from home.

Van smiled indulgently. "You know anything about Vietnam, Michael?" Christ, I didn't even know then it was south of China, let alone that it bordered Laos and Cambodia. "No, I'm sorry to say I know nothing of your country."

"The honcho running it, Diem, is a mandarin and patronizing, and his family is corrupt and greedy. I miss my wife like crazy, but the country not at all. In fact, I wish I could make a life for myself in the States, but that's impossible."

I told him, half-kiddingly, that in America anything was possible.

"How can I turn my back on my father?" Van asked painfully. "Also my mother's buried there, and my wife's family lives in Saigon. You know your General Lee was an upright man: He didn't believe in secession as a constitutional right, he wanted to abolish slavery, and he didn't even think the South would win without foreign intervention. But when he finally had to decide, he chose the state of Virginia, his forebears, his ancestry." It was a subject Van often returned to during the year he and I became close friends.

When he asked what I planned doing after I got out of the Army, I told him I'd probably wind up going to law school.

"Well, those guys are supposed to make big bucks, only what's the famous line—'Let's hang the lawyers first?'" and Van laughed good-naturedly.

I must have looked slightly pissed off, however, because he quickly added, "Only kidding, Michael, only kidding. I mean, I didn't write it. Blame Shakespeare."

I always remember the Sunday evening bus ride from Fayetteville back to Bragg as among the most forlorn of my life. It would take about an hour. You'd sit in a darkened, packed bus bouncing along, and once you reached the post, the driver would begin calling out, "503" or "415 MP's" or "Smoke Bomb Hill," as the bus snaked through the winding Army roads, depositing returning soldiers to their units. And my heart would contract as I walked back to the barracks, the hillbilly music, the petty harassment, KP and Guard Duty, the arbitrary decisions, bullshit inspections and GI parties— all the Mickey Mouse that made the peacetime Army the always potentially humiliating, monumental bore anyone who experienced it never forgets.

But that particular Sunday, I rode back to the base with Van in his 1941 Ford, and the Sunday evening loneliness I'd learned to anticipate no longer seemed quite so formidable.

"You pulling any details next weekend?" Van asked.

"I'll have to check the duty roster next few days, but I don't think so."

"I'll probably see you in town Saturday, then," he said.

"Thanks for the ride." I got out of the car, and he waved goodbye before heading over to the parking lot near his BOQ.

**

The following weekend, I had to pay a guy to take a Sunday KP for me to get off the base. That meant still having enough money for my hotel room, bus fare, and maybe two or three bucks left over for some bread, fruit, candy bars, and the Sunday *New York Times*. But that was okay, because getting off the post and doing exactly what I wished when I chose to do it meant everything to me.

Van was already in the library when I arrived there shortly after having checked into the hotel. It was three-thirty.

"Kind of late for you to get into town, isn't it?" he asked with a smile. We finished working Saturdays at twelve, and I usually ran back to the barracks, changed into my civvies, and caught the first available bus heading for Fayetteville.

"There was a last-minute switch, and I had KP tomorrow. It took a while and some persuasion to find someone willing to take it for me for twenty bucks." The usual price was ten.

He asked what I was doing for dinner that night, would I like to join him?

"Sorry, but those twenty bucks leaves me a little short."

"It's on me," Van offered.

"Thanks, but no thanks."

"At least for some coffee?"

"Sure." I liked him for offering to spring for dinner, and liked even more that he did not press me about accepting his first offer.

It was when we were walking back from the library to the hotel later that afternoon that we came across Sergeant Markowinski and Leslie.

Leonard Markowinski was the first sergeant of Headquarters Company, 1st RB&L.

"Hello, Michael," Leslie said. She was a striking blonde, who wore her hair long, and her eyes were a malachite green I've never seen before or since.

"Leslie," I said. "Hello, Sergeant Markowinski. This is my friend, Captain Thi."

"A pleasure to meet you, sir," Markowinski boomed out in his rich baritone. I don't exaggerate when I say that Markowinski had the bleached white teeth and flaring nostrils of a born paladin.

Van shook their hands, and we wished each other a pleasant weekend.

"Who are they?" Van asked, as we resumed our way back to the hotel.

"Markowinski's my first sergeant," I said. "Leslie's my wife. They're living together."

He stopped walking, looking at me to see if I was kidding. Then he smiled slowly, as if he still suspected I'd told a joke he'd somehow missed.

"My God, you're serious," Van finally said.

When I first met Markowinski, he almost immediately reminded me of Mr. Posner. Mr. Posner was a French teacher I'd had in junior high school. He had curly hair, luminous eyes, was handsome, brilliant, and charming. It was obvious even to a pimply thirteen-year-old that Mr. Posner should have been Secretary of State or writing stylish novels; or he should have been a Park Avenue surgeon or a dazzling Broadway actor. The great mystery was why a man possessing his many obvious gifts had settled for teaching junior high school students how to conjugate French verbs.

Well, Markowinski had that same fluorescent combination of looks, brains, and personality, and why he'd remained a sergeant in the peacetime Army was another mystery I never got around to solving. He was in his mid-thirties and twice divorced when he'd met Leslie and me in town shortly after we'd arrived at Bragg. Later, Leslie told me he'd looked her up within a month and they'd gone to bed the following week.

***

I could see that Van was still slightly stunned when we sat down in the coffee shop in the hotel. "Why don't you request a transfer to a different unit or to a different post?" he asked after the waitress brought our coffee. "I'm sure if you went to the chaplain, your battalion commander, someone in authority, and explained the situation, something could be done."

"I'm not going anywhere, Van," I said evenly. "I'm staying in 1st RB&L until my discharge, which is next June. Markowinski wants to request a transfer and move on, that's his business."

"How long has your wife been living with him?" Van got out a pack of cigarettes and lit up. I didn't smoke cigars then.

"About three months." It was ironic she'd left me to have an affair with a sergeant, a military man. We'd been married a year before I was drafted. I'd had a heart murmur as a kid and could have probably ducked the Army. But my father had sat out World War I, and I didn't wish my son to ever wonder about me as I'd occasionally wonder about my old man. So when I went for a physical, I never mentioned the murmur, and the Army doctors didn't find zilch. Although Leslie came to live with me off-post at Bragg after I'd finished basic, she never forgave my temporarily leaving her by going into the Army when I could have gotten out of it so easily.

"Is the reason you haven't transferred because you think she might return to you if you stick around?" Van asked, stubbing out his cigarette.

"You never know." Leslie was one of those chronically envious people who invariably thinks the folks next door have it better. She was also easily bored. It wasn't totally inconceivable that Markowinski would find her envy grating or her impatience insufferable. Keeping Leslie amused was a twenty-four-hour vocation.

I finished my coffee, which was a big improvement over that mud they served in the mess hall.

Van shuddered. "I don't think I could stand your situation, Michael."

"Markowinski doesn't think I can stand it either. 'I won't have to lift a finger, young trooper,' were his words. 'Knowing she's sleeping with me, not you, will drive you nuts, and after a couple of months you'll beg for a transfer.'"

Van shook his head in disbelief. "And you've decided to prove him wrong?"

"If it *fucking* kills me," I said.

***

A month later, Leslie called and said she wanted to meet Saturday about two in a parking lot behind one of the supermarkets in downtown Fayetteville. I freely confess I was stupid enough to hope that she and Markowinski were about to split up and she wanted me to take her back.

"Thanks for coming, Michael," she said, as I got in the car and sat beside her. A blue ribbon trailed in her hair. She was wearing a blue and pink striped sleeveless jersey. The down on her arms was silvery from the sun. It was pathetic—four innocuous words from her, and I was getting a hard-on.

"How are you, Leslie?" I said.

"Fine. How's your friend, Captain Thi? Did I pronounce it right?"

"Van? Nice guy. He's Vietnamese," and I told her all I knew about him. I was trying to conceal my nervousness. Of course, the more I kept talking, the more I kept hoping she was about to say she'd made a terrible mistake leaving me.

But what she said when I finally ran out of gas was, "I want a divorce, Michael. Leonard and I want to get married." Leslie gazed at me with those appealing green eyes, and for a second my heart seemed to stand still.

"The day after I get discharged and go home is the day I go to a lawyer and file for divorce," I repeated. I'd first told her that the morning she'd walked out on me, believing if I could keep to that date everything else in life after would be a cinch.

"I'm pregnant with Leonard's child," Leslie said reluctantly.

But I didn't believe her, as I hadn't believe her the time she lied when she first began sleeping with Markowinski before she left me.

"I'll take you to an obstetrician in Fayetteville," I said reasonably. "We'll tell him you think you're pregnant. Only the pregnancy results come to me. If you're pregnant.

I'll agree to a quick divorce, clean and simple. Otherwise, nothing doing until I'm out of the Army."

I suppose she'd tried to anticipate how I'd respond, and what I wound up saying wasn't a possibility that ever occurred to her, because she looked genuinely stunned. "You're just being willful and inflexible," she finally said. "They're your worst qualities, always were."

We'd been together, one way or another, since high school, and for all I knew she was absolutely right about identifying my worst faults. But they had nothing to do with this. "I'm not about to ever again be manipulated to suit your convenience, Leslie. The day after I get discharged, not twenty-four hours sooner."

"You know," she said confidingly, "as first sergeant Leonard could make your life rather miserable if he chose to."

I laughed. "How's he going to look, Leslie, if he messes around with me and I tell the IG my wife's been living with him for the last four months?"

"You bastard, you have an answer for everything, don't you?" she hissed. "Get out of here! Get out of my sight!" She switched on the ignition, and the car roared to life as I opened the door.

I watched as she drove away, her back wheels releasing an angry spray of small pebbles. Then, instead of meeting Van in the library, our Saturday afternoon rendezvous, I went back to the hotel. It was one thing to act tough sitting next to Leslie in her car. But alone, with no legitimate target off which to bounce my defiance, I felt empty and beaten, and in my hotel room it was difficult not to weep.

Van showed up there a couple of hours later. I must have appeared pretty shaky, because he almost immediately said, "You look ill, Michael, what's the matter?"

"I saw my wife this afternoon. She definitely wants a divorce so she can marry that prick Markowinski."

"Ah, my friend," he said sympathetically. "My friend."

I shrugged and laughed. What else was there to do? "I feel like getting a bottle of Scotch and tying one on."

Van nodded approvingly. "It's over, so divorce is better, a fresh start, Michael, a fresh start."

"You're right, I know you're right, only I'm not going down on their timetable."

He put his hand on my shoulder. Wanting to be helpful in a practical way, he said, "I'll get us a bottle. What's your brand, Michael—Chivas?"

We did not get drunk that afternoon but we certainly had more than a few, before going in Van's car to the Charcoal Steak House, which was the one decent restaurant near Bragg. Not only were the steaks delicious but they also served large salads as a main course plus all the bread you could handle. You ate on pink tablecloths, used a matching pink linen napkin, and the lighting was subdued and civilized. I used to think, "Civility never meant more to me."

During the months that followed, whenever Van thought I was having a particularly rough time, he'd insist on our going to the Charcoal Steak House. "You must keep up your strength, Michael," he'd say. I wouldn't discuss Leslie or my failed marriage those nights, or any nights. Rather, I'd get Van to tell me about Vietnam. He didn't require much encouragement, because his distrust of Diem and the coterie surrounding Diem was intense.

The way Van explained it, a 1954 agreement had been signed in Geneva to hold a general election in all of Vietnam two years later. But because the north, with its population of fifteen million, outnumbered the south's twelve million,

Diem, as the leader of the south, refused to sanction the election. The reason he gave was that the election in the north would have been rigged. But Van insisted the real reason was that Diem, an unpopular leader, would have lost, rigged election in the north or not.

"Diem has powerful friends here—Cardinal Spellman, Justice Douglas, Senator Mansfield—which explains why America supported Diem in his decision," Van said. "Don't get me wrong, Michael, those guys in the north aren't angels. But a great democracy like America shouldn't support frauds like Diem and his miserable brothers. It will all lead to disaster, and I'll be swept up by a current I won't be able to resist. My father helped Diem break a coup in 1955 and is still tortured by having had to shoot a rebel officer, whose brother was a close friend. He told me before I left for Bragg, 'Don't make my mistake.' But when I asked him how to avoid it he simply looked at me and said, 'I don't know, my son, I don't know.'"

I told Van that whatever happened, his good judgment and generous instincts would see him through.

He smiled patiently. "My father also has good judgment and generous instincts."

"You'll be okay, Van, I know it." I put my hand on his shoulder.

"Old friend, you wouldn't be slightly prejudiced?"

Van left Bragg the month I was discharged, returning to Vietnam in the summer of 1960, and we kept in touch by mail.

***

The day after I got home, I consulted one of my father's close friends, a lawyer, and began the process of obtaining a divorce. For a considerable time after, I avoided getting involved with another woman. I attended Columbia Law

School and worked my tail off. Made the *Law Review,* clerked for a famous federal judge from New York's Southern District, then joined a prestigious law firm, and was on my way.

During this period, the Vietnam War kept heating up. When Diem was overthrown and assassinated in the fall of 1963, Van wrote me, "Perhaps the country will rally around its new leaders, the Army." A day after the coup, in which his father had participated, the old man suffered a fatal heart attack. "As surely as the coup killed Diem and his brother Nhu," Van wrote, "it also killed my father, whose loyalties were strained beyond the breaking point. I think of you often, Michael, and of our weekends together in Fayetteville. They seem long ago and far away. Will we ever see each other again?" He was then a major, fighting in the Delta.

When the war reached its height, a famous picture appeared in many American newspapers. It showed a general attached to security summarily executing a young man thought to be a Vietcong agent on a Saigon street. As I recall, it was actually a sequence of pictures. In the first, you saw the general, partially bald, lifting his snub-nosed revolver; in the next, you saw him extending it, practically brushing the face of the VC suspect, who was much younger and had a full head of hair; in the third, the general has squeezed the trigger and the suspect starts to fall; in the last, the suspect lies on the ground, and the general, pistol in hand, can be seen looking down at him, expressionless. The pictures caused a storm of outrage when they appeared in the States.

In 1970, another, similar shot was published in the *New York Times.* Again, it showed a Vietnamese officer summarily executing a suspected VC on a Saigon street. This photo elicited much less mea culpa than the first set, no doubt because by then the American public had become inured to the horror of the Vietnam War. The officer in the second picture was my friend Van. I recognized him immediately, although his last name was misspelled in the caption. Van was then a colonel.

I wrote him the following day. I didn't mention seeing the picture. Instead, I stated that the war seemed to me irremediably lost, and the generals leading South Vietnam hopelessly inept and corrupt. Through my law work, I knew people in the State Department and in the Pentagon who owed me certain favors. If there was anything I could do to help Van and his family leave Vietnam and enter the States, I wrote, I was fully prepared to approach my influential contacts.

Less than a month later, I received his reply. "Of course," he wrote, "I remember your waiting anxiously for the *New York Times* to arrive in Fayetteville early Sunday afternoons, and the pleasure you radiated when the paper actually appeared. Your eyes, Michael, would absolutely light up. I mention this, because without your having said so, I knew that before you last wrote you'd seen my picture in the *Times*. Quite unflattering, if you ask me, and I am surprised that, of all papers, the august *Times* should have misspelled my name.

"This war, Michael, is more wretched than you can possibly imagine. My wife was assassinated by the VC a week before I shot the suspect in Saigon. They cut off her breasts and stuffed them in her mouth, which is how I found her in our bedroom. It is, of course, no excuse for my action.

"Your General Sherman once wrote that 'War is cruelty and you cannot refine it; and those who brought war into our country deserve all the curses and maledictions a people can pour out.' I naturally attempt to comfort myself with such sentiments. But they are like poultices, and what I require is quite different—a new heart.

"I tried to prepare myself for this trial as early as the time I spent at Bragg. But I have obviously failed, and I will not survive this war. I don't deserve to, and I no longer even wish to. When death comes, believe me, I will embrace it eagerly. Remember our friendship during an odd moment or two, dear Michael, and pray for my soul."

Of course, I wrote him again, immediately, "Here, Van, you'd be able to make a fresh start, a new beginning. As you told me the day Leslie asked for a divorce, it's over, done with, you must begin again. Your father is dead, your wife is dead, your country has lost its war and will soon be in shambles. Nor will the victors treat you with generosity. Come here where you will have a blank check on whatever money and influence I possess. Give me the word, dear Van, and I will turn Washington upside down to get you out as soon as possible, certainly before the Vietcong enter Saigon."

I regret to say that he did not answer my letter. Nor did he answer any of the others I wrote him that year. None were returned to the sender, does that mean Van received them? I've no way of knowing, but I've no doubt that he did not survive the war. He knew he was a marked man if the VC captured him. He would, I am certain, have taken his life first. Plus the opportunities to die under fire were so numerous during the last years of the war, Van would surely have found one that satisfied his deepest longing.

***

About a year after Van's last response, I received a letter from Leslie. She wrote that her husband, Sergeant Markowinski, was killed in Vietnam the previous year and she was now living in Portland, Oregon. It's a beautiful city, Leslie wrote, the air is clean, there are green mountains nearby and rivers clearer than crystal. If I ever got out that way, she'd be happy to see me, although she wasn't sure I'd want to see her. It was a long, chatty letter, broad with hints that we might even get it going again if I came.

I considered ignoring the letter. I hadn't seen or heard from her since our divorce in 1961, nor had I wished to. It had taken me ten years, but I was about to remarry—to a lawyer from the same firm, a terrific lady, smart, loving, good-looking, worldly. I was a lucky man, and I wasn't about to do anything so foolish as fly out to Portland.

But that didn't mean, I finally decided, Leslie didn't deserve a response. After all, her husband had been killed in Vietnam, and that must have been terrible for her. I wrote, offering my sympathy. No, I didn't often travel to the West Coast, I added. But I thanked her for the invitation and said if I ever did reach Portland, I'd be sure to look her up. I didn't mention that I was about to remarry.

***

Not too long ago, I had to go to Washington on business and found myself walking near the Vietnam Memorial. It was a beautiful spring morning. The forsythia were out, so were the daffodils and tulips. Clusters of visitors milled around the memorial. The visitors were mostly men who appeared ten years younger than me, men who, no doubt, had served in Vietnam. Occasionally, you'd see an older woman, alone or with her husband, only she did not walk among the different granite panels but stared inconsolably at a single name.

I thought about Van, and wished his name was on the monument. Then I recalled Leslie's letter, and, having some time to kill, began looking for Markowinski's name. There was no way I could have forgotten it, nor could I have possibly misspelled it. But the name was not where it should have been. I considered alternate spellings, searching back and forth among the monument's many black panels. I also considered that perhaps Leslie had misstated the year, and again retraced my steps. But try as hard as I could to find it, Leonard Markowinski's name simply was not on that monument. I must have appeared slightly frantic when I realized this, because people were beginning to look at me strangely.

Taking a deep breath, I made myself stand quietly in the leafy shadows, calming down but experiencing that same indelible emptiness I knew the day Leslie asked for a divorce and Van and I shared a bottle of Scotch. Because I never forgot that Van helped pull me through that long year at Bragg, it did not come as a complete surprise that after a while I could almost feel his hand, cupping my shoulder again. Van's touch was light, as always, and as always his words were unmistakably fraternal. "Hang in there, old friend," he kept saying. "It'll pass, it'll pass."

Garrison Revisited

Ned Molloy never did inquire how the Stolleys, mother and son, got his name. Perhaps they'd just flipped through the Yellow Pages until they came to "Investigators-Private," and the Irish-sounding Molloy caught their Waspish fancy. Of course, Ned's boxed-off advertisement did say he specialized in matrimonial cases—which included trailing one's spouse to see where he went, what he did, and with whom—but so did a lot of the other ads. Not that Molloy particularly cared how they came upon his name. Summoned to Mrs. Stolley's glittering Fifth Avenue apartment, Ned instantly realized that she could easily accommodate any slightly padded bill he might choose to submit.

Martha Stolley, it turned out, was the estranged wife of Harold Stolley, founder and chairman of the board Stolley and Associates, a leading New York advertising agency. She was one of those beautifully varnished women in her fifties you see stepping through the red door at Elizabeth Arden's for a facial, manicure, pedicure, and whatever other kind of cure they're offering these days in their never-ending war against oncoming age. Martha also had one of those thin, artistocratic noses that looked as if it had been pinched by a clothespin the day she was born, and a whispery voice that reminded Ned of Jackie O's. Not that she spoke a lot. In fact, Martha hardly said a word.

It was Peter, her only son, who did most of the talking. A stockbroker in his thirties, Peter wore a tie pin that held together the points of his blue shirt collar and a preppie striped tie. "Mrs. Stolley has been living estranged for almost two years," he told Ned, as if it wasn't Martha but another woman seated beside him on the claret-colored couch. "We're planning on her filing for divorce this fall. The grounds will be mental cruelty. Her husband's living with his current mistress, and our lawyers know all they need to about her and his several women over the years."

"Perhaps I missed something," Ned interrupted, "but it appears you already have more than enough verifiable grounds to file. Why call me in now?" Ned didn't want to seem impatient, but Peter, somehow coming on more like Martha's portfolio advisor than her son, made the detective slightly edgy. And while a vodka tonic, or any other cold drink, might have gone a long way toward helping Ned relax, neither Stolley thought to make the decent offer. Thank God their air conditioner was working, the living room unit humming in a purling monotone.

Peter Stolley frowned. He'd always been slightly bloodless, a trait that seemed to impress many of his Wall Street customers, although his father would invariably snap, "My God, Peter, you're worse than an overdose of Librium."

Suddenly, he cleared his throat. When Peter did that, even people he'd been boring for hours momentarily renewed their interest. "It seems that my father disappears every July fifteenth and sixteenth—simply vanishes—and this has been going on for as long as I can remember. No one knows where he goes or what he does. Not that we believe it will make a lot of difference, but July fifteenth and sixteenth are a loose end, so to speak, and we want to tie everything up before our lawyers file."

The job sounded simple enough now, although Ned was left only a week to do the required digging. Still, he nodded, telling them he charged $200 a day plus expenses. Peter immediately signed a $1,000 check as a retainer. He also gave Ned a picture of his father, as well as an index card listing the address of Harold Stolley's home and New York club.

"If you need any other information, don't hesitate to call," Martha Stolley added in her whispery voice.

Nodding again, Ned couldn't help fantasizing what it would be like going to bed with her. Married in his twenties but divorced before thirty, Ned hadn't lived with a woman for more than twenty years. Yet he believed he knew them better than he knew men, and he was sure that if Peter Pan wasn't around and he made a move, Martha would have been more than obliging. Frankly, though, Ned preferred his women with a little more meat to their bones. He would also have found it disconcerting hearing Martha, presumably experiencing an orgasm, moaning in that little girl's whispery voice. Maybe, Ned reflected, that's what compelled old Harold, God love him, to conquer other worlds.

In any case, Ned stood up now and shook hands with Mrs. Stolley and her son, saying he'd start working on their case next day and would certainly call if any pressing questions arose.

***

It was a typical, sweltering New York July afternoon; and though Central Park across the street looked lush with green, the sidewalk on exclusive Fifth Avenue had a baked quality, as shimmering heat waves rose off its burning stones. Coming out of the hummingly cool Stolly apartment, Ned felt as if he'd just been mugged with a discarded steam-bath towel, and in seconds, his fat face wore a garland of buttery sweat. "What I need is the coldest beer in town," he told himself, heading for a bar over on Madison Avenue and spinning the knob of his tie knot away from his pasty, confining collar.

Ned hadn't drunk in this particular bar in more that ten years, or when he was still a cop with the elite Special Investigating Unit, narcotic detectives who had city-wide jurisdiction. Like most of the other cops in SIU, Ned had been corrupted, but Internal Affairs couldn't lay a hand on him because he'd been more careful than the others—more careful, less greedy, and absolutely unapproachable about making a deal to save his own skin. When he told them he'd rather die than turn in a fellow cop, he meant it; and when he told them they'd have to prove he took a dime, let alone thousands of dollars, he meant that, too. And although he quit the force a year after the SIU scandal broke, because he'd never been convicted, or even indicted, getting a private-detective license from the sovereign state of New York proved no big deal.

While Ned's specialty of marital cases was an admittedly creepy way of making a buck, police work was all Ned knew, and getting the goods on cheating husbands and wives was a lot less confining than, say, employee theft or bodyguard protection. Even as a cop, he'd hated taking orders. But what was so great about being an SIU detective was that they operated almost like free-lancers, without supervision, yet they still belonged to a 30,000-member gang—a gang whose fraternity became obscene, Ned thought, when guys he shared coffee with decided they could only save themselves by throwing best friends to the wolves.

Ned quickly finished his beer and left. The bar, as did a hundred others in the city, still triggered too many bad memories. Splurging, Ned hailed a cab, which took him over to his West Side apartment. There he showered, then had a steak and salad sent up from the one neighborhood Broadway joint where his credit was still good. Dinner over, Ned took out Peter Stolley's $1,000 check, kissed it twice and then went to sleep dreaming the sweetest of middle-aged dreams – that one day soon, all his long-standing debts would be wiped clean.

***

The following morning found Ned patrolling Stolley's East Side apartment building. Stolley, still twin to the figure he cut in the photo, was a tall, slender man in his early sixties, who wore aviator glasses and walked with a slight limp. A chauffeured limousine took him down to his Fiftieth Street office, behind which Ned could plainly see St. Patrick's gaunt spires reaching for the heavens.

That week, Ned learned that Stolley's current mistress was a coat buyer for Bloomie's. In addition, Ned learned that during the last approximately twenty years, Stolley had not only been conducting indiscreet affairs with at least that many women, but had also fired at least that many men.

His reputation was that of a ruthless, driven millionaire, for whom no one particularly seemed to have a good word– not his old doorman at Fifth Avenue, not the black guy with white sideburns who ran the mail room in his office, not any of his former mistresses who still lived in New York, not an ex-partner he'd forced out when business contracted in the recession of 1970. No one. Ned knew, because he'd asked them all.

Stolley was one of those self-made tycoons who ruled with fear, giving, as the saying goes, rather than getting ulcers. Yet in Madison Avenue's clubby advertising world, he was considered a major creative force, a master administrator, and a magician at the numbers. In short, as a businessman, he had no apparent weakness. Nor did he brook any; while he paid his people well, he was brutally demanding of their time.

Anyway, just nosing about the guy for a week was enough to make Ned thoroughly despise Stolley, and although he didn't usually develop a rooting interest, he hoped the dirt he'd get on the bastard would help Martha maybe squeeze another million out of his miserable hide.

Of course, Ned couldn't help speculating why a guy like Stolley, who flaunted his sexual excesses and didn't seem to care what anyone thought of him, would make such a mystery about disappearing for a couple of days. Was he trying to conceal a bizarre sexual assignation? A kind of annual celebration with an old, cherished girlfriend? Secret admission to a hospital for a variety of tests, the results of which he wanted no one to know? Visiting some relative—an aged mother or father, maybe a loony brother or sister in an asylum on his or her birthday? One guess, Ned supposed, was as good as another.

Through various contacts, he'd acquired copies of old checks and credit card statements Stolley had received for the month of July for the last five years. But the cagey fucker must have made only cash payments during July fifteenth and sixteenth, because he signed neither a check nor credit card voucher during those two days.

Thus having absolutely no indication where Stolley was headed, Ned had to be prepared for a variety of possibilities, although if Stolley left the city, it didn't figure he was going very far, not for two days. At least, then, Ned didn't have to pack a lot of clothes in his bag. But he did carry $500 in traveler's checks, and he made sure he had his American Express card with him in case he quickly needed to purchase an expensive airline ticket.

Ned had parked his car, a battered Chevy station wagon, outside Stolley's apartment building, and had been waiting for the millionaire to emerge since six that morning. He was sure Stolley hadn't left yet, because he'd hired another ex-cop to remain outside the building all night, with instructions to immediately call and follow him if Stolley should take off before six.

But it was almost ten when Stolley's limousine appeared. The chauffeur went inside, notifying Stolley he'd arrived, then returned to the car. Five minutes later, Stolley came out of the building. He carried a small leather overnight bag and was wearing a Ralph Lauren blue cotton shirt under a light tan summer jacket. It was the first time Ned had seen him without a tie. The chauffeur took Stolley's bag and placed it in the car. Then he handed the car keys to Stolley and tipped his peaked cap. Stolley hailed him a cab.

What a sweet guy, what a swell boss, Ned thought, reaching for a cigarette as Stolley slid behind the wheel. It wasn't as hot now as it had been those earlier July days, and Ned preferred his car windows rolled down to running the air conditioner, which wheezed as if it, not Ned, smoked far too many unfiltered cigarettes.

Stolley drove crosstown on Ninety-sixth, then up the West Side Drive, but it was no problem for an old pro like Ned keeping the shiny black Cadillac in full view. Stolley kept wheeling north on the Sawmill River Parkway, until he got to Tarrytown, turning left on the Taconic, and for a while, Ned wondered if their destination was Sing Sing. But he eliminated that quaint prison possibility when they barreled past the Ossining exit some twenty minutes later.

It was a beautiful summer's day, and the lower Hudson Valley through which they were driving seemed to soak up the friendly yellow sun like a tired old dog. Stolley was moving along at a pleasant fifty miles an hour now; he seemed in no rush to get anywhere, and Ned was almost beginning to enjoy the ride. Small purple wild flowers Ned didn't know the name of dotted the grass on either side of the Taconic, and he felt as if he was in the country. But then, any town outside of New York, including suburban Long Island, was country to Ned.

Presently, they crossed over one of the Croton Reservoirs and continued north, then west, until they reached Route Nine. But they turned abruptly off the highway when they got to the coastal town of Garrison, where the gray, fortress-like buildings of West Point punctuated the bluffs high on the other side of the Hudson. Parking his car in front of a small two-story hotel near the littoral, Stolley got out of the Cadillac and carried his bag inside.

Ned had parked a block away and waited until Stolley went into the hotel before he left his station wagon. Guessing that Stolley was meeting a woman, he gave him perhaps ten minutes to check in, then entered the hotel himself without his bag, asking the white-haired lady sweeping behind the desk if he could have a room for the next two days.

"Why of course," she said, surprised but pleased.

Offered the register, Ned noted that Stolley, who'd been given room number five on the second floor, had signed his real name. Ned was also given a room on the second floor, number eight. No one else had signed the register today or yesterday, and Ned naturally reasoned that Stolley's mysterious lady friend hadn't arrived yet.

The lobby seemed pleasant, but not terribly prepossessing. The windows had starched white curtains and the floor was covered by a Persian rug, worn at the edges. Framed pictures of soldiers from Revolutionary times to the present hung behind the desk, and there was a huge map of the United States at the time of the Civil War tacked to the far wall.

Ned asked for his key, saying he'd either get his bag right away or take a nice walk around town.

The woman behind the desk, who identified herself as the hotel owner, said there was a bar a few blocks away facing the river that served sandwiches and beer; Ned might try there for lunch.

While he was still talking to the woman, Stolley came down the stairs. Stolley was no longer wearing his jacket, just that Ralph Lauren shirt and a pair of gray trousers. He nodded to the woman before stepping outside. "I think I just may see about that beer," Ned said with a nervous smile.

But he needn't have hurried, because Stolley only went as far as sitting himself in a high white chair under a blossoming cedar in front of the hotel. When Stolley glanced at his watch, it was obvious he was waiting for someone although for a high-powered businessman unused to waiting he didn't seem in a particularly impatient mood. Perhaps it was the sweet-smelling air, the majestic Hudson flowing past, or even the town of Garrison—a sleepy little river village, with a couple of antique stores, a bar or two, the hotel, a railroad station, and a brace of green hills rising behind the town's main street—that conspired to presumably calm Stolley's otherwise elevated blood pressure.

Getting into his car, Ned glanced at his own watch. It was almost 12:30. Reaching for a cigarette, he could still see Stolley in the white wooden chair, gazing out upon the luminous water.

***

It was almost an hour later when another black Cadillac parked outside the hotel. Stolley got to his feet. Two men Stolley's age emerged from the car. The shorter of the two looked vaguely Italian and had only one arm; an empty jacket sleeve hung limply at his left side. The second man smoked a pipe and wore a black patch over his right eye.

Stolley walked over to them, a huge grin creasing his otherwise ascetic-looking face. He threw his arms around the shorter man, then swung one hand on the shoulder of the guy wearing the eye patch, clapping his back fraternally.

Although the scene momentarily caught Ned unawares, he soon whipped out a miniature camera built into the false bottom of a cigarette lighter, and began snapping away.

Watching Stolley helping the two men with their bags into the hotel, Ned scratched his chin thoughtfully. Stolley limped, the shorter guy had only one arm, the pipe-smoker wore an eye patch—was that the connection between the three, Ned wondered? Then he wrote down the number of the Virginia license plate adorning the second Cadillac.

Ned's stomach rumbled twice, and he hoped his unholy trio was planning on going to lunch soon, maybe even to the bar the hotel owner had recommended to him earlier.

But when the men emerged from the hotel some ten minutes later, they walked away from the river and up a hilly street and Ned, hustling after them, cursed below his breath. The street was awfully steep, as steep as any Ned had ever seen, and he felt out of breath chasing them, hoping the lousy restaurant they sought was worth the arduous climb.

It wasn't a restaurant they were seeking, though, but a church, or rather, the little cemetery tucked behind the church, which was surrounded by a high iron fence filigreed with delicate-looking crosses. It was Stolley who opened the gate, after tossing his cigarette away, leading the other two into the cemetery. Ned watched them from behind a tree bordering the roadway outside the cemetery. He saw them approach a grave not too far from the fence.

The fellow with the eye patch took out a handkerchief, leaned over, and began cleaning the upright terra-cotta headstone at the head of the grave. Suddenly, the man with one arm fell to his knees, brought his armless jacket sleeve to his chest, grasped it with his good hand, and began to pray. The guy with the eye patch lowered his head. Only Stolley stood erect, his arms folded across his chest, in a studied effort at maintaining complete control. Ned took pictures of them, both singly and together.

After a while, Stolley and the guy with the eye patch helped the one-armed man to his feet. But he was awfully stubby, built low to the ground, and they had to struggle for more than a minute before he was actually able to regain his balance.

Then Stolley took out a pack of cigarettes and passed it around. Each of the men lit up, even the pipe-smoker. When the one-armed guy started to cry, the other two glanced at the bell tower crowning the white clapboard church.

Ned's stomach began rumbling again, and he was sure that now they were smoking they'd soon leave the cemetery to get a bite to eat. But none of them seemed able to make the first move, and they continued standing near the grave, lighting up fresh cigarettes and talking in soft snatches to each other.

It was only after the bell in the church tower struck three times, brassy and clangorous, did the trio, without even glancing at each other, begin walking toward the iron gate.

As soon as they left, Ned hurried into the cemetery before he forgot the precise location of the terra-cotta headstone. The inscription on it read, "PFC Ralph Curran, November 1922—July 1944."

Snapping a picture of the headstone, Ned couldn't help remembering that in July 1944, he was a twenty-year-old military policeman directing traffic on one of the roads leading to St. Lo, the Normandy juncture of several major highways and a town taken only after bitter hedgerow fighting.

For Christ's sake, July '44, Ned thought, hurrying after Stolley and the others. Spotting them entering the hotel, Ned slowed down. He wondered where PFC Curran had been killed and in what manner. And he wondered how, if Curran had gotten it overseas, he'd come to be buried in the sleepy river village of Garrison.

Sighing, Ned got his overnight bag from the station wagon and went up to his hotel room. Although he still hadn't eaten, for some reason, he was no longer hungry. If Stolley and the others had plans that afternoon, they were free to indulge them without being espied upon by the private detective. Ned felt unaccountably bushed, and now only wanted to get off his feet. Before six, he'd plant himself outside the hotel, letting Stolley and the others lead him to dinner. They had to eat sometime; and where they'd eat, he'd eat. And if Stolley spotted him and grew suspicious, well, fuck it.

Although the meaning wasn't yet clear to him, Ned knew he'd gotten what he came for. And stretching out on the sagging metal-framed bed, the stately Hudson lapping against the shoreline below his window, Ned thought, I must be getting too old for this private-eye shit.

***

That evening, Ned followed Stolley and company in his car, threading four winding roads in the hills above Garrison. They headed north. While it was still light, Stolley pulled up near a Victorian gingerbread house that had obviously been converted into a restaurant. There was an elliptic-shaped pond in front of the building, and a dense line of dark trees circling it. People were eating along the veranda, and the flickering candles on their tables, as well as the distinctive sound of silver clicking against bone china, seemed almost magical in a bosky setting Lee or Grant, wearing West Point gray, might have stumbled upon during a leisurely Sunday evening's canter. Stepping out of his car slightly dazzled, Ned wondered if he'd need a reservation.

But after tipping the maitre d', it turned out Ned had little trouble on this Wednesday night acquiring a table not too far from Stolley's, in a high-ceilinged room where leather-bound books still graced mahogany shelves built into the four walls.

Two Queen Anne sideboards stood at either end of the room, and people sat in cushioned chairs ornamented with elegantly curved armrests.

A waiter snapped a match, lighting the candle at Ned's table. Ned had never heard of most of the dishes listed on the menu. He ordered what turned out to be stuffed mushrooms and steamed blue trout. Because, three tables away, Stolley and the others were drinking a bottle of chilled white wine, Ned opted for one, too, although he'd have preferred dark German beer. The waiter brought Ned a bottle of Chablis, slightly green and flinty-tasting.

Stolley and the others seemed much more relaxed now than when they'd been at the cemetery, and watching them chatting, Ned guessed they were probably catching up on each other's triumphs and disappointments since they'd last gotten together. Perhaps it was the wine, but Ned found himself wishing he had a very old friend, an Army buddy he might see once a year, to share a bottle with. It was impossible tonight of course, yet when Stolley had a bottle of brandy set before his table, Ned did the next best thing by ordering his own Remy Martin.

Presently, Stolley and the other two men stood up, brandy snifters in hand, and touched glasses. "To Ralph," Stolley said. "To Ralph," the others echoed; and Ned, caught on the wing of an almost irresistible impulse, had to restrain himself from standing up with them.

Stolley and his friends drank for the next two hours, or until all the brandy was gone. Ned tried to keep up with them, but unused to the internal glow of fine brandy, there was no way he could match them drink for drink. When, finally, their bottle was quite empty, Stolley settled their bill and they all got up to leave. They seemed slightly drunk. Perhaps, Ned thought, they knew from past experience they needed that much sauce to sleep the night of the day they visited Curran's grave.

Although Ned was up bright and early next morning, Stolley and the others didn't leave their hotel rooms until it was almost noon. They went to a drugstore halfway up the steep street leading to the church, where they ordered toast and black coffee. None of the three had shaved, and each looked as if a patch of fur still lined the inside of his mouth.

After finishing their toast and coffee, the trio returned to their rooms and brought down their luggage. Standing in front of the two Cadillacs, Stolley hugged each of his friends before the two men got into the car with the Virginia license plate and drove away. Stolley himself sat in the same white wooden chair facing the Hudson he'd been using when his friends showed up yesterday. Ned couldn't be sure, but he thought he saw Stolley's hands gripping the sides of the armrests until his knuckles were as white as the chair. Only then, when Stolley thought he was quite alone, did he begin to weep.

That night, Ned called Peter Stolley, telling him that it would take about two weeks to put all the pieces together, mostly because he needed to get his hands on some old government files.

While it wasn't news Peter particularly welcomed, there was nothing he could do about it, because Ned refused to tell him anything else, claiming it was unprofessional. Of course, the longer Ned milked the case, the better were his chances of charging more and getting away with it.

*   *   *

Next morning, Ned called a contact who still worked in the Pentagon and made arrangements to have photostats of Curran's and Stolley's 201 Files sent to him by the end of the week; he was sure they'd served in the Army together. The second call he made that morning was to Richmond. An hour later, he had the name of the owner of the Virginia Cadillac, Leo Woodward.

What Ned guessed, Curran's 201 File confirmed. In the Tuscan hills above Florence in the summer of 1944, Ralph Curran had flung himself on a rolling grenade, saving the lives of three of his comrades, Harold Stolley, Leo Woodward, and Salvatore Tommasina, each of whom was nonetheless wounded by grenade fragments. Stolley had part of his heel blown away, Woodward lost one eye, and Tommasina his left arm. Curran was, incidentally, awarded the Congressional Medal of Honor, posthumously.

There was no mention in either 201 File how his friends managed to get Curran's body transferred back to his hometown of Garrison. It certainly wasn't normal procedure. But Stolley was awfully rich and resourceful, and Ned guessed that a lot of money probably changed hands and a lot of pressure must have been applied.

Staring at the photos of the three ex-soldiers he'd taken up at Garrison, Ned couldn't help wondering what it was really like over the years, knowing that someone actually laid down his life for you.

As an MP, Ned had never seen one soldier die for another, but he remembered that when the Allies finally took St. Lo in July of 1944 and the Germans plastered the town with screaming 88s, an American general walked down the center of St. Lo's main street, directing troop movements with his cane. And when a sniper's bullet went through his right arm, the general merely transferred the cane to his left hand and continued about his business.

The gesture, unspeakably brave, lifted Ned's heart as no other that war. And if Ned could still recall his valiant general, he could imagine how much more vividly Stolley and his friends remembered their Curran. Yet if Curran belonged to them in a special way, maybe because circumstances had given Ned an intimate glimpse of their homage, Curran now belonged to Ned as well. And perhaps that explains why he almost wished he didn't have to tell Stolley's family about what he'd learned. But Ned was a professional who'd been given a retainer, he had bills to pay, and the Stolleys were good for another two, three thousand. He really had no choice.

***

When he arrived at Martha Stolley's Fifth Avenue apartment two days later, Ned was surprised that only Peter was there to receive his report. "My mother's visiting friends in Newport," Peter said. Funny, Ned, touching all bases, had spoken to her the previous day, and she never mentioned going to Newport. Martha, he guessed, had decided to take in a movie, not wishing to hear news she might find upsetting, although God alone knows what she could have possibly found upsetting after a thirty-odd-year marriage to Harold Stolley, to whom an extramarital affair was a daily occurrence, practically a given.

Anyway, clearing his throat, Ned decided to make it short and sweet. "Each July fifteenth," he said, "your father and two Army friends meet in Garrison, where they visit the grave of a buddy who threw himself on a German grenade, saving their lives. Then they drink a bottle of brandy, and they don't get up till twelve next day." Ned shrugged. "That's it, your father's two mysterious days away from New York."

At first, Peter thought the private detective was kidding. But after Ned filled in the details—naming names, citing dates—and showed Peter photos of his father, Tommasina, and Woodward standing near the white church before Curran's grave, Peter bit his lip and turned pale.

"No woman wearing leather and wielding a whip, no fag who's been blackmailing him for years, no terrible secret he's been trying to keep from everyone—shit!" Peter exclaimed, angrily sweeping the photos to the floor.

It was most uncharacteristic, yet because of Peter Stolley's bitter disappointment, Ned wondered if there'd be a problem collecting the remainder of his bill, which he now presented. But Peter surprised him a second time that day by saying, "I want the negatives of the photos you took, all your goddamn pictures, all your records, and a notarized statement that you will never tell anyone about your investigation of my father, and I will pay you not another three but six thousand dollars. You heard me—six!"

That was an awful lot of money for a private detective in his late fifties, who often found making ends meet a problem these last few years. Still, Ned couldn't help asking, "Why are you being so generous to me, Mr. Stolley?"

It was obvious that Peter didn't give a damn about Ned nor did he particularly wish to answer, but it was also obvious he couldn't control himself, because he blurted out, "Because I don't want anyone else ever knowing that the son of a bitch has a human side to him, even if he can only show it two days a year!"

Not too long ago, Ned, offended by Peter's nasty tone, might have reached across and slapped the stockbroker silly. But now, he simply offered his most cynical smile. Really, it was none of his business if Stolley's kid burned the negatives and his badly typed report. Just long as Peter boy paid the bill. And if he decided to reward Ned with a $3,000 bonus, why, that was just so much gravy. As for Martha, she knew Ned was coming today, and if she'd wanted to learn the truth, she should have hung around to receive it. In short, Ned felt he'd satisfied his professional obligations.

"I'll take all but a thousand in cash, Mr. Stolley," he said amiably. "No point in sharing the wealth with you know who."

Ned's desire to shortchange the IRS reassured Peter, who said, "You bet," in his best preppie style, and they arranged to meet Friday in Peter's Wall Street office.

After Friday, when Ned turned over his files and got his money, he had nothing further to do with either Peter or his mother, although that fall, he did see in the *News* a clutch of stories discussing a particularly smarmy divorce proceeding involving Harold and Martha Stolley.

* * *

There's really not much else to add, save that the following July fifteenth, Stolley, Woodward, and Tommasina got together up in Garrison and visited Curran's grave again. Although Tommasina and Woodward looked about the same, Stolley had aged considerably the past year. Perhaps his messy, public divorce had taken more out of him than he would have cared to admit.

It was Tommasina who caught Stolley when he seemed to lose his balance, tripping over his feet, as they were leaving the cemetery that afternoon. "For Christ's sake, Hal, you okay?"

"I'm fine, fine," Stolley said, reaching for a cigarette. "Let go, Sal! Let go, goddamn it!"

Although both Tommasina and Woodward worried he'd make it back to New York in one piece, let alone get through the day, Stolley seemed to recover his strength, for he more than held his own at the restaurant that night. And when they toasted Curran's memory with brandy, it was Stolley who stood up first, proposing the toast as he'd done the previous year.

Sitting two tables away, Ned Molloy was awfully glad to see Stolley not only making the effort but actually bouncing back, and he couldn't help murmuring, "Fuck you, Peter Pan!" Then he lifted his own brandy snifter and joined the trio in their toast, as he'd surreptitiously joined them in their tribute at the cemetery earlier that day.

IV. Friends and Family

The Boss's Son

❧

"YOU WANT TO BRING some coffee to my office, Kitty?" Dave Birnbaum asked his father's secretary.

"I've got to type this letter right away," she said. "Why not grab a cup and take the coffee yourself?"

Dave gave Kitty his bad eye, but, hunched over her electric typewriter, she ignored him. Gritting his teeth, Dave thought, "If the old man wasn't banging you every other night, gee, I'd paste you in the teeth."

Listening intently, Dave could hear his father, Louis Birnbaum, carving up a slow-paying customer over the phone. What, for Christ's sake, did the old man—a live wire, if ever there was one—see in a surly type like Kitty? Twice Dave had tried to put the knock on her, but the last time, his father told him to cut out the hatchet job. "When you're running this place, you'll fire the help. But I'm still number one. Which means, only when I don't like them they get the ax."

Muttering under his breath now, Dave walked away from Kitty's desk without even going through the motions of pouring coffee for himself. "Kitty, sweetheart," he thought, "you just better be married or out of here before the old man either croaks or retires."

Dave walked down the hall to his own office. His father kept him at some distance, as if Dave, too close, might get notions of crowding L. B.'s style. Peering into the offices he passed, Dave checked to see who was at the old grindstone and who hadn't yet showed. A clumsy walker, he almost bowled over one of the bookkeepers, who was on her way to the ladies' room.

"Good morning, Dave," the bookkeeper said, dancing out of harm's way.

"Hello, Rose," Dave muttered without apologizing.

When he reached his office, Dave began sifting through the day's mail. Under the glass on his desk was a colored photograph of his wife, Ruth, and their three-year-old daughter. Ruth was slim, sunburned and very pretty. She was nuzzling the child, whose laughter was so apparent, even now Dave swore he could hear the kid giggling. His father had hoped for a grandson and, for that reason, Dave had badly wanted his first child to be a daughter. When the obstetrician told him Ruth had given birth to a girl, Dave's initial reaction was, "Tough shit, L. B."

One of the letters Dave opened was from a friend, Milt Zeigler, with whom he grew up on Long Island but who now lived in Miami and was running his father's business. Dave had tried to get his friend special prices, but the old man had turned down the last order, saying, "For the prices they're willing to pay, they'd have to buy triple the volume."

"But Milt's a buddy of mine. Can't you make an exception?" Dave had asked.

"What am I running, a fraternity house or a dress business?"

Dave had grinned sheepishly. "I sort of promised the order to him on lower terms. You're going to make me look bad, Dad, Milt doesn't get it."

'Well, then, that'll be a good lesson for you," his father had said. "I've told you once, I've told you a thousand times—don't promise any son of a bitch a special price without asking me first."

Dave had made one last try. "Maybe we give him these goods at a lower price, it'll encourage him to give us a larger volume of business."

"Listen," his father had said, growing impatient, "I wrote the rulebook on who to give specials to and why. Do us both a favor, *pisher.* Learn how to read before you write."

Dave glanced at his friend's letter. Naturally, first thing, Milt reminded him of the promise Dave had made about the lower price; wrote that he was counting on it; wrote that if he didn't get it, this would put him in a terrible money bind.

"Can I help it," Dave sighed, "the old man doesn't listen to reason?" And feeling like a bastard, he shredded Milt's letter. Then he made a mental note to tell Miss Switchboard that, should buddy Milt call during the next year and a half, she was to say Dave was out on the road.

Rubbing one eye, he saw Kitty standing in the doorway of his office. He wondered how long she'd been giving him the pleasure of her company and whether she saw him dumping Milt's letter into his trusty wastebasket. "Yeah, Kitty?" he said.

She sounded like the voice of doom: "Your father wants to see you."

"What about?" he snapped. He hoped his abruptness didn't betray jumpy nerves.

Kitty shrugged, but he suspected that she recognized his anxiety and enjoyed watching him squirm. Everyone squirmed when L. B. beckoned.

He hated asking her but couldn't help himself: "Is my father in a good mood?"

Kitty smiled maliciously. "He growled at me three times already, and that's one more than par for the course this early in the morning."

Groaning, Dave dismissed her with a wave of his hand. "I'll be in in a sec," he said.

As soon as Kitty left, he began to think of all the things his father might be angry about. But the truth was, his father was so unpredictable, Dave knew he was wasting his time trying to anticipate.

"Maybe the grouch just wants to pass the time of day with his sonny boy," Dave tried to tell himself. "Sure, sure, and some sweet morning, airplanes will fly flapping their wings."

Trying to look extra relaxed, he walked down the hall to his father's office. He took it for a good sign when he saw that the old man was dressed for golf. L.B. wore white loafers, sky-blue trousers and a pink cotton shirt with a soft collar open at the throat. He was almost sixty and had a paunch, but the flesh around his face was taut and when he wanted to turn on the charm, he seemed a much younger man.

Arthur Goldfarb, his administrative right hand, was sitting in the old man's office.

"Come on in, Dave," his father said softly, making himself comfortable behind his large mahogany desk.

Dave expected Arthur to excuse himself and leave father and son alone. But Arthur remained where he was sitting, though he looked as if he wished he was elsewhere.

"Did you want to see me for something, Dad?" Dave asked brightly.

"All right, Arthur, tell big shot here what you just told me," Louis Birnbaum said, gritting his teeth.

Arthur grimaced. A drop of sweat had popped off his forehead. "Louis, please—"

"Tell him!" Louis ordered.

Arthur took a deep breath. "Well, we have this buyer from Houston," he began. "He's flying to New York today and I wanted to set him up with a girl tonight."

"That goddamn call girl!" flashed through Dave's mind.

"Anyway," Arthur continued, "I just spoke to this girl we usually use for out-of-town buyers and she refused to have any part of the deal. And when I asked her why, she said the guy I sent her last week wouldn't give her the hundred she asked for but left only a fifty-dollar bill."

Though he was still on his feet, Dave felt as if he'd just had his legs knocked out from under him.

He heard Arthur saying, "I never sent her any guy last week, so I didn't have the faintest idea who she was talking about. 'Describe him,' I said to her. 'He's young, less than thirty,' she said, 'only he looks older, 'cause he's almost bald and has a paunch.'"

"Could I speak to you alone, Dad?" Dave said barely above a whisper.

"Well, Artie, my flesh and blood wants to speak to me alone," Louis said with a tight smile.

Arthur gave L. B. his best there-was-nothing-else-I-could-do-but-tell-you expression. Then he stood up and started for the door.

"But remember what I told you," Louis called out after him. "I want you to put a lock on your desk drawer where you keep the black book. And I don't want just any son of a bitch have a key to that lock, just you and me." And here, Louis nodded for emphasis. "Close the door after you, Arthur. Didn't you hear, sonny boy wants a private chat with his poppa."

Sitting down, Dave heard the door close softly behind him. "That tramp," he thought. "Fifty was more than enough for what she had to give away." When the girl had asked for a hundred, Dave thought sure she was trying to take him for double her usual price. How the hell was he to figure she was telling the truth?

Trying to look sincere, Dave said, "I didn't want to have to tell you this, Dad, but I've been having bad bedroom troubles with Ruthie."

"You're a liar, and that's bad enough!" his father shouted. "But what's worse is, you're not even a good liar!"

"No matter what I did, you didn't have to tell Arthur to pull the switch on me!" Dave shouted back. "You sure could have done it yourself, damn it!"

"You had it coming to you, sneaking into his office and getting caught going through his drawer."

"All right, so I cheated a little on Ruthie," Dave admitted. "What's so terrible?"

"I don't care you cheated on your wife!" the old man exploded again.

Dave was confused. "So what are you mad about, then?"

"I'm mad that you got caught sneaking into Arthur's drawer simply because you wouldn't pay what the girl asked."

"I thought she was trying to con me out of an extra fifty."

"So what, even if she was?" Louis answered. "You didn't want it to get back to Arthur or me you sneaked into his drawer, but by antagonizing the girl, you practically begged her to blow the whistle on you. Jesus Christ, is that so hard to figure out?"

"She wasn't worth a hundred," Dave insisted.

"You want to play and get away with it, you pay, you pay," Louis said. "What the hell makes you think you're so different you don't have to pay?"

What made him think he was different? A good question.

Looking for it, Dave spotted the photograph of his brother, Leo, on his father's desk. Leo was a physicist who lived on the West Coast, or as far away as he could get from Louis, yet the old man loved and respected Leo more than anyone else in the world.

"All right, so I can't figure out everything in advance," Dave said after a while. "All right, so I don't have a big brain like Leo."

"Leo? Leo?" Louis repeated. And it was obvious that he resented Dave's even daring to compare himself to his older brother.

Stung by his father's tone, Dave couldn't contain himself. "What the hell does Leo ever do for you? Does he write you? Call you? Does he know you're living, for God's sake?"

"And what do you do for me?" Louis asked with a sigh.

"I at least try to please you; only the harder I try, the more you seem to resent me."

The old man winced, and Dave felt good knowing he'd nailed a sore spot.

"Look," Louis said, after glancing at his watch, "we'll talk more about this tomorrow. But I'm supposed to meet Freddy Plesser over at the club this afternoon and, if I'm to get there on time, I have to dictate some letters to Kitty now."

It was his father's habit to cut conversations short whenever the going got a little rough—rough for Louis, that is. In this way, L. B. won all the arguments, or, rather, never lost any. It was, Dave recognized, a sweet ploy; and he looked forward to the day he could pull that same stunt on *his* hired help.

Dave stood up. He figured he was lucky that his father had a golfing date that afternoon. "Just let the old bastard have a good round," Dave thought, "and life tomorrow'll be easier on both of us."

"I'll see you in the morning, then, Dad," Dave said, grateful he was getting off this cheap.

But his old man just nodded, as if saying goodbye to Dave now was asking a bit much.

Walking out of his father's office, Dave saw Kitty watching him from her desk. He wondered if she'd heard them and prayed that his father's voice didn't carry through the walls separating their offices. It was bad enough that Arthur Goldfarb knew all the dirty details. Would Artie keep them to himself? "He'd better," Dave thought. There was, however, the possibility Artie no longer knew how to protect his interests. What was the sense, when you came down to it, in his reporting Dave's misadventures to the old man? Didn't Artie realize that one day soon Dave would, in fact, take over the business? "And come that day, Artie, baby," Dave decided, "come that day, you get the ax even before I fire Kitty."

The prospect of bouncing Kitty and Artie Goldfarb cheered Dave up immeasurably; but still, when he reached his own office, he found that his legs were quivering, and he had to sit down quickly or risk falling to the floor. Two salesmen walked past his door, sharing a joke. Their pleasure seemed so genuine and innocent, Dave almost envied them. Almost.

The rest of the morning dragged. Dave kept to his office. Above all, he wanted to avoid bumping into Arthur Goldfarb. He thought about calling his wife and/or his mother, but nothing they could tell him would make him feel as good as knowing that one day he'd be able to fire any son of a bitch he felt like getting rid of.

After a while, he heard some of the help leaving for lunch. Though he didn't have much of an appetite, Dave ordered up some coffee and a sandwich from a delicatessen around the corner.

Putting the phone down, he spotted Rose, the bookkeeper, passing his office. She was carrying a box from Altman's. Dave guessed she was returning a dress that was either too expensive or didn't fit well. Gee, for as long as he could remember, Rose had been working for his father.

Suddenly, Dave's phone rang. It was Milt Zeigler, his buddy from Miami. "Damn it!" Dave thought, after saying hello. He'd forgotten to tell Miss Switchboard he wasn't in to Milt for the duration.

"Did you get my letter?" Milt was asking.

"Sure, it's sitting in front of me right now."

"I'm sorry to bother you, Dave, but I'm really desperate for those dresses at the price you promised. I'm counting on you."

"Milt, I don't forget a promise to a friend," Dave said soothingly. "Of course, the old man is being a little rough about granting special prices these last few days, but I'll keep after him. And he'll come around, don't worry. Now, listen, old buddy, I'll get back to you on this either at the end of the week or, very latest, beginning of next week."

"Dave, I got a last chance to get these goods at a slightly higher price from someone else," Milt said. "You sure I can count on you to swing it with your father?"

"Absolutely, Milt," Dave said. He was goddamned if he was going to let himself get conned into admitting he couldn't deliver on a promise. "Don't give the other guy's price a second thought."

As soon as he hung up, Dave hustled out to the switchboard. "Sally," he told the redhead wearing the earphone, "Sally, don't ever put that bastard Zeigler through to me again. Ever. I'm always out to him. Always. You screw up on this, Sally, love, it's your neck. And I mean that. You better make a note to the girls who fill in for you during lunchtime, too, 'cause if anyone connects me to him, I'm holding you responsible."

Sally started to say how much she liked and needed her job, but Dave, spotting Arthur Goldfarb at the other end of the hall, broke away from the switchboard and hustled back to the privileged sanctuary of his office.

His sandwich and coffee arrived ten minutes later. He ate, looking out the second-story window, watching the pretty girls in their miniskirts. A blonde with long hair, who seemed as if she were carrying a pair of frightened mice inside her blouse, crossed the street, and Dave licked his lips. He even began to eat with an appetite, and though the coffee tasted like iodine, he savored every last drop.

After lunch, he finished going through his mail. He made a couple of unimportant business calls. More than an hour passed. Knowing that the odds were that Arthur Goldfarb was out to lunch, he risked going into the hall for a drink of water. That's when he spotted Rose, carrying a shopping bag from Altman's, on her way back to bookkeeping.

Frowning, he said. "You got a sec, Rose? I'd like to talk to you in my office."

Rose had curly hair that was dyed blonde. Though she couldn't have been more than in her early thirties, she was already beginning to put on some weight. She wore a wedding ring. Did she have children? Dave didn't know.

"Listen, Rose," he said, facing her in his office. "We give our people an hour for lunch. We don't ask you to sign any time sheet or punch any time card. Which means we trust you. Don't abuse that trust, Rose."

"I'm sorry, Dave, it won't happen again," she said, and looked as if she'd just eaten something disagreeable.

"It's painful for me to tell you something like this. But, Rose, one hour, that's it."

"It's just that I had to return something at Altman's and the lines were exceptionally long."

"OK, OK," he said. "Just wanted you to know how my father and I feel about it, Rose."

"Fine, Dave," Rose said, backing out of his office. "I can assure you, it won't happen again."

Chewing Rose out picked up Dave's spirits even more than seeing the pretty girls on the street. And contented with himself, he stayed behind his desk for the rest of the afternoon. He tried to keep busy. At three o'clock, he called his wife. At four o'clock, he called his mother. He would have slipped out and headed home early, except there was always the possibility the old man would call and ask to speak to him.

Five o'clock took its own sweet time showing up. Even then, Dave couldn't make a fast getaway. He still didn't want to bang into Arthur Goldfarb, so he pressed his nose against his office window and waited till he saw Arthur leaving the building. Behind him, he could hear some of the help rushing for the door, as if they were escaping from a prison.

Hell of a surprise he had when he spotted Goldfarb on the street walking next to Kitty. "That sneaky bastard," Dave muttered. Wide-eyed, he watched them cross the avenue together, then disappear inside the bar on the opposite corner.

"Louis takes an afternoon off, Artie goes after the old man's girl," flashed through Dave's mind. He tried to remember how long Goldfarb had been employed by his father; he knew it was more than twenty years, closer to twenty-five. "That's loyalty for you," he said to himself. "Some gratitude."

Dave wondered how the old man would react if he ratted on Arthur. Probably, L.B. would figure Dave was just getting back at Goldfarb for blowing the whistle on him earlier that day. Ratting wasn't the answer, then. Doing something was the answer. Doing something! What?

He knew Goldfarb had the upper hand between them and was in good enough with the old man to risk humiliating Dave if he either wanted or had to; yet Dave also knew that Artie was stepping way out of line by entertaining Kitty, for it was common knowledge in the office that Louis was having an affair with her. The question still was, what could Dave do about it? Better still, what would his father do in his shoes?

Ten minutes later, Dave left the office. He crossed the avenue and stood in front of the bar on the corner. Dave didn't relish the prospect of being humiliated, but blood is thicker than water, and the possibility that his old man was getting shafted infuriated him. If the old man could take a knife in the back, no one was safe. It was scary to think about.

Inhaling, Dave walked into the bar. He spotted the table where Kitty and Goldfarb were sitting and headed over in their direction.

"Looking for someone, Dave?" Goldfarb asked when Dave stood not a foot away from their table. Artie, who had a crewcut and red cheeks, liked his liquor and women. But he seemed neither guilty nor nervous that Dave had caught him with Kitty. Well, Artie Goldfarb hadn't managed to stick it out with the old man for close to twenty-five years without knowing how to handle himself when the going got a little tight.

"Actually, I was looking for Kitty," Dave said.

The girl stared at him. She had huge brown eyes and, though she liked to come on cool and tough, right now she looked frightened and vulnerable.

Dave said to her, "I need to buy a present for my wife tonight and could use a little feminine advice. So when I saw you and Artie dropping into the bar from my window, I thought I might impose and ask you to hop over to Altman's with me."

Kitty turned to Goldfarb. Obviously, she wanted him to tell her what to do.

Dave kept watching the girl while Goldfarb weighed the alternatives. It amazed Dave that he hadn't noticed Kitty's sexy eyes before this afternoon.

Though it seemed much longer, it didn't take ten seconds before Goldfarb said, with an easy laugh, "We were just having a quick one, and Dave does look like he needs a little help, Kitty. Why not go with him now? We'll have another drink some other time."

Kitty smiled. She seemed relieved at the clever way Goldfarb had made their having a drink together seem so casual.

"You're a good guy, Artie," Dave said. "Maybe sometime when you forget your wife's birthday, I'll be able to return the favor." He winked.

"It's been a hell of an interesting day." And Artie grinned, reminding Dave if he needed any reminding, that Artie knew all about shortchanging the call girl.

"Well, so long, Artie," Kitty said, getting up from the table.

"Peace, children," Artie said, reaching for his glass.

"It's swell of you to help me out like this," Dave told the girl.

"Glad to be of service," she said.

But when they arrived at Altman's, it turned out that that afternoon, the store had closed at 5:30, so the doors were already locked.

"I must have gotten the goddamn days confused," Dave said, apologizing for dragging Kitty away from the bar.

"Maybe Artie's still in the bar. Why don't we go back?" Kitty said.

Despite his father's high opinion of Kitty's intelligence, Dave never did think she was very bright. Or maybe by suggesting they return to the bar, she was saying, "I wouldn't dare tell you I want to go back there if Artie and me were really fooling around."

Not taking any chances, Dave said, "Let me treat you to a cab home, instead."

"That's not necessary," Kitty said,

"My pleasure."

Dave headed for the curb. There, he raised his right hand, flagging down a taxi that was about to swing up Fifth Avenue.

"Thanks for the help, anyway," he told Kitty. Then he closed the cab door behind her and slipped the driver a five-dollar bill.

"See you tomorrow," she said. Was she worried he'd tell his father he'd caught her having a drink with Artie? Dave couldn't decide.

Watching the cab drive away, Dave grinned. He felt pretty good about ending an almost disastrous working day on a positive note.

"Louis, baby. Louis, baby," he mused. "You think your precious Leo would have turned pimp for you like I just did?"

Every Other Sunday

After my father died, I made a point of visiting my mother every other Sunday. She had Hodgkin's disease and used to get IV shots of Velban every ten days, assuming her fickle white blood count could tolerate them. She lived in Forest Hills, I had an apartment in Manhattan, and it took an hour to get out there. I'd arrive about eleven, and when the weather was good and she was feeling up to it, she'd sit in a small park across the street from her building. I'd look for her and was always relieved when I saw her waiting for me because that meant she was feeling reasonably okay.

Often when I'd arrive at her front door, I'd smell the *cholent* she'd made. It's a beans-and-potato stew, some meat thrown in, which she'd let simmer overnight so that the potatoes would turn black. Talk about comfort food! The earthy smell used to drive me crazy, and I'd invariably smile after taking a series of deep, nourishing breaths. Usually we'd eat *cholent*, a small steak, and sliced tomatoes, three of my favorites.

"Ma, you could have made a fortune bottling and selling this stuff," I'd kid her.

She'd smile and shrug. "Grandma's *cholent* was better," she'd say, meaning her mom's.

"If it was, I'd have remembered," I insisted.

We usually ate around twelve-thirty, and to finesse our running out of things to say, we'd watch TV after. Mostly we'd watch the Yankee games. Barely a five-hundred club, they were an uninspired crew after the glory years of Maris and Mantle and before George Steinbrenner took over as owner, stocking the best damn team money could buy.

Watching the pre-Steinbrenner Yankees with my mother got to be sort of funny because she didn't know a thing about baseball.

"Ron Blomberg," she'd say, naming the team's first baseman. "Jewish?"

"He is," I'd tell her.

"Is he good?" she'd ask.

I'd laugh. "Not very."

My mother would moan exaggeratedly.

"That fellow Munson, he's always scowling," she'd say.

"Gee, say nice things about him, Ma. He's their best player."

"He looks like a good eater. I bet he'd like my *cholent.*"

"I bet he would," I'd say, laughing even louder.

Meanwhile, my team would be losing another close one, but I didn't really give a shit because my mother was having a good day.

One Sunday that summer I took her to a nearby restaurant. It was one of those dairy restaurants women who lived in Forest Hills and kept kosher went to and liked. The food was utterly nondescript, but my mother said she enjoyed the meal, and I was happy to see her finish her lunch. Happy, because since becoming ill my mother had lost a considerable amount of weight and didn't always feel like eating.

One of her so-called friends, Mrs. Litwin, stopped having anything to do with her soon after she became ill. It upset my mother badly, and at the restaurant she brought up Mrs. Litwin's name. "Would you believe she still crosses the street whenever she sees me as if Hodgkin's is contagious?"

"Come on, Ma, Mrs. Dorfman and Mrs. Korelitz remain good friends," I reminded her. "Screw Mrs. Litwin, think about the others."

My mother's face brightened. "I'm glad you mentioned Mrs. Korelitz," she said, "because that reminds me, she knows a pretty girl she thought you might like."

"Ma," I said, smiling, "how about some more coffee?"

"Eric, I worry about you," she said, the reason being I was in my mid-thirties and unmarried.

"Ma," I said in my deepest, most reassuring voice, "don't worry."

Two Sundays later, it rained all day. The Yankee game was postponed, there was nothing on TV worth seeing, and I wondered if we'd find enough to say to each other so that I could stick around without getting antsy until five, the usual hour I'd take off for the subway back to Manhattan.

It was after lunch, and I was sitting in my father's rocker, my mother half-lying, half-sitting up in bed. Her thin, drawn face made her large almost black eyes seem even larger. When I was a kid, I used to look into her eyes: they seemed like an infinitely soothing pool that I, her only child, could immerse myself in.

Trying to come up with an engaging subject, I said off the top of my head, "Tell me about how you and Dad met." Knowing that my parents didn't have a particularly good marriage, I probably shouldn't have broached the subject. On the other hand, I *was* curious, and maybe their initial encounter and what immediately followed might prove interesting.

Yet hearing me, my mother winced, and I thought, "Oh, hell, not such a great idea, after all,"

But then, after thinking about it a minute for some reason she decided to oblige me, and after propping her pillows, clearing her throat, and gathering her wits, here's what she told me.

***

"I never mentioned that your father first saw me in a restaurant that catered to the furriers on West Thirtieth Street? Well, it was April, 1929, and the city was surprisingly covered with ten inches of snow. It had been a beautiful spring afternoon the previous day, and people were stunned to wake up to white carpetted sidewalks the following morning.

"I didn't know it at the time, but your father and his brother Louie were already at the restaurant, sitting at a table near the cash register. It was a family-owned dairy place, run by my mother's first cousin, Ida Andron. They served gefilte fish, blintzes, potato pancakes. Their vegetables were overcooked, their desserts only so-so, but their soups were delicious.

"Ida was short and bustling, nosy and good-natured. She had curly, ringlet hair dyed a rusty red. She would gesture a lot with both hands when she spoke, and she had a high-pitched voice.

When I got to the restaurant, I remember I was wearing a sealskin coat and a white woolen cap. Ida was sitting behind the cash register, 'Boy, it's cold outside, Ida,' I told her, hanging up my coat on a rack that was really a metal pipe suspended between two tall wooden crates.

'Rachel, you had to work late tonight?' Ida asked me.

"I worked as a model and salesperson for this very nice furrier, Mr. Trumper. 'An old customer couldn't seem to make up her mind about the coat she wanted, and Mr. Trumper asked me to hang around until she decided,' I said.

"Then I took out this crumpled newspaper and presented it to Ida. It showed a picture taken of a smiling me that morning by a photographer from the *Sun,* me sitting in a nearby park, dressed for the snow and reading yesterday's paper. The caption mentioned my name and said not every New Yorker greeted last night's storm with dismay or displeasure.

"The photographer had stopped me while I was walking to work that morning, said I was a pretty girl and how would I like to appear in that afternoon's *Sun*. At first, I thought he was kidding. But he showed me his press credentials, insisted he was perfectly serious, and I thought, 'Oh, well, why not?'

"Evidently, your father's brother overheard me telling Ida about the photographer and, taking out his own copy of the *Sun*, began pointing to me while showing your father the picture.

"According to Ida, your father took one look at the picture, another at me, and was smitten. I'm sure she was exaggerating, Ida did like to dramatize; but that's the word she used, *smitten*.

"I of course knew nothing about your father's reaction at the time. Ida had one of her waiters bring me a bowl of barley soup, and it warmed me as I sat at one of the tables near the cash register.

"It seems that immediately after I left to go home, your father approached Ida and said, 'Excuse me, Mrs. Andron, but are you familiar with the young lady who just departed?'

"'Young lady? You mean my cousin Rachel?'

"'I think that's her name,' your father said. But to be sure they were talking about the same person, he added, 'Isn't her picture in today's *Sun?*'

"'Yes, that's Rachel,' Ida answered, beginning to catch on.

"'I was wondering, Mrs. Andron, if you'd consider it impolite of me to ask if she's married or engaged? And if neither, I was also wondering if you'd be able to give me her phone number?'

"Ida said she suppressed a knowing smile before saying, 'No, I don't think there's any special man in her life now. Of course I can't be sure. You never know about young, attractive women today. And besides, I'm not her mother although her mother is my first cousin Fanny.' Then, after maybe giving it ten seconds of additional thought, she jotted my phone number on the back of a blank restaurant check.

"Though Ida could, obviously, be impulsive, at least she restrained herself to wait until the brothers left before using the pay phone near her cash register to call me.

"We lived up in the Bronx then, about an hour's subway ride, and my mother answered the phone. 'Fanny, is Rachel home yet?' Ida asked. When I got to the phone, Ida said she hoped she hadn't done the wrong thing, but she'd given my phone number to an admirer who'd been sitting in the restaurant that night.

"'An admirer?' I said, not having the faintest idea who she was talking about.

"'I don't know what else to call him, Rachel. A very nice man, quiet, about forty, rich, owns his own hat business. He and his brother have been eating at my restaurant for a year. I think he's maybe a widower, Rachel.'

"I couldn't decide if I was pleased or annoyed, and asked where this fine fellow had been sitting, perhaps I might remember having noticed him. And though I did vaguely recall a face, I'd confused your father with his brother.

"'He's a little shorter than you, Rachel,' Ida said. She didn't want me to think she was touting Mr. Perfect, that would only have caused an inevitable letdown. Assuming, of course, your father did call and we'd get together.

"I thanked Ida for alerting me and asked to hear my mysterious admirer's name.

"'Harry Rosen,' Ida said and, as a lark, I thought to myself, 'Rachel Rosen. That doesn't sound too terrific.' And to tell the truth, it disappointed me that your father didn't also call the following day.

"When he finally phoned that weekend, he said he'd seen me in Ida's restaurant and had asked for my number, suggesting we meet at the same restaurant the following Wednesday for dinner. Meeting there, he knew, would put me at ease, or ease enough so that I'd find the nerve to risk one blind date. By the way, neither of us told Ida what would be happening Wednesday because, as I said, although she was benevolent, she was also terribly nosy."

Here my mother coughed and asked me to get her a glass of water. Going into the bathroom, I let the water run so that it would not only be cold but give her a little break, a pause. Surprised by how much she'd already told me, I think I needed a break, too.

***

After drinking the water a few minutes later, my mother perked up, saying, "Now where was I again, Eric? Oh, yeah, Ida's restaurant that Wednesday night.

"Your father arrived there early because he wanted to be in the position of approaching me rather than encouraging me to momentarily wonder if Mr. X sitting to my left or Mr. Y sitting to my right was the Harry Rosen who'd asked for my number.

"Me, I got there on time, after which your father quickly jumped up and introduced himself. Ida, no dummy, immediately realized what was happening and reacted with this complicated smile, suggesting she was glad we'd gotten together but was also a little hurt neither of us had confided in her.

"While we were eating, your father mentioned how old he was and what he did for a living. He'd been married, he said, but his wife had died a few years ago and the following year his only son, age three, had contracted polio and also died. He said, 'I tell you this not because I want you to feel sorry for me but because these are things you ought to know.' Then he asked me to tell him about myself. 'I've wanted to know since I saw you here and my brother showed me your picture in the *Sun*,' he said.

"Your father's nervous frankness appealed to me, and I told him I worked as a model and saleswoman for a furrier up the street. Also told him, and God only knows why, I'd once dreamed of becoming an opera singer and had taken singing lessons, even appeared on the radio a few times. I guess I was vain about it and showing off. Yet I shouldn't have, because although my singing teacher thought I had the voice and looks, too often my nerves betrayed me before going on. I'd literally become ill, eventually realizing I just didn't have what it took to perform.

"When your father nodded as if he understood, I appreciated his sympathy. His hair was wavy then. He had blue eyes, Eric, remember, and a bony nose. Yours is more like mine, thicker. He had a nice mouth and small hands. Smallest hands I'd ever seen on a man.

"After a while, your father asked if I ever went to the opera. I told him that, years ago, my singing teacher had taken me to the Met where we heard Caruso, one of the great thrills of my life. 'But I'm one of six,' I said, 'and help support my parents and younger sisters and brothers. So the Met's a little expensive for me now.'

"'I'm one of six, too,' your father said, and he seemed happy to learn we had that in common. 'Perhaps you'll let me take you to the Met soon.'

"I remember smiling, Eric, as if to say, let's wait and see how we both feel at the end of the evening.

"Anyway, at this point, Ida came over and asked how the food was. She couldn't resist.

"'The food is delicious as always,' your father said. And he tried to sound appreciative, but I could tell he was annoyed she'd intruded.

"Meanwhile, Ida was so charmed by what was happening, she kept hanging around and would only leave when it occurred to me to say, 'I have to be at work early tomorrow and should probably start getting ready to go home.'

"Your father signaled our waiter for the check. 'I hope you'll let me accompany you home,' he said.

"'Well, it's not exactly around the corner,' I told him. 'I live way up in the Bronx.'

"Smiling, your father said, 'That's nothing but a pleasant ride in a taxi. Besides, it's a beautiful spring night and I also once lived in the Bronx. So it'll be like going back to my old neighborhood.'

"He made no attempt to kiss me in the taxi but said. 'Please, Rachel, you really must let me take you to the Met. I'd like very much to.'

"Because dinner was okay and he seemed a gentleman, nice enough and I loved music, I found I couldn't say no, and your father suggested we make a date for the following Thursday.

"'But are you sure you can get tickets for Thursday?' I didn't want him putting himself in the possibly embarrassing position of promising tickets for a night that might already be sold out.

"Here your father smiled reassuringly. 'Not a problem,' he said with the perfect confidence of a man who wore a flashing stickpin and carried a roll of bills.'"

Suddenly my mother reached for the half-filled glass on her side table, finishing the water. "Give me a minute, Eric," she said, smiling. "I seemed to have temporarily run out of gas."

"Take as long as you want, Ma," I encouraged her because she looked as if, having gone this far, she was determined to finish what she'd started and I was even more curious now than when she'd begun.

"Want some more water?" I asked.

But she shook her head twice, then took a deep breath...

***

And resuming without wondering where she'd left off this time, my mother said, "Rich men loved taking well-appointed women to the Met those days; probably still do. In any case, your father must have gotten the best, most expensive seats available. Because after we entered the Met, we kept walking closer and closer to the stage. It was the old Met, Eric, a horseshoe-shaped theater on West Thirty-ninth Street, not the current one at Lincoln Center.

"I remember I wore my best dress, a burgundy velvet dinner one with long, tapered sleeves and a white satin collar.

"Soon the lights dimmed and the conductor's bobbing head appeared above the orchestra pit. The huge curtain slowly lifted, and we saw a Parisian garret of the 1830's, Puccini's *La Bohème*.

"That night, Rodolfo was sung by Beniamino Gigli, whose voice wasn't as virile as Caruso's. But Gigli phrased beautifully, and his high notes had a natural, unforced sweetness that completely won you over. I forget who Mimi was or the mezzo who sang Musetta. During the intermission, your father pointed out the famous banker Otto Kahn and Lieutenant Governor Lehman, who later became governor when FDR was elected president.

"I had never seen so many beautiful women and courtly men mingling together, talking and laughing. It was all quite dazzling—Gigli singing Rodolfo, hearing the great aria 'Musetta's Waltz,' the women's diamonds and pearls, the prosperous men so assured the way they comported themselves. The stock market crash was maybe six months away, but standing among the rich and powerful, who could possibly have forecast the *tsores* soon to descend and envelop so many?

"When Mimi died and Rodolfo cried out, the curtain fell to deafening applause and I felt tears coming to my eyes. Puccini once wrote a friend, 'I wish to make grownups cry,' and, boy, did he get to me that night.

"Your father suggested we hail a cab, then walk through Central Park. So we did, and it was one of those gorgeous spring nights when even the park's coppery green monuments seemed to preen and come to life.

"I told your father I'd never attended a performance as wonderful as the one we'd just seen.

"'It was beautiful,' your father said, 'but no more beautiful than you yourself.'

"Of course I figured he was working up his nerve, about to make a pass. But as we crossed a small, bow-style bridge near the center of the park, he said instead, 'I'd really like to get to know you better.'

"When I didn't answer or otherwise respond, he blurted out, 'I think I've fallen in love with you, Rachel, and want to marry you.'

"Well, his words just stunned me. 'But we hardly know each other,' I said.

"'Sure, exactly so,' he acknowledged, 'and that's why I just said I wanted us to get to know each other. How could you, a beautiful young woman, agree to marry me if you didn't get to know me better?'

"I'd had no idea the evening would take this abrupt, serious turn. Had he really proclaimed he wanted to marry me? Or was he simply trying to seduce me? He didn't seem the kind of man who'd glibly offer a proposal on such short notice.

"'I live on Central Park West, not far from here,' your father said. 'Why don't you come up to my apartment and we could talk, have a drink, or some coffee. It would make a real beginning, be a start for us.'

"I confess it occurred to me then that if I married him I'd be able to help my parents, maybe help put my youngest brother through college. Also, I was twenty-nine, had had a couple of marital chances but had passed them by, and twenty-nine was relatively old to be unmarried then. All this, and probably more that I don't remember, flashed through my mind.

"'Okay, I'll come up to your place for a few minutes,' I finally said, because it wasn't every night a wealthy manufacturer took me to the Met and less than an hour later proposed marriage, or seemed to. I still couldn't believe it.

"Coming out of the park, we crossed the street and soon found ourselves standing in front of a large apartment building that had an inner courtyard lit by two shiny globes of frosted glass. I was nervous when we entered the building despite the doorman tipping his cap and saying, 'Good evening, Mr. Rosen. Good evening, madame.'

"Riding up in the elevator, I wondered how his apartment was furnished, guessing that your father had retained some of his late wife's furniture. But, really, what did I know?

"It must have been close to midnight when we got up there, yet the apartment seemed to blaze with light as if we'd been expected. Your father wordlessly reached for my coat.

"A woman was dozing in the living room. She looked about sixty, had a Scandinavian's light coloring, and wore a dark dress with a starched white collar that seemed a kind of uniform. When she heard us moving toward her, she belatedly stood up and seemed surprised to see your father accompanied by a strange woman.

"'This is Mrs. Larson, my housekeeper,' your father said, clearing his throat. 'Mrs. Larson, this is my friend Rachel.' I think at that moment your father in his nervousness forgot my last name.

"Wishing us goodnight, Mrs. Larson quickly excused herself. Your father was still standing, I was sitting on a rose-colored couch under a large, circular mirror when I heard rather than saw someone running in bare feet behind me. It turned out to be a girl about ten, in pajamas. Her hair was cut in bangs, and she flung herself into your father's arms.

"'Daddy, Daddy!' she cried out, happy to see him.

"A second girl, perhaps two years younger than the first, also ran into the room, embracing your father and shouting, 'Daddy, Daddy, we're so glad you're home! We missed you!' Prettier than the older girl, she had puffy red cheeks.

"At first, I was bewildered, confused. Then it hit me that your father had two daughters, and bringing me here was his way of telling me what he couldn't bring himself to tell me at Ida's restaurant.

"Your father looked at me with a desperate expression, while his younger daughter buried her face in his hip and the older one stared, her expression that unmistakable combination of astonishment and anxiety a young girl experiences upon seeing a strange woman with her widowed father for the first time.

"I remember that the room seemed to contract, as I felt this distinct, unpleasant urge to get up and immediately leave without uttering a single word.

"But your father reached for my hand, saying, 'This is Sandra, my ten-year-old, and this is Arlene, who's seven.'"

And here my mother paused, wondering I suppose what else she might wish to add as a minute passed, then another.

Deciding otherwise, however, she abruptly said, "Well, that's it, Eric, how I not only met your father but learned he had two young daughters and realized if I married him I'd be a stepmother and trapped. Trapped, because it was a role I immediately understood I was totally unfit to assume."

***

Ten minutes later, I made us tea, and we sat drinking it in her kitchen, opposite a red cuckoo clock that my mother must have had forever, or at least since I was a kid.

"Your sisters and I didn't get along from the beginning," she recalled as if, having begun the story of her life, she couldn't on second thought just let everything come to a dead stop. "And two years after I married him, your father lost his business. Poor fellow, lost his first wife, then his first son, then his business all in five or six years. After that, he seemed unable to regain his resiliency, and who could blame him.

But after that, our marriage never really had a chance. We separated for a year when you were two, and only reconciled because I didn't have the courage to divorce him. I said I'd move back on the condition that we live near my family, no more than a block away. I needed to know they'd always be there, close by."

Taking a drink of tea, I nodded, telling myself, "This part of the story I know."

"I was a good mother, a good daughter, a good sister," my mother said, nodding to herself. "But I was a disappointed, unhappy wife and a lousy stepmother."

I also knew that, yet hearing my mother spell it out was disturbing, like seeing her naked for the first time when I was twenty.

"You weren't a good mother, Ma," I said, "but a terrific one. No kidding, A-plus."

I meant it, but was also trying to distract her and, although my mother smiled appreciatively, she said, "The truth hurts, but why kid you or myself at this stage of my life?"

I nodded again, realizing there was no further point in trying to distract her.

"You okay, Eric?" my mother asked, probably wishing she hadn't been so frank.

"I'm fine, Ma, fine," I assured her.

But that evening after I got home, I was far from okay and didn't feel like eating. I loved my mother and, not wishing to think about her having been unhappy, 1 poured myself a Scotch and put on some Haydn trios. I'd become very fond of Haydn. He's inventive without being self-indulgent, accessible without trying to ingratiate himself, moving without tugging at your heartstrings. My kind of composer, probably my kind of guy as well. In a word, I've found that drinking Scotch and listening to Haydn comforts me in a way drinking Scotch and listening to other composers rarely does.

But getting back to my parents, as I said, theirs was not a particularly happy marriage. Yet they do rest, next to each other, in one of those sprawling Jewish cemeteries out in Jersey, approximately a street's distance from where my mother's family is also buried.

"That's the way I wanted it," said my mother last time she was in the hospital. "Because my family will be near, they'll give me courage after I die, the way they gave me courage all their lives and the way you give me courage now."

I was holding her hand and could see her bony wrist, her network of blue veins. Yet despite her generous words, I was afraid to be alone with her and didn't myself feel very courageous just then. My mother was dying, and trying to think of something that would relieve my anxiety, I remembered all those losing Yankee games we'd watch together and the questions and funny comments my mother would make about the different players—Blomberg, Munson, Jerry Kenney, Gene Michael, Roy White, Bobby Murcer, Horace Clarke. Horace Clarke, who wore glasses and looked more like a college professor than a second baseman who could turn two.

And smiling, I thought, "You're the guy today, Horace, not Haydn nor a couple of shots of single malt. It's you and me, bud, and the night's young, so stick around."

And there I sat in my mother's hospital room up at Sloan-Kettering, remembering that Clarke was a switch-hitter, usually led off, not a big guy, stole something like twenty-five bases and batted around .250. Why'd I choose Clarke? Not only Munson but Bobby Murcer and Roy White were both far better players. Probably because Clarke and me were the same size, five-nine.

Meanwhile, my mother seemed to have drifted off to sleep, and, trying to be braver than I am, I kissed her, saying, "There's no other place I want to be tonight, Ma, so take your time, as long as you want, as long as you need."

A minute or two passed before Clarke nudged me. That's exactly the way it felt, as if someone nudged me.

"Tell her you love her and are never going to forget her," Clarke whispered encouragingly. "It'll make her happy."

I smiled, grateful to him for prompting me, then said what he'd suggested, word-for-word.

Badge Of Honor

Even at fourteen, Nora felt strange addressing the priest as "Uncle Peter." Though he insisted Nora call him that, Peter Corey was not really a friendly or loving man. Then there was the fact that he served on the Cardinal's staff as a financial administrator and had an office at St. Patrick's Cathedral, while Nora and her parents lived in a two-family house not far from the elevated subway tracks in Sunnyside. The vast differences separating herself from the priest were obvious to even someone as young as Nora. But she felt desperate and he was, after all, of her blood and marrow.

"I'm awfully sorry bothering you, Uncle Peter," she said, twisting one hand in the other. She was a thin but pretty girl, with green eyes and long black hair that highlighted her pale, bony face in an intensely dramatic way. They were sitting alone in her uncle's spartan office in the cathedral. There was an old-fashioned adding machine on his desk, next to a pearl-gray phone connecting him directly to the Cardinal. "It's my father, Uncle Peter," the girl was saying. "He's been impossible the last few weeks, punching my mother practically every other night. This happened once before, about six, seven years ago, and then it stopped. But now it's started again, and it seems to be going on forever."

The priest tried to maintain an impassive expression, but felt his heart contracting in a spasm of loathing. His brother, Michael, a detective with Safe and Loft, had a vicious temper even as a kid and his cop's reputation was that of a nasty man. And the priest, who considered himself an ambitious man of refined sensibilities, hated to be reminded of his brother's essential coarseness.

Though annoyed that his niece had thus thought to burden him, he had the wit to tell the girl, "I'm glad you came to see me, Nora. Of course, I'll have a word with your father. I'm sure you're not exaggerating, and though there's no excuse for his violence toward your mother, perhaps there's some explanation, some reason for his behavior." He looked up at his niece, offering his thin smile, and wondered if she caught each implication of his many-sided response.

For reasons she didn't understand, her uncle's words unsettled Nora, and biting her lip, she said, "Please don't tell my parents that I came to visit you about this. I'm not sure I should have, but I had to do something."

The priest put his glasses back on. He had a sharp nose and hardly any mouth to speak of—a scholar's face, a critic's aspect—and he gazed at his niece thoughtfully. In his way he was fond of Nora. Naturally, she attended parochial school, and Peter, making it his business once to look up her grades, was astonished to discover that Nora ranked in the top five percent of her class and had an IQ even higher than his own. A cum laude during his seminary days, the priest placed a high value on such matters as grades and tests.

"Don't worry, Nora, I won't tell your parents," he said reaching over and patting the girl's fine hands. "Leave it to me; I'll know how to handle this. You know, as a priest, I've had to deal with this sort of thing in the past." And he winked, trying to put the girl at her ease.

But the gesture, coming from so dry a man, struck Nora as faintly ludicrous, and she almost burst out laughing. Instead, she lowered her head, offering an attitude suggesting grateful respect.

Her uncle stood up now, signaling an end to their interview. When he took her hand, walking her to the door, she felt oddly touched, and impulsively kissed him on the cheek. He smelled of talcum powder.

"Now I don't want you worrying," he said, bidding her goodbye. "Your job is to maintain those wonderful high grades. Mine will be to attend this very week to the matter we've just discussed."

It was said with kindly authority, even verve, but closing the door and returning to his desk, the priest couldn't help grimacing. He was sure that some day his thuggish brother would shame him in the Cardinal's frosty eye. And how glad he was their parents weren't alive to witness this latest example of Michael's brutality. God knows, the insight didn't originate with the priest, but he believed that if his brother wasn't a cop, he'd have wound up behind bars, and it amazed Peter that he and Michael had been raised under the same pious roof.

Seeing his brother any time was a strain. But seeing him about the matter Nora had just brought to his attention would prove doubly so, and he was tempted to forget his promise to his niece. But duty beckoned, and what was a priest if not a man taught to respond nobly to the weight of freighted obligations.

***

Michael Corey picked up his brother outside the cathedral, and they drove to an empty lot in the Nineties, near where York Avenue begins. Michael was a solid six-footer, with a ruddy face. He had a wrestler's muscular neck and a drinker's bright red nose. His car stank of cheap cigars and when they parked, the priest lowered the window on his side to get a whiff of fresh air.

From where they were sitting, they could see the East River and Astoria on the far shore. When he was a teenager,

Michael and some beer-drinking buddies used to invade Astoria, looking for Greek kids to punch out. On a nearby handball court, the brothers saw a young man in a blue sweatsuit playing tennis against the wall, hitting the ball with the ferocity worthy of a Davis Cup participant.

"What's on your mind, Bishop?" Michael asked, looking up from the handball court. Though he was proud that his brother was a big shot priest working out of St. Paddy's, he didn't much care for Peter and enjoyed showing his disdain by calling him "Bishop."

"This is a difficult subject for me to discuss with you, Michael," Peter began, "but I feel I must. Never mind how, but it's come to my attention that you and Kathleen haven't been getting along well lately, and I wish to know if there's anything I can do to help. All marriages, I know, have their ups and downs, and I'm sure this trouble, too, will pass. But perhaps I can help make it pass more quickly."

The detective's face hardened. He should have known when his brother called, saying there was an urgent private matter he wished to discuss, it would be something as foolish and annoying as this. "You know, Peter, if you weren't a goddamn priest, I think I'd smack you, brother or no brother, messing in my private affairs like this. The only thing I'd really like to know is whether it was Kathleen or Nora who came to you with this packet of treacherous lies."

But ignoring his brother's question, the priest asked, "What's bothering you, Michael? Something happen with your work that perhaps upsets you? You know, if you gave yourself a chance to let me help you, you might find it comforting."

Here the priest slipped off his glasses and began polishing them. It was what he usually did when he didn't know what else to say or do. How he wished he was back in his office in the cathedral, where he felt totally safe and useful. Out among the flock, so to speak, as he was now with his brother, he'd always experienced a feeling of bewilderment and insecurity, and he wondered vaguely if the people he spoke to beyond the church building sensed his profound discomfort.

Shaking his head in disgust, Michael started the car. He got out a cigar and lit up without removing the cigar's red and gold brand. Then he released the brake and headed down York Avenue.

The priest sighed. He was afraid to ask his brother to put the cigar out, but the smell was making him truly nauseous, and he surreptitiously lowered the car window as far as it would go. He was somewhat disappointed but not really surprised by his brother's uncompromising hostility, although he did feel he'd done his duty and kept his promise to Nora. Hell, he hadn't yet met the man who could handle Michael.

"I deal with informers every day of the week," the cop was saying, as the car headed crosstown. "I need and use them, but I never forget what they are—rats! And Jesus Christ, to hear from the Bishop himself that I got a rat in my own house, living under the roof I provide, eating my bread and salt..." And he became so enraged by what he was saying that he tossed his vile-smelling cigar out the window.

"Thank God for small favors," the priest thought irreverently, as they turned down Fifth Avenue. But the cigar smell remained in the car and the priest resorted to breathing through his mouth until they finally reached the immense cathedral. The sight of the church, with its soaring steeples cleaving the heart of the metropolis, quickened Peter's faltering blood. "Even in the midst of their plenty, the rich and powerful need us," he reflected. He felt his spirit somewhat refreshed by this thought, and when he got out of his brother's car, he said, boldly for him. "Be kind to your family, Michael."

"Suck off!" the cop hissed, and the car's wheels spun away from the curb in a vicious snarl.

***

When Nora got home that afternoon from school, she found her mother weeping bitterly. Kathleen's face was puffy and she had the beginnings of a nasty "mouse" under her left eye. Nora didn't have to be told who had hit her mother, but she did want to know why, and pleading for her to stop crying, she asked, "But what did he say? He's got to have said something, mother."

Kathleen Corey got a grip on herself and blew her nose. Once a pretty woman, whose looks she'd passed on to Nora, Kathleen knew her face was an ugly mess that afternoon. "He walked in and just hauled off," she said, shaking her head in utter dismay. "It was only after he hit me that he said if I ever went to see his brother again about anything, he'd divorce me. No ifs, ands, or buts."

Nora felt like crawling into a hole and disappearing. But to mask her fear and guilt, she said, "He had the nerve to threaten you with divorce! My God, mother, you're the one who ought to divorce him! I mean, you ought to go out and find a lawyer today, now!"

"Divorce? Divorce?" Kathleen said, and pure horror infiltrated her voice. Although she wasn't a devout woman, she went to mass every Sunday and would sooner have died than be party to a divorce action. "I don't want you even mentioning that hateful word," she said, touching the bruise beneath her battered eye.

"Why don't we just leave him, then? Walk out?" Nora suggested. "Find ourselves an apartment, a new way of life? What he's doing to you is terrible, terrible, and no church could or would sanction your remaining with him." And talking about churches caused Nora to wince. A lot of good her going to see the priest had done. Oh, a lot of good!

Meanwhile, Kathleen sat there, a woman in her early forties going on sixty, as if she were seriously considering her daughter's suggestion. But she knew she would never leave Michael. She was too afraid of the unknown, of what life might be without him. She was a woman who'd wanted to be a good wife and the mother of many children, but only Nora was granted her. Still, she'd have considered life rich and fulfilling had her husband loved her and allowed her to do her daily chores in relative peace and quiet. It didn't seem too much to ask. But a month ago, Michael had been told by a superior he judged a fool that he'd never be considered for further promotion. Michael's humiliation was so great, he was unable to tell anyone, even Kathleen, although perhaps his battered psyche believed his repeated assaults were delivering that very message. But Kathleen wasn't a naturally curious person, and all she wished was for Michael to stop raining blows upon her battered head.

Yet her craven passivity offended Nora, who went into her room now, slamming the door shut. She wondered where her father was. Probably in a Queens Boulevard bar with some other detectives, getting filthy drunk and feeling like a hero because he'd given his unsuspecting wife a shiner without so much as a by-your-leave, madame. Rather than wind up like her mother, Nora knew she'd kill herself first. But she also knew she was indulging her anger now. The point was, her mother seemed lost, and what good were Nora's brains and high marks if they didn't help when it came to everyday life?

She thought and thought, but the best she came up with was getting in touch with Kevin Cunningham, her mother's brother, who'd been living in Costa Rica the last few years. Kevin had also been a cop, a corrupt detective who, when he heard that his partner in the narcotics division had been called to testify before a Federal grand jury, fled to Costa Rica that same night—a country that had no extradition treaty with the United States. Perhaps, Nora reasoned, if Kevin, who was fond of her mother, wrote her father, Michael might come to his senses. Kevin had been a cop, and Nora knew that while her father didn't like Kevin, he respected him. What was the worst her father could do, hit her mother in the other eye?

So that night she wrote Kevin, beginning in the traditional way, "Dear Kevin." She wondered if she should call him "uncle." But, remembering what little good calling Peter "uncle" had done, decided to leave the salutation as it was. "My father seems to be going through a difficult time and takes out whatever is bothering him on my mother. I'm very worried about her and was wondering if you could possibly write my father a letter. Perhaps if his peer, another cop, took an interest, he wouldn't feel the need to slap my mother around. I know that, alone, in Costa Rica, you must have plenty of your own problems, so please forgive in advance my asking you to become involved in something messy up here. But I don't know who else to turn to, and your sister needs help."

Next morning, without telling anyone, she mailed the letter. She wasn't sure of Kevin's response, if any, but just sitting around doing nothing struck Nora as the worst possible alternative, total defeat.

***

When he read the letter a week later, Kevin Cunningham turned pale. Some years ago, he'd found out that his brother-in-law had been banging Kathleen around, and Kevin had gone to him, saying, "You son of a bitch, you ever slap my sister again while I'm still around, I'll give you three in the head. Hell, she'd be better off a widow, collecting your pension and Social Security, than taking any more of your crap."

Michael had wanted no trouble from Kevin—the word about Kevin was he'd once shot to death a junkie who'd tried to blackmail him, then gone to Patsy's a half-hour later and washed down a plateful of veal and peppers with a bottle of Chianti. In any case, Michael told his brother-in-law there must have been some misunderstanding. He might have gotten drunk once or twice and lost his head, but that wasn't likely to happen again.

Kevin had been a detective with the Narcotic Division's Special Investigating Unit. During their heyday, a columnist from the *News* had called them "princes of the city." That was because they had jurisdiction in all five boroughs, chose their own targets, and roamed New York with the impunity and arrogance of paladins. Most of them were eventually busted for corruption, but in their prime, they made some incredible arrests. They would dress for the occasion, wearing leather or suede overcoats in January, tapered silk shirts and loafers with tassels during the summer. In those days, it was a ritual for SIU detectives to go to an expensive barber shop immediately after breaking a big case. There, luxuriating under a tent of hot towels, they were manicured, scented, pampered and had their boots polished. Until one or another of them talked, eventually implicating most of the others, they were practically a law unto themselves. Kevin was one of the few who had the foresight to flee just before it all unraveled, thus avoiding arrest, trial and imprisonment in a Federal penitentiary. In short, he was tough and smart, yet a man with a price still on his head.

Reading his niece's letter over a second time, he found himself muttering, "That mick bastard probably thinks just because I'm not in New York he can get away with banging Kathleen around."

Kevin wasn't tall, maybe five-nine, but he was built like a construction worker, with massive shoulders and forearms resembling tree trunks. He was in charge of security for a huge auto replacement-parts factory on the outskirts of San Jose. Fortunately, he'd learned Spanish, working alongside the junkies and stoolies in Spanish Harlem. Not that it was all that meaningful, but he had a facility for foreign languages, as well as a higher IQ than both the priest and Nora.

Despite his questionable reputation, Kevin never considered himself an evil man, and seeing an opportunity to do his sister a good turn, he immediately decided to return to New York incognito. Besides, not only was Kevin fond of Kathleen, but having introduced her to Michael, he felt partly responsible for their lousy marriage. So he'd face down his asshole of a brother-in-law, setting Michael straight a second time. He'd fly into New York, make contact with Michael and return to Costa Rica the following night. Getting a phony passport was no problem. Kevin would wear a beard and a wig. The only person who'd recognize him would be Michael, and that would occur when he removed the wig and beard. "I want the son of a bitch to look in my face," Kevin told himself. "I want him to see my eyes and know who he's fucking with."

***

He flew to New York three days later. His blessed mother, could she have risen from her final resting place in Calvary Cemetery, wouldn't have recognized her precious boyo when he stepped off the plane at Kennedy Airport.

Passing through customs was a breeze. Driving in a cab to a midtown hotel, Kevin looked out the car window excitedly. The streets seemed dirtier than he remembered, and the cabby, thinking Kevin a green out-of-towner, took a longer route getting to the hotel than was necessary: but the ride still thrilled Kevin, and he had the momentary but infinitely pleasant illusion that at long last he'd come home.

That night, though, he took no chances and had dinner sent up to his room. He went to sleep early. Next morning, while it was still dark and the streets deserted, Kevin hailed a cab and drove out to Sunnyside. He hoped to recognize Michael's car, jimmy the backdoor, and wait for his brother-in-law hunched over the floor in the rear of the auto. If he didn't recognize the car, he'd follow Michael, then force his way into the back seat just as his brother-in-law was settling himself behind the wheel. Because the second procedure was riskier, he preferred the first and, luckily, recognized Michael's fire-engine red Pontiac parked in front of the cop's house. Kevin hadn't lost the touch, and getting into the car was a cinch.

It was five in the morning, and he figured he had at least a three-hour wait. Though it was April, the air was chilly and Kevin, living in Costa Rica the last few years, was unaccustomed to the cold. Sitting in Michael's car reminded him of those pre-dawn stakeouts just before he and his partner collared an unwary suspect.

He was faintly amused at the recollection, but then quickly focused on the reason he was back in New York. His square sister, he knew, would never leave her jerk of a husband. "Kathleen, Kathleen," he thought, shaking his head. She'd been sending him packages of food every four, five months since he'd been in Costa Rica. Small earthen jugs of marmalade, jars of raw honey, tins of skinless sardines, kosher salamis that, the rabbis swore, wouldn't dare spoil in passage. The first time he'd received one of Kathleen's "CARE packages," he'd wept. Manly, tough Kevin, the rogue cop, cried like a baby. He'd wept only that once, but each package stirred fresh feelings of love for his foolish, passive sister. Because, who else in the wide world gave a royal shit whether he lived or died?

So, while it was cold and cramped slumped on the floor in Michael's foul-smelling car, it wasn't that cold, it wasn't that cramped. Kevin straightened his phony beard and wig. He wore a trench coat over a black turtleneck sweater. Because he wanted to be sure his arms had maximum freedom, he wore no burdensome jacket. He patted the shoulder holster containing his service revolver, which he'd sneaked out when he left the States and brought back with him last night. Without quite realizing it, he nodded off to sleep.

But his old cop's instincts still seemed to work, because as soon as Michael put the key into the car door, Kevin became instantly awake and alert, arranging himself so that if he had to make his move more quickly than he wished, he'd have as much maneuvering room as possible.

Sitting in the front seat, Michael cleared his throat and spit out the window, then lit one of his awful-smelling cigars. If Kevin had any lingering doubt he was in the right car, the sound of Michael's hawking and the smell of his cigar reassured him. "Christ, some stiffs never grow, never change," he thought.

When the car started moving, Kevin braced himself. He guessed they were spinning down Queens Boulevard now, on the way into Manhattan. He would make his presence known before they reached the Fifty-ninth Street Bridge, because Michael, startled either on the approach or on the bridge itself, might accidentally swerve and have an accident.

When they stopped for the next red light, Kevin eased the gun out of his holster, then quickly but quietly emerged from behind the seat, placing the cold nose of the revolver firmly against the base of Michael's thick skull. "You make any funny move, friend. I'll whack you out so fast you'll see your brains falling in your lap," he said, just loud enough for Michael to hear.

"What the hell is this, some kind of shakedown?" the cop said in a choked voice.

"When the light changes, you move with the other cars," Kevin told him. "We're going into Manhattan, then up to the Cloisters, where we can talk, just the two of us. I've got nothing to lose, so any monkey business, cocksucker, you're flapping your wings." To emphasize the point, Kevin pressed the nose of the gun harder against Michael's skull. Then, because he didn't want any pain-in-the-ass innocent bystander possibly becoming nosy or heroic, he said, "I'm going to lower the gun, friend, but you better believe it's out, the safety's off, and it won't be a contest if you reach for yours and try to swing around."

The voice was vaguely familiar, but Michael couldn't place it, and feeling sick to his stomach he stubbed out his morning cigar. He tried to remember a suspect who'd threatened him, or one he'd worked over unnecessarily, but none came readily to mind. Putting his foot gently on the gas, he drove in silence. At the next red light, he tried to get a good look at Kevin's face through the rearview mirror, but the beard and wig were totally convincing, and he did not recognize Kevin.

"After we go over the bridge, you're going to head up the FDR Drive, then turn off at the George Washington Bridge exit," Kevin directed. "And stop looking at me in the mirror. When I want you to know who I am, I'll tell you."

Deliberately murdering a New York policeman wasn't the smartest thing to do, because cops were merciless toward cop-killers. And the guy seated behind him, despite his threatening talk, seemed too knowing and professional to foolishly call down upon himself thirty-odd thousand other cops, or "the biggest fucking gang in the world," as one of Michael's Safe and Loft buddies fondly referred to them. So despite the fact he was frightened and guessed he wasn't going to like what was in the offing. whatever that was, Michael did not think he was going to die. Cops killed by hoods were those who committed an act of betrayal: but among his many sins, Michael had never knowingly gone that dumb, treacherous route.

He wished he knew what this was all about. Then perhaps things might be worked out minus the customary rough stuff. Probably it was a case of mistaken identity. Or perhaps a Mafia honcho wanted to talk a deal and had sent this conscientious hood in the backseat to fetch him. Oh, who the hell knew? And that was the trouble. Michael hadn't the faintest idea. In any case, he drove carefully following Kevin's directions to the letter.

When they reached the Cloisters, Kevin directed Michael to park in a lot near the museum, then get out of the car. "Leave the keys on the front seat." As soon as they emerged from the car. Kevin reached for Michael's gun and put it in his trench coat. Then he patted Michael down, feeling for a second, smaller weapon.

They were standing on a hill overlooking the fabled Hudson and the distant Palisades. "We're going to walk in the woods where we can talk," Kevin said. "You in front, me behind. Start walking; I'll tell you when to stop." They headed away from the river and into the trees which were still bare. The sun was out now but no buds yet greeted it. "Okay, we've gone far enough." Kevin said.

It was then, Kevin, gun in hand, swung, raking the side of Michael's face and knocking him to the ground.

Michael, stunned and bewildered, struggled to his feet. "What the hell?" he shouted. His pants near one knee was torn and his cheek felt sore and bruised.

"Look at me!" Kevin directed. "Look at me, cocksucker!"

Michael stared at his brother-in-law with ignorant eyes. "I wish the hell you'd tell me what this is all about, fellow," he said, patting his swollen cheek. No bones felt broken, but the skin beneath his trembling touch was hot and tender. "There's probably been some kind of misunderstanding."

"Misunderstanding, my ass," Kevin said, pulling the beard off and removing the wig.

"Kevin! Kevin!" Michael exclaimed. "What the hell are you doing here? You crazy? Man, they'll put you away for ten years, if they catch you!"

Kevin smiled at this incongruous show of concern on Michael's part, or was it surprise? But no matter, really, because using a compact, choppy motion, he smashed the gun into the other side of his brother-in-law's face, knocking him down a second time.

"What the hell's the matter with you?" Michael shouted. "The sun down there made you loco?" He got to his feet slowly, trying to figure out what Kevin was so teed-off about and why he was back in New York. But his brain drew a blank, and his head was starting to buzz with pain. While he was relieved that his assailant was Kevin—at least it wasn't some psycho—at the same time he recalled Kevin's reputation and felt a chill, like a blast of arctic air sweeping the length of his colon.

"Listen to me, you son of a bitch," Kevin said, grabbing him with one hand around the collar. "I ever hear that you hurt my sister again. I'll kill you. I'll put three in your thick head." And before Michael could show surprise or insist that Kevin had it all wrong, his brother-in-law smashed the gun barrel into his nose, producing an instant spurt of foaming blood. Kevin jerked Michael's head aside, so that the gushing crimson river did not stain his spotless trench coat. Then he swung the gun against the other side of Michael's nose, and this time he heard the bone breaking. It sounded like a thick sheet of cardboard being torn.

For a minute, Michael thought he was going to faint, and spinning wildly he fell to the ground. The humiliating taste of bile sprang to his mouth and he kept trying to swallow the bad taste away so that he would not vomit. How long he lay there he did not know, but after a while, he felt Kevin lifting his head.

"Open your eyes! Open your eyes!" Kevin said, shaking him until he obeyed. He was too afraid not to. "I won't be in New York after today, but I'll know the same night you hurt Kathleen. I came back yesterday. I'll come back again. You can count on it. The only reason I don't kill you now is that you're a brother cop: I owed you this warning. But that's all I owe you." Then he dropped Michael's head and practically heard it bounce. Before he left, Kevin added a last touch, a well-aimed kick that landed in Michael's rib cage, momentarily lifting him off the ground. Landing, Michael clutched his side with both hands, as if to plug a leak of hissing air.

***

Fifteen minutes later, Kevin took his brother-in-law's car and parked it near the cavernous bus terminal on upper Broadway. Then he grabbed a taxi and headed downtown to his hotel, where he packed, got some magazines from the news stand in the hotel lobby, and caught a second cab back out to Kennedy. Altogether he'd been in the city slightly more than 14 hours. He glanced at his watch. His plane to San Jose was due to take off in about an hour. His timing couldn't have been better, and sitting in the cab he pressed his back against the seat, sighing with satisfaction. It was the same feeling he used to get when he and a partner clinched an important case with a big collar.

Kevin checked in at the airport without any problems. God knows, it made good sense getting into and out of the city as quickly as possible. It would be harder leaving if he stayed a few days, and who could predict what Michael would say to his superiors.

A young, good-looking woman holding a little girl of two or three—Kevin, not being a father, never could tell about children's ages—sat next to him in the airport lobby. She, too, was flying to San Jose. Her husband, she told Kevin, was a mining engineer whose company had sent him down to Costa Rica for a year, and she and her daughter were joining him. It was her first trip out of the country.

Kevin told her that the people in Central America were friendly and parts of the countryside startlingly beautiful, and taking in the woman's fresh, all-American looks, he found himself envying the mining engineer. He was even sorrier he wasn't a father, and his heart gave a slight tug as he gazed at the woman's little girl, dressed in a salmon-colored jacket and matching corduroy pants. She had huge brown eyes, hair cut becomingly short and big cheeks, the kind fathers invariably pinch and kiss.

When the call came for the passengers to line up and board their plane, Kevin offered to help tote the woman's carryon luggage. She reminded him of a girl he had lived with for three years, when he first became a detective and got his gold shield.

"You're very kind, thanks," she said, lifting her child. She had chestnut-colored hair that skirted her shoulder and was smartly set off by a leather jacket. Long-legged, she stood perhaps two inches taller than Kevin.

Kevin couldn't resist patting her daughter's cheeks, and the child smiled in response. Then he leaned down for the mother's luggage. As Kevin began straightening up, the friendly child reached across and in one affectionate, sweeping motion knocked off Kevin's wig and pulled askew his false beard. Though the child giggled, the mother, staring at Kevin, couldn't help letting out a startled scream. Two custom agents, standing near the boarding tunnel to the plane, saw Kevin, his face deathly pale, reaching to retrieve the lost wig. They looked at each other, instantly realized they had a live one not twenty feet away, and quickly approached him without a word passing between them.

Kevin saw them out of the corner of his eye. He knew that if they detained him, they'd get around to taking his fingerprints, which meant he'd be arrested. Straightening up, he dropped the wig and began heading away from the milling passengers lining up to board the plane.

"Hey you, hold it!" one of the custom agents yelled at Kevin.

Glancing over his shoulder, he saw them breaking into a trot, and he, too, began running. He looked for a door, some exit, a corner to quickly turn and so possibly lose his pursuers. But none appeared, and glancing behind him a second time, he saw a Port Authority cop joining the chase. Sprinting wildly, Kevin told himself, "I will not spend one goddamn day in the slammer!"

Rounding a corner near a newsstand, Kevin saw an unsuspecting cop approaching him. Before the cop could react, Kevin knocked the guy down and grabbed his gun. Whirling, he got the drop on those chasing him, and they halted in their tracks. All around them people began shouting and diving for cover.

"Drop it! Drop it!" Kevin heard someone calling out behind him. "Put your hands behind your head, asshole, or I'll blow you away!" He knew it was a cop, because they'd all been taught to shout intimidating obscenities at the top of their lungs, and that's exactly what Kevin would have said in the other guy's place.

He thought the cop would have more sense than to try shooting him with so many innocent people around them, and he was counting on that when he whirled, hoping to get the first shot in. But the cop was an ambitious rookie and Kevin didn't know what hit him as two quick slugs tore the side of his head off.

***

Of course, the New York papers splashed the story across their front pages. Some police department higher-ups suggested that Kevin was in New York because he was part of a South American drug ring; they also hinted that it was known he was in the city, but he hadn't been arrested in the hope he'd lead them to bigger fish. All bullshit!

Only Michael Corey, lying in his Bellevue Hospital room knew the truth, and he wasn't talking. His brother, the priest, couldn't get over how terrible Michael looked. His face, from his forehead to his chin, seemed one huge patch of black and blue, punctuated by a nose that seemed to go off in four different directions. Two ribs were fractured; he was lucky they hadn't perforated his lungs. Michael had told his superiors he had no idea who'd worked him over; there were two of them and they wore ski masks. The probability was they were a couple of thugs paying him back for having been over-zealous in the lawful pursuit of his sworn duties. God knows, it made sense. New York was a violent town, and there were a lot of rough people roaming the streets— people it was dangerous to bang around, cop or no cop, and

Michael did have a street reputation for being both violent and tactless.

It was the day after he'd been admitted to Bellevue that Michael had learned what happened to Kevin. Kathleen and Nora told him. They were both in terrible shape. Because Michael couldn't possibly get out of the hospital, even if he'd wanted to, his brother took charge of Kevin's funeral. Peter, being Peter, felt as if he was soiling his hands; but, considering the circumstances and his vocation, he knew he had no choice but to perform a charitable act.

He visited Michael the day after the funeral. "That brother-in-law of yours was some piece of work." the priest said. "To return to New York knowing the FBI and Internal Affairs of the PD were still looking for him, what a fool! But to come back because he was involved in drug traffic meant he was worse than a fool. He was a degenerate!"

"You really think so, huh?" Michael said quietly. But his eyes suddenly blazed with outrage and could he have bounced off his bed, fists flying, the priest would have seen stars. Because how dare his brother say such things about a man he barely knew! How dare he assume a morally superior attitude that was totally insupportable!

"Why is it," Michael thought, "everyone really hates cops, and tears them apart given the slightest encouragement?" Clearing his throat, he asked the priest to close the door, there was something he wanted to tell him, something he had to tell him. It hurt to sit up, but Michael, twisting and turning, managed it after a struggle.

"Bishop, it wasn't a couple of asshole hoods who worked me over," he confessed. "It was Kevin, and the sole reason he came to New York was to beat the piss out of me because of the trouble I was giving Kathleen."

"Kevin?" the priest said, with a disbelieving groan. "Kevin did that to you?" He held one hand against his startled mouth. "Why are you telling me this?"

"Christ, you are my brother, even if you are a dumb-shit priest," Michael answered brutally.

"That's not what I meant," Peter said, smarting yet still trying to make sense of Michael's words. "Why didn't you tell the police who questioned you?"

Michael laughed bitterly. "I was questioned before I knew Kevin was killed, and talking about him then would have alerted them he was back in New York. What do you take me for? Rat on a cop who'd once been a great detective? And unlike many prima donna cops, never implicated others to save his own skin? Never was humiliated by a finger-pointing prosecutor before a grand jury? Never served a day of time? Rat on a detective most cops, me included, considered a hero? Flawed, but still a hero?"

"You mean he came to New York, risking arrest, just to beat you up?" the priest asked, still unable to believe his brother.

"I hate that prick for what he did to me a few days ago," Michael said. "But let's face it, Bishop, you and me, we wouldn't have come to New York from Costa Rica to help each other, or a sister."

"How do you know I wouldn't?" the priest protested, but suddenly felt as if Michael had casually stripped away his white collar and peered into his soul. "Why did you have to say something like that?"

"Oh, Peter, it's the truth, that's why, and it applies to both of us—both." Michael hadn't meant to hurt his brother's feelings; that wasn't the point. "Look, just don't call Kevin stupid, and, for God's sake, don't parrot that crap those newspaper reporters are writing. Okay?" His ribs were killing him, but it would have been unseemly, saying what he needed to say lying flat on his back.

Though the priest was surprised by the generous passion of Michael's words—frankly, he hadn't thought his brother had it in him—he found both Michael's logic and morality profoundly suspect, and his face must have reflected his skepticism.

"Peter, Peter, there are bad guys and there are really bad guys. Take it from someone who knows the difference," Michael said. "Kevin was in the first group, no matter what the big shots in the Department would like everyone to think."

Peter still wasn't sure that Michael was right, but when he left his brother's room, the disturbing possibility occurred to him that if Kevin hadn't turned out a corrupt cop, unlike Peter himself, he might have made a great priest.

It Felt Like A Slap

My appointment with Dr. Graber was for one-thirty, but he didn't get to me until two-fifteen. I'd felt better this last week but because my gut had been acting up, I'd decided to check in again. I'd had four colonoscopies with Graber, plus he'd treated me for a gallbladder attack a while back. Last time I saw him was four years ago.

Entering the examining room, he grinned. "When I spotted your name, Eric, I smiled."

I was two months' shy of eighty-three and, laughing, I said, "You didn't think I'd make it this long, right?"

At first, he didn't know how to respond. But after a minute, he winked. "I didn't think *I'd* make it this long."

Because I had twenty-odd years on him, I gave Graber points for not taking either of us too seriously.

After he listened to my song-and-dance, feeling around and sticking his finger up my ass, I inquired if he thought I needed another colonoscopy. He said colonoscopies weren't a great idea after the age of eighty and since I was starting to feel better and hadn't lost any weight, why not give it another ten days. He thought I'd be okay, but if I started feeling uncomfortable again to call, and we'd discuss what to do next.

"Okay with me if it's okay with you," I said, and why not? He'd not only successfully excised five polyps from my gut, but *New York* magazine kept naming him one of the city's best gastroenterologists. Besides, he was a guy I liked and trusted.

It was a sunny May day, a good one to be out and breathing, especially after leaving a doctor who often diagnosed patients with cancer. I caught the Third Avenue bus a block away. I'd lived longer than my mother, longer than my father; I had no legitimate span-of-life gripe.

Getting off the bus, I started walking toward First. East Eighty-sixth, a crosstown street dense with fast-food takeout and discount stores, is always crowded mid-afternoon and today was no exception. Suddenly, between Third and Second, I saw Marie Brombert walking toward me, saw her before she noticed me. The street was too crammed for either of us to veer off or do much else about it. She still wore her hair down to her shoulders but, as I kept getting closer, I could see it was pure white now. When our eyes finally locked, she looked stunned, then violently turned away as if I was the single worst guy she'd ever known.

She lived, I knew, four blocks from me, and we'd see each other, oh, about every five years. Once I spotted her in the nearby Barnes & Noble, another time in the supermarket at Eighty-ninth and First. Last time I saw her, she was talking to a panhandler on Lex near the stale entrance to the downtown subway station. Neither of us had acknowledged the other, ever said a word.

But today—the violence of her reaction making it singularly so—today was utterly different. And feeling as if I'd just been slapped, I had to literally restrain myself from grabbing her and saying, "Hey, after you broke up with me and got yourself in a jam, you asked for help and I came through, remember? Remember? So you don't have to say anything, but don't turn away as if you wished I'd never existed. Okay? Got it? Catch my meaning?" I was that incensed, pissed, so utterly furious I had a hard time sleeping that night.

Next day, I went crosstown to 106th between West End Avenue and Riverside Drive. It's where I go to calm down instead of entering a synagogue or engaging a shrink.

Although, if truth be known, I still couldn't stop thinking about Marie the whole damn week after she'd blown me off.

***

I was twenty-seven when we met, Marie maybe five years' younger. We were both assistant editors at a trade magazine called *Supermarket Merchandising*. The magazine was as boring as it sounded, but getting that job was a way to break into publishing.

The draft was still going strong. I'd served two years in the Army and had marked time another two years before meeting Marie. Marking time included driving from New York to California with a boyhood friend, Richie Graf. I'd taken driving lessons and was scheduled for a driver's test; but impatient Richie kept urging, "Oh, come on, Eric, fuck waiting around," until I finally, foolishly, said, "Well, okay, it's your car." Fortunately, I didn't kill him, me, or anyone else, although driving out to L.A., I was one nervous wreck. Coming back, no problem: I hit sixty, seventy MPH and couldn't have cared less.

Marie, from a small town outside Boston, had graduated from Barnard that June and landed the job at *Supermarket Merchandising* in October, a month after me. A dirty blonde then, she was a Philip Roth fan even before he'd written *Portnoy's Complaint.* I preferred Malamud who was, I thought, less talented but wrote stories like "The Magic Barrel" that I couldn't forget, stories that stuck to me, a guy also interested in writing short stories.

Marie's desk and mine were separated by a row of filing cabinets. I remember her once standing on a chair so that I could see her over those filing cabinets when she told me that Belmondo, her favorite actor, had an even more broken nose than mine. Marie often referenced movies, for which she had a passion: loved Truffaut's and Fellini's, Godard's and *Singin' in the Rain.* Anyway, seeing Marie's blue-green eyes bouncing above those filing cabinets, I fell for her.

The magazine was run by an editor named Nat Shlagel. His right-hand man was his brother Sidney. It was hard to believe they were brothers. Nat was short and fair; Sidney, who had a big brown mustache, was maybe a half foot taller. Another thing, Nat was also often petty, sarcastic, and unpleasant, Sidney invariably friendly and kind.

From the beginning, I liked Sidney but considered Nat a certifiable prick. Still, it was a job and, as I say, a way to break into publishing.

Instead of writing the word "recur," I once wrote the nonexistent word "reoccur." Nat made it sound as if I'd committed a mortal sin and was an idiot. That night, I told Marie, "One of these days, I'm going to punch that sucker in his nasty mouth."

He fired me before lunch on a Friday preceding the July Fourth weekend. "I'm letting you go, Eric," he said. "Nothing personal. But we need to economize, and you're odd man out. Good luck."

I left his office, walked over to where Marie was sitting, and told her, "Don't get upset, Brom, I just got fired."

For a second, Marie looked stunned. Then she burst into tears. "Go back in there, Eric, and punch him in the mouth. Do it, goddamn him, do it!"

I laughed. "Come on, Marie, let's go to lunch before you get fired, too."

"But what reason did he give? What'd he say?"

"Oh, Marie, who cares what he said?"

"Eric, you didn't deserve this. It's just that he sensed you couldn't stand him."

"Hey, it's probably a blessing in disguise. Besides, I got what I could out of this place and will probably land another, a better job in a month or two. So it's no big deal, Marie, no tragedy."

Brave words but, as everyone knows, getting fired anywhere hurts, and I felt rotten during that long weekend though Marie and I screwed our brains out in her apartment on West Eighty-eighth.

Leaving Marie late Monday afternoon and before heading home to Queens, I walked up Broadway to the aforementioned 106th between West End and Riverside Drive.

At the end of the street is a pedestal overlooking the Hudson and the statue of a horse facing Riverside Park. The guy riding the horse is a Civil War major general named Franz Sigel. He's hatless, a sword hanging down his left side. He holds a pair of double reins and his stirrups have a flap on top. Sigel looks his age, not quite forty, is lean, has lank hair, and a brief chin beard. Of course, none of that meant a thing to me or to my boyhood friends, Harry Kotlowitz, Andy Rabin, and Bruce Kamen. Nor to my other boyhood friends, the said Richie Graf and Ira Zeller, Alex Novokov and Gerard Schumann.

One-hundred-and-sixth was where our crowd and a handful of hangers-on grew up playing stickball. I've read about other men recalling trout streams, rugby fields, and hunting camps that made their boyhoods memorable. For me, a city kid born and bred, 106th was just as meaningful, my stony venue just as hallowed as any trout stream, rugby field, or hunting camp.

Hovering near the general and his horse, I can still see, after all these years, how each of my friends hit, his stance, who could field, who had a lousy arm, who could steam around the bases, who couldn't run worth shit.

I can even see the old minister who lived at the end of the block, shouting at us from his second-floor balcony. We'd disturbed his mid-afternoon siesta, made too much of a racket, as spirited, raucous boys playing stickball inevitably would. A retired bishop, he'd wave his angry arms, howling at us, "You're all moral degenerates!"

"So are you, you old fart!" said Alex, who never backed off, waving his arms just as indignantly.

Soon the cops would come, stepping out of their green and white patrol cars, grab our stick and, using the indentation in the nearest manhole cover, snap it in two, telling us to get lost and not come back.

Were they kidding? Because two, three days later back we were—same street, same guys, same bouncy, pink Spalding, different broomstick.

Afterward, we'd go to Pollock's, a nearby candy store on Broadway, have a soda and eat a pretzel, arguing who was better—Mantle or Mays, Reese or Rizzuto? *Who was better?* Like it really mattered. I can't stop smiling when I think of how passionately we debated.

Kotlowitz, Andy, Bruce Kamen, and I still get together for lunch three, four times a year. Sadly, Gerard and Alex both died of prostate cancer. Ira Zeller disappeared off the face of the earth. Boorish Richie Graf was eventually ignored by the rest of us.

That last is a lousy thing to have to acknowledge, particularly when I tell myself I never felt safer or happier than when I was playing stickball. Which is why, feeling unusually depressed, I gravitate to 106th and inoculate myself by circling where I remember first, second, third, and home stood, touching each as if I just launched one, the pink ball soaring above the spine of the street before bouncing with compressed top spin toward the estimable statue, Kotlowitz and maybe Ira chasing it down between them.

God, I love that statue, love 106th, still love my boyhood friends, or at least most of them.

***

I began submitting short stories to the old *Saturday Evening Post* at the same time I started working at S*upermarket Merchandising*. To my astonishment, two fiction editors there liked my stories, tried to get them accepted by the powers-that-be, and kept encouraging me to submit more. One took me to lunch, the other suggested I send my stories to an editor/friend at Random House. The first began a subsequent letter, "As part of my campaign to assist you in winning the Nobel Prize, I discussed your work with the agent Teresa Pinero, and she asked me to ask you to send her some of your stories. Her address is..."

One morning the following October, he called where I now worked, at *Drycleaning World*, another trade magazine as dull and heart-numbing as *Supermarket Merchandising.*

"What's on your mind, Don?" I said.

"That last story you submitted, Eric, 'At the Beach,'" he said and paused.

"Yeah, what about it?"

"Congratulations, we're going to publish it."

I almost fainted. "You're kidding."

He laughed. "No, I wouldn't kid about that, Eric," he assured me.

First to hear my good news was Marie, whom I'd been seeing for a year now. "Oh, my God!" she exclaimed. And because she was still working at *Supermarket Merchandising,* I made a point of adding, "Be sure to tell brother Sidney this morning," knowing he'd be sure to tell brother Nat before lunch. Call me a son of a bitch, but I couldn't resist.

I phoned my parents next. Told my mother, who started to cry. Then I called my uncle Danny, who was more like an older brother. Danny, a kind of producer/packager, provided music and entertainment for banquets, conventions, and sales meetings.

"Oh, Eric, Eric, Eric," he kept saying, and I couldn't tell if he was laughing or crying.

It was the first story I'd gotten someone to accept. Of course, that day was one of the best of my life. The night wasn't bad either, and I told Marie, "When I get the *Post's* check, I want to buy you a coat." She'd been wearing a frayed blue one since I knew her.

Believe it or not, the *Post* paid in two weeks. Their acceptance letter began, "We hand you herewith our check for $1,000.00 in payment for the following editorial material (herein called 'material'): Author: Eric Rosen. Title: AT THE BEACH (Story)..."

It sounded ridiculously formal and legal, but considering the sum and how quickly I received it, who's complaining?

The first Saturday after depositing their check, I took Marie to Saks, where we spent a couple of hours as she kept modeling one coat after another. "What do you think?" she asked.

"Hey, it's going to be yours, up to you," I told her. "And if you don't like any here, we'll go to Bloomingdale's or wherever you want to try next. Take your time, Marie, we got all day."

She finally selected a stylish black coat with pleats and a belt that extended from and was sewn into the back of the coat. Marie had shapely legs, and seeing the coat on her was a treat, a genuine pleasure.

"It'll be the nicest coat I've ever owned, Eric." She squeezed my hand, her blue-green eyes brimming with happiness.

A month later, I saw the illustration the *Post* had commissioned to accompany my story. It was an aerial view of a thronged beach, the people like dots, the surf swinging in toward the shoreline like a plunging roller coaster.

I didn't know it, but a month after I saw the illustration, the *Post* hired a new chief fiction editor. A couple of months passed, and when my story didn't appear I called to find out why. Turned out, the two editors who'd befriended me were no longer there, and the new honcho didn't like my story and refused to schedule it. I'd acquired an agent by then, and, after an unpleasant phone call, she requested the guy return my story. Which he did, with the understanding that in the event of a resale the *Post* would receive fifty percent of the sale proceeds. He ended his letter with: "I am now enclosing the author's manuscript and an edited Photostat of it." The Photostat wasn't enclosed, and his last six words were crossed out as if *he* was pissed off.

Next day, I told Marie the story wouldn't be appearing anywhere soon. Had to tell my parents and Danny, too.

I tried to claw my way out of this embarrassing dark hole by writing two other stories. Both were terrible, the characters cardboard, the dialogue dry as dust. Pallid sentences ran into each other, paragraphs appeared out of nowhere, like unrelated orphans. I barely kept my editing job at *Drycleaning World,* but was unable to concentrate on much else. Marie kept trying to cheer me up, but I was poor company and knew it. We hadn't stopped sleeping with each other, but it was far less enjoyable, more obligatory now. Not her fault: admittedly, totally, utterly all mine.

***

This particular Sunday morning we were over my place and had just finished breakfast when my phone rang. It was a little after nine.

"Eric, it's Danny," my uncle said.

"Hey, Danny," I said.

"Listen, I'm worried about you, kid, and want to come over this morning."

Oh, Christ, my big brother/uncle, I thought, glancing at Marie, who was wearing a yellow T-shirt and a pair of my purple running shorts with a Queens College logo.

"Gee, Danny, it's nice of you wanting to come over now, but I'm really okay, fine; so no need to bother, to be concerned."

"Eric, I spoke to your mom yesterday. She's worried about you, too," he said. "I promised I'd check in with you today."

Oh, shit! I thought. Close families—great and not so great.

"Please, Eric, I promised your mom. You know how anxious mothers get. So do us both this favor, kid."

I sighed, but because I hated turning Danny down about anything, I said without trying to sound grudging, "Well, okay. But I need to shower and shave, Danny, so give me an hour."

When I got off the phone, I stared at Marie. No one in my family had ever met her or even knew we were involved, the reason being she wasn't Jewish.

"That was my uncle Danny," I said. "My mother and Danny are worried about me. He wants to come over now and reassure himself I'm not about to jump out the window. I've a lousy favor to ask, Marie. Please go to the park near the high school two blocks from here, maybe read the Sunday *Times* there, and come back in a couple of hours. He'll be gone, and we'll have lunch and take in the new Bergman movie. I know it's a crummy thing to ask, but your not being here will finesse a slew of complications I don't want to have to deal with just now." I thought Marie winced, but maybe I was imagining things.

Later, I told myself the problem was I hadn't thought fast enough. Hadn't simply said, "Hey, Danny, my girlfriend slept over and is here with me now. So, bad time to get together. Why don't we make a date for tomorrow?"

Twenty-twenty hindsight—it's enough to make any Jewish mother's son despair.

And talking about twenty, I was twenty-eight. I mean, even if Danny met Marie and guessed she wasn't of the Hebrew persuasion, so what?

Yet after Danny had come and gone, none the wiser because Marie wasn't around, I felt not only stupid but cowardly and dishonorable. Why? Because there was no way my parents, Sabbath observers who kept kosher, would ever accept Marie, and I'd understood that from the get-go yet kept seeing her. In short, unless I broke with my folks, I'd gotten in over my head and today proved that in spades. I add, unconvincingly, the possibility of Marie converting never entered my pea-sized brain.

When Marie finally returned, I apologized for asking her to leave, but she said it was okay, nothing major, no big deal. But I knew it wasn't okay. Yet I still couldn't face the truth. Instead, I told myself that my unpublished story was weighing me down. Told myself that today was the single worst day of a stifling summer I'd grown to hate, one that couldn't end fast enough. Blaming it on the weather—how's that for one sadder-than-sorry, half-assed evasion?

***

On the other hand, it did soon begin to cool off, and I clearly remember Marie and me getting together the Saturday night following Labor Day. She'd moved from Eighty-eighth to a larger apartment on Ninety-fifth, near the Orthodox synagogue between Broadway and Amsterdam which, incidentally, my father attended when my parents had lived on Ninety-sixth. Nice reminder, as if I needed one, that I was in trouble.

Anyway, whether I knew, let alone accepted it, the clock was ticking, and I couldn't have been in Marie's apartment for more than ten minutes when her phone rang.

The caller was a guy she knew from work. She was now a copy editor at *Town and Country*; he was one of the magazine's sale reps.

"Phil," she told him after a minute or so. "I'd love to have dinner with you Tuesday and take in a movie after. Great idea, and thanks for calling. See you Monday at work."

Putting the phone down, Marie, who'd been looking the other way, now glanced at me, gauging my reaction.

Standing up, I said, "What's going on, Marie?" Neither of us had been seeing anyone else for more than a year. "What's the idea?"

She took a deep breath. "I need fresh air, Eric, need a change, need to see someone else besides you," she said.

"You serious?"

Biting her lip, she nodded.

"This your shrink's idea?" I asked. She'd been seeing this shrink since college and thought he walked on water.

"This is strictly my idea, Eric," Marie said nervously.

God knows, I didn't have the right, but I could feel myself growing angrier by the second. "You stage this call, Marie?" I said, looking for a fight. "Told the guy to phone now, knowing I'd be here?"

Suddenly Marie's eyes got watery.

Undeterred, I raised my voice. "This your great notion, Marie, of how to kiss me off, how to say bye-bye, let's be friends?"

When she looked away, I took that for a yes.

"You know what, Marie? The hell with this!" I said, reaching for my jacket. And I left, slamming the door. My heart was hammering, so was my head. First, my goddamn story a couple of months ago, now Marie. I don't remember how I got home, got back to Queens.

I thought of calling her that night, but I couldn't seem to calm down, cool off enough to pick up the phone. Amazing, I knew the score, yet kept telling myself I was the wounded party, the victim. I even felt blindsided, overwhelmed, and, in despair, I didn't know what to do that weekend, how to cope.

The summer, dominated by my rejected story, had been a disaster, but at least I'd had Marie then. Now it was almost fall; I no longer had Marie, and September was casting earmarks worse than my worst summer.

I quit my two-bit job at *Drycleaning World* the following month. Quitting, another dumb mistake I made that year I'll never forget.

Dumb in part, because Marie called at the beginning of November, saying she wanted to see me at my apartment, would tomorrow be okay? And I thought: so, the other guy hasn't panned out, and now she has second thoughts about dumping me, but I have no job. Well, okay, I'll somehow still make it work.

But five minutes after she got to my place, Marie said, "I've done something stupid, Eric. Got myself pregnant, and not only need an abortion but your help."

I was pleased she'd turned to me but upset because of the reason. Yet that night, she stayed over. Why? Let's be honest. One, I was horny as hell. Two, she was frightened. Three, I naively, selfishly thought her staying over meant we'd be able to get it going again after her abortion.

***

The following Saturday, Marie and I went to the Port Authority where we caught the next bus to Newark, arriving before nine. Marie's abortion was going to cost six-hundred dollars. No longer employed, not being a saver, and having spent all of my *Post* money, I was obliged to call Danny. Told him I needed to borrow six-hundred dollars yesterday. It took Danny three seconds to add two and two.

Marie had been instructed to stand in front of the Military Park Hotel where she'd be picked up before nine-thirty. When we got there, another woman was also waiting to be picked up. Next to her stood her husband and five-year-old pigtailed daughter. After saying an awkward hello to us in English, the couple spoke to each other in German.

Promptly at nine-thirty, not the doctor, but a guy with a pepper-and-salt beard pulled up near us. The car was a dark green Buick.

"I'll be back here with the ladies between three-thirty and four," he said to the German guy and me. "Nothing to worry about, fellows. He's a good doctor, done a lot of these procedures."

Then he opened the near rear door of his car. "Ladies," he said, gesturing to them like a genial MC. Marie got in first.

After they drove off, the husband smiled but the little girl looked furiously at me, as if her mother's departure was somehow my fault.

I felt like telling the kid: sorry, but you're pissed off at the wrong guy, sweetie.

The day dragged and was probably the longest of my life. I walked around a lot, careful not to get lost. What would I do if Marie wasn't back by four? Abortions were illegal. Would I go to the cops? Yet what would I tell them? What could I tell them? Dopy inexperienced me forgot to ask Marie the name of the doctor. Nor was I an especially prayerful man but better believe I said more than one that Marie would be okay and I'd see her by four.

Sitting in the park across from the hotel, I wondered if, before asking for my help, she'd approached the guy who'd gotten her pregnant. Also wondered if the kid wasn't his but mine. Later I wondered if Marie had been testing me, wanted to see if I'd offer to marry her and we'd raise the child, whoever the father was. In a word, the craziest possibilities occurred to me that afternoon. Or maybe they weren't so crazy.

A little before three-thirty, I walked to the hotel. The German guy and his kid were already there. Clutching a doll this time, the little girl appeared apprehensive rather than angry, and I said a quick one for her, too.

Thank God, the Buick pulled up ten minutes later. The bearded guy climbed out of the car, smiled reassuringly at us, and offered each emerging woman a helping hand.

Marie looked pale.

"You okay?" I asked.

"Let's get out of here," she said weakly.

I stayed with her that night and most of Sunday. She didn't want to talk about any of it. I called her a couple of times during the week. But when I asked if I could come over that weekend, she said, no, didn't think it was a good idea.

I wrote her a long letter telling her how much I wanted to see her, how much I still liked her and hoped we could start over. Knowing what I now knew, realizing all I now realized, I still couldn't let go.

She wrote back saying she began to cry as soon as she started reading my letter. She blamed herself for our breakup, saying she'd always been insecure and her relationship with any man at this point in her life wouldn't last. "When I began to feel you didn't want to sleep with me, when I began to feel too many blows to my pride, a desire for revenge was nurtured and spread that I wasn't even aware of until it did irreparable damage to us. But if it wasn't this, I think it would have been something else. Maybe that you weren't paying enough attention; I did feel that from time to time." She also wrote she was frightened by the idea of marriage, of permanence.

Finally, she thanked me for my letter and hoped I wished her luck because she needed it. If I got a story published, she also hoped I'd let her know. Her last hope was that I'd forgive her for what she did to me.

Even if she didn't know or realize it, I knew her letter was far better than I deserved. Whatever revenge she took on me I had coming, even if I thought she'd taken it for the wrong reasons.

A year or so later, I sent her a copy of a story I'd published in *Redbook*. She wrote back, saying how much she'd liked the story. By then, she was an editor at a small publishing house in Jersey; I was an editor of a men's adventure magazine. Her last line was, "Keep writing." She added a P.S. "Did I tell you I met Philip Roth?"

I had to laugh at Marie's P.S., but three guesses about the four words I said after laughing. Let me give you a hint. The first was "Oh," the last was "Roth!"

***

I married eleven years after Marie and I broke up. For maybe two, three years during that interim, I'd get these three-in-the-morning phone calls.

I'd had a couple of girlfriends after Marie and before I married. So it could have been Marie or one of the others, although I didn't like the others the way I'd liked Marie, and they didn't like me the same way Marie had once liked me. Put a gun to my head, and I'd say my late-night caller was probably Marie. My guess was she called but, in the end, couldn't finally announce herself because her pride wouldn't let her. Or was that me punishing her by not saying, Marie, is that you?

Of course, it could also have been a total stranger. There are a lot of lonely hearts in New York plus I don't know how many screwballs. Yet I tried to be sympathetic, kept asking who my caller was, but never got a response. Nor did the person calling ever hang up first.

During those two, three years, I must have received more than a dozen calls. Finally, out of patience, I said, "Look, if you keep phoning and don't say who you are, I'm going to change my number. So please, tell me who you are or, for Christ's sake, enough's enough!"

I remember getting one last call, a kind of tuneless encore, but that was it.

***

If I'm still living and next see a living Marie at our usual every five years, I'll be eighty-eight. She'll be eighty-two or eighty-three. I still remember her birthday, April 4, but don't recall the exact year she was born. The more I think about the last time we saw each other, the more I realize that seeing me on Eighty-sixth must have been like reliving an infrequent but terrible dream, one that recurs when you least expect it.

When I stitch that realization to those three-in-the-morning calls and to the belated observation that I never saw Marie wear a wedding ring nor ever saw her walking with a guy, I ask myself how I could even remotely have considered wanting to confront her. By all that's right and fair, Marie, not I, would be justified in compelling a confrontation.

Should she flinch, whirl away again five years from now, or sooner, I'll not say a word; but, unnerved and distraught, I'll board that Eighty-sixth Street crosstown next morning and find my way to 106th.

I'll probably appear a limping, wide-eyed relic, senescent and lost. But don't you believe it. I'll circle the bases once more, touch the manhole that used to be second, hit the other manhole cover that was home plate, and a great calm will, I hope, descend as it almost always does.

Only this time I'll make a point of also remembering how Marie burst into tears that Friday Shlagel fired me, and I'll remember how happy she was when she wore that pleated coat a year later. Both will grab me.

Then I'll wish for the impossible—that I could give Marie my go-to 106th, that I could somehow have it shipped FedEx First Overnight so she'd receive it first thing following the morning I thought it might help.

Of course, sending Marie 106th, with the street actually calming her as it's helped calm me all these years, is sheer nonsense. But indulge me, because it's not so much wishful thinking but rather a desperate response, as desperate as those three-in-the-morning phone calls I've begun receiving again a couple of weeks ago.

The Paranoid

❦

Sitting in his office with nothing better to do one morning, the advertising executive Larry Polansky decided he wanted his wife to have a baby. After giving it five minutes of intensive thought, he phoned his sweetie, who worked for a rival advertising agency. Whenever something out of the ordinary occurred to either of them, one would call the other.

"Edith, I've been thinking, let's start a family." he said.

But Polansky must have caught his wife on a bad morning, for she answered, "Jesus, Larry, I'm busy as hell. Just fired two assistants and getting ready to ax another two. If that's the only reason you called…"

It infuriated Polansky whenever his wife tried brushing him off, and making a terrific effort to cool his explosive temper, he said, "Okay, then, baby, so for two cents, Gene Hermanski?" It was the opening question of a quiz game he often played with his wife to head off potential trouble.

Edith got the message and said with a sigh, "Dodger outfielder, late Forties."

"Ching Johnson?" Polansky shot right back.

"Defenseman, Rangers, nineteen-twenties."

"Dizzy Dean?"

"Pitcher, Cards. Nineteen thirty-four."

"You still love me?" Polansky threw in.

"If I didn't, do you think I'd play this nut game whenever you want to?"

"I'm talking seriously now, Edith, seriously. Do you?"

"I love you, I love you, I love you," she said.

After putting the phone down, Polansky got out the file he kept on his wife. Dating the entry, he wrote: "Edith claims she still loves me, but today she violently objected when I suggested we have a kid. Maybe she's starting to take me for granted. Maybe she's got a boyfriend. Maybe I have to prove to her that I'm still *Numero Uno*. Who the hell knows? But this rates my constant attention, if not surveillance." He got out his silver key, put Edith's voluminous file away and locked the drawer.

Polansky was one of those certified paranoids who kept files on everyone he felt was out to get him, which meant everyone he came in contact with. While he didn't exactly think Edith was out to get him, to be on the safe side, he kept a file on her, too.

Edith, a solidly built blonde with hazel eyes had just turned thirty, and though she'd been married to Polansky before she was twenty, they had no children. Polansky, all five-feet-five of him, hadn't wanted children till he was sure of success. The trouble was, in his volatile racket you never could be sure. But sensing time passing him by this morning, he concluded he wanted a kid, success or not. Only his wife, who was making as much money as Polansky, immediately realized that raising a child and maintaining her independence was a tough combination to handle. Maybe too tough. In part, Edith was Polansky's business equal because he – a natural teacher who couldn't resist lecturing – had taught her every dirty trick he knew. A willing pupil, Edith learned early in their marriage that though Polansky was lovable and sometimes touchingly foolish, he was also terribly overbearing. To live with him and maintain a semblance of self-respect, she'd realized, she would have to be as tough and high-handed as he was.

So that night when he said again, "I'm hot to have a kid call me daddy," she responded by saying, "Why should you be the only one who's free?"

"What's that supposed to mean?" he snapped.

"You once told me you wanted absolute control over your life, that you didn't want to be at the mercy of just any son of a bitch including me. Well, damn it. I'm your equal and what's good enough for you is good enough for me." And without waiting for an answer, she turned her back on him and walked out of the room.

"Come here!" he ordered.

But she kept walking, her nose in the air.

He ran after her, vaulting the couch. As she was about to lock herself into the sanctuary of the bathroom, he grabbed her arm.

"Who do you think you are – walking away when I'm still talking?"

She looked him in the eye.

"You hit me, I'll slam you back." Edith was shorter and lighter than Polansky and if it developed into a knock-down, drag-out fight, he'd come out on top. But he knew she'd never give up.

"I guess you're okay," he conceded.

"Just as long as we both know that," she said.

While Edith's independence was a mutually recognized fact of their married life that hardly meant Polansky was about to abandon his becoming a father and, attempting a different tack, he said, "You don't want a child because you don't trust me to take care of you."

"No, it's not that I don't trust you," she corrected him. "It's that I don't want to be placed in the position of having to trust you."

"Oh, well, since you put it that way, everything's cool again." Which made absolutely no sense, except tomorrow was another day.

And next morning when Edith woke, she saw Polansky in his pajamas, sitting in a chair opposite their bed and staring at her. He'd been awake most of the night wrestling with various schemes designed to force Edith into agreeing to have a child. A little before four that morning, he thought he'd hit on the best one, and he smiled sweetly now, as he said, "If you don't want to have my kid, we'll adopt one."

"That would make it seem I'm unable to give birth, no dice," Edith said, swinging her chunky legs out of bed; she was nothing if not a competitor which was precisely what Polansky was counting on. "Is that supposed to shame me?" she asked. "You trying to scare me?"

"Who cares if you're scared or not?" Polansky replied, delighted with the results his strategy was eliciting so far.

Edith thought fast. "How are you going to adopt a baby if I don't agree to it? If I don't sign the papers?"

"Don't be naive," he answered. "There are ways of finding an unwanted baby without having to go to adoption agencies."

"So, you've thought it all out," she said.

"I'm not fooling around."

"Okay." she said softly. "Okay."

"Okay what?" Polansky grunted. He hated misunderstandings.

"I'll stop taking the magic pills." she said. "If you have to have a brat, I suppose we might as well have our own."

Polansky grinned. "I thought you'd finally see it my way."

"But if and when I get pregnant, you're going to have to agree to certain things."

He didn't like her tone. "What are you talking about?"

"Let's first wait and see if you're man enough to make a baby."

Polansky planted himself in front of her, extended his double chin and gave her the time-honored response: "I'll fuck your brains out if I have to!"

And from that night on, every time he made love to his wife, Polansky duly noted such privileged goings-on in Edith's file. One such entry read: "We must have screwed three hours last night, and I got the feeling I scored during the second hour."

But when a month flew past and Edith didn't say boo, Polansky began to wonder why his sperm cells were betraying him. It was bad enough the whole world was out to get him, was his own body now conspiring against him, too? But if Polansky was a certified paranoid, he was also a genuine competitor, even if that meant competing against his own sperm cells. And during the following month, he called upon sexual powers he didn't know he had, for even more compelling displays of night-long virility.

After seven weeks of the heaviest lovemaking of his life, Polansky hit pay dirt. That is, one morning Edith woke and realized she'd missed her period. She didn't tell Polansky the big news though she knew he was one anxious bed partner, nor did she tell him she'd made an appointment to see her doctor a few weekday mornings later. "Let lover boy sweat a little first," she thought.

He guessed that his house wasn't in order when he called her office that morning and her secretary reported that Edith had phoned earlier to say she'd arrive about noon. A born alarmist, Polansky immediately dialed his apartment, thinking that perhaps Edith had become ill. But no one picked up the home phone either, and when he tried her office again a half hour after the first call, her secretary said that Edith still hadn't shown up.

Putting the phone down, Polansky wondered if his wife was having an affair with one of the men at her office or perhaps with the superintendent of their building, a tall, hairy Lithuanian who liked pinching girls. And straining at the bit, he was about to call her office a third time, when his own phone rang. It was Edith, and she was calling from work.

"Where the hell you been?" he asked.

"What's biting you?" she said.

"You sick or what?"

"Why are you getting so excited?"

"You having an office affair?"

"What are you talking about?"

"Or is it that you're hot for what the hairy super's got?"

"Stop it!" she said. "Stop it!"

"I want to know what's going on with my wife!"

"You're impossible, impossible!" she cried out. "Here I am, going to tell you something important. But the way you're acting, who can get a word in, and now I don't even want to. Forget that I called," she said, hanging up.

As soon as Polansky put the phone down, he leaped for his coat, told his secretary that his wife was having a nervous breakdown, and ran out of the office building, jumping into the first empty cab.

In the cab, his heart was thumping wildly, and his head whirling, but he made a point of asserting control, if only because poise was required to make notes so that Edith's file could be maintained with fresh, perhaps revealing quotes. Polansky particularly remembered to jot down that when he referred to the super, Edith didn't deny it directly but merely said, "Stop it!" cutting off conversation in general.

He arrived at his wife's office less than ten minutes later. Plowing past an indifferent receptionist, he aimed himself like a cannonball toward Edith's office. He'd visited her before, so he knew his way around the hallways and, more important, he made moves as if he knew his way around. Consequently, no one stopped him, and he burst into Edith's office while she was discussing an ad campaign with one of the agency's top clients.

"Larry, what are you doing here?" Edith said, standing up and turning deathly pale when she saw him.

"I've got to talk to you, Edith!" her husband said. "Now!"

"Please wait outside till I'm finished with Mr. Troyat. He's an important client," she whispered, appealing to Polansky's business sense.

"Wait outside? Not on your life!" Polansky said, ignoring Troyat. "Not when my marriage is hanging by a goddamn thread!"

Troyat, a thin, nervous man with an ulcer, knew better than to remain caught in a marital crossfire, and looking at the combatants with bulging, frightened eyes, he jumped to his feet. "Perhaps I can come back later," he said, sliding out of Edith's office without turning his back on Polansky.

Wringing her hands, Edith called hopelessly after the retreating client, "I can explain everything."

"That's what I'm here for, too, explanations," Polansky muttered.

Turning to him, Edith said icily, "You call this acting professionally?"

But Polansky had no time for any such business amenities, and he said, "Listen, I want to know where you've been this morning and, if you're seeing some other guy, I want to know that, too. Just let's get everything aboveboard. Clear the air, I always say. My marriage may not be one of the ten greatest of all time, but it's mine and I like it and want to try and save it."

"What *are* you talking about?" his wife asked, totally bewildered.

"Stop stalling. Answer yes or no—where were you this morning?"

Edith sat behind her desk, collecting her wits. Polansky had called, she knew, and she wasn't around, and he must have been so anxious for good news the past two months that the strain of not reaching Old Reliable had proved too unsettling. This much, anyway, was clear to Edith, when she said, "I tried to tell you when I called, but you were so nasty on the phone, it was impossible."

He sighed. "Okay, so I'm here now. I'm all ears. Couldn't give you more of my undivided attention if I tried. Talk. Speak. Open your mouth. Articulate. Say words."

But all she could do now was look at him. Sweat poured from his forehead. And he leaned forward, over her desk, breathing hoarsely like someone about to explode. No wonder old Troyat had fled from the room.

"For a girl who's got something to say, you sure don't seem to be doing so hot," he prodded her.

Showing him more mercy than he probably deserved, Edith said, "I was at the doctor's this morning, and it looks like you're going to have that precious brat you want so badly."

"Brat?" Polansky said, the truth slowly sinking in. "A baby?"

"Well, it's not definite. I'll know for sure in a few days."

Polansky collapsed into the nearest empty chair.

Despite the bad taste left by the embarrassing Troyat business, Edith said to her husband, "Now don't you feel foolish for having burst in on me like you just did? Now, don't you?"

But catching his second wind, Polansky leaned forward in his chair and coolly asked, "Who's the doctor?"

"My mother's cousin, Milton Gold."

Afraid of exactly that, Polansky winced. Gold had taken care of Edith in the past, when she'd had fallopian tube troubles, and Polansky hadn't gotten along with the stiff then. "Gold's out," he said. "I'll find you a ten times better obstetrician tomorrow."

His wife rubbed her eyes and counted to ten. "Do you remember when I told you that if I was pregnant we'd have to come to certain agreements?" Edith said. "Well, the first one is, Gold's the doctor."

"Gold," Polansky said, swallowing the name as if he was swallowing castor oil. "Okay, Gold," he consented. Although he hated losing any argument, he figured he could let his wife win one on the day she told him she was pregnant.

Still, when he got back to his office that morning, he tried to find Gold's old file, but for some reason was unable to locate it. Polansky was meticulous about his files, and he couldn't believe he hadn't initiated one describing Gold when the doctor had treated Edith years ago. Then Polansky wondered if someone had filched the file during the intervening years.

He was the only one who had the silver key to the drawer containing the files, but you never know. Mother of God, sometimes it seemed even eternal vigilance wasn't good enough.

That night, both Polanskys were exhausted from the confrontation they'd had in Edith's office. They didn't say much after dinner but watched TV. Edith, however, did have something on her mind, and after building up a sufficient amount of adrenalin, she turned the TV set off.

"Hey, what's the big idea?" Polansky said, jumping to his feet and making a fist. Just because she was pregnant was hardly enough reason for her to act as if she was boss in the house.

"The time's come to talk turkey," Edith said, and she got him to sit down, then made herself comfortable opposite him.

"If I'm pregnant, Gold will want me to quit work after a couple of months," she began. "He'll say I'm over thirty, this is my first pregnancy, I shouldn't take any chances. But I don't want to take a leave of absence from my job until I absolutely have to—a day or two before I'm due to give birth. You see, I've decided I want to go back to work after I have the child."

Making two fists, Polansky began muttering under his breath.

"Don't be mad," she said. "The way you are makes me have to protect myself, and retaining some independence is the best way I know how. I guess what I'm trying to say is that I can accept having the child as long as you don't smother or swallow me in the process."

"Thank God for small favors," he said.

"The point is, you've got to back me when I tell Gold I'm not quitting my job," she said. "If you both gang on me, I won't be able to keep working and if I don't, I'll be impossible to live with. But if we stick together, Gold will have to go along with us."

"Let me think about it," he said, stalling for time.

"No," she said, "because swearing to back me's got nothing to do with thinking."

"Ten years ago, you wouldn't have dared set conditions."

"To have survived living with you, I've come a far piece," she agreed amiably.

The following day, Gold called, telling Edith she was officially pregnant. Gold was a tall man in his fifties with a shock of white hair atop a granite-like but pleasing face. He had neither a smooth nor a charming manner and was often heard talking tough to his pregnant patients. But they sensed he genuinely liked them, and he did. He treated husbands as necessary annoyances. They sensed he wasn't crazy for them, and that, too, was the truth.

During the third month of Edith's pregnancy, she went to the doctor's office for an examination and brought Polansky along for support. As Edith knew he would, the doctor told them that he wanted her to quit her job as soon as possible. Hearing Gold out, Edith kicked Polansky's foot, reminding him of his solemn promise to back her when the time came.

Lifting his double chin with an air of self-importance, Polansky said, "Psychologically speaking, it's important for Edith to work."

But since it had been Gold's contention through the years that psychology was a ripe field for fakers, lay and professional, he answered, "I never told Freud what to write, I don't see why he or his disciples should advise my patients to assume physical risks I consider unreasonable."

"Well, other women seem to be able to work till a few weeks before they give birth," Polansky countered.

"Look, I know your wife has a good job and makes a potful of dough. I'm just telling you that from my point of view, it would be a less risky pregnancy if she stopped working soon."

Polansky's favorite ploy when he found himself on shaky ground was to fire a series of questions at the bastard giving him the hard time, and catching Gold's eye, he opened up with, "How does Edith seem to you as of today?"

"Pregnancy looks good so far," the doctor conceded.

"Can she eat any kind of food she wants?'"

"Nobody can," Gold frowned.

"Should she exercise?"

"Keep it confined to the bedroom," the doctor suggested.

Blushing furiously, Polansky asked, "Are you talking about sex?"

"In my line of work, it's what I usually end up talking about."

"Frankly, I don't think you're taking my questions very seriously," Polansky said.

"Frankly, I make it a point of never taking husbands' questions very seriously," Gold said, standing up and making it clear that his time with them was fast drawing to a close.

Before they left, the doctor told Edith he wanted to see her again in four weeks. "Only this time, bring your husband along only if *he* wants to come."

In the cab after they'd left the doctor's office, Polansky asked his wife, "What did he mean by that last crack?"

"He understands I'm going to keep working and he knows you're on my side. And, spoilsport, I guess he doesn't like losing an argument.'

"Tough shit," Polansky said, puffing out his chest. "I'm not about to let my sweetie down."

When he got back to his office that day, first thing Polansky did was type a dated memo. The page read: "RE MILTON GOLD, M.D.—Took Edith to his office this morning, and Gold gave her a clean bill of health. Pregnancy looks good so far. Said he didn't want her to work, but when we stood up for our rights, he realized he wasn't dealing with the usual two submissive schmucks. Also implied we could have sex as often as we wanted. Did he remember that he and I didn't get along when Edith went to him five years ago? He asked then if we wanted children. 'None of your goddamn business,' I told him. 'Women aren't getting pregnant like they used to, and I have to hustle for new patients. So it's my business, if it's anyone's,' he said. 'Well, you shouldn't hustle relatives,' I answered. 'Best people I know to hustle,' he said. Conclusion: Since Gold's answers today resembled those of five years ago, he's still a putz and will keep my bad eye out for him."

That was Friday. Saturday, Polansky and his wife woke late. Smart fellow, he waited till it was after twelve before he broke the bad news, saying he had to go to the office to finish some work that had piled up last week.

"I don't feel so great today; don't go," Edith pouted.

"What's the matter?" Polansky asked.

"I feel jumpy."

"You feel jumpy now and it's only your third month. What the hell you going to do when it's your sixth or seventh?"

"I don't know what I'll do then, I only know how I feel now."

But Polansky was counting on catching up on his paranoid files in the office today, and "jumpiness" was far too vague a reason for him to pass up this opportunity. "Edith, I backed you to the hilt with Gold yesterday! To the hilt! So be reasonable today. Given my compulsive personality, I can't afford to let my work at the office swamp me.'"

Edith made two small fists. "If three or four lousy hours staying with me today is going to make you lose your lousy job..."

Then she started to cry.

Seeing his wife in tears infuriated Polansky. "You play rough and tough, you want me to treat you as an equal, but when you don't get your way, you turn on the tears. Well, no way, Jose!'"

And he put on his coat, whipping it around him as if it were a cape and stormed out of the apartment.

"Drop dead!' he heard his wife shout after him.

"You shout that loud, you can't be so jumpy!" he screamed back.

That night, he brought legitimate work home with him so he wouldn't have to go to the office Sunday. There was so much to do—partly because when he should have been working for his clients, Polansky was busy maintaining his paranoid files—he even asked Edith to lend a hand next afternoon. And although she had a bad headache, Edith, grateful that hubby chose to hang around the apartment instead of going to the office, pitched in without a whimper.

She felt much better Monday morning, and it was a relief that she was able to go to work. In the office, she was about to settle into her routine when Polansky phoned to say he'd just had a terrible fight with his secretary, Connie, who'd called him 'paranoid' in front of two other secretaries. Polansky wanted the girl fired on the spot, but the people in personnel wouldn't go along.

Edith listened and tried to sound sympathetic, but remembering her own uncertain nerves Saturday, she couldn't help saying, "Maybe the girl doesn't feel well; maybe her boyfriend's holding out on her; maybe she's having a hard time with her period. Or maybe it's just that I'm pregnant and the pressure's getting to you."

"Pressure getting to me? Bullshit!" he said. "If you let one lower-echelon type person take advantage, the word'll get around, Edith. No, this girl has to get the ax, and I'm just surprised that someone with your executive know-how doesn't grasp that immediately!"

After speaking to his wife, Polansky got out the file he kept on Connie and recounted, using direct quotes, what had transpired between them that morning. His last three sentences later read: "Told Edith what had happened, and she seemed to side with the girl. Pregnancy seems to be softening her up. Hope that doesn't mean she's having a hard time carrying, like me, my naturally feisty kid in her belly."

But Edith felt remarkably well during the following month, and when Gold examined her, he said, "You're in excellent shape, couldn't be better." Naturally, she told Polansky, and he dutifully noted the conversation in his Gold file next morning. He caught up on Connie's file then, too, noting that she'd been officially transferred to a different department over his strenuous objections. Polansky wrote: "By refusing to fire her as I demanded, Blanton, head of personnel, is now Number 4 on my shit list." Ahead of Blanton were the two partners who ran the advertising company where Polansky worked and Milton Gold, M.D.

Gold, however, vaulted to undisputed Number 1 the night Edith felt nauseous and couldn't keep her dinner down. It was a memorable night. Although Polansky desperately tried to reach the good doctor, it took his exchange an hour to track Gold down.

"My wife's turned green in the face, could you come over and take a look at her?" Polansky asked the doctor excitedly.

"Not blue but green, huh? What exactly seems to be the trouble?" Gold glanced at his watch. It was past ten.

"Goddamn it, details don't count! I want you to come over and examine her!" Polansky insisted.

"Put your better half on the phone," the M.D. said, stifling a yawn.

Polansky's initial reaction was to rip the phone from the wall. But controlling his temper, he shoved the receiver into Edith's cool hand. She dutifully told the doctor her symptoms, after which Gold suggested she have the nearest druggist on duty buzz him; he'd issue a prescription for tranquilizers. "Have your husband take two every four hours," Gold said.

"What about me?" Edith asked.

"You? There's nothing terribly wrong with you. Who doesn't get an upset stomach once in a while?"

While Edith had been talking, Polansky reached for a pencil and scratch pad. On the top of the page, he jotted down the date and time. Then he wrote: "Gold refused to come over to the house tonight and examine Edith, despite my telling him she'd vomited massively and was hysterical with fright."

"What are you writing?" Edith asked, after calling the druggist.

Polansky's eyes shot off fiery sparks. "If anything happens to you or the kid, that fag doctor's ass is mine!"

Edith turned a shade greener than she already was. "Can't you ever stop thinking about your ego?" she asked tensely.

"Can't you ever stop injecting yourself into the center of everything that ever happens?'"

Polansky appeared bewildered. "What's that supposed to mean?"

Remembering the pills Gold had just prescribed for Polansky, Edith said, jabbing a finger against her swollen belly, "I'm the main one involved! Not you! I'm the woman! Not you! I'm the one pregnant! Not you! Me, you son of a bitch, and don't ever forget that!'"

Luckily for everyone, Edith had a normal pregnancy and gave birth to a bouncing baby boy. The beaming parents called him Jeremy. Polansky was bursting with pride and did not give friends and business associates cigars with his announcement but boxes of cigars. This was because he considered himself a classy man, generous to a fault.

But with all the generosity in the world, he was totally unprepared for the problems he encountered when his wife and son came home from the hospital. The kid turned out to be a crybaby.

He even dared to cry when Polansky was trying to sleep, and it often seemed to Polansky that the kid would cry all night long just to spite him. "Can't you get him to stop bawling?" he once asked Edith.

"What about you?" she answered, black rings circling her eyes. "You helpless?"

This answer so infuriated Polansky, he reached for his pencil and scratch pad. "RE JEREMY POLANSKY," he began writing. Below the date, he scribbled: "The kid is keeping me awake all night again tonight. When I went over to his crib earlier and told him to knock it off, he smiled, then gave me the finger. Maybe the kid wants to keep me awake so I'll get fired. This is not as farfetched as it sounds because he's already competing with me for Edith's attention; and if

I get fired from lack of sleep, *I'll* come off the schmuck, not him, though he's the one who cries the whole goddamn night, not me."

It really wasn't all that surprising that Polansky had begun keeping a file on his kid. Think about it. Ask other paranoid fathers. Just because Jeremy was his kid, and only a few weeks old, hardly meant Jeremy wasn't also a possible, if not probable, threat.

In any case, the following week the entry in Jeremy's file read: "The kid spit his milk all over me this morning. It seems obvious he hates my guts. What have I done to deserve this? Edith keeps giving me dirty looks and seems to blame the kid's tantrums on me; maybe she thinks it's a trait he inherited from my side of the family. I finally told her, 'Hey. I'm not the one crying, I'm not the one who can't keep his food down, I'm not the one who keeps everyone else awake all night. Give him the dirty look, not me.' Edith, and her bright idea that we had to have a kid..."

My Father, My Sisters, The Rabbi, And Me

"Since I was six, I keep having this recurring dream and had it again last night," Arlene said. She'd just turned ninety-two, and my wife and I had her over for lunch. We make a point of inviting her at least twice a year—before Rosh Hashanah and for her birthday. Her daughter Sophie, who was supposed to come with her, cancelled at the last minute, but that didn't stop Arlene. She took a bus from Fair Lawn and made it to where we live on the corner of Eighty-ninth and First. That's actually three buses she has to take. Where my sister gets the energy and guts at ninety-two to travel by her lonesome from Jersey to NYC, God alone knows.

We'd finished lunch and were sitting in the living room, talking. I invariably try to get Arlene to reminisce about our father. Why? Because she's thirteen years older and knew him longer. She and my deceased sister Sandra were the old man's first wife's children. Their mother died in 1927, and their three-year-old brother Stanley died not quite a year later.

"In the dream," Arlene's saying, "Sandra's wearing her new red velvet dress and goes to answer the door. The big bad wolf is there and invites Sandra to go with him. Sandra turns and says goodbye to me. I yell out she shouldn't go with him, but she smiles and says she'll see me later."

Here Arlene interrupts telling about the wolf to fill in some additional background.

When my sisters were kids and my father was a rich man before the Depression, they used to get new dresses twice a year—before Rosh Hashanah and before Passover. Sandra, the eldest, always got red, because she was pale and red dresses were thought to give her color. Arlene, who didn't need color because she had big red cheeks, always got blue because that matched her striking eyes.

Arlene said she used to dread saying goodbye to anyone when she was younger because her mother once called both daughters into her bedroom to tell them she'd be going away for a while and would return soon, but never did. Arlene remembered her mother was wearing a pink nightgown and seemed okay, not sick. What neither sister realized because no one told them, was that their mother was going into the hospital for an operation—one from which she never regained consciousness.

"After that," Arlene confided, "I used to think when anyone said goodbye, it meant I'd never see them again. And, believe it or not, a goodbye today still makes me occasionally fearful."

It's really odd hearing her talk this way, because Arlene's a cheerful, bubbly, amusing woman. Still has a hundred friends—okay, gross exaggeration because lots of them have passed—and before she married seemed to have had fifty boyfriends, five of whom, she told me a year ago, had actually proposed marriage. Because she was both pretty and fun to be around, the kind of girl guys like, I take her at her word. Certainly compared to my father and to Sandra, Arlene seemed far less affected by her mother and younger brother's deaths. For as long as I can remember, Sandra and my dad were equally withdrawn. And yet even Arlene, it turns out, had and still has bad dreams, lousy premonitions, lifelong fears. Well, you never know, although maybe I should have.

"But getting back to Sandra," says Arlene, "remember when she got married, Eric? It was the day before Thanksgiving, 1942, during the war. I was so happy, her marrying Bernie. But after the wedding, she left with him and went down to Texas where he was stationed. I didn't see her for two years, and there were days after her wedding it felt as though she'd also died. See? See what I mean about me and goodbyes?"

Even though I was only seven at the time, I, too, have retained vivid, if different, memories of Sandra's wedding, and soon Arlene and I began trading recollections, my wife, Elaine, sitting opposite us, listening with interest...

***

First of all, the circumstances were intrinsically dramatic because Sandra's *was* a wartime wedding. Then there was the fact that Bernie had three older sisters but, as the only son, was made to think he was special. Moreover, he was halfway through a master's in psychiatric social work when he was drafted and his sisters felt that Sandra, who hadn't attended college, wasn't worthy of their prince and tried to discourage him from marrying her even after learning they'd become engaged.

Complicating matters still further, Sandra and Bernie abruptly decided to marry in the midst of Bernie's furlough that Thanksgiving week. Sandra told my old man on a Sunday morning, which gave him three days to engage a rabbi, figure out where the ceremony would be held, decide whom to invite, and choose which restaurant the guests might repair to after the ceremony. My father, although anxious to a fault, somehow managed to pull it all together.

Yet when Bernie told his family, his father, fearing he'd have to help support a possibly pregnant Sandra while Bernie was overseas, refused to attend the wedding. Bernie's mother, a shy, birdlike woman, deferred to her husband. Bernie's sisters were divided—one agreed to show up for the wedding, the two oldest sided with their parents.

That night, Bernie told Sandra most of his family wouldn't be attending the ceremony, suggesting maybe marriage then wasn't such a great idea; probably the smartest thing was to wait until after the war.

Turning a milky white, Sandra told him in a trembling voice that if they didn't get married that week, everything was over between them.

Being the kid brother, I, of course, knew nothing of the contretemps preceding Sandra's wedding. What I *did* know, or rather what I remembered, was that the ceremony was held in the rabbi's apartment. His name was Solomon. He had a goatee, spoke with a slight English accent, and lived on 103rd and West End. The rabbi's wife played the piano before the couple exchanged vows. Someone else served champagne after; I think it was my father's cousin Irving and his wife Bertha. Then everyone piled into cars and taxis, and drove down to a large kosher restaurant in the Garment District.

Here Arlene laughed, saying, "I was supposed to be maid of honor. But we all sat at this long table in the restaurant, and you and I, Eric, were relegated to the end, away from Sandra and Bernie, away from Daddy and the other principals. I was kind of hurt they'd exiled us to Siberia."

While Siberia didn't ring a bell, I had an explanation. "You were stuck with seven-year-old me, that's the most likely reason. But, aside from us cast as poor relations, what else you remember?"

Arlene thought a minute before saying, "Oh, one other thing that didn't strike me as important at the time. But before the ceremony, the rabbi asked Sandra and Daddy to come into his study where he closed the door. Then he put his hands on Sandra's head and blessed her in Hebrew. Did the same to Daddy. Sandra knew that wasn't part of the regular service, and she later told me it gave her a funny feeling.

"When they left the rabbi's study, Sandra asked Daddy why the rabbi did that. Daddy shook his head and didn't answer directly, only saying that the rabbi was a wonderful man, and it meant a lot to him that it was going to be Rabbi Solomon who'd be presiding at her wedding."

Oh, incidentally, Arlene added, when they came out of the rabbi's study, guess who'd just entered the rabbi's apartment? Bernie's parents. And not only his parents, but both sisters who'd also said they wouldn't come, plus their husbands.

"And they probably got to sit near the head of the table," I said, "honored guests, while you and me, banished to the bleachers, kept getting more and more teed off. Oh, Jesus, Arlene, life's unfair."

My sister laughed, said she was thirsty from talking so much, and would I mind getting her a glass of water.

*****

When I came back after getting water for both Arlene and Elaine, I said, "Now that you've mentioned Rabbi Solomon, you've jogged memories of my *bar mitzvah*."

And I reminded Arlene that Rabbi Solomon had been rabbi at the synagogue on Ninety-third off Broadway, but that we'd lived on 104th and attended the large synagogue at West End and 100th Street, which was closer. Yet when it came time for me to be *bar mitzvahed*, my father insisted for some reason that the service be held at the synagogue at Ninety-third. It upset me because my older friends, who'd already been *bar mitzvahed*, had celebrated theirs at the synagogue on 100th.

"'My being *bar mitzvahed* at Ninety-third makes no sense, Dad,' I told him. 'That's not where I go to Hebrew School and not where you worship. I don't know anyone there, nor do you.'

"'No,'" Daddy contradicted me. 'I know the rabbi there; he performed Sandra's wedding, remember?'

"'But it's my *bar mitzvah*," I said. 'What's any of Sandra's wedding got to do with me?'

"'Listen to your father,' he insisted."

Hardly a decent, let alone good reason. But my father could be a painfully stubborn man, and at a certain point I remember telling myself, "Well, if that's the way he wants it, screw it!" Only knowing me, even at thirteen I didn't say screw it!

No big surprise, my saying worse. But how's this for one —a week before my *bar mitzvah*, my father took me up to the rabbi's apartment, same apartment where Sandra had been married six years before. My father said he wanted me to meet Rabbi Solomon, or he said Rabbi Solomon wanted to meet me; I forget which.

It was the rabbi's wife who answered their apartment door and led us to the rabbi's study. She had the same curly white hair, only this time she walked with a bad limp, and I remembered her playing the piano before Sandra's wedding. The rabbi had been sitting behind his desk when we entered his study. He stood up, placing the palm of one hand against his desk for support, shook my father's hand, then mine, after which he gestured for us to sit down. I took him to be a dignified eighty.

He had, I remembered, unusually dark eyes and was wearing a white *yarmulke*. There was a red bookcase behind him stacked with books, most of whose bindings were naturally imprinted with Hebrew letters that read from right to left.

Soon the rabbi began conversing with my father in Yiddish. Not really knowing the language, I not only couldn't understand a word but had the feeling they didn't want me to understand.

After a while, the rabbi stood up, gesturing for both my father and me to do the same. Then he came around his desk, placed his hands on my head and said a prayer in Hebrew. He did the same to my father, who closed his eyes, rocking back and forth as if he was in a trance, and we left a few minutes later.

When we got downstairs, I asked what that was all about, but my father merely shrugged and otherwise acted as if the matter was of no importance.

Listening and smiling, Arlene kept shaking her head.

"What's so funny?" I asked.

"Not literally funny; but hearing your *bar mitzvah* story, you're going to find it especially interesting when I tell you about my wedding which, you probably don't remember, was presided over by guess who?"

"Of course I remember," I said. "The old man assigned me to get you there, saying it would upset Rabbi Solomon and disgrace the family if you showed up late as usual. How could I possibly not remember?"

Giving me an obligatory stuff-it-you-know-where grin, Arlene said, "A week before I got married, Daddy stipulated he wanted to meet me so we could see Rabbi Solomon together. Or exactly what happened to you shortly before you were *bar mitzvahed*. I was married in 1954, so this was six years later, my turn, and the rabbi blessed me and blessed Daddy. But, unlike what happened to you, Eric, that wasn't the end of it. After blessing me, the rabbi hugged Daddy, embracing him."

"He embraced him?" I asked.

But rather than answer me, Arlene said, "And after they embraced, he started crying."

I shook my head, thinking I must have missed or forgotten a relevant detail.

Elaine must also have been confused, because she said, "You lost me, Arlene. Cried? Who cried? The rabbi or your father?"

"No, no, the rabbi," said Arlene. "He cried and couldn't seem to stop."

"So, how'd it get resolved?" I asked.

"Daddy helped the rabbi sit down, told him everything was going to be okay, and after a couple of minutes the rabbi stopped crying, apologizing to both of us."

Arlene said when they got in the street, she, like Sandra and me, asked what the rabbi's unusual behavior signified.

"Daddy shook his head, saying, 'I think he got me confused with someone else. That sometimes happens to people in their eighties. And I just hope he makes it to your wedding in better shape. It would be terribly disappointing if we had to find someone else at the last minute.'"

Standing up, Arlene said she needed to use the bathroom, walking there slowly, and I had the sense that age might finally be catching up to my ageless sister. That, or something about what she'd just been saying had upset her.

While she was gone, Elaine asked with a puzzled smile, "Eric, have you heard any of this before?"

"I only wish," I said, gesturing with both hands, palms up.

When Arlene came out of the bathroom, she resumed making herself comfortable in the middle of our sand-colored couch, me still sitting in the blue wing chair to her left, Elaine facing her across the room in front of our ceiling-high white bookshelves. Seeing Arlene smile, I was frankly relieved that my irrepressible sister had seemingly regained her composure. That is, if she'd ever lost it.

"It's funny, and don't know what this is apropos of, Eric," she said. "But in the bathroom I remembered you once asking if Daddy ever spoke about my mother before she died; and I told you he did after I got engaged, and that was the only time. But just now, I remembered the other time. It was when I was a kid and it was *Yom Kippur*, and Daddy took Sandra and me to *shul* to say *Yiskor* for my mother. That's a special prayer for the dead recited on the most important holidays," she explained to Elaine who wasn't Jewish.

"Before he took us, he said it was important to remember and pray for my mother because she loved us. In response, I said that my mother had promised to come back before she left, but didn't, so why should we have to pray for her? He said she wanted to come back, but God called her because God needed her help. I told him only old people are called to help God, and she wasn't old. But Daddy said she was also special, that was why God had called her. I said God must have made a mistake, because even if she was special she was still young. And suddenly, Daddy turned away, as if he didn't want me to see him."

Neither Elaine nor I said anything for a minute. Then, standing, Elaine said she felt like some tea. "Me, too," I said, and Arlene made it unanimous by nodding, after which she said, "I guess I've always had a big mouth, unlike Sandra, who was smarter but a lot quieter which, in the end, is probably better."

***

Following Elaine's strong tea, to which I added an even stronger shot of single malt, Arlene said, "Eric, did you know that Rabbi Solomon died a month after my wedding?"

Gee, that was news to me, and I shook my head.

Arlene remembered clearly because the morning after Rabbi Solomon passed, my father called her before seven. He called, because he'd just read of the rabbi's death in the *Times* and wanted Arlene to accompany him to the funeral scheduled for eleven-thirty. Arlene tried to say it would be difficult for her to make it, but my father insisted, saying it was important that at least one of his three children attend the service with him. Because Sandra was vacationing in Canada with her family and I was a camp counselor up in Pittsfield, Arlene, living in nearby Jersey with her recently minted husband, was chosen.

Unfortunately, predictably, she arrived late, and the synagogue was so crowded they couldn't get in.

"Daddy was angry, terribly upset," Arlene said, "and I kept apologizing, but he said I was going to be late for his funeral, too."

Wondering what to say or do to make up to him, Arlene heard herself finally asking, "'But, Daddy, why is this so important to you?'

"'Why? Why? Because the rabbi saved my life, that's why! A good enough reason for you?'"

Arlene said before she could tell us what my father meant, she had to back up by saying that after her brother Stanley died, soon after her mother had died, my father used to come home from work and sit for hours in a chair in the living room, his head down. Everyone told Sandra and Arlene to let him alone when he sat like that. Arlene would always go to her room to play or draw; but Sandra remained in the living room, saying she wanted to be near him.

"It was during this period, Daddy sought out Rabbi Solomon," Arlene said. "It was Rabbi Solomon, you see, who'd married my parents and presided over my mother and brother's funerals. Anyway, he went to Rabbi Solomon and told him that each day felt worse than the other and every day felt like a nightmare; and he wasn't sure how long he could keep going, nor even sure he wanted to keep going. There were nights, he told the rabbi, he wished he was dead.

"Daddy said the rabbi put his arm around his shoulder, saying Daddy had two young daughters, it was a dangerous world, and no one would care for them the way a father who lost his wife would. He also said Daddy should remarry in a year or two and try to have another son. Both obligations were, the rabbi told Daddy, what he needed to fulfill as a man and as a Jew."

Arlene recalled reaching for my father's hands then, and asked if I remembered how small they were. I told Arlene I could still envision them and the crescent shape of his unusually small fingernails, and used to think how unfair it was for a man with such small hands to have had to cope with so much grief slamming into him during the course of a single year.

"The rabbi," said Arlene, "made Daddy swear he wouldn't commit suicide or otherwise give up. For his part, the rabbi promised, *promised* he'd officiate at my wedding and at Sandra's, and preside over Daddy's son's *bar mitzvah* should Daddy be blessed with another son."

"And you say he died a month after your wedding?" I asked my sister.

Arlene nodded. "A coincidence, right? Yet you know what Daddy said the afternoon of the rabbi's funeral? 'Pray for the rabbi the way you pray for your mother next time you say *Yiskor*.'

"'Why?' I asked him.

"'Because he kept his promise,' Daddy said, 'and that meant he was there for me until you married.'

"'But more important, Daddy,'I told him, 'you kept your promise, too! You didn't forsake us! You never abandoned us!' And I kissed him maybe five times, one kiss right after the other, the frantic way I used to kiss him after Stanley died and I thought it was maybe my turn next year."

***

An hour later, I walked Arlene to the crosstown stop. It was a Sunday. We must have just missed a bus, because next one didn't show up for another ten minutes. Killing time, Arlene, sole curator of a more than ninety-year-old archive, told yet another story I'd never heard before. But unlike the others today, this one left me laughing.

As a kid, she'd always been picky about food. And after her mother died and before my father remarried, they had a live-in cook who offered one inedible dish after another, which only made Arlene an even more finicky eater.

Often hungry, she'd ask my father for a nickel to get some ice cream. Only instead of ice cream, she'd walk to a nearby shoe repair store. The owner was an Italian with a handlebar mustache. Besides repairing shoes, he cooked and sold hot dogs as a sideline. To satisfy her hunger, Arlene gave him her nickel and bought one.

"Arlene," I asked, blinking three or four times in pretended astonishment, "were they at least kosher?"

"Are you kidding?" she said. Her mother died when she was five and my father didn't remarry and move until Arlene was eight. So we 're talking about the years Arlene was a resourceful six and seven.

"Not only weren't they kosher," Arlene reported, "but the shoe repair man's hands were always dirty from the shoe polish he kept applying during the day."

I practically fainted, and here's why. After her brother died of polio, my father became obsessed about washing his children's hands. Not only Arlene's and Sandra's, but he was still a fanatic after I was born and it used to drive me up the wall.

Anyway, glancing over my left shoulder, I could see Arlene's bus turning right at York and begin heading our way. Grinning, I said, "My God, Arlene, if the old man knew how you'd spent that nickel he'd have had two major strokes: one, because of the guy's dirty hands; the other, because the hot dogs weren't kosher. How many you figure you ate?"

Nodding penitently, Arlene said, "Oh, I don't know, twenty, thirty. Thank God Daddy never found out and thank God I never got food poisoning."

"Twenty, thirty?" I said, and couldn't stop myself from laughing.

Less than a minute later, the bus pulled up and people began boarding it. But Arlene seemed reluctant to leave, reluctant to say goodbye, and today, at last, I knew exactly why.

"See you soon," I told her instead of saying goodbye. And smiling, I reached for my sister's hand, picturing her at seven furtively eating a forbidden hotdog.

She smiled back, grateful I hadn't said goodbye.

"Arlene," I said, kissing her twice, "you're a pisser."

Opening Day

At Katz's Delicatessen on Houston Street, which had been around forever, there was still a World War II sign that read, "Send your soldier boy a salami." Seeing it and grinning, Harry Steinhardt ordered two pastrami and two corned beef sandwiches, four pickles, a large container of coleslaw, and a couple of cans of cream soda. He and his friend of more than fifty years, Lionel Kirshbaum, would be lucky for each to ingest a single pickle plus a sandwich, even luckier not to suffer heartburn later that day. But eating sandwiches from Katz's and watching the Yankee home opener on Lionel's TV in Baldwin was a venerable tradition with them.

From Katz's in lower Manhattan out to Lionel's would take about an hour, provided the traffic on the Long Island Expressway wasn't a nightmare. Harry usually drove listening to WQXR, because a little Mozart went a long way. This time, however, he traveled to Lionel's without turning on the radio.

For the last ten years, Harry had been sending Lionel checks totaling twenty thousand dollars annually. Lionel, a painter, had been experiencing, he said, a terrible time selling his work this past decade, and Harry, who'd done exceptionally well in the stock market, had promised to help out as long as he could. Today Harry was going to tell Lionel that he could only afford to keep sending him ten thousand a year. The reason being, Harry had taken a number of recent hits, and his money manager had advised to quickly cut down on expenses or his financial situation would start to seriously deteriorate.

Two Jewish boys from New York, Harry and Lionel had served in the Army together, beginning in 1943. Each spoke

Yiddish fluently, which was why they'd been assigned to a military government detachment based near Munich. There Lionel fell in love with a German-Jewish girl, Trudie. Yet he decided not to marry her because she'd had a kid a year before with a German officer who was later killed. It was Trudie who'd introduced Harry to her cousin Lisel, and rather a miracle that both girls had survived the Nazis. In truth, it wasn't really a miracle but a German officer who, at great risk to himself, had saved them. Why saved them—guilt? infatuation? perversity?—Lord only knows. But talk about irony, luck, talk about surprises.

Another was that the more conventional Harry wound up marrying Lisel. Two years later, back in New York, Lionel married a Bronx girl, Sylvia Roth. While Sylvia was neurotic, possessive, and congenitally unhappy, Trudie had loved to laugh. She ended up marrying a Canadian soldier and lived in Toronto. Lisel kept in touch with her, although they'd had a falling-out a while back and were no longer close friends.

Because Sylvia was aware of Lionel's wartime affair—he was the kind of man who couldn't help telling everyone—she wasn't wild about either Lisel or Harry. Besides, she knew they both thought Lionel had made the mistake of a lifetime not marrying Trudie, even if Trudie had been saddled with a kid.

"You guys planning to make yourselves good and sick this year, or just anticipate some mild indigestion?" said Sylvia, who had watery eyes and long gray hair she wore in a bun.

"How are you, Sylvia?" Harry said, as the enveloping smell of brine and garlic quickly perfumed the kitchen. In the old days, he'd kiss her on the cheek to be polite. Now he no longer went through the motions.

"I ought to be back by five," Sylvia told her husband. She was on her way to meet her sister and go to a movie. "Don't forget to take your pills after you eat, Lionel. Not that they'll do you any good today."

God forgive Harry, but he was always happy to see her leave, and Lionel seemed to exhale gratefully as well.

Lionel was on the short side, heavyset, almost completely bald. He wore bifocals and had large brown eyes and a generous mouth. His appearance suggested a man born to be cheerful, but Lionel had a bad temper. It not only got him into trouble in the Army but unnecessarily complicated his life in the notoriously contentious New York art world.

Harry had been sending him checks because he believed in Lionel's talent. But it was really Lionel's gruff way of speaking and brotherly heart that Harry had found so appealing from the beginning. That, plus the three years they'd spent together in Germany during and after the war. The sheer power they wielded as military governors, dispensing justice, Hershey Bars, and cigarettes, was never greater, and the sex they encountered there never more touchingly desperate. Because of Germany, they considered themselves friends forever.

**

It was during the seventh-inning stretch, just before the Yankees came to bat against the hated Red Sox, that Harry finally managed to say, "I'm no longer able to send you twenty grand a year, Lionel. But you can still count on me for ten."

At first, Lionel looked shocked, then angry. But recovering his composure, he said, "Gee, Harry, I guess I took advantage and milked you."

"No, it's nothing like that, and I'm just sorry I've got to cut down on expenses."

"If I haven't thanked you sufficiently in the past, don't think I was ever ungrateful."

But Harry waved him off, as if gratitude or even its facsimile was unnecessary. "I feel badly about this, Lionel, just can't help myself."

"Don't feel badly," Lionel told him.

Because he seemed to take the news with equanimity, even graciousness, Harry experienced a sense of relief.

Yet when Lionel moved his car from the driveway after the game, presumably making it easier for Harry to subsequently pull out, he almost ran Harry over. Fortunately, his friend managed to scramble clear of Lionel's Buick at the last second or Lionel's fender would have smashed into his knee.

"What the hell's the matter with you?" a shocked Harry said when Lionel emerged from the car. "Have you gone nuts?"

Of course Lionel apologized, said it was an accident, he was really getting too old to continue driving. But there had always been something violent, unpredictable, even wild about Lionel. It was there in his paintings as well. While this quality drew you toward his work, it often left you shaken rather than satisfied, as though the emotion binding the pigments encapsulated only anger.

"It's not because you cut down on the money," Lionel insisted.

"Yeah, right," Harry answered, making a fist without realizing it.

Harry didn't tell his wife about his near miss. But then, he never told Lisel about sending Lionel money over the years either. He was one of those men both generous and suspicious, which explained why he'd give Lisel a blank check any time she asked but always refused to purchase even the most innocuous form of life insurance.

They lived in an apartment on Fifth Avenue overlooking Central Park near the Metropolitan Museum of Art. Their daughter, Miriam, was a writer whose second novel was slated to be published the following month. They'd had a son, Robert, but he died in a plane crash several years before. Learning about the crash via a phone call from his wife, Lionel had immediately arranged to board an overnight flight and returned from a Los Angeles art show, arriving bleary-eyed at Harry's apartment before nine the following morning.

Surprised to see him, Harry had said, "I thought it was important for you to remain in L.A. with your paintings till the end of the week."

Lionel shrugged. "Turned out it wasn't that important," he said.

Harry was just under six feet, slender, had a long, aquiline nose, a high forehead, and thinning, sandy-colored hair. While he genuinely enjoyed acquiring a lot of money, he believed that freedom and art were just as valuable, another reason he'd felt so attracted to someone like Lionel.

Yet Harry didn't hear from him after the incident involving the car, although Lionel usually called to thank his friend for the pastrami sandwiches.

Grudgingly, it was Harry who called the last day in April, and they talked pleasantly for almost a half hour, neither of them mentioning the money nor Lionel's car. They talked, in short, as if nothing had changed between them. But hanging up, Harry promised himself he would not call again if Lionel didn't return his call. "I've bent over backwards," Harry thought. "If he can't find the courage or grace, get over his embarrassment or anger, well, the hell with him."

***

May came and went without their speaking. This was the first month, excluding when either went on vacation, they hadn't spoken since they were discharged from the Army, and it depressed Harry to think that their friendship had suddenly gone awry.

He remembered their wild nights in Germany, recalled the Knick games they'd attended at the old Garden, meals they'd shared in Chinatown and Little Italy. He remembered taking in Lionel's art shows down in the Village and going to Lionel's parents' funerals, even recalled Lionel visiting his mother at Mount Sinai Hospital after her heart attack, making her smile and laugh. And who could forget Lionel showing up early that morning after learning Harry's son had been killed?

"Lionel, for God's sake!" Harry muttered.

In June, he tried to entice a call by sending Lionel a copy of his daughter's recently published novel. It was inspired by her brother's death and told through the eyes of a terrorist planning to blow up a plane filled with American tourists. Lisel absolutely refused to look at the book. Harry thought it was brilliant but found it excruciating to read. Unfortunately, Lionel never acknowledged even receiving a copy.

Not hearing from him that summer was hard to take, as if Harry had lost someone he'd come to think of as irreplaceable.

It wasn't until the end of October when Lionel finally called, blithely telling Harry, as though the connection between them had remained alive and well the last six months, "Guess what today is?"

Harry cautiously answered he hadn't the faintest idea.

"It's my birthday. Can you believe I'm seventy-five? I can't. That a *meshuganah* guy like me actually made it this far is a bloody miracle."

"Happy Birthday," Harry said without his usual enthusiasm. "*Mazel Tov.*"

"I guess you're wondering why I haven't phoned for a while," Lionel responded. "Who's kidding who? I was teed off about the money. Now I'm over it. You want to know why, Harry? Because life's too short not to be. Hell, life's too short, period."

Neither of them mentioned Miriam's new novel, yet they spoke for almost an hour, catching up on what each had done over the summer. Lionel and Sylvie had spent a couple of weeks in the Poconos. Harry had finally convinced Lisel to get away for the first time since their son died, and they'd stayed with old friends in Maine.

"So, what do you think the Yanks will do next year?" Lionel asked, and he resumed phoning Harry during the next several weeks, signaling that the call on his birthday was not a one-shot affair.

Hoping to re-energize their hemorrhaging friendship and wanting to keep his decade-old promise, Harry sent Lionel a check for ten thousand the first week in January.

When Lionel stopped calling that February, Harry thought, "My God, he played me for a jerk, a *shlemiel* just to get one more check," and enraged, he phoned Lionel. But it was Sylvia who answered. Lionel wasn't home, she said nervously, but she'd tell him Harry called.

A week passed, ten days, two weeks. When Harry called a second time, Sylvia said Lionel was indisposed and quickly hung up.

Slamming the phone down, Harry wanted to kill them both.

"Your old friend gives and takes offense too easily," was Lisel's reaction when Harry bitterly criticized Lionel without going into detail. "But that's exactly the way he was in Germany fifty years ago." Lisel never really forgave Lionel's disappointing her cousin.

It was Sylvia who phoned the following month to say that the reason Harry hadn't heard from Lionel was that Lionel had been ill and didn't want anyone to know. Now, the diagnosis definitive, there was no point any longer in hiding the truth. "Lionel's going to die this spring," Sylvia announced. "He's got pancreatic cancer."

The news stunned Harry, who asked if Lionel could come to the phone.

"No," said Sylvia, "because the prospect of talking to you seems to particularly upset him." It was as though she'd chosen the precise words she knew would hurt Harry most.

Still, desperate to hear about his friend's condition, Harry began to call at least twice a week, and Sylvia would report *ad nauseam* that her husband was too sick to come to the phone. As for visiting Lionel, actually seeing him, Sylvia pronounced that out of the question. "If he's too weak to talk on the phone, Harry, how could he possibly find the strength to tolerate a visit?"

Putting the receiver down, Harry told his wife, "He's been my closest friend for fifty years. How can she make me sound like a perfect moron? And forget about me, doesn't she realize what that says about her husband?"

***

Fortunately, Harry happened to call once when Lionel's son answered the phone. The last time they'd spoken had been at David's wedding ten years before. Harry clearly remembered, because a clumsy photographer had accidentally pushed Sylvia, almost knocking her down. Losing his famous temper, Lionel angrily demanded an apology. When the photographer refused, Lionel uncorked a right and sent the guy flying. It was a family scandal, typical Lionel.

"How's your father doing today, David?" Harry asked, knowing the news wasn't going to be terrific.

"About the same." David, an accountant who didn't always get along with his father, had Lionel's gruff voice. "He's sleeping now, Harry."

But just then, Lionel woke, and when David told him it was Harry on the other end, Lionel asked to speak to him.

"I'm sorry I wasn't up to talking to you before," Lionel apologized, covering for Sylvia.

He sounded painfully weak, and Harry felt helpless, worse than how he'd felt when his mother was at Sinai after her heart attack. "I wish to God there was something I could do for you, Lionel."

"Don't give up on me yet, okay?" Lionel answered.

"For crying out loud, Lionel, when have I ever really given up on you?" Harry said.

But two nights later, when David called, Harry was sure that Lionel had just died. Instead, David said that his father had asked to see Harry. "You're welcome to come anytime." Yet David added that people from the local hospice, however, had begun administering morphine to Lionel since the day before yesterday, which meant that if Harry came he might find Lionel sleeping.

Because Harry no longer drove at night, he decided, "I'll be out there late tomorrow morning."

"My father said to tell you that you don't have to bring any sandwiches from Katz's this time, whatever that means."

Harry explained that he and Lionel used to celebrate the Yanks' home opener by watching the game on Lionel's TV while eating pastrami and corned beef sandwiches, and weren't the Bombers opening at the Stadium that week?

"You flaky old guys, talk about heartburn heaven," David said, and couldn't help laughing. "See you tomorrow."

Yet when Harry showed up the following morning, Sylvia practically refused to let him enter the house, and if David still wasn't around, Harry would have been forced to leave.

David had grown a heavy black beard since his wedding, and it made him look fierce when he told his mother, "I don't know what you've held against Harry all these years, but Dad asked to see him, and you're not going to prevent it even if I have to drag you out of here kicking and screaming. You're too possessive, Ma, you always were."

"Go to hell, both of you!" she told them, storming out of the house. Her husband was dying and that morning Sylvia, a born dyspeptic, hated the whole world.

***

Lionel was dozing when they entered his bedroom. He must have lost thirty pounds since Harry had seen him almost exactly a year before. He was lying in bed, freshly shaven and propped up on a couple of pillows, wearing a long-sleeve red golf shirt rather than pajamas. Three of his paintings hung opposite the bed. The most striking, least characteristic, and one of Harry's favorites, showed a boy and dog running past a deserted house on a sandy hill. The contrast between the boy's innocence and the forlorn, abandoned house somehow broke your heart.

"Dad, you awake?" David asked. "Harry's come to visit you."

Lionel opened his eyes, focusing on Harry. "I'm not going to be my usual charming self," he warned, his voice sounding less gruff than usual.

Harry smiled nervously. "That's okay, Lionel. I've seen you uncharming before."

"David, I want to be alone with Harry for fifteen, twenty minutes. Don't want you or your mother up here, okay?"

"Whatever you say, Dad." And starting to leave, he added over his burly shoulder, "I'll be downstairs. If you guys need anything, just give a holler."

"Sit down, Harry, take the load off," Lionel said after David left them alone. The blinds were up and the room, which smelled of witch hazel, was filled with bright sunlight.

What a day for a ballgame, Harry couldn't help thinking, and pulling up the nearest folding chair, he asked if Lionel was in any pain.

Lionel said the hospice people had been giving him enough morphine to knock out a horse, and he was only sorry he hadn't gotten in touch with them sooner. He could have saved himself a lot of unnecessary suffering. Then he closed his eyes.

He seemed to be drifting in and out, and sitting there, Harry tried to engrave his memory with his friend's features —Lionel's blunt nose, sensitive mouth, his stubby, muscular fingers.

"I hope I haven't disappointed you too often, Harry," Lionel muttered without opening his eyes.

Reaching for Lionel's hand, Harry said, "You've been my dearest friend, Lionel. Sometimes difficult, but always interesting, always interesting."

Lionel smiled, opening his eyes. "You wouldn't shit a guy on his deathbed, right?"

Grinning, Harry refused to flinch. "Not a chance."

Instead of going to Katz's that morning, Harry said, he'd stopped off at Sherry Lehmann's where he'd purchased a bottle of Mouton-Rothschild. He'd read somewhere, he told Lionel, that the French used to wet the lips of their newborn kings with wine of the finest quality, and he was hoping they might share a drink together now.

"I'll need a straw," Lionel said, "if that's okay," and he couldn't help laughing. "Imagine, the famous Mouton-Rothschild drunk with a plastic straw—probably first time in the history of the Medoc."

Lionel managed a sip or two with Harry's help, after which Harry lifted his own glass. "Here's to friendship," he toasted with a shaky hand.

Lionel nodded, and Harry kept looking at him as he enjoyed sipping the wine which went down like nectar.

"I apologize for not acknowledging your daughter's book last year," Lionel said. "I wanted to hurt you badly, Harry. I know I've mentioned it before, but cutting down on the money infuriated me. It's especially embarrassing to admit now, because I'm about to ask for another favor."

Harry stiffened but didn't pull back. "What's on your mind, Lionel?"

"After I'm gone, I'd like you to notify Trudie," he said. "I can't ask Sylvia to do that and I'd rather keep my son out of it." He added that he knew Lisel occasionally corresponded with Trudie, so Harry could get her Canadian address from his wife.

Harry was surprised that Lionel knew the cousins still corresponded infrequently. "Sure," he said. "I'll take care of it."

"I've never told you before, Harry, but I've been in touch with Trudie for the last ten years," Lionel said. "Her husband ran off, disappeared with all their money, and she was ashamed, didn't want you and Lisel to know. But she was also desperate, which was why she contacted me." Here Lionel paused, as if he was about to add something; but thinking better of it, he shook his head, saying, "No, I've covered everything I want to tell you, Harry. You can figure out the rest for yourself. And now I need to say goodbye. Actually, what I really need is to take a wicked leak, and would you ask David to come up when you get downstairs."

Standing and nodding, Harry blinked twice. Lionel was right, it didn't take a genius to figure things out. "I'll leave the bottle here, Lionel, in case you want another drink," Harry said.

When Lionel thanked him for the wine, Harry leaned over and kissed his friend's forehead. "My lawyer'll keep sending money to Trudie that I would have sent you and write that it's from a trust you left her," Harry promised. "That sound okay, Lionel, what you maybe had in mind?"

Sighing, Lionel nodded again before closing his eyes. "I guess I turned out to be an expensive friend. But tell you what, Harry—I'll put in a good word for you when I get to where I'm going."

Lionel always could induce a bounce from him, even now, and Harry smiled. "Oh, hell, Lionel," he said, his heart banging away. "What am I going to do without you?"

The Visitor

～

The pulmonologist Bernard Lowenthal made a point of picking up his mother's mail before visiting her in the hospital. Suzanne had been there since Wednesday night, and it was now Saturday afternoon. The prior Friday, she'd had a cyst removed from her right palm. Unfortunately, the palm had become infected. A neighbor suggested she take antibiotics, but they didn't help. Not wanting to worry her son, she hadn't alerted Bernie until Wednesday evening. He took one look at her purulent hand and immediately drove her to Mount Sinai. A good friend of Bernie's operated early next morning. By Saturday, the infection had receded, but she was still receiving a new antibiotic.

Suzanne, a widow, was in her early eighties. She'd emigrated from France soon after the war. Bernie was her only child.

"Ma, brought your mail from the last four days," he said, entering her room and kissing her. Her hand was still heavily bandaged and had a caudal block.

"Bernie, darling," said his mother. She was wearing a wine-colored robe the hospital had provided and was sitting in a chair, her right hand raised at the urging of her surgeon.

"How you feeling, Ma?" Bernie asked, noting lipstick for the first time since she'd been hospitalized.

"Oh, much better. I could see that my hand wasn't as red when the doctor changed the dressing this morning."

Suzanne had been an exceptionally good-looking woman, a genuine beauty, and even now, in her eighties, she'd retained those high cheekbones and striking green eyes men had found so alluring.

Bernie left her mail next to a rectangular box of pink tissues. The envelope on top was a blue airmail with a Paris postmark. Bernie wondered who the letter was from. As far as he knew, his mother's French relatives had all been killed during the war.

"So, how's Judy and the girls?" Suzanne asked, as Bernie sat up on her bed. He'd been jogging in nearby Central Park, had muscular calves, and wore a pair of blue Nikes with grey laces.

"Everybody's fine, Ma, good, said to say hello." Bernie and his wife Judy had two daughters. The oldest was a singer with the Chicago Lyric Opera, the youngest attended Harvard Law School. Suzanne was only sorry that her late husband Bobby wasn't still around. He would have been so proud—a lawyer-to-be and a diva. Not bad. Bobby himself had been a big shot newspaper editor at the old *Herald Tribune.*

"When am I getting out of here, Bernie?" Suzanne asked. In Bernie's experience, restless female patients wearing lipstick, were usually patients heading north, not south.

"Figuring you'd ask, I made sure to call Harry Crowder who thought you'd be going home Monday." Crowder was Suzanne's ortho.

"Nice man, Dr. Crowder. By the way, he said you were a very good doctor, Bernie, best pulmonologist here."

Bernie burst out laughing. "For Christ's sake, Ma, you're my one and only. What 'd you expect him to say?"

"Oh, Bernie, don't be so cynical."

"Ah, my son the doctor, the dream of every Jewish mother." Bernie winked and mentioned the beautiful weather, before patting Suzanne's shoulder after bouncing to his feet. "I was jogging, Ma, this is a quickie visit. But Judy and I will stop by tomorrow. Bring you a couple of *croissants* and spend some time here. Anything else you want us to bring?"

"The Sunday *Times*," she said cheerfully before he kissed her goodbye. While Suzanne missed the late, lamented *Trib*, she'd grown to love the *Times* and still kept herself avidly informed of the big wide world beyond New York, home-sweet-home for the last sixty years.

***

Yet an hour later, the hospital called, telling Bernie that his mother had disappeared from her room and, so far, they hadn't been able to find her.

"Disappeared? What do you mean, disappeared?" Bernie asked. Had his mother been jinxed from the start by this stupid, harmless cyst? "I'll be right over."

Fortunately, by the time Bernie arrived one of the security people found his mother sitting behind a post in one of the stairwells near the roof, five floors above the floor where Suzanne's room was located.

She'd taken a walk, she told Bernie calmly, couldn't find her way back and, feeling tired, sat down in the stairwell and must have dozed off.

Bernie asked what day it was, her late husband's name, how old she was. Suzanne smiled when he began and kept smiling, which was why Bernie kept asking.

Finally, she told him, "Bernie, I'm sorry I upset you so much, sorry they called and you felt you had to come back," and she began to stroke his face as if he was the one who'd gotten lost, not her. Then she said, "Today's Saturday, your father's name is Bobby, and I'm eighty. So, I still have all my marbles?"

Bernie nodded.

"Say it, Bernie," she insisted.

"You still have all your marbles, Suzanne." Bernie only called her "Suzanne" when she seemed not so much his mother but rather a beautiful woman fated to break his heart.

"Good," she responded. "So please stop worrying. Go home. Have dinner. Give Judy an extra hug for me."

Yet Bernie remained disturbed, because Suzanne was hardly the type either to get lost or to become lost and doze off.

***

Nevertheless, he took her home Monday after she'd had a final IV of antibiotics at ten-thirty.

Earlier that morning, Bernie and his wife had shopped for Suzanne, filling her refrigerator. Their housekeeper, Loretta, who'd been working for Bernie and Judy for twenty years, would be coming over later to cook for Suzanne. Judy, a violist with the New York Philharmonic, was a lousy cook; Bernie even worse. The reason Judy hadn't accompanied Bernie when he'd picked his mother up was because she was attending a rehearsal at Lincoln Center for a concert the orchestra was scheduled to perform the following evening.

Five minutes after arriving from the hospital, Suzanne's phone rang. "Want me to answer it, Ma?" Bernie asked.

"No," she said, reaching awkwardly but assertively for the receiver with her left hand. Using her left hand in the hospital had taken some getting used to.

The person on the other end must have asked if she was Suzanne Lowenthal, because she answered, "Yes, I'm Suzanne Lowenthal."

After which she listened for almost a minute before saying, "I received your letter but was in the hospital, which is why I couldn't answer it. I'm sorry to disappoint you, my friend, but you've simply got the wrong person, and our getting together would therefore be quite pointless, make no sense."

Suzanne's caller, however, must have continued talking about meeting her, because Suzanne soon began rolling her eyes helplessly.

Bernie gestured for the phone, gently removing it from his mother's hand. "I'm Suzanne's son, Bernard," he said. "Can I help you?"

"My name is Charles Corbet," the fellow on the other end replied. He had a pronounced French accent. "I don't wish to shock you, but I believe your mother is also my birth mother, and I would like to meet her."

Suzanne was alternately shaking her head and shrugging, as if the poor fellow was crazy, or, more likely, it was one of those sad cases of mistaken identity.

"My mother's quite elderly and just got home from the hospital," said a suddenly distraught Bernie, stalling.

"It must be difficult receiving this call at your mother's," Corbet acknowledged sympathetically. "I'm staying at the Wales Hotel on Madison Avenue and Ninety-second Street. Perhaps we could meet there, have a drink, talk."

Bernie's protective instinct prompted him to say, "Sir, you've made a mistake, so please don't call my mother again." Then he abruptly hung up, in the belief that nothing was to be gained by prolonging the conversation, at least in Suzanne's apartment. Yet knowing within seconds the guy deserved better, Bernie felt like a shit.

"I really don't understand how such crazy things happen," Suzanne was saying. "Imagine the poor man believing I gave birth to him. I've read stories like his in the *Times*; but actually, getting a call like this is quite unbelievable."

"Of course, Ma," agreed a seemingly accommodating Bernie, and rather than pursue the subject, he asked if Suzanne would like a bite of lunch, maybe soup, a cheese sandwich, or both. Even a bum cook like Bernie could manage that.

"Bernie, darling," said Suzanne, relieved he'd dropped the prior, touchier subject. "I couldn't wish for a better son."

"Oh, Ma, come on, cut it out." It always embarrassed Bernie when she'd praise him to his face. It was probably genetic, because his father used to react the same way.

***

That evening when Judy got home, she naturally asked Bernie, "How's your mom doing?" Judy was slender, with a slightly upturned nose, melting brown eyes, and a curvy, sensuous mouth. While she liked Suzanne, she sensed early on there would have been a problem dealing with her if she wasn't successful, an accomplished musician.

"You'll never guess what happened today," Bernie began, sipping a Scotch. "A guy called out of nowhere, saying my mother gave birth to him before coming to the States."

Leaning back against their sand-colored living room couch, it didn't surprise Judy that Suzanne had a dubious past. Suzanne had always struck her as the kind of woman men found irresistible, women less so.

"I'm sorry, Bernie, it must be terribly upsetting," his wife said. "But I don't know there's anything you can do about it."

"I'll be damned if I know what to do either." And putting his drink down, Bernie related for the first time that when his father was dying, the old man told him to be kind to his mother because before arriving in the States, she'd had a wrenching experience in wartime Europe. "When I asked my father what he meant, he refused to elaborate, saying he'd promised never to tell anyone. My guess was she'd been raped."

"Funny," Judy interjected, "you never mentioning this before."

"Oh, I don't know, maybe not so funny, maybe not so strange, after all." Because hadn't he been aware at least since his father died that there was something secretive, painfully unsettling about his mother's past?

Bernie's parents had become involved when his father had served as an infantryman over in Normandy. It was his father who'd arranged for Suzanne to come to the States after the war. There, to please his father's parents, she'd converted to Judaism before marrying a head-over-heels in love Bobby.

"So, how 'd it end at your mother's today?" Judy asked.

"I told the guy to back off, that he'd made a mistake," Bernie said. "But before I hung up, he quickly mentioned where he was staying. Clever fellow, fast on his feet. But, frankly, I'm afraid if I went over there I'd be opening a Pandora's box. At the same time, while I don't want to upset my mother, I'm curious as hell. Wouldn't you be?"

"Maybe the answer is to meet him without your mother knowing," suggested Judy, guessing with a pang of guilt that probably sounded unfair to Suzanne.

"I can't tell you why," said Bernie, frowning, "but I have the feeling this is one of those situations that I'm going to bitterly regret whatever I do or don't do."

**

The following day, Bernie saw patients at his Park Avenue office from nine to four. His specialty was asthma and emphysema. Not having been in the office Monday because he'd wanted to be completely available to his mother, meant catch-up time, a particularly busy office day, and he was beat when he left.

It was on his way home that a man his size approached him, saying, "I'm Charles Corbet. We spoke on the phone yesterday."

Adrenalin kicking in despite feeling exhausted, it took all of five seconds for a startled Bernie to realize that Corbet could easily have passed for a sibling.

Like Bernie, Corbet had Suzanne's striking green eyes, the same full lower lip and appealing, knifelike nose.

Momentarily tongue-tied, Bernie considered shaking hands. But his arm seemed incapable of moving as well. Yet forcing himself to focus, he zeroed in on Corbet, who was wearing a navy pinstripe suit, blue shirt with a spread collar, and a red polka-dot tie.

"I looked up your name in the phone book," Corbet was saying, "took a chance the Dr. Bernard Lowenthal was the same Bernard Lowenthal I spoke to yesterday, and decided to wait outside your office. Frankly, I knew it was you as soon as I saw you—we have the same eyes. Listen, there's a bar near the Hotel Wales where I'm staying, and it's within walking distance."

Bernie knew the street. He'd eaten with Judy and another couple in an Italian restaurant directly across from the Wales less than a month ago. But a bar, any bar, would hardly offer the privacy this kind of meeting required. The man, after all, could almost have passed for his twin.

"Let's get a cab," Bernie heard himself nervously saying. "I live across town, on the Upper West Side. Do you know New York at all?" Corbet spoke English so well, Bernie wouldn't have been surprised had he responded that he'd visited the States often.

Corbet said he'd never been to New York before but had lived in Chicago for two years as an exchange student.

Nodding, Bernie hailed a taxi at the corner of Eighty-sixth. It was one of those newer cabs that have sliding doors and look like an S.U.V. When Corbet stepped into the cab, Bernie noted for the first time that he was carrying a shiny black briefcase with a large gold clasp shaped like a heart.

They drove past the Lehman Wing of the Metropolitan, winding through Central Park, shrubs of forsythia doing their best to cheer Bernie up. He said that his wife, a violist with the New York Philharmonic, would be performing at Lincoln Center that night but that their cook, Loretta, would be home.

"My wife is an editor at *Le Monde*," observed Corbet, relieved that Bernie seemed to have gotten over his initial shock.

"My father was also a newspaper editor," said Bernie, grateful they had something else in common.

Neither knew what to say next, though, how to follow up, and a minute or two seemed to descend like a sheet of lead between them. Mercifully, their cab soon turned right at West End Avenue, pulling up less than a mile away.

***

"Loretta, this is a friend from Paris, Charles Corbet," said Bernie, the word "friend" striking his inner ear as less jarring than any other under the circumstances. "We're going to be in the living room, having a drink or two."

Loretta nodded, knowing Bernie well enough to understand that meant he didn't wish to be disturbed. Standing almost six feet, Loretta, born in Jamaica, was taller than either man, with skinny legs, ebony-colored skin, and frizzy hair.

"When I left your mother an hour ago, she said to tell you she was feeling better and to stop worrying," Loretta reported in her singsong voice. "But I told her it wouldn't help, because you always worried about her."

Bernie laughed. Loretta was a naturally uninhibited woman, visitor or no visitor, and Bernie, broken in over the years, had grown to like her that way. So did Judy and their daughters. Loretta kept them all alert, loose, often amused and only occasionally embarrassed.

The men went into the living room, which was dominated by a trio of floor-length bookcases. Bernie asked if Corbet preferred brandy or Scotch. Corbet surprisingly said Scotch, and Bernie poured them each a stiff shot; then, without asking, he went into the kitchen and returned with a crystal bowl of clicking ice and two tall glasses of water.

"My mother, Suzanne, lives across the street, a block away," Bernie said, sitting in one of two green suede chairs. It was, he thought, as good a way of getting the ball rolling as any other.

Blinking, Corbet understood this was it, why he'd flown to New York, or another step in the right direction. He sat opposite Bernie, on the couch, to the right of an inlaid table that had a copper rim.

"I was born in 1944," he began, "an orphan adopted by a French civil servant and his wife. They'd lost a young daughter to cancer. My childhood was happy and I attended the Sorbonne, where I became interested in art. I'm a curator at the Louvre, married, have two sons."

Trying to reply in kind, Bernie said that he was born in 1949 and that his specialty was pulmonology. "You already know that I'm married. We have two daughters, and, as you might have noticed, a number of their pictures are scattered throughout this room."

When Bernie paused to take a drink, Corbet decided it was his turn again, and plunging ahead, he said, "I learned last year the truth about myself when my adopted mother was dying. She told me that my father was a German officer and that my mother was a young Frenchwoman who'd placed me in an orphanage days after I was born. I suppose she wanted a clean break, a fresh start. Of course the news was devastating, because before then I'd had no idea I was what is called in France an *enfant de Boches*, a child born during the war to a Frenchwoman and a German soldier."

Corbet subsequently discovered that about 200,000 such children were born as a result of those wartime liaisons. "We are in our sixties, most of us now, and those like me, who were recently told the truth, are attempting to seek out our birth parents before it is too late."

Curious because of his mother's involvement, about which Bernie had absolutely no doubt now, he asked if Corbet had met his father yet.

"My birth father, I learned from German military archives, was an artillery officer killed in early 1945. He was in his thirties, had a wife back in Hamburg, and, like yourself, two daughters. I've met both. Although our DNA's match, one wants nothing to do with me; the other, quite friendly, was a dentist but is now retired."

Here Corbet opened his briefcase and withdrew a colored photograph of a German soldier in his grey/green uniform standing, hatless and smiling, near a glinting lake with his two daughters. He has a round face, dark curly hair, and there is a distinct scar trailing across his forehead. His arms are draped around each girl, both of whom have bangs and look less than ten years old. Yellow flowers dot the countryside, and you can practically smell the velvety grass.

"The little girl who is frowning is the one who wishes to be friends," said Corbet, smiling ironically.

At this point, both men had finished their drinks, and Bernie got up and poured each a second shot.

"Please do not be offended that I ask if you are close to your mother," Corbet said, both hands nervously stroking his tall glass.

Bernie nodded, saying frankly, "I love my mother dearly."

Corbet reached inside his briefcase again and withdrew a second photograph, handing it to Bernie, saying, "I know this will upset you. You must try to forgive me."

The nine-by-twelve black and white shot showed a cobblestone French street with a crowd of people, a ragged procession, marching along. Dominating the foreground is a young woman whose head is shaved. She's holding an infant. Walking next to her, talking to her, is a French policeman wearing a helmet, a leather strap under his chin. To the woman's right is an older man, carrying a laundry sack and wearing a beret. Women are in the background, children, too, and another policeman, this one wearing a kepi. Many of the women are smiling. A little girl about seven is not only smiling but pointing, jeeringly, at the woman carrying the infant. You can see a French flag hanging, dipping, from the second floor of a stone building that has a chipped balcony.

Even shorn and humiliated, Bernie immediately recognized his mother's beautiful face.

Corbet said, "Your mother was hounded in her village. I understand why. It was war, and her neighbors hated the Germans with good reason."

Staring inconsolably at his mother's picture, Bernie retained enough composure to ask how Corbet finally tracked Suzanne to America, New York, to the Upper West Side.

"When my mother was dying, she mentioned your mother's name, saying your mother had gone to America. The French government was not helpful in the beginning. But a new foreign minister, whose grandparents were killed at Auschwitz, recently offered the country's cooperation; and having your mother's name, I was able to follow her via her French passport to New York. Here an investigator discovered her wedding license, citing your father's name. After that, learning your mother's address and phone number was child's play. I wrote two weeks ago, called yesterday, you know the rest..."

It made sense to Bernie, certainly the sequential steps fit logically, and he could easily see himself doing the same thing in Corbet's shoes.

"I do not wish to cause your mother additional suffering, but it would mean a great deal to me if we could meet. I am trying to put my life in order, make sense of things, come to understand who I am and accept who I came from. But it is complicated and, I confess, still troubling."

Bernie could hardly blame the guy, yet he said, "I really don't know that I can assist you. My mother's in her eighties. If she refuses to see you, if it's too painful for her to face you, I'm not sure there's anything I can say that would help. Nor would I wish her to think I in any way betrayed her."

"Please try to understand," Corbet said, "I've come so close."

Bernie's phone rang, and he guessed it was his service, calling to say an asthmatic patient was in trouble or needed to consult about a prescribed medicine. But no, it wasn't his answering service, rather his youngest daughter Ella phoning from school, wanting to know how Suzanne was faring.

"Good, better, why don't you give Grandma a call now," Bernie suggested impatiently.

"I will after dinner, Dad, but wanted to check with you first. By the way, you sound kind of strange. You and Mom okay?"

"We're fine. Your mother's performing tonight. I think it's Mozart's 40th, but I forget the rest of the program. Someone's with me, sweetie, a visitor from Paris. Can I call you back?"

"Oh, sure, Dad. You should have said so right away. Love ya to pieces."

Bernie smiled. Ella had been signing off that way since she was five. The phrase had become a kind of signature.

"I'm sorry," Bernie apologized to Corbet. "That was my youngest who's away at Boston studying to be a lawyer."

Corbet was staring at the picture of a shorn Suzanne carrying her firstborn, and it seemed to Bernie that Corbet was holding the photo so tightly his knuckles had turned white.

The doorbell rang, hell, another interruption.

"Loretta, would you please answer the door!" Bernie called out.

Loretta was in her room, reading her Bible. She'd been living with the Lowenthals since their older daughter Leila had move to Chicago five years ago.

"It's me. Loretta," said Suzanne, walking into the apartment. "I made some *cholent* for Bernie." It was an East European stew consisting of beans and potatoes. Bernie's grandmother had taught Suzanne how to make it because Bernie loved it so. "Has he eaten yet?" Suzanne asked.

"No, he's with a friend," explained Loretta. "They're in the living room, talking and drinking. You know Bernie; once he gets started he can go for hours."

"An old friend?" Suzanne wondered. "I probably should leave the *cholent* in the kitchen." But then Suzanne smiled, her striking green eyes by turns willful, appealing, irresistible. "On the other hand, age has its privileges, Loretta, right?" she said, and began heading toward the living room.

"Suzanne, you sure you want to bust in on them?" a trailing Loretta called after her. "Maybe it's better not to."

Suzanne whirled around, giving Loretta an incensed look that made her appear almost young again, full of fire and passion. Then she kept going, boldly and purposefully, until she reached the living room. Bernie was her son, her one and only in New York. No one was going to stop her, certainly not meddlesome Loretta.

"Bernie, darling," she announced, carrying the red Creuset pot of *cholent* with both hands, as if it were a celestial offering, a gift she couldn't possibly resist imparting that instant, immediately, that very moment.

A minute passed. "This is Charles," Loretta heard a startled Bernie finally say, introducing his guest, as both men stood. "You spoke to him on the phone yesterday."

Suzanne blinked twice. Another minute passed. "You fellows been friends for a long time?" she asked and tried to smile.

It was impossible to tell if she knew what she was saying, or knew exactly what she was saying, or even what was happening, and the men looked at each other bewildered, Bernie wishing he was a million miles away.

"Sit down, Suzanne," he said, pulling up his chair for her.

V. Encore

Lake George
The Second Son
Shirt Talk

Lake George

⁓

The night before Bruce Kamen called, we'd attended a surprise seventy-fifth birthday party for our mutual friend Andy Rabin.

There was Bruce and his girlfriend of more than forty years, Harry Kotlowitz and his wife, me and my wife, a couple the rest of us didn't know, and, of course, Andy and his wife. Bruce, Kotlowitz, Andy, and myself were part of a group of about ten who'd grown up around 104th and West End during the Forties and early Fifties.

Calling me next afternoon, Bruce said he'd just talked to Alex Novograd, another guy from the old neighborhood who'd been living in California for the last twenty years. Bruce had called Alex, wanting to tell him about Andy's party.

Alex, however, had interrupted him, saying he had stage four, prostate cancer.

Closing my eyes and swallowing twice, I said, "I'll give him a ring in a day or two."

But Bruce said, "Alex doesn't want anyone calling him."

Neither of us had too much to say after that, and I got off the phone a few minutes later. Then I got out a bottle of Scotch, tossed down a shot and felt a restorative jolt, before sipping a second and third. Didn't feel like doing much of anything the rest of that afternoon and, sitting in my living room, soon remembered the last time I spoke to Alex, which would have been two years ago this coming fall...

***

We'd wanted to get away, see the fall foliage, and my wife had heard from a friend that Lake George was particularly beautiful in October. So we rented a cottage for six nights, packed, didn't forget to take the dog, and drove up on a bright Sunday morning. There was little traffic. We stayed on 87 all the way, stopping between Kingston and Albany for lunch and to give Molly a chance to take a leak.

The cottage was one of five owned by an ex-New York cop, who told us he used to work out of a drug-riddled Bronx precinct. He was a heavyset guy, bald, and wore a black tee shirt with a white motorcycle stamped on the front. His Puerto Rican wife spoke with a lisp and said she grew up in Brooklyn.

She offered a two-bedroom cottage, charging us what she would have charged for a one-bedroom because the season was winding down and none of their cottages were occupied.

They were all located within a few blocks of the stunningly gorgeous lake, foggy mountains in the distance, clearer mountains on the near side of the water. But even more spectacular than the lake was the foliage. Both in the village and up on the mountains the leaves were scarlet, lemon-colored, gold, almost black, and dark green. Of course I'd seen fall foliage over the years, but never so much of it and never had the colors seemed so intense.

I'd been to Lake George once before, but that was in mid-June, fifty-five or fifty-six years ago. No fall foliage then, nor did I remember the lake being so wide, blue, and lovely.

The trip fifty-odd years earlier was one I've never forgotten. I had driven up with five boyhood friends, and it was there we'd almost all gotten killed, also there I'd gotten laid for the first time. Almost killed and first time I got laid— Christ, who's going to forget that weekend?

Five of us were born in 1935, which made us nineteen or twenty when this happened. The youngest, Bruce, was born in 1937. He was seated up front, on the passenger side of the light blue 1953 Chevy we were riding in. Next to him was Richie Graf, whose car it was. Driving that night was Alex. In the back seat behind Alex sat Harry Kotlowitz. I was in the middle. To my right was Gerard Schumann, whom everyone called Gee.

We'd completed college finals a week before except for Gee, who'd started working immediately after graduating from high school. I think it was Alex who suggested going up to Lake George, because he 'd worked the prior summer in one of the nearby hotels and knew the area.

That night, we'd been drinking and looking for girls. I'd known these fellows since I was seven or eight. Knew their parents, even remembered Gee's grandmother and Graf's grandfather. Kotlowitz's grandparents were incinerated in the ovens back in Europe. All the guys were Jewish, except Alex. They'd attended my *bar mitzvah*; I went to theirs. There was little we didn't know about each other.

It was late, dark, maybe eleven, and we were driving along a two-lane road, probably 87. We were either north of Lake George or driving between Glens Falls and Lake George, when Alex began speeding up. He was feeling the booze, no pain. Next to him, Richie Graf began reading the speedometer aloud, egging him on. "Seventy-five, seventy-eight," Richie said. I was half asleep in the back. But when I heard Richie saying, "Eighty-six, eighty-eight," I woke with a start as Alex lost control of the car. Another car was coming our way, but we spun past it and kept spinning, as a second car flew past us, the guy blaring his horn angrily. Wide awake, I was frightened we were going to turn over or keep spinning until we hurtled off the road and slammed into one of the nearby trees. Finally, after what seemed forever, the car came to a blessed stop. For a minute, no one said a word. Then we all stumbled out of the car. It was on the other side of the road, in a ditch.

"Holy shit!" said Kotlowitz, or maybe it was me.

"Jesus Christ!" said Bruce Kamen, or maybe it was Gee.

We must have stood there for at least ten minutes discussing our narrow escape, it being the general consensus that if there weren't six in the gyrating car it would surely have flipped over.

It was Alex, I believe, who eventually said, "Guys, we're living on borrowed time. I think we ought to get laid and I know a couple of whorehouses near here."

If he was aware of them, that meant he'd been to one. I knew that Richie Graf often went to a whorehouse near the University of Florida called "The Green Lantern," because he repeatedly wrote of the glorious times he'd experienced there. Also knew that my buddy Kotlowitz had screwed a hooker in the Hotel Marseilles, which was a block from where he lived. That left Gee, Bruce Kamen, and me. They never mentioned getting laid, and I knew I hadn't.

Richie Graf was the one who cheered up, saying, "Yeah, let's all get laid. Great idea, Alex." Kotlowitz offered no dissenting opinion. What could the three others, including me, say at that moment without sounding like a bunch of frightened jerks?

Alex soon found the right street and spoke to a thin black guy with a mustache, who ushered us over to a nearby cottage that was lit and had a wraparound porch. Alex went inside first, then Richie, followed by Kotlowitz. Given the luxury of time, Gee decided he wasn't going to do it. Bruce said he didn't have the money. I had the money and was petrified, but said, "My turn, guys."

The woman said her name was Ruby and once I undressed it took less than two minutes. Relieved coming out of there, I told myself, "Thank God I did it and thank God it's over."

Anyway, that's the way I remembered it at Lake George fifty-odd years later, as my wife and I waited to be served, sitting in a timbered restaurant that had once been a hunting lodge.

Next day it rained, but the crisp, bracing fall weather was otherwise splendid, and we all had a good time, including Molly, returning to New York the following Saturday.

***

It was late Sunday afternoon when I got in touch with Alex Novograd, whom I hadn't seen or spoken to in twenty-five years. He was a psychiatrist and lived in a small town near San Diego.

I wanted to talk about what happened that memorable Lake George night to someone who'd been there. Couldn't discuss it with Gee who'd died. Nor could I talk to Bruce Kamen, who'd left a message on his answering machine that he was away and wouldn't be back until the end of the month. Didn't want to talk to Richie Graf, because I'd stopped being his friend in 1991. Kotlowitz and I spoke every week, but he was also away, off in Europe with his wife. That left Novograd, so I called him.

"How you doing, Alex?" I said, after his wife put him on the phone. I said it casually, conversationally, without identifying myself, as if I expected him to recognize my voice after twenty-five years.

Of course he didn't. "Who's this?" he asked suspiciously.

"Oh, come on, Novo, cut the bullshit! Just because we haven't spoken this century is no reason you don't recognize my voice. You must have heard it ten thousand times at the corner of West End and 104th."

"Gee, that you?" he asked after a second.

"Strike one," I told him.

"Kotlowitz?"

"You're hurting my feelings," I said.

"Eric?"

"Bingo!" I declared.

"Eric, you son of a bitch!" he laughed.

When I asked how he and his family were, he quickly informed me that he had four children and six grandchildren. Two of his children were lawyers, one was a doctor. Alex, who'd almost got us killed, *paterfamilias* and grandfather of six—unbelievable!

"I got back from Lake George yesterday," I told him. "Haven't been there since that night fifty years ago, and wondered if you were still around."

Alex laughed again. "Still around," he said, and began asking about the others starting with Gee.

It was Gee who'd introduced Alex to our group. They were in the same seventh grade class, although Alex lived on 109th and Gee, like the rest of us, lived between 103rd and 105th.

When I told him Gee had died, he asked me when, but I didn't remember exactly. "Between five and ten years ago," I said.

I'd had little to do with Gee the last fifty years. No one did. We were all supposed to get together thirty years ago, a kind of reunion, but Gee had refused to come.

"He never married, did he?" Alex asked.

IVAN PRASHKER

"No, never married and ended up living with his mother," I said.

"God, the poker games up at Gee's," Alex remembered. We often played cards Saturday nights, almost always at Gee's, and occasionally his old man sat in.

"Poor Gee," Alex said.

"I often thought that you and Gee were particularly close, the way I was with Kotlowitz and Graf," I said.

"No," Alex contradicted me. "I liked Gee a lot, but it wasn't so much Gee or anyone in particular; rather it was the group on 104th that attracted me. The group."

Alex had the high cheekbones of a Tartar and a strong, bony jaw. I remembered that when he'd call for me, he liked talking to my mother. She'd ask if he'd had lunch and make him a sandwich. "He's different from your other friends," my mother would later say. "More aggressive and at the same time more alone."

Alex wondered if I was still in touch with Kotlowitz.

"We talk once a week and get together, he and his wife, me and my wife, maybe six, seven times a year. Kotlowitz, my old asshole buddy."

Laughing, Alex said, "I forget, what's an 'asshole buddy?'"

"Someone you call when you're hurting who'll say, 'Where are you and what do you need? I'll be right over.'"

"Never had one of those," Alex acknowledged and asked how Bruce Kamen was, saying he remembered Bruce was in the passenger seat that memorable Lake George night.

I told him that when Bruce turned seventy, he celebrated by gathering together Kotlowitz, myself, and Andy Rabin, who hadn't made the trip to Lake George—the three of us

376

guys who hadn't seen Bruce for more than twenty years. Andy, probably the most resourceful among us, had lived in Europe for ten years, yet seamlessly rejoined the group as if he'd never been away.

Unlike Andy, Bruce was shy. Yet during these last years, Bruce had become our social glue, the one who'd call, getting us together for lunch. He was unmarried, I told Alex, still seeing the same woman for the last forty years, and don't ask me why because I don't know the answer.

It was at that point Alex said he and his wife were meeting another couple for lunch in ten minutes. But he'd call back in a few days because he wanted to hear about Richie Graf and learn what I was up to.

I gave him my number, saying it twice.

"Gee, I'm really glad you called, Eric," he said. "Talk to you soon."

***

But a week flew past and I didn't hear from him, although Kotlowitz phoned that Saturday. Back from Europe, he was checking in. He and his wife had traveled to Marseilles, then spent a week on a boat cruising up the Rhone before disembarking at Lyon. The countryside was terrific, Harry said, the food even better, first-class. And I let him describe a few of the more sumptuous meals before not only telling him I'd revisited Lake George but mentioned calling Alex.

Curious, Harry asked, "How come you looked him up?"

"I wanted to talk to someone about that crazy night fifty years ago. You weren't around, Gee's dead, Bruce is away, Graf for me is *persona non grata*. That left Alex." I said that we'd talked for a while before he had to leave, promising he'd call back in a few days but that was a week ago.

"I'm not surprised. I liked Alex but never trusted him," Harry said. "Don't mean to suggest he was dishonest; it was always a more visceral reaction on my part."

They were both tall, same size, and guarded each other when we played basketball. Also blocked each other when we'd play touch football. Both played hard, both wanted to win. That led not to out-and-out fights but to physical confrontations. I was there; remembered how rough they used to get. If I didn't forget, Harry certainly hadn't.

"I wonder if Alex has changed much since he was a kid?" I said.

"Oh, Eric, you frame too much in the past," Harry answered.

It hardly seemed a response, but I understood Harry to mean the time I was growing up, my boyhood, which I thought was rich. I'd had my friends, my parents, especially my mother, my grandparents, and various aunts and uncles who lived a block away. I was the only child in that family for years. Harry had his friends, his parents, neither of whom he thought should have been parents, a sister he currently tolerates and a brother he can't stand.

On the other hand, Harry now has two daughters and three grandchildren, and I have neither. Harry married when he was twenty-three, I married when I was thirty-nine. Yet we remained strong friends during those sixteen years. A lot of the credit for that goes not only to Harry but to Harry's first wife, Ruth. I liked Ruth independent of the fact she was Harry's wife, and she liked me independent of the fact I was Harry's boyhood friend. Nor did she regard it strange that I remained single for so long. Or, at least, she never made me feel uncomfortable about it. Other wives did. In any case, it bothered me a lot when Harry and Ruth divorced.

As for us, Harry and I agree more than we disagree, although we did differ on the Iraq war. I was for it, Harry against. I'm tougher on Israel, he despises Kissinger. I love Haydn's string quartets, he's more a Beethoven man.

"Think Alex will call you back?" Harry asked.

"I'm not sure," I said. "It's not as though I know him now the way I knew him fifty years ago."

"I wouldn't count on it," Harry cautioned.

Yet I confess it would have troubled me if a friend from the old days had promised but didn't eventually return my call which I'm happy to say, he, in fact, did.

"Sorry I didn't get back to you last week," Alex began, and mentioned having caught a cold that seemed to last forever. Can't say I believed him totally, but, okay, because in the end there he was.

Before Alex could ask, I told him I'd stopped being in touch with Richie Graf twenty years ago. I wanted it off my chest without any hemming and hawing.

Surprised, Alex said he remembered we were close, so what happened? Richie, I said, was a sad case of someone who never grew up, a guy spoiled from the beginning. He and I were in the same third grade class, but being spoiled didn't seem to matter then.

Sounding like the shrink he was, Alex said, "Tell me more about it."

"Sure," I said, more than happy to oblige. Richie was the kind of guy who talked of retiring with a great pension at the age of thirty. Yet he never seemed to do anything of substance or find a job that satisfied him. He drifted and never stopped drifting. His wife eventually divorced him and one of his children refused to have anything to do with him. The other guys gradually pulled away. I believe I was the last who kept in touch with him.

"You'd invite Richie for dinner at six, he'd show up at two, and it was never with a bottle of wine or a handful of flowers. 'Goddamn it, Richie,' I used to think, 'bring something, anything, a Mars Candy Bar for Christ's sake. Make that two, I'm married.'

"One interminable night after entertaining Richie, I ran out of patience, telling myself, 'Your sense of entitlement, your willfulness, your lack of civility has made you a boorish man, Richie. I'm embarrassed for you and I'm embarrassed having you for a friend. And despite my abiding belief in the virtues of loyalty, I've grown tired of putting up with it and tired of putting up with you.' I never saw him again, Alex."

Sighing, Alex said it sounded as if dropping Richie still bothered me.

"It does," I confessed. "I hate to think I acted like a prick. Yet I tell myself if I was a better man, I wouldn't have done it. After all, I'd known Richie fifty years. Long time, Alex, long, fucking time. Maybe if I hadn't known him so long it wouldn't still bother me."

It was only then that, tapped out, I finally said enough, enough my talking about Graf, no doubt too much, that I wanted to hear what Alex remembered about driving us that night up at Lake George. That was, I told him, the real reason I'd called a couple of weeks ago.

"My turn to recite, huh?" said Alex, sounding relieved to hear it, and who could blame him. "Well, okay, Eric, here goes.

"We'd already had a few drinks and were looking for girls. We were heading toward Lake George on a curvy road, two lanes. I was moving along at a good clip, and Richie kept announcing our speed as I kept going faster and faster.

I remember that the right side of the road went up, not much shoulder. The driver side, also not much shoulder. We were going about ninety when the road curved to the right and I lost control. We started to spin completely around, three-sixty, as one guy passed me on the passenger side. Another car was coming toward us as we kept spinning, and he also went by on the passenger side. I remember that the guy in the second car was with his wife or girlfriend, and they both had these horror-stricken expressions. Finally we came to a stop. No one said a word until we all got out of the car. A third guy who passed us stopped, came back, and asked if we were okay. You know what Richie said to me as we looked over his car? A hubcap was missing, and he said, 'Alex, you're going to have to replace that hubcap.' Hell, this was two minutes after we'd all just escaped getting killed. Typical Graf. Class all the way..."

"No kidding," I thought, asking if Alex remembered what happened next.

Alex laughed, saying of course he did.

I asked if going to the whorehouse was his idea.

He guessed it probably was.

I told him I thought it was between Lake George and Glens Falls.

"No, it was Glens Falls. I'd been there a couple of times the year before, Eric. Remember what happened at the whorehouse?"

What a question! "Sure," I said, "we got laid. It was the first time for me and I was petrified."

"Remember anything else about it?" Alex asked.

His voice sounded odd, different, and I hadn't the faintest idea what he was alluding to. "What do you mean?" I said.

"I told you not to do it."

"What?" He startled me. I didn't remember that. "Why?" I asked him.

"That's what you kept saying when I kept telling you not to do it."

"But I would have felt embarrassed not pursuing it after you, Harry, and Richie had gone in."

And mentioning Richie again, I knew I shouldn't have jumped all over him minutes ago. Richie was Richie. I should have felt badly for him being estranged instead of growing angry because I no longer wanted anything to do with him.

Anyway, after a minute, Alex said, "I never told you the reason why I tried to discourage you, but I'm going to tell you now. It's probably going to sound a little strange. I liked your mother. She was the only mother on West End who'd make me a sandwich, offer me a glass of juice on a hot day without my having to ask. The only one, and I knew it would have upset her if she'd somehow found out or sensed you'd screwed a prostitute. I would have felt responsible because I'd almost gotten us all killed, and that's why we went."

Alex mentioning my mother stunned me. "Because of my mom you tried to dissuade me from getting laid?"

"What can I tell you?"

Of course I could have replied that all this occurred during a less sophisticated time, a more ingenuous one. Kennedy hadn't been shot, Vietnam hadn't imploded, Watergate hadn't destroyed Nixon, the Twin Towers hadn't come crashing down. People, it seemed, were far less cynical; people like my mother were around, and outliers like Alex responded to them.

"Eric, you still there?" Alex said.

The lingering bad taste in my mouth over Graf had dissipated for the time being, and nodding, I remembered

Alex had an older brother and asked if his brother was still living in Philadelphia, suggesting next time Alex came east to give me a ring.

Gee was dead, Richie was gone by choice, mine. Bruce and Andy Rabin had come back into my life, Kotlowitz never left it. I guess that's par for the course. And then, as I just said, there was Alex, a kind of unexpected bonus, who never figured to hear from me again.

"I'll be in touch," he said, and the confiding way he said it made me believe we'd get together during the next few months.

From past experience I knew that the New York to Philly train takes a boring two hours. But I'd be whistling all the way down. Any guy who tried to protect my mother at the cost of my remaining an innocent nineteen-year-old not only cheered me up, but had to be a singular fellow I wanted to see again.

Unfortunately, it was not to be, not in the cards or, more likely, Alex got there but never called me. In the old days, I would have said, "Well, fuck you, too, Alex!"

But the old days were long gone, and the morning after I learned he was dying, I decided to be a grownup and write him a letter. By the way, so did Harry.

I wrote Alex the end of April. Told him that for me he'd always be one of the guys from 104th, one of my oldest friends, and how much I'd liked him. All true. Plus, I wrote that if I could hug him today I would just as I'd hugged Andy Rabin last Sunday on his seventy-fifth birthday. I signed off, "Your friend, Eric."

Alex died early that June, six weeks later. After Bruce called, telling me, I got out that same bottle of Scotch and poured myself a stiff shot. Then I sat back, and remembering Alex saying he'd tried to discourage me from getting laid,

I couldn't help shaking my head and smiling. Alex—my mother's knight in shining armor, her cavalier, her champion? Funny what you wind up remembering about a guy.

The Second Son

"Daddy loved you, too," said my sister Sandra over the phone after spotting Gino Carbone's lead obit in Saturday's *Times*.

Gino, seventy-nine, had written three or four best-sellers and had been one of my closest friends. Sandra had met him not only when Gino came to my mother and father's funerals but also when we were sitting *shiva*.

I was sixty-three now, and first got to know Gino when I was thirty. He was fifteen years older than me, the fifth of seven children of a poor Italian family who'd grown up in Hell's Kitchen during the Depression. I'd seen them all at Gino's kids' weddings to which my wife and I were always invited.

We'd worked as editors at the same quartet of men's adventure magazines for a couple of years before Gino extricated himself by writing his first best-seller. Fortunately, we'd hit it off before he became famous. I don't often connect with a guy from the beginning because I'm not that sociable. But I'd loved another book Gino had written before his first best-seller, so I was a fan from the start. I think what attracted Gino to me was I embodied the admiring young friend he'd long sought—an insight I'd realized after reading that book of his I'd loved.

In any case, I got to know Gino far better than I knew my father. Why? The short answer is, my father lost his first wife to lung cancer, leaving him with three children: eight-year-old Sandra; Arlene, three years younger; and Stanley who, less than a year later, died of polio, after which my dad became kind of shell-shocked the rest of his life.

I only learned my father lost a son when my sister Arlene happened to casually mention Stanley. I was eighteen then, in college, my father's second wife's only sheltered child. What saved me from becoming a mama's boy was not my withdrawn father but rather my mother's two younger brothers, Marty and Danny.

The night I was born, it was Marty, not my absent father, into whose startled arms I was placed. A harbinger of things to come, because it was Marty, not my father, whom I tried to please as a kid. I'd write him long letters and send him maps I'd drawn of Italy when he was stationed there during the war. That's where he'd contracted leukemia. Before he died when I was eleven, he gave me his Army dog tags. I still have one and carry it on a key ring next to my own dog tag.

After he died, Danny, who'd been in the Coast Guard during the war, immediately assumed his role, as if Marty had told him I needed another older man to look up to and lean on. And that, too, worked out, until Danny died in his early fifties.

To cite one example of how well it worked—when I was in the Army it was Danny I called when I thought I was coming down with pneumonia, asking him to send me antibiotics to help me get through Basic; otherwise, I'd have had to restart from week one the Army's wretched eight-week training cycle. Not in a million years would it have occurred to me to call my father, who served neither during World War I nor World War II.

Yet when I thought about Sandra telling me, "Daddy loved you, too," it struck me as doubly ironic, because it was just as difficult for me to connect with her at it had been for me to connect with my father.

Of the old man's three surviving children, Sandra was the most like him—inaccessible, remote, and withholding. Nor was I the only relative who found Sandra hard to reach.

Arlene's take was that while she and Sandra were close and would talk about everything, Sandra simply didn't talk a lot to anyone else.

"Sandra was always more reserved than me," Arlene tried to explain, "but Sandra was reserved because she was so self-assured. She didn't need to ask people what to do or tell anyone what she wanted. She just did it, got over our mother dying young far more quickly than I did. I don't know if you remember, Eric, but Sandra married at twenty-three. It took me until thirty-two, though I had a few proposals before then."

"How many?" I asked, your typical, wise-guy kid brother.

"Oh, more than one," said Arlene, and, unwilling to quote a number, she laughed nervously. "It was after the war and I was pretty, the girl-next-door, and the boys getting out of the Army wanted to make up for lost time and start a family. But I was enjoying myself and couldn't make up my mind."

Of course, I was too young at the time to remember any of that. What I did recall was my father assigning me, almost a decade later, the questionable task of making sure that Arlene, who was chronically late, arrived at her wedding on time. I remembered that and my father being enormously relieved at the conclusion of the service. But then, I never knew another man more anxious, or more repressed than my father.

***

I suppose that explains why for weeks I couldn't stop thinking about Sandra's words, "Daddy loved you, too."

Her remark particularly disturbed me because I knew I didn't love my father the way I loved my mother, my two uncles, or Gino Carbone.

What bothered me most was that my father died thirty years ago when I was thirty-three and that should have given me more than enough time to come to terms with how I felt about him.

Instead, it was only after my father passed that, in a half-assed way, I'd periodically try to get Arlene to tell me what she remembered about him. I'd ask if he had been different before I was born. "Not really," Arlene would answer. "He was always quiet and reserved."

It wasn't the answer I was looking for. I wanted something more visceral, more nourishing, a bone I could chew on.

Once, trying to disarm Arlene by making a game of it, I'd asked, "Tell me the first four things you remember about Daddy."

Loving that sort of brother-sister banter, Arlene grinned. Although she was in her sixties then, she still had a girlish, chirpy voice, and, humoring me, she said, "Daddy had the smallest hands I've ever seen on a man."

I nodded. That was my recollection, too, and I could still picture my father's tiny hands and his small, squared-off nails. As far as that goes, I remembered my dad standing five-four or was it five-five? Sandra was his height, Arlene and me both taller.

"What else do you remember?" I asked.

"After my mother died, he used to take Sandra and me rowing in Central Park," she answered, only this memory, unlike the first, seemed to upset Arlene, turning her voice two shades darker.

I have a photograph of the three of them in a rowboat, my father feathering the oars. He's wearing a diamond ring and a stickpin below the knot of his tie, which meant he was still rich then, still ran a successful hat business. It was obviously before the Depression had wiped him out—another blow that broke his spirit.

Anyway, my sisters are sitting behind him, their heads pressed against each other, their hair bobbed. They look about six and nine, and I try to see in their young faces if they understand what their mother's death meant.

"Hey, Eric, how come it's 'four-question' time today?" Arlene asked. "Something recently happen to prompt this?"

"Oh, nothing in particular," I said, shrugging.

I think her question suggested she didn't want to continue. But curiosity and guilty conscience kept firing me up, and I heard myself saying, "So, Arlene, tell me a third thing you remember."

Arlene was quiet for a moment and then said that after graduating from high school and obedient to my dad's wishes, she trooped off to secretarial school. But she'd hated working in an office, hated filing and typing. It was deadly dull, and she got fired twice for being late. For a while, she recalled, she worked as a saleslady at Macy's.

"But one afternoon, Daddy showed up there," Arlene said. "He told me he was upset I was working at Macy's, that I should be working in an office, which was far more respectable. I was so embarrassed, Eric, because the other salesladies could hear him.

"Later, I got a job with a public relations firm that turned out okay because we did publicity for Perry Como, who was not only a good singer but a sweet man." Arlene giggled. "Daddy didn't know Perry Como from Frank Sinatra, but he was happy because I now worked in an office, not as a saleslady at Macy's anymore."

Happy? Not a word I associated with my father, and I couldn't help asking Arlene if the old man ever spoke about her mother and Stanley after they died.

"No," she said. "But that's the fourth thing I'd mention: he'd tell me I should visit my mother's grave every year before Rosh Hashanah. Annoyed, I once asked if he ever went. He said a rabbi told him he should concern himself more about his second wife and about getting on with the rest of his life, that it was his duty as a Jew to have another son, to have you."

"Me?" I said, and couldn't help laughing self-consciously. "Good God, me, a redemptive figure?"

***

That night I told myself that if I fused the first four things that occurred to me about my father with what Arlene had related, I might be able to come up with a credible composite portrait, without which there was no resolving how I felt toward him. It was, admittedly, a schematic, inelegant way of going about things, but I was groping. Vis-a-vis my father, it's been that way for as long as I can remember.

Sadly, the first thing that occurred to me was that I couldn't recall the old man ever having a single friend. When I was a kid, I had about ten, one of whom turned out lifelong, plus I'd made a pretty good one in college, an even better one in the Army, and then there was Gino.

Nor was I the only member of my family who had a talent for friendship. Arlene was still friendly with two women she'd met in high school, and my mother always had neighborhood friends. About Sandra I couldn't say, I simply didn't know her well enough.

The second thing that jumped out about my father was that he'd constantly wash my hands. It upset me terribly because this was still going on when I was eleven and twelve. Angrily, irritably, I'd tell him to stop, cut it out, let me alone. My hands were clean enough. "You don't understand," my father would say furiously. "People become ill and get polio from dirty hands; people die from dirty hands. As long as you live here, keep your lousy hands clean."

But that wasn't the angriest I saw my father. The angriest was the third thing I remembered. It was when I was seventeen. I'd been a waiter at a boys' camp that summer and had been home for just a few days after my stint at camp. We were eating lunch when my mother mentioned that an elderly granduncle, a World War I veteran who'd been wounded in France, had passed away over the summer. I was fond of the man, liked hearing his war stories, and found tears running down my face.

"What are you crying for?" my father said to me. "Moe was in his late eighties, lived a full life, what's to get so upset about?"

Embarrassed, I swiped at my eyes, brushing away the tears. "I wasn't crying," I lied. "But even if I was, so what?"

My father seemed to explode. "Moe was in his eighties, for God's sake!" he shouted. "And besides, who was he, a distant uncle? That's someone to cry for? To mourn? I can't believe you're acting so childishly. And don't lie to me either!"

My mother sprang up. "Let him alone!" she shouted back. "Let my son alone!"

I sat there, bewildered. I'd never seen my father, whose face had turned a blistering red, react so violently. And I thought that's the way you react when you really don't like someone.

"Ach, the tiger defending her cub!" my father snapped, getting to his feet. "I need to take a walk, get out of this hothouse, breathe some fresh air," and we heard the front door slam behind him.

His eruption seemed so completely out of the blue that I couldn't make sense of it until the following year when Arlene happened to remark that her brother Stanley, who died at three, would have been twenty-eight that week.

"Brother? What brother?" I asked, squinting. And thinking Arlene was kidding, I even smiled. "Hey, I'm your brother, your one and only."

A minute passed. "No, Eric," said Arlene in an unusually quiet voice. "You're not my one, you're not my only."

I flinched. "What are you talking about?"

And that was the fourth thing I recalled about my father —he never mentioned he'd had another son. Nor had anyone else, as if it was a dark family secret, until Arlene's unexpected aside.

Unfortunately, my memory of my father joined with Arlene's still left me high and dry, without a satisfying resolution. "Christ," I used to think miserably, "three-year-old Stanley probably got to know him better than I ever did."

***

It was toward the end of the week after Gino died and Sandra told me, "Daddy loved you, too," that the need to finally come to terms with how I felt about my father became something I had to resolve or tell myself once and for all, "Just fuck it! The hell with it!"

I decided if I could somehow place myself in my father's shoes that would probably go a long way toward opening a closed door. But I wasn't sure I could do it on my own, that is, without some kind of prop or device. Then it occurred to me that the way to proceed was to literally walk where my father had walked after his first wife and Stanley died. And the easiest way to do that would be by visiting the cemetery where they were buried. Because I hadn't the faintest idea of its location, I called and asked Arlene.

"Gee, Eric, that's a funny thing to ask," she said. "Are you serious?"

"Yeah, I'm serious."

"You okay?" she asked.

"I'm fine, fine," I said, laughing to reassure her.

"But my mother wasn't related to you and you never knew or met Stanley."

"You're right, Arlene. On the other hand, Stanley was a brother even if I never knew him, and it seems I ought to pay my respects once. At any rate, I've been thinking about it and I'd like to go there."

"Well, I guess, if you really want to," said a still puzzled Arlene.

"Hang on." And she went to look up the name of the cemetery, the plot number, and told me how to get there.

***

Next morning, I took the C train out to Queens.

A New Yorker born and bred, I've always loved subways —their hurtling speed, their noise, the smell of their musty stations, their clicking turnstiles, the engineer's narrow booth on the right side of the front car, the red and green lights inside their black tunnels. Subways always struck me as arterial blood circulating throughout the city's several boroughs, without which New York couldn't possibly function, breathe, live. Oh, hell, name a great city that doesn't have a bustling subway. London? Paris? Tokyo?

The ride took over an hour. Plenty of time to think. Plenty of time to brood. Plenty of time to speculate.

Arlene had once shown me a three-by-five picture of Stanley. It was an exterior shot taken in the summer—I could tell by the short-sleeved, skimpy shirt Stanley was wearing —taken, by the way, two or three months before he died. He had my father's pale blue eyes and light coloring. So do I, and I couldn't help wondering what it might have been like to have had a considerably older brother.

Would he have told me that throwing a ball meant using your shoulders, your hips, your legs, not merely your arm? Would he have advised that when I found myself in a fight, to figure out and nail the other guy's weakest spot with everything I had? Would he have said that when a girl invited me up to her apartment, that meant I had a great shot at scoring and, be cool, but go for it? God knows, advice I could have especially used. And, practically hearing him, I found myself smiling...

***

An hour later, following Arlene's directions, I got off at the elevated Hudson Street Station out in Ozone Park.

When I descended into the street, I could see slanting bars of yellow light as I walked under the El. A train heading back into Manhattan rumbled above me across the avenue, the street vibrating as the sun's beams passing between the tracks were momentarily obliterated.

Almost immediately, I approached three small cemeteries, each extending the width of two city streets. I walked to the last of them where a sign read, "Acacia, 83-84 Liberty Avenue." To my right were the neighborhood's storefronts, most of them body shops with Italian names. Also a laundromat with a broken window, the glass spidery with cracked, haphazard lines.

Acacia was built above the level of the street, its entrance up an inclined macadam road, an arch beneath a three-story building straddling the entrance. A chain-link fence enclosed three sides of the site.

It was an old, sorry-looking cemetery, probably built before 1900, and no one else seemed to be around. Its length measured more than twice its width. The headstones were often large and bulky, decorated with baroque carvings and floral designs.

Looking for plot number 76, I proceeded down the length of a dirt road, almost to the end before turning left.

I was walking on grass now, between occupied graves, and when I came to a headstone taller than the others I did an abrupt about-face. Arlene had told me to look for it.

Near the top of the headstone was an oval-shaped, wallet-sized picture of a young woman, sealed with shiny porcelain. Immediately below the photograph was a heart carved into the stone, inscribed with Hebrew lettering. Below the Hebrew letters, it read, "My Beloved Wife and Our Dear Mother, Miriam Rosen. Died October 24, 1927. Age 29 Years."

Approaching the monument, I could see that the woman had large eyes and her hair was bobbed. She was wearing a scarf above an opened coat. Her lower lip was full, sensuous. She wasn't pretty so much as vivacious. The picture had been taken outside, and I could see blotches of indistinct flowers dappling the background.

Directly in front of this grave was a second headstone reaching no higher than my knee. The writing in English read, "Beloved Son Stanley Rosen. Died September 7, 1928. Age 3 1/2 years."

There was a stone bench in the plot facing the two graves, and sitting on the bench, I could still see the white rim of porcelain and imagined my father visiting here before he married my mother. I could see him standing where I now abruptly stood up, staring at his first wife's plinth-like memorial, then at his son's smaller headstone. In my mind's eye, I could see my father's familiar but inscrutable face. Was he weeping? Probably, but I never saw him weep. Nor can I remember ever hearing him laugh either.

Suddenly it struck me that accompanying my father to this cemetery was something I might have proposed during the last decade of his life. No big deal, but it would have been something, not the nothing, the zero, I wound up doing.

So, why had it never occurred? Was I really that obtuse?

No, preoccupied comes closer. But at the same time I was preoccupied, I'd had Gino in my corner. Before I married and was having woman trouble, it was a sympathetic Gino who told me, "You'll be okay, don't worry, you'll meet someone else." And when I tried writing a novel and was flailing, he also said, "Jesus, Eric, don't give up, never give up." That was the other side of Gino, the tougher, undefeated side. I admired both.

I'd met Gino less than a month after my Uncle Danny died. Gino, in effect, had succeeded Danny who'd succeeded my Uncle Marty.

Not to belabor the obvious, there was no gap between them, and I was deeply fortunate that each—Gino, Danny, and Marty—had taken an interest in me. But I was also unfortunate because, as a consequence, I never needed my father, something I knew for years but had never confronted before now. Well, better late than never, no?

Walking over to Stanley's grave, I hunched down, my finger tracing his name, and I thought how easily that could have been me buried there. Same eyes, same coloring, same father.

"Look, I'm sorry I screwed up," I apologized to this older brother I never met. I needed to apologize to someone and felt that Stanley, blood of my blood, would understand better than most. And carried away now, I began telling him about Marty and Danny, also about Gino, and how seamlessly each had followed the other from, literally, the night I was born until almost now. And I must have gone on for ten, fifteen minutes trying to explain why I never needed my father before Stanley broke in, interrupting me.

"Listen," he said in a gravelly voice, "our old man was broken and hurt. I wasn't around to comfort him, but you were; and while you may not have needed him, he needed you. But let's face it—you were in the habit of ignoring him for years, and you continued ignoring him when you were old enough to know better."

I didn't answer him. How could I when his every word rang true?

"Tell me," Stanley said, "do you finally understand that your love and gratitude toward Gino and your uncles doesn't excuse you?"

"Hell, if I thought it excused me why would I be here?" I asked him.

I assumed he believed me, because he said, "You're my younger brother, Eric. I wish I could help you."

"Stanley," I said, "it keeps bothering me more and more."

"Oh, Eric," he sighed, "it's fucking supposed to."

***

Arlene called a couple of days later. "Did you visit the cemetery?" she asked.

I said I did.

"And did you find what you were looking for?"

"Sure," I told her, because what else was there to say? What else could I say?

"You asked a while back if Daddy ever spoke about Stanley and my mother after they died, and I told you no, he never did," Arlene said. "But last night I remembered the only time he talked about my mother. It was after I got engaged, and he remembered all sorts of details, especially about their honeymoon. They'd gone to Atlantic City, swam in the ocean, rode on the boardwalk in a jitney, ate cotton candy. It amazed me. I mean, I thought that during all those in-between years he'd forgotten about her, and I just wished he'd mentioned Atlantic City and their honeymoon before then. But that was the only time he opened up to me about her. Although I guess he never did forget, because he insisted that the same rabbi who'd married him and my mother marry both Sandra and me."

I remembered the rabbi. He'd lived on 103rd Street and West End, had a goatee, and spoke with a slight English accent.

"Don't get pissed off, Eric," said Arlene, "but Sandra happened to call yesterday and I told her about you asking where my mother and Stanley are buried, and that you were going to visit their graves."

I wasn't pissed off, had no reason to be, but I was curious. "What'd she say?"

"She seemed upset and asked why you were going. I hope you don't feel I betrayed you is what I'm trying to say."

"No, of course not," I reassured her.

"I have a big mouth and probably shouldn't have mentioned it."

"Don't be silly," I told her. "You didn't do anything wrong, and if Sandra wants to talk to me about it, fine, not a problem."

Sandra didn't call but sent me a birthday card which I received the following week. I was sixty-four. "I'm glad you're my brother," she wrote. "Take care, keep well, and stay in touch."

Well, that was Sandra—dutiful and taciturn, a replication of my father. Although I took her writing "I'm glad you're my brother" to mean that, despite my visiting the cemetery without her knowledge, as if I needed her permission, we were still okay, sister and brother.

Arlene's birthday card arrived two days later. She mailed it the day of my birthday. "Late again," she wrote, which made me laugh. And wasn't that typical Arlene—girlish, chronically late, yet endearing? My father, rest in peace, used to say she was going to be late for his funeral.

"Oh, hell, Dad," I'd tell him if he was still around. "Better late for your funeral than late for your life."

Shirt Talk

When he heard his wife leave the apartment to go shopping in the afternoon, Moe Sohn, a retired shirt manufacturer in his late seventies, called his ex-partner, Sam Lipshitz, who'd bought him out and was running the business alone.

Moe hadn't spoken to Lipshitz for more than a year; they hadn't gotten along when they were partners, and they'd fought bitterly over price when the partnership broke up. Lipshitz, seventy years young but in good health save for slight prostate trouble, was surprised to hear from his ex-.

"It's been so long we spoke I almost don't recognize you," Lipshitz couldn't resist.

"Big deal," Moe countered.

"What do you want?" Lipshitz asked tonelessly.

"I'm calling about business."

"What 'business' a rich, retired stud like you has to worry about?" Lipshitz needled.

"Did you ship the goods to Kuflik?"

"Goods? Kuflik?"

"I know he doesn't pay so fast, but he's proved to be a solid account over the years, so maybe you got to be a little lenient."

Lipshitz looked like a boss sitting in his Thirty-fourth Street office opposite the Empire State Building. An oily black cigar rested amiably between his fat lips and his feet were propped comfortably on his desk. Now whether or not he shipped goods to a customer was simply no longer Moe's concern. Besides, six months ago, it became company policy to stop selling small-timers. All of which meant that Lipshitz didn't owe Kuflik beans, let alone shirts.

"I'm not following you, Moe," Lipshitz said. "Maybe it's because today I'm thinking a little slow."

"Today is no different than any other day."

Lipshitz gritted his teeth. Moe always could get under his skin. "Look," he said impatiently, "I'm a busy man, and I don't quite get your train of thought. You're out of business, what's Kuflik got to do with you these days?"

"What do you mean I'm out of business?" Moe said indignantly. "I sold him six weeks ago for fall delivery. I want you to ship him even he does pay a little slow."

Lipshitz swung his feet off his desk. He put his cigar in the fancy copper ashtray on his desk, closed his eyes, and bit his lower lip. "Where's your wife, Moishe?" he asked. "Where's Ida?"

"I know Kuflik from the old country yet, seventy years I know him," Moe was saying. "How's it look, he buys and we don't ship cause he doesn't pay like a goddamn IBM machine."

"I want to talk to Ida," Lipshitz said.

"Ida's downstairs shopping. What's she got to do with shipping Kuflik? This is shirts I'm discussing."

"I'll tell you, Moe, let me think about it. I'll get back to you tomorrow about the Kuflik shipment."

But Lipshitz didn't wait until the following day to call back. He dialed Moe's number when he was reasonably sure he would catch Ida in the apartment later that same afternoon. She was preparing dinner.

"Ida, how's Moe feeling?" Lipshitz asked.

"I'll be right back," she said, wiping her hands on her apron. She went into the living room. Moe was taking a nap, sprawled in his favorite chair. His mouth was wide open.

Closing the kitchen door, Ida picked up the phone. "Why are you calling?" she asked Lipshitz. "Did something happen today?"

"Is Moe acting 'funny' lately?"

"'Funny?'" Ida stalled. But she had a good idea what Lipshitz meant. Not two days ago, looking Ida in the eye, Moe had asked, "Where's my wife?"

"Please," she said to Lipshitz, "why the questions?"

The ex-partner sighed. He hated to be the bearer of bad news but felt obliged to tell Ida she had to keep her husband from calling the office. Between the time Lipshitz had spoken to Moe and dialed Ida, he'd learned that for the last two weeks Moe had been discussing nonexistent business with office personnel—the bookkeeper, two salesmen, an inside man, even the mailroom boy. And they'd all been afraid to tell him about Moe's calls, but once Lipshitz had broken the ice that afternoon, every other gossip with a contribution to make eagerly chimed in. And Lipshitz, who half enjoyed working himself up over shaky office morale, had decided to put a stop to the older man's foolishness before it got out of hand. "I'm sorry to have to add to your troubles, Ida," was how he began.

She listened patiently, as Lipshitz spelled out the telephone calls Moe had made to the office the past two weeks. Ida was not surprised. Moe had lived for his work. After his second heart attack a year and a half ago, she'd forced him to retire. It was a wifely duty she had had to perform for his own good. But sitting home with time on his hands after a lifetime of hard work, Moe suffered misery Ida became aware only even existed this last year; and now she hated herself for having laid down the retirement law to her husband.

"You know," she told Lipshitz, "I'm sorry I didn't send him back to the office with my blessing after the second heart attack. It would have been better for him to die on Thirty-fourth Street than be unhappy for a year counting the money other shirt people were raking in."

"But that's crazy talk," Lipshitz cut her short. Even just imagining Moe dropping dead in the office gave his ex-partner goose pimples. "About why I dialed you, Ida, dear," he said, bringing the conversation back to essentials. "Moe's calls got to stop."

Ida had an inspiration. "Is it really so terrible he telephones, talks business to you or someone else in the office once in a while?" she asked.

Somehow the question struck like a blade to the belly and Lipshitz squirmed. "Ida, I'm a manufacturer, not a psychiatrist."

"I know it's a big favor to ask, but couldn't you kid him along? Talk business to him as if he were still a partner?"

Lipshitz had always liked Ida and wished he could grant her request. Screw office morale! You pay your people good money, that's office morale.

But Lipshitz couldn't forget that after selling to him, Moe had spread the word in the industry he'd been taken for a one-way ride by his former partner of twenty-five years.

"Ida, I wish I could go along with what you're asking, I really do," Lipshitz said. "But in the first place, I'm a busy man. Since Moe isn't here, I do two jobs. And in the second place, it's hard to forget Moe told everyone I took advantage he was sick and only offered a lousy price. I mean, my heart just isn't in the right place for him these days."

"What he said about you is nothing to what he says about me because I made him retire," Ida answered. "He can't work, and it's killing him, so he leaves it out. But if he could talk shirts to you, it might make it easier for him at home. He's got no friends. All his brothers and sisters are dead. Talk business to him. Do it. And if you can't do it for him, then do it for me."

Once, when everyone was younger, Lipshitz had gotten a woman buyer in trouble and needed money quickly. He was ashamed to ask Moe, a Sabbath observer, and in desperation turned to Ida. She gave him cold cash the following day, telling him explanations between friends were unnecessary. And now, twenty years later, she was asking this favor of him, and though Lipshitz hated getting involved he found he couldn't say no. "All right, Ida," he told her. "But remember, this is only for your sake."

***

Moe was still dozing when his wife went back into the living room. He looked shrunken. She knew he couldn't have weighed more than one hundred and ten pounds. Sometimes at night she would watch him put on his pajamas, and seeing he was all bone it was difficult for her to keep herself from gasping. He was almost seventy-nine-years-old, and she knew she was lucky he'd lived this long, and in relative good health. But still, he was her husband, they'd been through a lot together, and she didn't want him to die.

Because he'd been having trouble sleeping during the nights the last two weeks, Ida gave him a sleeping pill that evening. The pill didn't do much good, however, for sometime after one o'clock she heard him getting out of bed. She thought he was going to the bathroom and said nothing. The next thing she knew she heard him opening the front door. She jumped out of bed. "Moe, what's the matter?" she called out.

But he didn't answer her.

Snapping on the hall light, she said, "Moe, where are you going?"

He was standing near the front door, wearing only his pajamas, which no longer fit him. "I was looking for the paper," he said. A delivery boy dropped the *New York Times* opposite their apartment door each morning between seven and seven-thirty.

"But, Moe, it's only one-thirty in the morning."

He stared at her, squeezing the door's brass knob.

"It's still pitch-dark outside," she said.

"One-thirty?" he said, closing the front door.

He went into the kitchen, where he studied the clock hanging over the kitchen table. "Are you sure this clock is working?"

"Come back to bed with me," Ida told her husband.

"I'm not sleepy."

"Would you like a cup of tea?"

"What's today?" he asked.

She forgot. "The day after yesterday," she said with more assurance than she felt.

He nodded. For some reason satisfied with her answer, he found his way back into their bedroom. He started to groan almost as soon as he fell asleep. And hearing him, Ida herself could only toss and turn. He mumbled a sentence; some words were in Yiddish, others in English. She caught his oldest brother's name.

Moe came of a family of four sons, two daughters, and when he was just past thirty he was supporting one of his sisters, paying the business debts of two brothers, shelling out rent money for his parents, sending his youngest brother through New York Law School, and maintaining his own family in an apartment near Central Park. He had carried them all, and whenever Ida rode a bus down Fifth Avenue and saw the statue of Atlas supporting the world on his shoulders, she couldn't help wondering, "But was Atlas as reliable as my Moe?" And it struck her as incredible that Moe now only weighed a little more than a hundred pounds. And still hearing his groans, she suddenly sat up in bed and prayed that Lipshitz would understand what forced retirement meant to a man whom everyone used to depend on; in a word, she prayed that Lipshitz would keep his promise and talk shirts.

And the next day, at the breakfast table, she purposely brought up the ex-partner's name. While she didn't expect miracles from a couple of phone conversations, she was prepared to be most grateful for any breaks that came her way, and for that reason she didn't want too much time to elapse between Lipshitz's promise and a call from Moe.

But Moe didn't need any prompting. The customer Kuflik was still on his mind, and when Ida went down shopping in the early part of the afternoon, Moe dialed the Thirty-fourth Street office and asked to speak to the boss.

"Moe, how are you?" Lipshitz greeted him as a long lost friend.

"Have you shipped the goods to Kuflik?"

Lipshitz, who would keep his promise to Ida, so help him, had decided not merely to talk to Moe but to sound convincing, in character.

"I've been thinking about what you said yesterday, Moe, and the truth is I don't like dealing with small potatoes," he uttered for openers. "Now I got nothing against this Kuflik personally, but when, in addition to only giving us peanut orders, he doesn't pay on time, then that's one kike who's more trouble than he's worth."

"But I sold him goods," Moe protested. "You can't let him keep expecting delivery and not ship. That's treating a man like a dog."

Lipshitz stayed in character. "He doesn't pay on time, he doesn't like our terms let the greaseball buy from some other house."

"I, Moe Sohn, personally promised him fall delivery!" Moe declared. "You dirty louse, ship him!"

Lipshitz's ears sprang to attention. He wasn't used to people calling him bad names; but remembering Moe's rotten ticker, he held his explosive temper in check. "The way you talk about Kuflik, one would think he was your brother, at least a relative," he temporized.

"I always argue with you, Lipshitz," Moe was saying. "We're partners, fifty-fifty, and we're always fighting. I guess the truth is I never liked you."

Suddenly Lipshitz forgot he was play-acting. "I'm not exactly crazy for you either."

"Your opinions couldn't make me care less," Moe shrugged.

"Goddamn it, we don't have to stay partners forever." Lipshitz was so angry he didn't know what he was saying. "Maybe I ought to buy you out, or vice versa."

"Don't threaten me," Moe said. "Make me an offer. A *fair* one."

Emphasis on the word "fair" brought the ex-partner back to his senses. The past was finished. If Moe was nuts, confused past with present, that didn't mean Lipshitz had to do likewise, could only talk to Moe by forgetting he was making believe they were still partners. Cooling off, yet remembering his promise to Ida, he took a deep breath.

"Look, Moe," he said after a while, "we don't have to agree on every single customer, but that doesn't mean we're still not good for each other. We've built a profitable business these last twenty-five years, and it wasn't by luck or accident either. There are things you know I don't, and there are tricks I can perform you're not so hot at. I mean, we do good as partners. But even in the best of families there are some disagreements, no?"

Moe, however, was implacable. He said one word: "Kuflik."

"All right, all right, we'll ship the *pisher*. But tell him, Moe, tell him from me, he doesn't pay on time this once, he should find himself another shirt firm to drive crazy."

"Ship him," Moe sighed.

"I said okay."

"Kuflik's a proud man, and he's ashamed for people to know, but he's blind in one eye and the other has a cataract; also, sometimes he doesn't remember, and he can't always make out the due date on his bills."

"But why didn't you tell me this before?" Lipshitz asked.

"I knew it before," Moe said. "It was enough I knew."

Lipshitz had a premonition, he shivered. "Moe," he whispered, "is there anything else I should know?"

Moe thought a moment. "Don't let them make you retire."

"Is that all?" Lipshitz asked, disappointed.

"Don't kid yourself, I'm telling you a lot."

Lipshitz squinted. Was Moe supposed to think he was still a partner or not? Sometimes he sounded like he did, sometimes not so. Lipshitz was confused. "I don't want to keep you," he said, hoping Moe would take the hint.

Moe complied. "I got to go now."

"Be okay," Lipshitz said, grateful the call had come to an end. And putting the phone down, he sighed. Talking to Moe, in character, had proved to be a bigger favor than even Lipshitz had bargained for. And sighing again, he lit up an oily cigar and, remembering his past prostate trouble, called his doctor and made an appointment for the following week.

***

Moe didn't mention the phone conversation he'd held with his ex-partner when Ida returned to the apartment that afternoon. He had strange, faraway look in his eye, and she guessed that Lipshitz had said the wrong thing; everyone knew the that the ex-partner wasn't exactly Mister Tactful. Besides, psychology was a tricky affair, you never could tell how it would work out.

Now she asked Moe if he'd like something to drink, maybe a glass of orange juice before supper.

But instead of answering her, he went to the hall closet and got out his coat and hat.

"Where are you going, Moe?" Ida asked. She didn't want to stop him, but it upset her when he went into the street alone, and the fact it was getting close to dark now made her even more jumpy.

"I'm going home," he said, putting on his hat.

"You're going where?"

"Home. I'm going home."

The perfectly calm expression on his face alarmed her even more than what he said. She tried to smile; she tried to smile the way a mother does to reassure a bewildered child. "But this is your home. You live here, Moe."

"No, you're mistaken, I work here." Then he went over to the desk in the living room and withdrew from one of its drawers a small blue-velvet bag containing his prayer shawl and phylacteries.

"What are you doing?" she asked.

"I'm taking these home with me," he said, stuffing the velvet bag into his coat pocket. "I need them for *shachris* tomorrow morning."

"Come to the window with me," she said in the calmest voice she could manage. He let her lead him through the living room. They looked out the window together. "Don't you recognize this neighborhood? The apartment buildings? You've lived on this street for more than ten years."

"But why are you trying to fool me?" he asked angrily.

"I'm not trying to fool you," she said.

He pointed to a group of men. "You see those guys across the street? They've just left their offices. This is Thirty-fourth Street. I wouldn't mind sleeping here, but it's not safe; too many *goyim* around."

"Let's go out into the hall and ring Mrs. Feder's doorbell," Ida suggested. Mrs. Feder was their next-door neighbor. "She doesn't work downtown. If you see her, will you admit this is your home?"

He said nothing, and she took him by the hand. His fingers were cold to her touch, but she wouldn't let them go. And man and wife, they walked out of their apartment together.

Ida rang Mrs. Feder's doorbell, but there was no answer. She thought to try another neighbor's apartment, but frightened at the way fate seemed to be conspiring against her, she hurried back to the safety of her own living room, holding Moe tightly by the hand.

Stalling for time, she said, "Stay just tonight. If you still want to leave tomorrow, then okay, *gey shon.*"

He seemed undecided.

"I work hard all day, I'm tired it comes five o'clock. Is that so terrible?" he asked.

"Of course not," she said, letting go of his hand.

"It may not sound hard, but today I had to tell Lipshitz how he should handle my friend Kuflik. Educating a dummy, that's not such easy work. And now I want to go home."

"How is Lipshitz?" she asked, trying to get his mind off leaving the apartment.

"I never hurt you. Why do you torture me like this?" Moe said bitterly.

"Shhh," she calmed him. "We'll eat supper soon, and you'll feel better."

She reached for his hand again. It was still cold, but she saw fat drops of sweat popping from his forehead.

"Take off your coat," Ida coaxed.

"I wish you wouldn't try to confuse me," he said. "It only makes it worse."

"I'm sorry I tried to confuse you," she apologized. "It was a mistake, won't happen again."

She took the bag containing the prayer shawl and phylacteries out of his coat and put it back in the desk drawer. Somehow it comforted her to know he wouldn't leave the apartment without his phylacteries.

www.ingramcontent.com/pod-product-compliance
Lightning Source LLC
Chambersburg PA
CBHW032047020426
42335CB00011B/224